The Breath of Spanish Oaks

by

Dr. Sue Clifton
and
Nyoka Beer

Daughters of the Way, Book 1

The Breath of Spanish Oaks

Cover Art by *Kim Mendoza*

The Wild Rose Press, Inc.
PO Box 708
Adams Basin, NY 14410-0708
Visit us at www.thewildrosepress.com

Publishing History
First Fantasy Rose Edition, 2019
Print ISBN 978-1-5092-2524-8
Digital ISBN 978-1-5092-2525-5

Daughters of the Way, Book 1
Published in the United States of America

The moon popped from behind its cloud and beamed so brightly at one time that she thought she had made daylight, only to have the light disappear again. But before it left her, she saw him, horse and rider, staring at her from across what could only be a mirage, a vast field of knee-high yellow flowers. He motioned for her to come, and this time he did not leave her.

Without taking her eyes off him, she waded into the flowers waving in the night breeze, beckoning her on. But when she was midway, she felt the ground beneath her soften and, as suddenly as it appeared, the yellow faded, replaced by slimy dark water and cypress and willow trees. Each step grew more difficult as the mud sucked at her, making it harder to lift her feet.

When she was waist-deep, she pulled the bag over her head and tried to lasso a cypress knee a yard away. On her third swing, the strap caught, and she pulled hard but to no avail. The harder she pulled, the more she sank. Panic set in, and she kicked her feet hard as if she were treading water, but the harder she kicked the more she sank, until she was forced to let go of the bag. Knowing she was about to perish, she flailed her arms and yelled, begging the man to help her, but he only stared the cold hard stare of one who had no compassion as she slowly descended.

Screaming! Flailing! Sinking! A gargled last plea for help emerged as only her wide horror-filled eyes remained above the mire swallowing its prey. As her eyes disappeared, the rider threw back his head and gave a ghastly, satanic laugh that echoed through the swamp, heard only by the swamp creatures.

Praise for Dr. Sue Clifton

Dr. Sue won many first place awards for her first novel, *THE GULLY PATH*, at the Arkansas Writers' Conference, as well as being named Panola County Author of the Year for five consecutive years in her home state.

In 2015, Dr. Sue was cast in A&E's five-part TV series *Cursed: The Bell Witch*.

~*~

Other Books by Dr. Sue Clifton
published by The Wild Rose Press, Inc.

Daughters of Parrish Oaks series:
The Gully Path
Under Northern Lights
Heart of the Beartooths
Mountain Mists
Wings on Mountain Breezes

~

Coming Soon in the
Daughters of the Way series:
Keeper of the Lambs

Dedication

To our sister Minnie Lee,
Even though you are no longer with us
in the physical world, you are forever with us in spirit.
We travel, we search, we write,
but mostly we share joy remembering when
we were the three Nelson sisters
from Pope, Mississippi.

Acknowledgements

With thanks to Mary Michael, Montana sculptor, who approved the use of her name in this book.

Prologue

South Mississippi, 1848

Evil stole through the woods, prodding his horse to go faster as lightning lit his path. He knew the trail well, having used it several times in his efforts to trade with plantation owners in the area. Some slaves he had bought outright, always paying far less than their market value and taking advantage of plantation owners he knew were in financial straits. But this trip was different. He was not seeking the property of another plantation owner but property already belonging to him, a gift from a female admirer. The thought of the beautiful she-devil brought a smile to his face, a handsome, rugged face beset with scars won in many personal battles, each scar hiding past evils deep within their human walls.

As horse and rider swerved to avoid low-hanging limbs, something caught Evil's eye, forcing him to turn his horse back, closer to the lowest limb. Plucking the piece of woolen fabric from the limb, the man gave a deep-throated laugh, a terrifying duet with the deafening thunder. The heavens opened and sheets of rain poured down as if God were trying to wash away the sin of what transpired below. Turning his horse, Evil spurred his steed, hastening what he knew would soon be the recapture of his prize.

****

"You gotta hold tight, Chloe girl! This old hoss be tired and sore, but we gotta run like da devil chasin' us. Dat storm comin' so close I can feel da cold wet of it creepin' up my backbone." A shiver crept up the woman's spine, but it was not from the dampness. Deep in her senses, she knew he was close.

"I'll hold tight, Auntie 'Liza! I won't let go. I know my mama waitin' for me wi' de attic light blazin' to light my way. Hurry, Auntie 'Liza!"

The human horse rose from her resting spot where she had insisted the little girl rest a bit and eat the few remaining crumbs of fried fatback and cornbread. After shaking off the remaining loose crumbs, Eliza folded the grease-streaked muslin and laid it on the log beside her. Opening the worn leather satchel at her feet, she dug into a side pocket and removed a piece of oilcloth tightly wound around a rolled-up document. After unrolling it, she took out a wrinkled, torn poster. Though she lacked the ability to read, Eliza knew what the paper said. Dicey, one of the house servants on the Fairchild Plantation, could read, unbeknownst to her ruthless owner, and the girl had secretly stolen the wadded-up paper from the slave master's trash and brought it to Eliza.

Dicey had explained to Eliza how she had been dusting in the library of the big house, uncomfortable with the gaze of her master, Rathbone Fairchild. She was young and knew from experience what lecherous desires were feeding her master's stares. To her good fortune, his intentions were interrupted when Mr. John, the plantation overseer and the only person the slaves hated more than Massa himself, entered and thrust the paper into his boss's hands. Fairchild's scars deepened into angry scarlet gullies as he read. His curse thundered through the library, causing Dicey to dust faster in an attempt to get away before he took his wrath out on her.

That night in the slave quarters, Dicey read the poster to Eliza, confirming in Eliza's mind what she had to do. No longer could the slave woman listen to the whimpers of the little girl or the cries for "Mama" in her fretful attempt at sleep. Eliza remembered the separation from her own mama when she was ten, only four years older than Chloe, and the cruel pain he had inflicted as he forced her into womanhood two years later. She had watched with sadness and anger as Dicey had become a plaything of the master and knew she, too, would be discarded as younger, prettier girls were brought to the plantation. Eliza knew the same fate awaited Chloe and had vowed not to let this happen to another child even if she had to die trying to prevent it.

The poster was the answer to Eliza's prayers, and she began making preparations for her mission that same night. Dicey added names to locate each important landmark and made Eliza practice recognizing each name.

Mose Fox, the strongest of the field hands, also helped by telling Eliza it was a hard three-day walk. Mose had been bought from Spanish Oaks Plantation many years ago. With the skill of one who claimed to have the natural senses of a fox, thus the reason for the self-imposed last name, Mose had drawn a map on the back of the poster, locating woods and river trails to follow that would keep the runaways from public roads.

****

Rain fell in rapids, making it impossible for Eliza to travel at the gait she knew she needed to go. Chloe began to squirm on her back.

"Chloe, you gotta hold still like a church mouse iffin we gonna make some time. I don't think it far, but my old legs 'bout to give out."

"I'll try, Auntie 'Liza. But da rain so cold!"

"I know, Baby Girl, but it won't be long 'fore you see yo' mammy again. She'll wrap her warm arms 'roun' you and you forget all 'bout da cold you been through to get back to her."

Eliza recognized the sharp curve in the river ahead from the map and knew they had almost reached their destination. Hurrying, sloshing through the mud and rounding the curve, she saw the road lined on both sides with giant Spanish oaks. The wet moss clung to the limbs and swayed in the storm like long thin fingers reaching for them, beckoning them to hurry, directing them down the path Mose had told her would lead to the plantation and safety. Soon her mission would be accomplished and Chloe would be safe.

The rescuer could only hope Master Broussard would be as kind as Mose and Chloe had described him. Perhaps he would reward her and would not return her to Fairchild Plantation. A slave had no need for monetary reward, and Eliza knew freedom was an unrealistic dream, a dream to hide in spiritual lyrics sung in the fields or hummed as if no words existed while serving in the massa's house. To live under a kind master would be enough. But whatever the outcome, the important thing was to get Chloe away from "the devil massa."

As she stopped to catch her breath, lightning ripped

over the oaks, illuminating a sight causing her to slide to an abrupt halt. The horse and rider stood watch halfway up the oak rows, and Eliza, gripped with fear, went weak. As she dropped to the ground, her tiny passenger tumbled into the mud beside her.

"We gotta go back into da woods, Chloe. Someone watchin' for us, and it ain't yo' nice massa. We go 'roun' and come in back of da big house. Maybe we can get to da massa befo' dat devil man see us."

Chloe crawled again onto Eliza's back and held tight and still, burying her face into Eliza's shoulder, not wanting to see what lay ahead. In her mind, the child imagined herself napping in the small bed in the attic room of the big house while her mother worked in the kitchen. The featherbed was warm and fluffy, and every afternoon she went to sleep with her mama rubbing her back, singing "Hush-a-Bye" until the little girl's eyes closed.

"Chloe, you gotta grip now. There da house! We gotta race 'gainst da lightnin'!"

Peeking around her auntie's head, Chloe smiled through chattering teeth.

"I see it! Mama got da light burnin' for me! Run, Auntie 'Liza! Run fast!" Chloe locked her legs around Eliza's waist and tightened her grip around her neck. The girl watched as the lantern light flickered wildly as if fueled by her breath.

Eliza clutched the satchel under her arm, lifted her skirt high with the same hand while holding tight to Chloe with the other hand, and waited for the lightning to subside. She knew their only chance was to run straight for the house before the next streak gave them away.

****

His gaze caught movement, and Rathbone Fairchild moved toward the back of the house, keeping close to the gnarly, moss-laden oaks. Leaning forward in his saddle, making sure of what he thought he saw through the downpour off the brim of his hat, he readied himself to kick his horse into a gallop.

****

Across the spongy grounds, the human horse and rider trotted, the horse glancing right and left, never looking back for fear of seeing the devil-man on her tail. Eliza seemed to have gotten her second wind, but even so, the house was hundreds of feet ahead. As the house grew closer, her step quickened. She thought she detected the sound of hooves behind her once but refused to deny or confirm this by wasting precious energy looking back. Besides, escape would be impossible at this point.

Four hundred feet to the house…

Lawd help me, Jesus!

Eliza did not waste breath speaking aloud but mouthed her silent prayer as she ran. The rain grew harder, beating down as if funneled through the clouds directly above them.

Three hundred feet to the house…

Run straight! Run straight!

The dark grew thicker as Eliza ran blindly.

Two hundred feet to the house…

Don't look back! Don't look back!

The house seemed to be moving backward, and the rescuer's burst of energy gave way to fatigue.

Running! Stumbling! Sliding! The sky spasmed as thunder rolled through its depths like a tidal wave.

Lightning torched heaven and earth like the apocalypse.

Eliza's senses perked up, hearing the sound of what could only be the devil's horse behind her. Once again her adrenaline kicked in, and she ran.

One hundred feet to the house, then…

SILENCE!

Chapter One

South Mississippi, The Present

The young man floor-boarded the old Chevy, doing seventy on the crooked gravel road, but he knew it wasn't enough. His eyes darted from steering wheel to rearview mirror, hoping against useless hope not to see what he knew was inevitable. Then he saw them—the glaring eyes of a monster so terrifying he would risk everything, even what lay on the seat beside him, to be able to outrun them, but he knew escape was impossible. The young man pumped the gas pedal, then stomped it again in a vain attempt to get more out of the old car than it could do. He had to think fast. One thing he would not risk was the girl with him, but if he could get her out of the car, she could take the bag and maybe he could keep them both. Besides, without the bag with him, his chances of survival would be better.

"Here, take it!" He pushed the leather bag toward the girl. "Hang it around your neck! Quick! When we round the curve up ahead, I'll slow down enough for you to jump out of the car. You've got to run and not look back!"

"No! I won't take it! It's the reason we're in this mess! It's cursed and so are we for taking it! Just stop and let them have it!" The young woman's terrified gaze froze on the driver.

"We don't have a choice! They'll kill us for sure, once they get it. I can't outrun them, but if I don't have it when they catch me, they'll let me live thinking I know where it is. Run into the woods and don't look back. I'll catch up with you later! I promise."

He reached across the seat and gave her hand a reassuring squeeze. She was shaking so badly she could hardly maneuver to put the strap over her head with the bag under her right arm.

"I'm scared!" The girl began to sob. "What if they see me?"

"They're still far enough back they won't see my brake lights after we make the curve. Besides, they think I'm alone. You've got to be ready when I slow down. You can do this, babe!"

The curve was coming fast, and there was no time for them to change their minds. The glaring eyes were approaching fast.

"Get ready!"

The young driver turned the curve, swerving as he hit the brakes, coming almost to a complete stop. Reaching across her, he pushed the passenger door open and yelled at her when she hesitated.

"Jump, damn it, or we'll both die!"

He only had time for one quick look back but was sure he saw her bolting into the woods, the bag flapping at her side. Stomping the accelerator, he slung gravel, knowing he had to put as much distance between himself and his pursuers as possible. A temporary sense of relief settled over him as he saw the stoplight ahead indicating the intersection and more traffic on the highway, more witnesses who might save him from the brutality the two thugs had promised would follow if he didn't hand the prize over like agreed.

But his relief proved short-lived as the lights behind him shone so bright he had to shade the mirror with his right hand while trying to steer with his left; he was sure the car would bump his at any moment in an attempt to stop him. Then, as quickly as they were on his tail, they disappeared. He glanced into the mirror to see what had happened without checking his speed, knowing the intersection was only a few hundred yards away. He felt they were still behind him but with their lights off.

As he looked back at the road, something shattered the back glass and left a hole in the front windshield. Cracks splintered off in all directions, extending across his view like a giant spider ready to grasp him and inject poisonous venom into his body.

"Shit! They're shooting at me!"

But it was too late. The next bullet came so close he ducked, jerking the wheel wildly and losing control. The car catapulted from the road, airborne like the bullet that had jarred him into the reality that escape was impossible. Every organ in his body felt torn loose and lodged in his throat as he hit ground; the car careened on the driver's side for what seemed minutes, tearing away the door and the young driver's flesh as he watched his life fly by with the glass and metal of the old Chevy. The car stopped when what was left of it wrapped around a giant oak tree several yards off the road. The black car stopped for only a few minutes before speeding toward the intersection when headlights appeared in the distance. Eternal darkness took control, and the young man's nightmare ended.

****

Her nightmare had just begun. When she first entered the woods, she became entangled in rusted, downed barbwire covered with kudzu vines that had wrapped themselves around it, hiding it from trespassers. Knowing she didn't have time to get herself loose, she lay still and flat with the bag under her, hoping whoever followed her boyfriend would not see her. It wasn't long before the car, a fast, sleek, black sedan, bombed past, leaving her a little relieved and glad she was not with him if and when he was caught—and he would be caught. She only hoped they would go easy on him when they saw he did not have what they were seeking, what he had carelessly told his thief boss he had discovered.

As she untangled the vines, the barbed wire ripped her khakis and bit into her leg. She felt the blood drip as she removed the wire from her pants leg, but there was no time to whimper. She had to run deeper into the woods, the ones she had been warned about when she'd had her fortune told. Mama Tee had also warned her about him, but the girl was young, and the boy was good-looking, just the kind of rough-and-tumble guy she had always found attractive, the kind her sister had kept at bay when she was a teenager and still at home under her sister's watchful care. But she was on her own now. She had made some mistakes, but who didn't when they were young? He wanted to marry her, and with the money they'd get for this treasure they could live in luxury on a beach somewhere, maybe the Cayman Islands, with no worries and no low-paying jobs.

She felt for the bag as she stood up, making sure it was still with her. Then she ran like he'd told her to, trying not to think of the snakes and alligators she knew were in the woods that would turn into swamp.

I'll go in deep and wait until daylight before I come out. With luck, he'll be waiting for me on the other side.

"With luck" was the key phrase in her thinking. Several times she had to slosh through black and slimy water, the mud sucking at her tennis shoes and making running impossible. Able to see only by the moonlight, she wouldn't let herself think about what might be underfoot. Once the strap to the bag caught on a willow limb and bounced her back like a slingshot, causing her to fall on her rear; the water oozed around her waist like thick oil. She had no idea how far it was to the other side of the bog; nor did she know if she was running in the right direction to get out of it, but she kept assuring herself she was safer here than with him.

What seemed like hours passed, but she attempted to keep a steady pace. As the moon hid behind a cloud, her path became as black as the swamp water, forcing her to stop and try to get her bearings. The slight breeze she'd felt when she entered the woods had given way to an eerie wind playing the tree limbs and vines like the deepest minor chords on an organ, background music for a horror movie and she was the only actor.

In the distance she heard sirens and hoped it had nothing to do with him. She wished she could pray, but her praying had ended when she was twelve, the night her mother died from cancer. Her father, distraught over his loss, had followed a few hours later from a self-inflicted gunshot wound.

Rather than mouthing a prayer, she began to hum a song her mother had sung to her as a toddler, but the song could not stop her heart from racing. She trudged on, holding tight to the bag that held both hope and risk of death. In her mind, she pictured herself on a white beach, lying beside this young man she loved, as he caressed her back with suntan oil. So intent was she with her reverie that she became complacent, unaware of any dangers lurking in the shadows of the willows and cypresses.

The moon reappeared, and she saw the strange man for the first time, directly in her path. He sat on a tall, black horse, staring down at her without expression or concern.

"Can you help me, sir? I'm lost. I need to get to the road on the other side of the swamp." But all the young woman could do was watch as the nonresponsive rider turned his horse and galloped away, the tail of his old-fashioned black coat flying behind him.

Thinking he must be showing her the way, she trudged through the mud, following him, but he disappeared too quickly. Discouragement took control as she found herself lost, once again left in the dark by the moon that seemed to be playing tricks on her. Trudging through the mud, she thought she heard hissing, followed by something sliding into the water behind her. Her adrenaline boosted her on until, panting, she plopped down on a knoll to rest, a temporary reprieve from the gross muck and its slithering beings. Her throat was parched, but there was nothing to drink but fear. Even though it was cool in the swamp, she was wet from sweat and needed to rid herself of her thick sweatshirt that hung heavy with mud. After pulling the bag over her head, she removed the muddy sweatshirt, laying it beside her. It was then she realized she was missing a tennis shoe, probably sucked off by the mud as she pulled herself up on the knoll. After pulling the bag back over her T-shirt, she looked around again, hoping to see a path leading out of the miserable swamp. Again the horseman appeared, and once again she pleaded with him.

"Please, mister. I need help!"

His answer was the same, to ride away without acknowledging her. Once again she took his leaving to mean she should follow, and she did so with haste. Anxious to end the nightmare and rid herself of the rest of her mud-soaked clothing, she held tight to the bag and tried her best to sprint. This time she would not stop to rest but would move fast in an effort to catch the strange rider. Whenever she thought she could go no farther, she would catch a glimpse of him and begin running again, fueled by an unidentified strength.

The moon popped from behind its cloud and beamed so brightly at one time that she thought she had made daylight, only to have the light disappear again. But before it left her, she saw him, horse and rider, staring at her from across what could only be a mirage, a vast field of knee-high yellow flowers. He motioned for her to come, and this time he did not leave her.

Without taking her eyes off him, she waded into the flowers waving in the night breeze, beckoning her on. But when she was midway, she felt the ground beneath her soften and, as suddenly as it appeared, the yellow faded, replaced by slimy dark water and cypress and willow trees. Each step grew more difficult as the mud sucked at her, making it harder to lift her feet.

When she was waist-deep, she pulled the bag over her head and tried to lasso a cypress knee a yard away.

On her third swing, the strap caught, and she pulled hard but to no avail. The harder she pulled, the more she sank. Panic set in, and she kicked her feet hard as if she were treading water, but the harder she kicked the more she sank, until she was forced to let go of the bag. Knowing she was about to perish, she flailed her arms and yelled, begging the man to help her, but he only stared the cold hard stare of one who had no compassion as she slowly descended.

Screaming! Flailing! Sinking! A gargled last plea for help emerged as only her wide horror-filled eyes remained above the mire swallowing its prey. As her eyes disappeared, the rider threw back his head and gave a ghastly, satanic laugh that echoed through the swamp, heard only by the swamp creatures.

Chapter Two

The South, Three Months Later

"Good Lord, Cayce! Can't you dispense with the Fat Bastards for at least one trip? You're in the South, not Montana, you know."

"Nice to see you again, too, Sister. And by the way, my boots are Fatbabies. Fat Bastard is a wine." The two hugged as they headed for the baggage claim in Memphis.

"Babies! Bastards! Same thing if you're talking about cowboy boots on a woman who could be a real looker if she cared anything at all about fashion. Besides, what woman in her right mind would wear something named Fat?"

"Give it up, Harri! Yes, we are in our twin months, but we made an agreement. Even if we're old, we're still more Mary Kate and Ashley than the Doublemint twins, so we don't have to dress alike. Besides, these boots are real ostrich, $300 on eBay. You just wait and see. These thick-soled Babies will be worth something in another thirty years as vintage western boots."

"Well, thank God you don't have on your ten-gallon hat, small miracles and all that. My feet hurt just looking at those cowboy boots. If I could find a pair of Crocs with a two-inch heel, I'd buy them to complete my wardrobe. Meanwhile, I'll stick with my designer flats and diamonds." Harri waved her hand in Cayce's face, flaunting her four-carat oval diamond wedding ring. "Oh, well, I guess if I can be be-dangled, you can be be-footed."

Harri—preferred nickname for her official moniker of Harriet Wellington—and her twin sister for two months of each year, Cayce McCallister—nickname for Cathryn Celia McCallister—were on their yearly adventure to places and sights unknown and, even better, unplanned. The sisters had started these yearly trips at the young age of forty and had not missed one in fifteen years. At one time, the trips had taken more planning and definitely more cajoling with their then husbands. Both were now single, Cayce by choice, Harri by act of God.

"You know we will never be twins, Harri. The ten months in age difference made us two distinct persons, but I do enjoy pretending we're twins during the two months a year we are the same age. Good thing we had the same dad to give us each a little of what he inherited from his father. To think our father was the great-grandson of a Native American shaman, tribe unknown and credibility questionable, but the implication certainly explains much about what seems to lead us, the gift he gave each of us."

"Yeah, we not only don't look alike, but our lifestyles are totally different. Just look at us. Here I am, once married to a doctor, until he decided to up and die on me, and now I'm the owner of a teahouse in an exclusive and historical part of Germantown, Tennessee—a Victorian teahouse in which I, Harriet Wellington, am a culinary genius." Harri curtsied before standing straight and rolling her hands forward, directing her next statement to Cayce. "And you, my sister, are a Montana rancher who wears cowboy boots and rides horses. I rest my case."

"TEACAKE?" Cayce stared at the personalized tag as she loaded her bags into the trunk of her sister's new red BMW convertible. "I know Teacake is your teashop, but to a complete stranger looking at this car's license plate, it probably sounds like some rich old codger's twenty-five-year-old bride, or mistress, complete with short skirt, exposed midriff, cleavage the size of the Grand Canyon, and four-inch stilettos accentuating mile-long legs. Guess the mourning period is over, huh? What happened to the 'I'm going to take good care of Stan's money' I've been hearing for the two years since he died?" Cayce asked the question as she climbed in to ride shotgun in her sister's luxury car.

"I am taking care of my husband's money. Taking care to spend whatever I want, whenever I feel the need to be 'Teacake,' with or without a sugar daddy. And don't be such a smart ass. If I didn't complain last year when I rode all over the West in that school-bus yellow, '52 Chevy street-rod, pickup truck of yours, then you certainly shouldn't be critical of my Beamer."

"You chose your lifestyle, and I chose mine. So I ended up marrying a rancher turned construction boss, a marriage not made in heaven even though it lasted many years. I ended up with a degree and a career in education, a ranch in Montana, and, most important, a beautiful daughter—Piper—whom you and I both adore, not to mention our father, who named her after the movie star our mother hated. Mom was so jealous of the way Dad ogled at the famous Piper on the big screen!"

"Well, Piper is one thing you have that I don't, Cayce, and I thank you for letting me share in the adoration of her. Piper, even though you taught her to be a cowgirl, still has my feminine qualities."

"I'll have to agree with you there, but I'm glad Piper grew up in the West. And even though Cody and I split, he and Piper have a wonderful relationship. The money Cody worked so hard for when he started his construction company provides Piper and me both with comfortable lifestyles."

Cayce became quiet, thinking of how things had turned out. She and Cody had been married for twenty fairly happy years when the trouble started. A short time later, by mutual consent, they ended their marriage, splitting their assets peaceably and vowing to remain friends. Piper was not happy about the divorce but soon set off on her own adventures. Cayce had stayed in Montana and turned her ranch in the Beartooth Mountains into a guest ranch offering backcountry trips by horseback in the summer and horse-drawn sleigh rides along snow-packed trails in the winter.

"So how is the teashop doing, and how are you, really? Are you coping with Stan's death? You can lie to me over the phone, but you know I can tell if we're face to face."

"I'm just fine, Cayce. My life is moving forward just like Stan would want. The Teacake is doing better than it's ever done, with the new catering room booked for three months. Thanks to Peggy, my new manager, and a dream staff, I can travel or do just about anything I want and the shop will run smoothly, business as usual, with me only a cell phone away. This leads me to the main goal of this year's trip. My turn to pick, remember."

"And that would be…?"

"Any old, preferably antebellum, recipes I can use in the Teacake. Any guesses as to where we're going?"

"Let's see. We're heading south on I-55. Think antiques…think our love of bed-and-breakfast inns…think antebellum."

"Natchez!" The sisters laughed after their synchronized answer.

"We've still got it, Harri. Pop would be so proud."

The sisters headed south on Interstate 55 until they reached Jackson. As soon as they saw the Natchez Trace Parkway sign, Harri looked at Cayce and, without saying a word, turned onto the Trace, their love of the historical taking precedence over speedy traveling. Once they turned, Cayce began telling Harri what she remembered from Mississippi history about the bloody marauders and robbers on the Natchez Trace, known in the 1700s as the Wilderness Road. Harri related stories of the Mason gang, the most notorious of the criminals who robbed travelers on the trail that ran from Natchez to Nashville. Cayce gave dramatic retellings of blood-curdling tales she remembered from reading Harnett Kane's *Natchez on the Mississippi* when she was in high school.

"I read where one of the Mason brothers got so irritated when his baby was crying, he smashed its head against a tree. How cruel could any thug be?" Cayce turned to see if Harri shared the disgust, and intrigue, she had for the historical but disgusting Mason gang.

"Cayce, are you sure you want to be discussing the blood-and-guts sagas of the Natchez Trace? I'm halfway expecting you to scream for me to stop at any minute because you need to help some weary traveler dressed in pre-statehood attire and lying in the woods off to the side of the Parkway. Your gift of seeing visions from the past is not for the faint of heart."

"You and I both live with pain from the gifts Dad left us. Yours is just more emotional feelings of the dearly departed, while mine is actual physical and mental seeing, being there when the event happens, sometimes a hundred or more years ago. The worst part of my visions is not being able to control or change the outcome."

Cayce became quiet, contemplative, remembering some of the scenes from the past—ghostly participants conjured up by simply touching a relic from a historical period or even touching something from the present. Cayce had helped law enforcement solve crimes on a couple of occasions in Montana but was always hesitant, afraid some criminal would seek revenge and hurt Piper.

"Well, I don't plan on stopping the Beamer and risking you joining past foot travelers on the Trace, especially the Mason gang. Thank goodness I don't have to see what you see. Feeling the sadness, fear, and pain of those experiencing these past events is more than I really want."

"If I did see something, it would just be one of my cheap shots that lasts a second and then it's gone. No big deal, Harri. To become involved, so to speak, I'd have to get out and walk through the woods, and I'm not doing that. Snakes are out."

As soon as Cayce got the words out of her mouth, she experienced a "cheap shot," seeing a man knocked off his horse with the butt end of a rifle. Cayce jumped and turned toward her sister, hoping Harri had not noticed her double-take. Cayce was relieved to see Harri's eyes were on the highway straight ahead.

"Only you would find a new meaning for 'cheap shot,' but I guess it fits. Your seeing is an attack on your emotions if not your self, per se."

A few hours later, Harri and Cayce headed for Natchez Under the Hill, one of the oldest and most historic sites in the United States and once the hangout for some of the most notorious thieves in Mississippi history. Harri had heard it was full of unique shops, and she could hardly wait to begin her recipe search.

Disappointment soon replaced enthusiasm when the sisters realized the historic district that stood under the levee of the Mississippi River was no more. Natchez Under the Hill had been erased by the floodwaters of greed and malevolent disregard for history, falling prey to the philosophy, "When money talks, history walks."

Fortunately, Franklin Street still existed downtown, and the sisters put their disappointment on hold as they dove into one magnificent antique shop after another.

"Whoo-wee! I believe the thieves have risen from the grave! Look at these prices!"

Harri had found one shop in particular that had a huge old book section, and she knew they would probably close this one down. She paid no attention to the fact her sister had covered almost the entire shop by the time she, herself, had moved only a few feet. A glass case holding a few rare and very pricey books caught Harri's interest, and she was quickly mesmerized.

"Look at this, Cayce." Harri spoke loud enough for Cayce to hear her from the back of the shop, and soon Cayce was by her side. "The card says this handwritten cookbook predates the Civil War and contains recipes from a plantation in south Mississippi. I really want to look at it, but check out the price."

"Good lord, Harri! Is the Teacake doing that great?" Cayce put her head close to the glass, not believing the price tag.

"I'm not sure, but I'd really like to see what's inside those covers." Harri battled, trying to convince herself she really did not need to spend this kind of money, and began walking her fingers across the glass top away from the precious journal and her sister.

Cayce shook her head, left her sister to her self-haggling, and headed to a section of primitive antiques, her personal favorite. Over her shoulder, she glanced back to see if her sister might win the battle and laughed when she heard Harri talking aloud to her conscience.

"I'll just walk on by this glass case and not give that cooking journal another thought." Harri realized she was losing the battle as the book beckoned her back to it as if she were not in control of her own footsteps.

"Not now, Pop. It's too much." Harri was talking to herself but knew she would not be able to overcome the pull when she felt it and, as always, attributed said pull to her deceased father. She didn't make it five feet from the case before she giant-stepped backward.

"Could I possibly take a look at this cooking journal?" Harri looked toward the sales person who was heading in her direction, most likely sensing here was a sale in the making.

"This is a very rare book, as you can see by the glass case. You will have to put on white gloves before handling it. Also, please be very careful. The pages are somewhat brittle. You can sit at this table while you look at it." Before removing the book from the case, the woman covered the top of the table with thick felt.

"Just keep the book on the felt while you're looking at it. You need to know we have a university museum from Louisiana interested in purchasing the journal. The curator is due to come by later in the week."

The woman pulled out two pairs of white gloves from a drawer, handed a pair to Harri, and put on a pair herself. After taking the book from the case, she gingerly placed it on the felt, handling it as if it were a first edition of *Gone with the Wind* or *To Kill a Mockingbird*.

"Actually, we just bought this two days ago from a dealer who buys from estate sales. Even at this price I doubt it will be here very long. Handwritten books are a hot item right now, especially from the antebellum period. I guess because handwriting is becoming obsolete, with email and text messaging."

Harri thought the sales lady must have been on commission the way she was pushing the book.

"Cayce, I need you to come look at this."

Cayce knew from the excitement in her sister's voice there was more here than just a cookbook. By the time she reached her sister's side, Harri was pale and very quiet as she meticulously turned each page, running her fingers over it as if reading Braille.

"Do you have any questions about the book?" The saleslady stared at Harri, waiting for her answer. When she didn't answer, the lady repeated her question but once again got no reply. Harri seemed to be pulled in by the pages.

As Cayce took a seat by her sister, a bell jingled, signifying another customer was arriving. The saleslady looked anxious as a young couple with two small children entered the shop. The children took off in different directions, one licking an ice cream cone and the other slurping an ice drink covered in sickeningly pink flavoring. The parents, oblivious to the No Food or Drink sign, demonstrated they were even more oblivious to the antics of their two rambunctious children. The dad headed for the Civil War memorabilia and his wife to the china section. The sales lady headed after one of the children, who was trying to climb feet first into a two-hundred-year-old wicker baby carriage while balancing a drippy ice cream cone in the other hand. The girl's brother, about four years old, headed to the table where Cayce and Harri were looking at the book.

"Look at this section, Cayce. It seems to be several pages stuck together. Looks like something spilled on it, judging by the dark shadow coming through on this page. I feel so…so mixed up—sad, angry, vengeful, frightened—a stew of emotions." Harri's voice was dramatic, some of it spoken through pursed lips.

"That dark shadow is probably just spaghetti sauce, very old spaghetti sauce, so don't let your imagination run wild. And as for those emotions you're feeling…maybe your blood pressure is up. Did you bring your meds?"

"You know I haven't had blood pressure problems since I started dieting and exercising and lost all that weight after Stan died. Skinny one-hundred-ten-pound bitches, as we used to call them in our obese days, don't have blood pressure problems."

"Your bragging is not bothering me this year, Skinny Minnie." Cayce directed her gaze away from her sister and back to the journal. "So why the feeling? You think it's...you know?"

"The gift? I haven't experienced it in a long time, but I think it could be. Do you feel anything?" Harri looked Cayce in the face, waiting for her answer.

"You know it has to be more tangible for me to have an experience. Besides, this thing is over one hundred fifty years old. I'm sure there are some hard memories there, and probably some things that need to stay hidden. Better to leave it with the white gloves. I'm not ready to go on a vision quest right now." Cayce scooted farther from the table to emphasize her point.

As if some greater power was saying "na-na-na-na-na-na" to the vision quest remark, Cayce found herself grabbing the book from the table without the shield of white gloves. The boy had crawled onto the chair across from the sisters and, while attempting to stand on the table, dumped his slush. Pink glob raced toward the fragile book. Cayce only had time to react, not think.

As she clutched the book to her chest, Cayce became engulfed in thick mist, like that rising from Montana mountain streams on a cold morning. As the fog dissipated, she found herself in a kitchen, a very old kitchen with a big stone fireplace on one wall, a dry sink and table on another. Adjusting her vision, her focus zoomed in on a poplar work table with its scrubbed top filled with a large wooden dough bowl, flour, eggs, and a stone pitcher overturned, with milk running to the edge of the table. The milk raced along, stopping only when it hit cold, hard steel, where it changed from white to pink, the color of the Pepto-Bismol slush of only seconds ago.

Her gaze magnified, and she realized the steel object was a butcher knife, a blood-covered butcher knife. The knife lay precariously near the edge, the blade extending over the end of the table, with dark pink liquid dripping from its sharp point to form a puddle on the floor. The pink puddle turned into a dark red river heading to another corner in the room, but was it the source or the end?

Too much red, not enough pink!

Cayce's head spun as her gaze followed. The red stream meandered over the uneven stone floor until it merged with a pile of elegant emerald green taffeta. The taffeta entombed the body of a small woman whose waist was the size of Scarlett O'Hara's—the waist made even smaller by a gaping hole, a small green volcano erupting blood. Cayce's gaze traveled on, climbing over tight bosoms, the victim's cleavage forming a deep pathway to a thin, ghostly-pale neck.

Candlelight ricocheted off the woman's body. One hand rested on the wound as if attempting to stop the flow of blood, while the other hand clutched something around her neck. Sparks of green and yellow light danced against the ceiling like lightning bugs on a steamy southern summer night. The victim's face was hidden under a blanket of tousled thick red hair that exposed only a delicate chin.

As the candlelight faded, the dancing orbs gave way to more fog engulfing the room again as Cayce was shaken back to the present.

Harri took the book from her sister and laid it carefully on the table. "Cayce, are you all right? Here. Drink this water." Harri grabbed the cup of water the saleslady had brought and forced it into her sister's trembling hands.

After guzzling the water, Cayce looked from her sister's questioning face to the bewildered stare of the saleslady. Without hesitation or second thought, Cayce spoke.

"We'll take it. Wrap it up."

Chapter Three

As the sisters headed out of Natchez, a long line of traffic going nowhere stopped them.

"Oh, great! Construction!"

Harri's theory was disproved as an ambulance and a police car sped by on the shoulder of the road. Within minutes, the traffic began moving slowly. As they made a sharp turn, they could see lights flashing up ahead. When they passed the wreck, Cayce saw a man, blood on his face and on his white shirt, being helped into the back of the ambulance. When they were side by side with the ambulance, the man looked toward the BMW, making eye contact briefly with Cayce, who had peeked around her sister. His navy blue SUV was wedged against a concrete railing, facing the wrong direction. The passenger side of the vehicle was crunched in, but the door had been pried open by rescuers from the fire department with a jaws-of-life tool. A beat-up pickup truck sat off the other side of the road, and an old farmer stood talking to a police officer taking notes.

"I bet whoever was riding on the passenger side didn't fare as well as the driver. At least the man didn't look like his injuries were too serious. Maybe it's a sign. Keep your designer shoe light on that accelerator, Harri. Better to get there later than never."

****

By the time they were out of Natchez city limits,

the sisters' nerves had settled down and both were looking forward to the scenic drive down the historic old trail to the inn where they had just booked a room.

"Spanish Oaks Plantation. Look at the pamphlet we found at the visitor's center and see if they give specific directions how to get there."

Harri had forced herself to remember the name Spanish Oaks Plantation while she was entranced in the book in the shop—not by the worn leather cover where a faded coat of arms had been skillfully etched with the name, but by the content of the book. Harri had been intrigued most by the notes written journal-like throughout, telling the occasion or occasions on which each special dish had been served. All notes had been written in a fancy, almost calligraphic script, different from the simplistic writing of the recipes. Many recipes had dates written before or after them by the author with the fancy handwriting to indicate the dates on which the recipes were made. These included comments about difficulty or possible variations.

Cayce was hesitant but unfastened her seatbelt to dig through pamphlets on the back seat. As she reached for the stack, she practiced caution, trying not to disturb the rare and very expensive cookbook, even though it had been wrapped in plastic and placed in a cardboard box before leaving the shop. No way did either of them want to risk another experience with miles to go before reaching the plantation. In fact, they had purchased two pairs of white gloves from the antique shop before they left so they could have some control over the magical qualities of the book.

The sisters had decided not to spend even one night in Natchez, both anxious to continue what was already a memorable twin trip. As luck would have it, although neither of them really believed in luck, Spanish Oaks Plantation was now a famous inn, complete with its own ghost stories.

Harri had suggested they Google Spanish Oaks before leaving Natchez, to get as much information as possible, but Cayce talked her out of it.

"You know what Pop always said."

"Keep an open mind and an open path, and the Way will find you." Once again the sisters answered in synchrony.

"I hope we're not making a mistake, booking for a week. The cookbook—or cooking journal, as the shop labeled it, was definitely talking to us, but the rooms aren't cheap. At least if I'm looking for recipes for the Teacake I can claim it as a tax deduction."

"Good! Then you can pay for the room, the gas, and the food. You know I don't have much need for recipes at the ranch, not with a freezer full of Lean Tasties."

"You are such a food junkie, Cayce. You better start worrying about what you put in your arteries."

"Did you not hear the word 'lean' in that name brand? If I want a real meal, I just go down the road to one of the saloons. That's the good thing about Montana. There's at least one saloon in even the tiniest community, but I go for the food, not the drink."

Not finding a good map in the pamphlet, Cayce dug the atlas from under the seat and turned to the page showing Mississippi. Using a highlighter, she outlined the best route to follow.

"Our best bet is to work our way back to I-55 and head south. We can cut across the southeast corner of

Louisiana and be at River Town in two or three hours, depending on how heavy your foot is."

"You're the navigator. Just tell me when to turn."

The day had turned warm, and Harri put the top down a few miles out of River Town. She laughed when Cayce confessed to feeling like Thelma and Louise. Late in the afternoon, TEACAKE headed down a long private drive shaded by ancient Spanish oaks whose limbs overlapped the road, playing a permanent game of London Bridges with those lucky enough to be traversing below.

"Those limbs are so heavy with moss, I think I could just grab a handful." Cayce grabbed at the air to prove her point.

"Don't you dare, Cayce, or you'll be cleaning that moss out of this luxury car."

****

The sight of the Spanish Oaks Plantation home caused the oohs and ahs of minutes before to give way to silent, mouth-wide-open, speechless awe. This place even surpassed Twelve Oaks from *Gone with the Wind* as the most beautiful antebellum home the sisters had ever seen, with its roof seeming to reach to the sky. The mansion was Greek revival, surrounded on all four sides by deep, columned porches held up by Tuscan columns. On its steep roof, two small doghouses stood guard over the front of the exquisite plantation home.

In the yard, Spanish oaks gave way to giant magnolias surrounded by perfectly manicured grounds perfumed with lilacs, camellias, and magnolia blossoms. To the rear of the house, perhaps a hundred feet away, lay a row of fifteen rustic board-and-batten, tin-roofed cabins, the slave quarters still standing after over one hundred fifty years.

A long building of antique red brick was located to the left and rear of the mansion; it had probably housed expensive and magnificent horses in its early years. On its roof, four weathervanes with prancing horses turned in the warm May breeze, keeping time to the swaying of the magnolia leaves. Stable doors had been replaced with rows and rows of large-paned windows overlooking grounds that included a small pond complete with white lattice bridge and gazebo. Over the double-door entrance was a sign painted in calligraphy: The Stables Restaurant.

"Oh, my gosh!" Cayce spoke first after several minutes of the two sitting in the driveway staring at the impressive spectacle before them.

"The pamphlet does not do it justice. I may never leave." Harri's gaze settled on the Stables. "I cannot wait to check out the local cuisine. Maybe they have a cookbook or two of their own."

"Speaking of cookbooks, something tells me we should keep our purchase to ourselves for a while. Do you have the same hunch?"

"Odd you should mention it—well, not really odd, but I was just thinking the same thing. It will be interesting to see if they serve some of the recipes from the book."

The front porch was filled with white wicker rockers, most empty as guests roamed the grounds, strolled around the pond, or loitered in the gift shop almost hidden by camellias between the restaurant and the mansion.

The sisters were even more wowed when they entered the mansion. No one was at the desk, so the two took the opportunity to go room by room admiring the well-preserved décor and architectural features. Cayce picked up a brochure from a table in the entry and read from it, taking over as tour guide:

"The main entrance hall, or lobby, has a ceiling reaching to the top of the second floor and is embellished with circular arabesques covered in fleur-de-lis. An oversized bronze chandelier with hundreds of crystal prisms hangs from the center of the expansive ceiling. A long, heavily carved mahogany desk, a later addition, awaits the arrival of guests. Two enormous gold-trimmed mirrors hang on each side of the entry."

"This is fabulous! Keep going, Cayce."

"On the left side, two huge parlors with seventeen-foot ceilings provide entertainment space. The first, for ladies, is also called the music room and includes a square rosewood grand piano. The larger adjoining room—wouldn't you know it would have to be larger," Cayce interjected, "is a smoking parlor for the gentlemen. Both parlors are filled with elegant antique sofas and armchairs, ornate tables, and Old Paris Porcelain pieces. Above the mantel in the gentlemen's parlor hangs a large coat of arms, the family crest of the Broussards. It is a work of art with fleur-de-lis, knights, and castles painted in bold colors. The two rooms can be opened to form a large and stately ballroom eighty feet long by unfolding the floor-to-ceiling paneled doors dividing the rooms."

Harri led the way to the opposite side of the entry as Cayce continued as guide, reading from the brochure.

"On the other side of the entry is a large formal dining room, more of a banquet room, with its elongated mahogany table and sixteen matching empire chairs. Two magnificent punkahs hang over the table and were manned by servants to shoo away flies during the hot, humid Mississippi summers."

Cayce and Harri returned to the entry to await the desk clerk. They admired a spiral staircase with a mahogany railing, shined to perfection, standing in the center of the lobby. At the top of the stairs, fifteen doors opened onto the open hallway that wrapped around like a balcony looking down on the entry and eye to eye with the giant chandelier.

"Welcome to Spanish Oaks. You must be Harriet and Cathryn." The receptionist came through the front door and greeted the two with a firm handshake. "I'm sorry I wasn't here when you came in, but I had to give a radio to the maintenance man before he got away."

"That's fine. It gave us a chance to look around at this spectacular mansion." Cayce gestured with her hands at the expansive entry. "Please call me Cayce. Cathryn is legal but definitely not a good fit."

"And I am Harri, although Harriet might be a better fit."

"I'll remember, Cayce and Harri. And my name is Monica." Monica took her place behind the desk and pulled out two cards.

"Just fill out these registration cards for me while I get your keys." As Cayce and Harri began filling out the forms, Monica continued. "You have no idea how lucky you two are. Spanish Oaks never has cancellations. In fact, we don't even keep a cancellation list. We're booked up at least three months in advance, longer for the spring and summer months. The owner only allows cancellations if it is a serious emergency like a death in the family. Reservations have to be cancelled two weeks in advance or the client is charged."

"So the rooms just remain empty if people don't show, even though others might want to stay?" Harri asked, expressing disagreement with the cancellation policy.

"That's right. I know it sounds a little harsh, but the owner is very serious when it comes to business matters, and the policy has not hurt us yet. I can't remember the last time a room was available on such short notice, except of course when we were dealing with Katrina. The couple that had booked your room called after lunch today saying they had wrecked on their way here and were both hospitalized. Not serious injuries, thank goodness, but we allowed them to cancel without charging them. It was so strange when you called just minutes after they cancelled. I do apologize for only having the one room, but I think you'll find it comfortable."

"If another room becomes available, would you keep us in mind? We hate sharing a room. Bad childhood memories." Harri whispered the last sentence as if her sister was not supposed to hear.

"What she is trying to say is I breathe loud. Harri forgets her own tendency to snore when she's on her back. We haven't shared a room since we were preteens. Hope this doesn't cause us to fight like we did then."

"I wouldn't want that to happen." Monica began searching in a drawer behind the desk. "Here you go. Two pairs." The sisters laughed as they were presented with earplugs. Cayce gladly took her pair, but Harri refused, saying she had slept with her fingers in her ears since childhood, first with a loud-breathing sister and then with a husband who not only snored but talked in his sleep.

"If you change your mind, Harri, these earplugs will be here waiting for you—anything to make your stay more enjoyable. By the way, I don't suppose either of you are interested in our contest while you're here?"

"Contest? What kind?" Harri asked the question while Cayce was busy looking at a souvenir book giving the history of the house and the founding family.

"Our annual cooking contest. Each year Spanish Oaks invites the local chefs and anyone with cooking skills to recreate a dish that can be served in the Stables. This year the category is sweets. Do either of you have a talent for cooking?"

Cayce grinned at Monica. "Not me, but my sister here just happens to own her own tea shop, and desserts are her specialty."

"Can it be any dessert, or do you specify a certain category like cakes, pies, pastries, et cetera?"

"All that is required is it must be sweet and an old, preferably antebellum, family recipe. The two judges are chefs from famous restaurants in South Mississippi and Louisiana."

"What's the prize?" Cayce asked the question, sure her sister would win. After all, Harri had won the Betty Crocker Award in high school, not to mention a blue ribbon at the Midsouth Fair for her red velvet cake.

"Five days' stay at Spanish Oaks in our best rooms, Jacob and Victoria's Suite, and publication of the recipe under the contestant's name in our famous cookbook, first rights only, in case you want to include it in a cookbook of your own some day. But the prize that has seemed most valued by winners in the ten years we've held the contest is that the food is named for its creator and becomes the signature dessert on the menu at the Stables for a full year."

"Where do I sign up?"

"I can take care of that for you, but you might want to register later. We have our last tour for today starting in fifteen minutes. Usually there are two later tours, but our tour guide has something else scheduled this evening. I can get someone to take your bags up right away, if you'd like to join the tour."

"Just give us directions and we'll take our bags."

"I think you might want help. Unfortunately, your room is on the second floor."

Cayce looked up at the winding mahogany stairs. Later, she was glad they had listened to Monica. Cayce panted like a gelding with a broken windpipe after climbing the double flight of stairs, while her petite sister was either not winded or was doing a good job of pretending by swallowing her breath. She talked the whole way up the stairs.

The room was small but furnished nicely with matching three-quarter-sized four-poster beds and a child-sized armoire. A closet that looked like a late addition was to one side of a small fireplace with a guardian angel carved in the mantelpiece. The bathroom, too, was a late addition but had an old tub with claw feet. A small empire desk sat caddy-corner to one side of the fireplace, and Harri got busy setting up her computer on it.

"Hey, Harri! This should come in handy for you, and it's just your size." Cayce pointed to a rush-bottom potty rocker at the end of one of the beds. It must have been used for small children in the family.

"Very funny, Cayce." Harri continued to look around the quaint room.

"Any place in particular you'd like your bags placed?" The teenage bellhop was anxious to please, anticipating a generous tip.

"Just one on each bed will be fine. I'll take the bed next to the window. The red suitcase is mine." Cayce handed the boy several dollar bills, and Harri followed suit.

"Thanks. If you need anything else, just let the front desk know." The boy started to leave, then turned back. "And good luck to you, ladies." Tipping his hat, he closed the door.

"What did that mean? Do you think he knew you were entering the contest?"

"How could he? I haven't registered yet, and he wasn't in the room when we were discussing it with Monica. Did you see that little smirk on his face as he closed the door? Makes me wish we hadn't been so generous tipping."

"No matter. Just another surly teenager with a personality as bad as his complexion. Let's get back downstairs and join the tour. We can unpack later."

As they headed down, Harri stopped and faced Cayce. "You do know where we were today right after lunch when the would-be guests called saying they had an accident?"

"I know exactly where you were, but I have a feeling I was right here at Spanish Oaks." Cayce raised her eyebrows up and down and gave her sister a mischievous smile.

When they reached the front desk, people were already waiting for the tour.

"If you'll gather in the foyer, we'll begin." The tour guide was a beautiful young woman whose skin was the color of a Pacific Islander. Her hair was long, a tousle of thick soft crinkles outlining high cheekbones and small features only slightly giving away her partial African-American heritage. Her eyes were light brown and danced with flecks of gold.

Twelve people made up the tour group, all adults with the exception of a five-year-old girl and a boy who looked to be about twelve. The boy stood cross-armed, pouting after losing an argument with his parents concerning what he would rather be doing. The little girl looked angelic and could have been little sister to the guide. Anyone who looked at her got a deep dimpled smile, further evidence of heavenly origin, as she peeked from under a wide-brimmed straw hat such as a child might have worn back in the 1800s. Her long crinkly braids hung to the waist of her white ruffled sundress, accentuated by pink lace-up tennis shoes. Molly, as her mother called her, held her daddy's hand and seemed perfectly content to be in the company of adult strangers.

"My name is Sophia, and I'll be your tour guide. We will begin the tour on the grounds of Spanish Oaks, something the owners have taken great pride in over the years."

The lawns lay tranquil, meticulously mowed, with azaleas and every shrub and tree pruned to perfection. Walking over the manicured yard was pleasant and relaxing, but Cayce whispered to her sister she hoped this part of the tour would go quickly. Harri, too, was anxious to get to the people stories and was not interested in knowing the name or origin of every tree, bush, or plant on the grounds.

"The lilies and irises—or flags, as we like to call them—you see on the grounds have special meaning. When we tour the main house, I'll point out the coat of arms for the Broussard family, which incorporates the fleur-de-lis, the flower of the lily. The fleur-de-lis symbolizes the French ancestry of Jacob Broussard, the original owner of Spanish Oaks Plantation and builder of this magnificent mansion. Most of the lilies and irises are from the original stock of bulbs Mr. Broussard imported from France. But I'll talk more about the symbolism when I show you the coat of arms."

"What's with the area back there roped off with yellow tape? Is that a crime scene or something?"

The young man was pointing to a large area a hundred or so feet from the slave quarters. No shrubs, flowers, or trees were growing there except for a weeping willow looking like a social outcast, a sore spot in the midst of the formal, award-winning landscape. A few feet away from it stood a stone cistern, complete with weathered wooden water bucket attached to a pulley.

"The five owners since the Broussards would agree with you on it being a crime scene, at least as compared with the rest of these beautiful grounds. For some reason, nothing will grow there permanently. It's very boggy, possibly because of an underground spring. Different owners have tried to plant the area, and the willow has been cut down several times, but it always grows back, and eventually anything else planted there dies. But the present owner has found a solution. He's putting in a beautiful swimming pool, something often requested by our many guests but rejected by past owners, who thought it would modernize the place too much. It's quite a coincidence that the present owner would be the one to give in to the idea, since he is the one who has done the most to preserve the history of the estate and to keep it historically accurate in every detail. He says it will be a masterpiece of art and will fit in with the natural aesthetics of Spanish Oaks as inconspicuously as possible. He even plans to incorporate the old cistern into the landscape. But now to the personal history of the Oaks."

"Please follow me to the slave quarters. This is where the real story begins. Stay on the cobblestone path, and before we enter the quarters, I'd like to establish a few ground rules. Please stay behind the roped areas and refrain from touching the furnishings. And it would behoove you to stay with the group for the remainder of the tour. Wanderers in the past have often had strange things happen, things that drove them back to the group in a hurry, or forced them to leave the plantation altogether."

Sophia smiled as her gaze turned to the boy who had strayed off the path and was peeking in the window of one of the cabins. The boy's father rebuked his son and ordered him back to the group. After he was secured between his parents, the group continued down the pathway.

"If you have any questions, feel free to stop me at any point."

As the group followed their guide toward the quarters, Cayce heard the voice of the little girl calling her mama in a whisper.

"That little girl sounds as sweet as she looks." With her head, Cayce motioned to the girl up ahead.

"You mean the little girl behind us?"

"No, she's up ahead, a few feet behind the guide." Cayce looked around the tourists in front of them and saw only the couple with their son, who was now staggering off the path trying to play a game on his cell phone and walk at the same time.

Then she looked behind them and was rewarded with a big smile from Molly.

"I could have sworn her voice was coming from up there." Cayce and Harri continued walking, with Cayce still glancing around the crowd just in case she heard the voice again.

"Two of the quarters are part of the tour but are never rented out. The one you will see today is Milla's cabin. Her story is not for the faint of heart."

"Now we're getting somewhere," Harri whispered, rubbing her hands together in eager anticipation.

Milla's cabin, like the others, was one small room. The furnishings were sparse and utilitarian, consisting of a three-quarter-sized oak bed covered in a frayed and faded cotton patchwork quilt, a pine cupboard containing a few pieces of stoneware dishes, a poplar hutch table that could serve as additional seating by lifting the table top, two crudely built straight chairs with worn-down legs, and a primitive rocker. In the corner opposite the door stood an oak-framed full-length mirror, distorted by age and by dark splotches where the silvering had worn away. A fireplace occupied most of one wall, and on its stone hearth sat iron cookware, a Dutch oven, and a hanging pot. Two lamps were noticeable, one on the table and the other on the mantel.

"The furnishings are all original and have been in this cabin for over one hundred fifty years. That is, except for the few times different owners have tried to move pieces to other cabins or to the main house. Every time an item has been moved, it has mysteriously found its way back here, and always to the exact spot in the cabin where it was before removal."

"Yeah, right!" A young man who looked to be in his twenties gave a sarcastic laugh as his young wife nudged him with her shoulder.

"I'm sorry, but my husband is a real skeptic when it comes to the paranormal. But please just do like I do and ignore him."

"Oh, he's not the first unbeliever I've run into, but you might ask Tom, our maintenance man, if you want verification. About four years ago, the oak bed, a rope bed requiring much time to rope, was dismantled and moved to the porch while the sagging floor was being repaired.

"The carpenters returned the next morning to continue the project and found the bed back in place, fully roped and with the bedding back on. When the contractor complained to Tom about not wanting to waste time by having to dismantle the bed before starting work, Tom told him he had no idea what he was talking about. Tom took the bed down again and put it back on the porch.

"The next morning, the contractor found the same situation again. This time, he ordered his men to complete the project before leaving, even if it took all night to finish. If you'll bend down and look under the bed, you will be surprised to find that the floor still sags even though the sag was removed at the time. But I'm getting ahead of the story."

"Ouch! Stop it, Janie! Pinching me is not going to make me believe this crap." The young husband rubbed his upper arm.

"I didn't pinch you, Brad." Looking behind him, Brad found the spot empty where he'd thought she stood. His wife had moved to the other side of the room to get a better look at the floor. The look Brad gave his wife was one of bewilderment mixed with anger.

"I'm going to the Stables and have a drink. I'll wait for you there." Brad giant-stepped his way out of the cabin as the group followed Janie's lead in laughing.

"Oh, there's another detail I should mention. There is no electricity in these two cabins for the same reason nothing is moved from them. Electricity will not work in either cabin. It's been tried numerous times but never works longer than a day. That is why we have lamps in each one. It's the only light allowed. If you really want to get in the spirit of the quarters, no pun intended, you should sign up for one of the last two tours of the day, when the cabins are lit by the original coal oil lamps."

The tour members looked at each other, wanting to disbelieve what seemed a farfetched disclosure, but their faces revealed definite uncertainty.

"Now for the rest of the story." Sophia took a position in front of the mantel. "Milla was a house servant, a coveted position among the slave population. Her mother was Affie, the main cook, a wedding gift to the founding family, Jacob and Victoria Broussard. Milla was born the same year as the only Broussard child, Princeton, who would be the last Broussard to own Spanish Oaks. In addition to being the cook, Affie was also Princeton's nanny. Milla and Princeton became inseparable as children, not knowing, or refusing to believe, there was a color barrier to their friendship. Affie even gave them baths together as toddlers. At the big social balls held at Spanish Oaks, when Affie was required to cook, the two children were often seen peeking through the stair rails on the second floor late at night. Once the children were reprimanded by an angry male guest who caught them in the act of a southern faux pas—dancing the waltz under the magnolias, imitating the adults they had been watching in the ballroom."

"When it was time to school her son, Victoria also taught Milla, at Princeton's insistence, stopping only when she realized Milla was reading better and reciting her math facts faster than Princeton. Milla continued to practice her reading and writing at night with her mother, who had been taught by Victoria when she recognized Affie's culinary talents, wanting her to be able to record her recipes for posterity."

Harri looked at Cayce, and she nodded in acknowledgment. The same thought had occurred to her. Had they bought Affie's cookbook?

"Also, being a deeply religious person, Victoria wanted Affie to be able to read the Bible to the other slaves as well as to her own family, who at that time consisted of her husband Big Zed and Affie's son Caleb, who came with his mother as part of the wedding gift."

Harri punched Cayce, but she had not been paying attention to Sophie. She was too busy watching Molly waving to the mirror and smiling.

"Is that an original *McGuffy Reader*?" Molly's

mother was staring at a tattered, yellowed book on the table.

"Yes, it is. It was used by Mrs. Broussard to teach Princeton and Milla to read. Milla also used it to teach her own daughter, but, unfortunately, the child did not get to go past the first reader. But let's not get ahead of ourselves. This is where the story becomes a tragedy.

"As Milla and Princeton grew to be young adults, their interest in each other changed directions. Both knew the mutual affection they felt could never amount to anything, but they were young and impetuous. It was no surprise to Victoria or her husband when Milla became pregnant, even though Princeton had become quite the lady's man in his own society. At one point, Victoria and Jacob talked of selling Milla before the baby was born, but Princeton became enraged and a compromise was reached. Milla and her soon-to-be-born child would stay at Spanish Oaks, and Princeton would marry someone worthy of his position in society.

"Before Princeton could choose a suitable wife, Jacob Broussard suffered a stroke and died. Victoria, distraught over her husband's death, took to her bed and handed the plantation over to Princeton, a very eligible bachelor, who became the catch of plantation society in South Mississippi. At Victoria's insistence, Princeton married the most beautiful and sought-after girl in the county, a girl who just happened to be from a very wealthy family. I'll tell you more about Beatrice Broussard when we get to the main house, but for now, just picture Scarlett O'Hara, with flaming red hair.

"Milla gave birth shortly after Princeton and Beatrice married. Chloe was a beautiful child who, as a toddler, radiated joy to everyone she came in contact with, especially her father, whom she called 'Massey.' Victoria Broussard and her son were enamored with Chloe and spoiled her with love and attention while keeping her at arm's length socially. Victoria seemed to fare best physically when Chloe made her daily visit, plopping herself on Victoria's bed and brushing her grandmother's thin gray hair while singing a lullaby her grandmother Affie had taught her. Of course, Chloe did not know Victoria was her grandmother. Chloe called her Miss Victoria.

"Beatrice was so busy spending her husband's money and being the social butterfly she was not bothered by the presence of Chloe or her slave mother, whom she viewed as nothing more than a past fling for her young husband. That was until Beatrice herself became pregnant. Beatrice gave birth to a daughter who was beautiful like her mother. Princeton was proud of the baby and named her Lily after the fleur-de-lis emblazoned on the family crest, but his pride was short-lived. The young parents soon realized there was something wrong with the baby girl. Lily did not cry or smile or coo, and she did not recognize or react to anyone except her mother and then only when she was nursing."

"She had autism." The statement came from an older woman in the group. "I've worked with students with disabilities all my life. She sounds as if she had low-functioning autism spectrum disorder."

"Many people have recognized the traits when I get to this part of the story, usually teachers like yourself, or psychologists or doctors. I believe you are correct, but autism was an unknown mental disease in the early nineteenth century. Remember, mental disease was viewed as a curse treatable only by denial and secrecy.

"Once Princeton discovered his daughter's difference, he had nothing more to do with her. He began drinking heavily and ignored the affections and desires of his wife, possibly in fear of creating another child like Lily. He turned his attention back to Milla and heaped even more love and attention on Chloe. Chloe even rode behind him on many occasions when he went into River Town, something not viewed favorably by residents of the town, who suspected the truth.

"When Chloe was six, she had the run of the house. She dragged four-year-old Lily with her, treating her like a live baby doll. Beatrice began to hate Chloe, resentment eating away at her as she watched her own daughter being treated as a throwaway by the man who had fathered her.

"Victoria died when Lily was four, leaving Princeton with the responsibilities of a plantation suffering financial problems and with a wife and child he could not or would not love. His drinking got worse.

"In March of 1848, Chloe disappeared while playing in the yard with Lily. Princeton and Milla were distraught. Even Beatrice feigned concern. Since it was not uncommon for slaves to disappear off plantations after slave importation was banned, they surmised Chloe had been stolen. Princeton searched for the child for weeks and sent others to search as far as Louisiana and Alabama, but it was all to no avail."

"She is so sad. She misses Chloe."

Everyone turned to look at Molly, who had spoken while staring at the mirror. Leaving her mother's side, the little girl crawled under the rope and walked to the mirror. Her father attempted to retrieve his daughter, but Sophia beckoned for him to let her go and made no attempt to call her back across the rope, regardless of the rules.

"It's okay, Milla. I'll find Chloe for you." Molly caressed the mirror with her fingertips, consoling something or someone she thought she saw in the mirror.

"She's okay now. You can go on, Soppy." Molly returned to the other side of the rope and took her mother's hand as if this was nothing out of the ordinary.

Sophia smiled at the little girl before speaking again to the group, who were noticeably awed by the experience. Even the boy paid attention now, putting his cell phone in his pocket.

"Please don't be alarmed. Molly is not the first child on a tour to see Milla in the cabin. She seems comforted by children, especially little girls about the age of Chloe when she disappeared. But it is the first time anyone on the tour has called me Soppy. I was named after one of my ancestors, a grandmother too many greats ago to remember. That grandmother was the wife of Affie's son, Caleb, Milla's older brother. Only my father calls me Soppy, but I do know the original Sophia was also called Soppy. I have to admit I have goose bumps right now, whether from the temperature dropping in the cabin or from my own surprise. Anyway, I'd better go on with the story while I can still talk."

As they listened, the teacher gasped and Molly's mother wiped tears from her eyes as she held tightly to her little girl's hand. Cayce and Harri moved closer to Molly, hoping Milla might appear again. The others on the tour kept eyes and ears glued on Sophia.

"Milla became more and more distraught, convinced Chloe was dead. Finally, she could endure the suffering no longer. Some time before midnight on May 30, 1848, while Princeton and Beatrice were celebrating Princeton's twenty-sixth birthday, Milla ended her suffering with a self-made noose she hung from the rafters in this cabin. Caleb found her. If you look at the rafter there to your right, you will see a light mark, the scratch left by the rope where Milla ended her life. One of the chairs by the table is the one she kicked from beneath her."

The group was obviously upset by the story, giving out sighs of disbelief and horror. Harri became so upset she had to leave the room, and Cayce followed her.

"I could feel her pain from the moment we entered that cabin, even before the guide began the story. If I had looked in that mirror, I'm sure I would have seen Milla begging for my help, too. That was the saddest, most emotional experience I've had...ever." Harri wiped her tear-filled eyes as Cayce tried to console her.

"I don't think I can finish the tour today, Cayce. Right now, a little Jack would be helpful."

"Let's check out the Stables. If you feel like eating, we'll have dinner and maybe look through the gift shop before we retire. It's been a long, tiring day but definitely an interesting one."

****

It was dark by the time they left the restaurant. The grounds were lit up, and guests were walking around or mingling on the porches with cocktails or glasses of wine in hand.

"How about we walk off some of that delicious

meal before we go up? My pecan-crusted salmon was delicious, and I didn't even know I liked salmon. And what was that you had again?"

Cayce knew it was too early to go to bed and was leery of taking out the antique cookbook just yet. She felt Harri needed some recoup time. Psychic vibes beat like the drums of her shaman ancestors at every corner and turn of the property, and she knew Harri felt the vibrations, too.

"*Coq au vin.* I'd tell you how to make it if I thought you were interested."

"I'll just wait 'til Lean Tasties comes out with it."

"Yeah, right." Harri headed to the cobblestone path leading to the slave quarters.

"Are you sure you want to walk in this direction?"

"If you fall off a horse…"

"Would you look at those stars? And they call Montana the Big Sky Country." Cayce was trying to distract Harri from the quarters.

"Yes, it's pretty spectacular. It looked just like this the night Milla died. She looked out the window and prayed to God to let her be with her child before she got on that chair."

"I won't ask how you know this, but I bet you're right." Cayce started to return her gaze to the path, when she stopped.

"Look, Harri! There! In the window on the second floor!"

"You mean that light? It looks like an old timey oil lamp. Seems like that would be against the fire code."

"One, two, three…wait a minute! That's higher than the second floor. Must be some kind of attic, or maybe there's a third floor." The breeze they had been enjoying suddenly turned fierce, as if it wanted to push the two away from the quarters, but the sisters did not take their eyes off the lamp. Seconds later, it flickered and died.

"Are you ready?" Cayce watched as Harri took out her notepad.

"Got it. Quarter 'til eight. Third floor lamp. Strong breeze lasting only seconds."

"Let's go to the gift shop before it closes. I want to pick up a copy of the history of the plantation like I was looking at when we checked in, especially since we didn't finish the tour."

The gift shop was full of the usual souvenirs, T-shirts, cups, and calendars, along with some new, very expensive quilts and replicas of rag dolls, mostly African-American with calico dresses and bandanas around their yarn hair, or with a multitude of pigtails. Another doll they did not expect to see was small and made from straight pieces of wood like a wooden cross. The doll was covered with layers of brightly colored yarn and fabric, with eyes and mouth made of red beads. Many strands of red, purple, and yellow beads hung around its neck, draping to the waist. It, too, had a bright scarf tied around its head.

"I hope this is not what it looks like. You know how Pop fought those elements. Preached it was not Christian. If he were here right now, he'd give somebody what for. Remember, his hero was Edgar Cayce, the clairvoyant who, in addition to having visions, taught Sunday school all his life. Dad must have really idolized him to name me after him." Cayce couldn't help but think of her father's warning against such a talisman.

"I'm afraid it is what you're thinking. A voodoo doll." Harri picked the doll up to scrutinize it closer.

"Not bad voodoo! A love charm. Jus' what da world need!" The voice came from the door. A strange yet beautiful woman who looked to be in her fifties entered the gift shop carrying a wooden basket filled with the "love charms." Her hair was tied up in a bright purple silk scarf, and she was dressed like the Caribbean of the old days, or like some islanders dress when trying to attract the tourist business.

"You both had love but lose it. Am I not correct?" The woman spoke with a broken accent.

"Very perceptive, but we *are* two women traveling alone." Harri smiled at the woman while dismissing her ability to tell their pasts.

"Here. A gift to each of you." The lady balanced the basket on her hip as she handed each one a doll. "My senses tell me I like you. You have special seeing, useful gift at the Oaks. Maybe I help you some." The woman placed the basket on the table.

"These are quite unique, beautiful in a mystifying sort of way." Cayce turned the doll over and over in her hands. "My name is Cayce, and this is my sister, Harri." Cayce extended her hand to the giver.

"And who do we have to thank for these lovely charms?" Harri also shook the woman's hand.

"I am Sherone, but they call me Mama Tee. Maybe you come see me while you here? My address on da tag. I like to hear what you see. No charge." After shaking hands with the sisters, Sherone opened the door to leave.

"May da Way find you!" With that, Mama Tee left the shop.

Cayce and Harri looked at each other and then turned to the shop clerk, who had a big smile on her face.

"Oh, yeah, Mama Tee is for real. You know what people say—there's one in every town. I've never been to her, but a lot of tourists have their fortunes told. I'm too scared. She's been living here over thirty years. Inherited her grandmother's cabin and her gift for 'knowing all,' as she says. She's from the Caribbean just like her grandmother's ancestors. Her parents moved back there to learn about their culture—and probably to get away from the legends left by the first Mama Tee, if I'm guessing right. If you need directions how to get to her cabin, I'll give them to you. It's in a pretty desolate, out-of-the-way place."

"We'll think about it. Thanks for the information." Cayce paid for the history book before following Harri out the door.

"What do you want to do now? Mama Tee is a hard act to follow."

"Well, there's no TV in the room, but I wouldn't mind getting into bed and reading this history. How about you, Harri? Got any good books to read?"

"Yeah. One, but I've never worn white gloves with my nightgown. Think I'll make a fashion statement?"

No one was at the front desk, so Harri could not register for the contest. Cayce was disappointed for another reason. She wanted to see if there was an explanation for the lamp on the third floor, if there was a third floor.

Harri again talked all the way up the steep stairs, dismissing Cayce's idea her sister was faking not being winded by the climb. But Harri stopped chattering as they neared their room.

"Who left this door open? And more important, what was anyone doing in our room? We didn't ask for a bed turn-down, although chocolate mints—or better still, pecan pralines—on the pillow might be nice." Harri pushed the door open, and Cayce entered first, with apprehension.

"No bed turn-down, but a definite bed turn-upside-down."

Cayce's red suitcase was open and her clothes were strewn on the wrong bed, the one by the wall, not by the window. Harri's suitcase was untouched except to be moved next to the closet door. Everything in Cayce's suitcase was tumbled onto the bed. The little satchel containing her jewelry had been dumped on the floor.

"My gold chain and locket are missing. The locket isn't valuable, but the pictures in it of Mom and Pop are. Who would want to take something that's only special to the owner?"

"The box is gone!" Harri ran to the closet and threw open the door. "It's not in here. Look under the bed, Cayce!"

"Not here. We have to report this right now, Harri! The locket is one thing but the book is something entirely different."

"I'll go. You can clean up this mess and put your things in the drawers of the chest."

Harri was surprised to see Sophia working the front desk.

"Where is Monica?"

"She had to leave early, so I'm watching the desk for her. I usually run the last tours, but tonight I'm working the desk until midnight. You left the tour early.

I might be wrong, but I sensed you had some experiences of your own in Milla's cabin. Am I right?"

"Yes, but just some minor sensations. What I'm concerned about now is what happened in our room on the second floor."

"Let's see." Sophia ran her finger down the register. "Oh, I see. That's Lily's room, next to the staircase that goes to the attic room. I'll bet your suitcases got shuffled around. Right?"

"How did you know what happened? But it was more than shuffled. My sister's suitcase was dumped and she's missing a necklace. And I have a box missing."

"I am so sorry, but please don't be alarmed. It happens sometimes but hasn't in a long time. We were beginning to think our ghosts had left us, but all of a sudden, they're back in full force. Spanish Oaks is breathing again. You must be in tune with the paranormal."

"Seems that way. I'm not concerned with the suitcase, and my sister doesn't care that much about the necklace, but we are both concerned about the box. I want it back."

"Describe it for me. I'll let the staff know. Usually, things that go missing are found within an hour or so."

Harri described the box and requested an immediate search be made. Sophia picked up her radio to alert all staff on duty. Harri returned to the room thinking about what Sophia had said. As she neared their door, she looked just past it and saw a small hallway. Entering it, she found narrow, steep stairs, obviously going to the attic room, and couldn't wait to tell Cayce.

"I know where the room is where we saw the lamp, but I don't know where the box or the necklace is."

"Are they going to search for them?"

"Yes, Sophia was working the front desk and didn't seem surprised by any of this. I didn't tell her what was in the box. I'm glad I used that Sharpie to put my name and address on the outside. Now for the secret of the third floor. Come out in the hallway."

Harri and Cayce stood looking up the narrow staircase that climbed up partway, then made a turn to the right.

"I think that would be pretty tight even for you, Harri. I guess you want me to suck in and climb up there behind you to see if the attic room is open?"

"No. I want you to go first. You're the brave one, remember? You crawled under our grandmother's house during snake season and dragged those puppies out by their ears."

"That was almost fifty years ago! How much longer are you going to use that story?"

Cayce squeezed her way up the stairs with Harri in tow. After huffing and puffing her way up the two steep, curving flights of stairs, Cayce was halted by an ancient doorknob. After trying to turn the white enamel knob, she tried jiggling it.

"I figured as much. It's locked, and from the looks of the rust on it, it's been locked a very long time. It takes one of those big old antique keys to unlock it."

Cayce tried to peek through the keyhole, but all she saw was blackness.

"We might as well go back to the room and wait to see if the box turns up. Did Sophia say if things were always found?" Cayce asked.

"She implied as much. Said missing objects usually turn up within an hour or two. I just hope whoever finds it doesn't open it. I know we bought it legally, but I'm not sure Spanish Oaks knew it was for sale. I just have this feeling."

Cayce decided to soak her tired body in the big clawfoot tub while Harri sat worrying about the book. While drying off, Cayce heard a knock at the door. Anxious to see if the box had been found, she put on one of the thick robes supplied by the inn before getting completely dry.

"Sophia said not to worry, and she was right. They didn't find your locket and chain, though."

Having no scissors or knife, Harri dug her car keys out of her purse, preparing to use them to open the box. The tape looked secure and was still wound completely around the box several times over the opening. Her name and address were exactly as she had written it on the top.

"Thought you had decided not to look at the book tonight. The box doesn't look like it was tampered with."

"I know, but I have to be sure."

After several runs with her key down the seam, Harri cut the tape and began unfolding the layers of newspaper stuffed around the plastic-wrapped book. As the last piece of newspaper was thrown to the floor, Harri reached in to remove the treasure.

"Shit!"

As she jerked her hand out, blood dripped to the newspaper on the floor.

Cayce grabbed a wet washcloth from the bathroom and handed it to Harri, who immediately wrapped it around her finger. The sisters butted heads as they leaned in to get a closer look in the box as Cayce held open the cardboard flaps.

"What the hell?" The sisters responded in unison.

Chapter Four

"I've seen that butcher knife before, Harri! Don't touch it!" Cayce held her hands up as if she were trying to keep her sister from getting near the knife again.

"You mean, don't touch it *again*." Harri held up her finger with a bandage showing a red spot where the blood continued to seep through. "What do you mean you've seen it before? Have you lost your mind?"

"My vision, in the antique shop. The knife was lying on the edge of the table in the kitchen. A trail of milk from an overturned stone pitcher was running across the table." Cayce made a trail in the air in front of her with her finger. "The knife blocked the milk's flow and redirected it so it followed the blade, mixing with the blood that covered it and forming dark pink droplets that fell in a stream to the floor."

"You're sure this is the same knife, Cayce?" Harri held her finger up in an attempt to stop the throbbing.

"Yes. I remember the heavy brass brads in the handle and the long steel blade worn thin like it had been used for decades, a blade that must have been exceptionally sharp to form the gaping wound I saw in the woman's stomach." Cayce sat on the edge of her bed, waiting for Harri's reaction.

"But how did it get in the box?" Harri sat on her bed facing Cayce. "The tape had not been disturbed, and I know it wasn't in there when we left the shop."

61

"As Pop would say, 'There's an explanation for everything, but not necessarily the one you want.'"

"So what do we do now?" Harri held her hands open, waiting. "We need to find out where this came from."

"We'll just say we found this knife in our room. Unless you have a better idea, Harri?"

"Well, we did find it in our room. How exactly do we carry it? If we walk downstairs with this thing, we'll scare the other guests to death. Not to mention they'll think we're a couple of whackos."

"We *are* a couple of whackos. Family trait, remember?" Cayce left her bed and headed for the bathroom. When she came out, she was carrying a thick towel. "Let's wrap it up in this towel for tonight. We'll take it down first thing tomorrow morning and see if anyone will claim it, or know where its home is."

In addition to wrapping it in the towel, Cayce put it in her empty suitcase and locked it. Then, to make sure it didn't jump out of the suitcase in the night and murder them, the sisters put it in the closet and secured the door shut with a chair under the knob.

"There. That oughta do it. Now for that reading. I have so many questions, but I'm sure they won't be answered in this book. Still, I need to know about the families who lived here." Cayce picked up the history book and began pulling back the covers on her bed.

"I bet I have the same questions. For instance, how is it possible for furniture to return to Milla's cabin without anyone taking credit for moving it? And are we the only ones who are feeling the pain of the dead here?" Harri put her bandaged finger to her cheek in contemplation.

"My questions exactly, and now the added questions of who tumbled my suitcase and took the box."

"And most of all, where did the butcher knife come from and what is its significance to us?" Harri added as she gingerly opened the closet door, ready to retrieve the box.

"Well, I think I know what you are about to do. Let the seeking for answers begin!" Cayce clarified the situation with the statement as she crawled between the crisp Egyptian cotton sheets and propped herself up with fluffy down pillows.

Harri unlocked the suitcase and took out the box. After gingerly opening the box, she took the white gloves out and slid her hands into them, making sure she got rid of even the tiniest wrinkle by pushing hard between each finger, more as a delaying tactic than actual concern. Then, carefully, she bypassed the towel-wrapped knife and lifted the journal out of the box. Next, she placed the journal on the small desktop in the corner of the room. Before looking at the journal, Harri returned the box and knife to the suitcase, locked it, and placed it back in the closet, with the chair secure under the doorknob.

The sisters grew silent, totally engrossed in their respective reading materials. A few minutes later, Cayce broke the silence as she sat up fast, knocking one of the pillows off the bed.

"Oh, my gosh!" She held the book closer to her eyes to make sure she was seeing what she thought she was seeing.

"What is it?" Harri left her own reading and went to sit on the foot of her sister's bed.

"This picture! It's a picture of Beatrice Broussard with Lily. Even though it's black and white, you can just tell that thick, curly hair is flaming red." Cayce held the book so Harri could see the picture.

"My, my, what a beautiful child! Beautiful but with such a hollow, unnatural look in her eyes. How sad!" Harri went back to her own book.

"Anything interesting in your cookbook?"

"I'm taking it one page at a time and devouring, no pun intended, each recipe. It reads like a diary. There are definitely two sets of handwriting, one elegant, probably belonged to Victoria Broussard, and the second handwriting, a much simpler print rather than script, was probably Affie's. The recipe handwriting lacks elegance but is extremely neat, with each letter size measured in exactness. It has a curvy flow to it even if it is print and reminds me of when we were teenagers and tried to write with a ruler under our pens.

"The first few pages are missing lines from the top and bottom. Too bad! The dates are part of the worn-off edges, so I don't know when Victoria started keeping the cooking journal. About halfway through, the first date that can be deciphered is February 8, 1844. The last date shown is May 30, 1848, but the elegant handwriting stops earlier. Does it say in the history when Victoria died?"

"Let me turn to the end where I saw a chart of significant dates in the family history. Jean Paul Broussard...Jacob Broussard...Oh, here it is. Victoria Broussard died in her sleep on January 3, 1848."

"That pretty much cinches it. There's very little narrative after the last of Victoria's handwriting. That date was...let's see...December 24, 1847. That would have been Victoria's last Christmas in this beautiful mansion."

"What about the pages stuck together? Where do they fall in the book?" Cayce placed her book face down on her bed to give Harri her full attention.

"Toward the end, very near where the writing stops. There are a few blank pages, and it looks like a few pages were torn out at the end, probably to be used as writing paper. I bet there are several stories in here, but we'll never know unless it comes to you in one of your experiences. Of course, you could take a look through these pages yourself." Harri stood and held the book out to her sister, who moved as close to the wall side of the bed as possible.

"You just keep that book away from me. I'm not sure the white gloves would be enough, that book is so potent. Even having the knife locked in the closet gives me the hibby-jibbies!" Cayce shuddered as she looked toward the closet as if expecting the chair to move away on its own.

"I know what you mean. I'll be glad when we can return it to wherever, tomorrow. Speaking of tomorrow, I'm ready to call it quits for today. How about you?"

After putting their books away, Harri crawled into her bed, and Cayce turned out the bedside lamp between them.

Sleep came fast after the emotionally draining day. At some point in the night, Cayce awoke and began feeling in the dark for the earplugs. Harri had turned onto her back. As Cayce was inserting the second earplug, she thought she heard a bump overhead. Sitting up and pulling the earplug out, she listened, straining to hear over Harri's snores that were growing louder.

Bump! There it was again, but this time a noise like some object being dragged replaced the bump. As she listened, a slight shuffle followed by a rhythmic "creak…creak…creak" sounded from overhead. Her curiosity, always stronger than any fear she might have, forced Cayce to leave her bed and fumble around in her purse until she found the penlight she kept for just such emergencies. After tiptoeing across the room, Cayce inched open the door to the hall, careful not to awaken Harri.

The hall was illuminated only slightly by low-burning lights made to resemble candles and giving an eerie ambiance to the hall—not creepy, but with the right shadows it could have been. No guests were stirring in the hall or down below, and Cayce wished she had looked at the clock so she could journal in her mind the exact time of the noises. A few steps later, she stood looking up at the narrow stairs leading to the attic room and had almost decided to go back and wake Harri before going any farther. But from the staircase, the creaking grew louder, and she decided to continue on her own.

Cayce stepped lightly, glad she had on soft slippers and not her boots. Lingering at the fourth step from the top, she pondered whether she really wanted to approach the door. Shining her penlight up, she noticed the door looked exactly as it had earlier and wondered if it would open this time.

Third step…second step…top step. Cayce was about to turn the doorknob when she heard the sound of a child humming softly, keeping time to the creaking that had started again. Putting her ear to the door, she recognized the words to a lullaby her father had sung to her and Harri as toddlers.

Hush-a-bye, don't you cry,
Go to sleepy little baby.
When you wake, you'll have cake,
And all the pretty little horses.

Cayce was mesmerized by the sweet but melancholy voice and could not move. It was as if she had lost all control of her faculties as well as any recollection of the original intent of her trespassing.

Way down yonder, down in the meadow,
There's a poor wee little lamby.
The bees and the butterflies pickin' at its eyes,
The poor wee thing cried for her mammy.

"What are you doing, Cayce?"

Cayce shrieked, threw up her hands, and dropped her penlight, which rolled all the way down to where Harri retrieved it at the curve of the stairs.

"My Lord in heaven, Harri! You scared me out of ten years' growth! Well, that wouldn't be such a bad thing, but for gosh sake, don't sneak up on me like that anymore."

"I didn't sneak. If you hadn't had your head glued to that door, you would have heard me. I repeat. What are you doing?"

Cayce motioned for her sister to come on up but knew there would be nothing for her to hear. Cayce and Harri pressed their ears to the door but heard only silence.

"I swear there was a child rocking and singing 'Hush-a-Bye.'"

Harri placed her hand on the doorknob and turned, but nothing happened.

"I think you had a nightmare and sleepwalked. This

door is just as rusted and locked as it was earlier."

"It was not a nightmare, and I've never sleepwalked and you know it. I heard noises up here, even louder than the noise going on in our room when you turned on your back. I had to check it out."

"Well, next time wake me up. Two sets of ears are always better than one." Harri led the way back to their room.

No "next time" was required the rest of the night. Cayce slept little, waiting for the attic room noise to return, but when she did nod off, it was short-lived. For whatever reason awakened, Cayce would sit up and listen, turning her head in all directions in case one ear was more acute than the other. Not hearing anything, she would lie back, disappointed she could not hear the angelic child's lullaby again. Harri had no trouble sleeping, but fortunately for her sister she slept on her side for the remainder of the night.

****

Morning sunlight streamed through the bedroom window and caressed Harri's cheeks, awakening her from a restful though eventful night. The draperies had been opened, after they'd turned out the light for the last time, so the moonlight and stars could sing their own lullabies to the sisters.

Cayce was just coming out of the bathroom, drying her long hair with a towel. She had, as usual, gotten up earlier than her sister, and Harri could see the history book open where her sister had been researching for no telling how long this morning.

"Let me guess. You were trying to identify your little ghost singer, right? How long have you been up anyway?"

"Long enough to have my body screaming so loud for caffeine I couldn't concentrate anymore, and yes, I was trying to find out about any children who lived here. Hit the shower…uh…make that the tub. I'll tell you everything I know at breakfast."

Over the biggest and most delicious butter-packed cinnamon rolls either had ever tasted, Cayce began sharing the history of Spanish Oaks.

"Jacob Broussard was given the plantation by his father, Jean Paul Broussard, who owned two distilleries and a shipping business in New Orleans, as well as a large plantation north of New Orleans which he referred to as his hobby. But get this! According to the scuttlebutt in the New Orleans community in the early 1800s, Jean Paul was involved in illegal slave importation, mostly by way of the Caribbean, and other black market buying and selling—the other not specified."

Cayce took a sip of coffee before continuing. "Also, Mr. Broussard was a miraculously lucky gambler. Shall we say cheater? The two thousand acres that became Spanish Oaks was won in a high-stakes poker game. The man he won it off accused him of cheating and challenged him to a duel. Not a good thing to do, since Jean Paul's other hobby seems to have been dueling."

"Quite a character, huh? I wonder which of the distinguished-looking portraits in the lobby is Jean Paul. So who all did he kill in exercising hobby number two?" Harri took a bite of cinnamon roll and then pushed it away from her. "That is wonderful but way too rich for me. Continue, please." Harri took a drink of ice water while nodding to Cayce.

"It doesn't give specifics but says more than a dozen duels were recorded, and it was not known how many unrecorded duels he fought. No specifics about the duels either, except for two—the one with the original owner of this land, and then one with some dude from France, P. Bruser, who spoke little English. The story goes he confronted Jean Paul in one of the elite gambling houses he frequented, called him a thief, and demanded the return of some family heirloom he called '*La Fleur*.' Jean Paul, usually cool, calm, and collected, became so angry he challenged him immediately. No 'meet me at sunrise.' The two men went into the street, paced off, and J.P. shot Bruser, a bullet straight between the eyes. Jean Paul had Bruser buried in the pauper's cemetery with no attempt at notification of next of kin and no grave marker erected. J.P. called his opponent a crazy man who obviously had mistaken him for someone else. He refused to ever speak of the incident again."

"Any information on Affie, or Milla and Chloe?"

"The story of Chloe's disappearance takes up several pages and includes Milla's suicide. There's a whole section on the ghosts of Spanish Oaks, but I'm saving that. I want to know as much as I can about the Broussard family first, and I bet there will be much mention of our little Chloe in that section, and possibly Lily, too."

"What about Affie?" Harri wiped her mouth on her napkin, folded it, and placed it on top of her plate, signifying she was finished.

"Affie was given to Victoria by her father-in-law as a wedding present, a personal servant, said to be the most 'refined' of the slaves Jean Paul owned. She was only seventeen at the time and had a one-year-old son, Caleb."

"What about Big Zed? Isn't that what Sophie said Affie's husband's name was?" Harri was anxious to know as much about Affie's family as she could.

"Zed came later. The book didn't mention Affie coming with a husband. Zed was the trusted personal attendant of Jacob and accompanied him everywhere he went. When he wasn't by his master's side, he was in charge of all the house servants, something unusual given the size and strength of Zed. Ordinarily, he would have been a top field hand. Affie and Zed 'jumped the broom,' so to speak, two years after Affie's arrival at Spanish Oaks, and Milla was born a year later. Let's see, that would make Caleb her older brother by about four years. Zed had the last name of his previous owner, Devaux, so I assume Milla and Affie's last name was Devaux. Caleb possibly was given the name of his stepfather, but the book doesn't say. There isn't much written about Affie except to say she was Victoria's devoted companion throughout her mistress's married life and was at her side when she died in 1848."

"Sophia said she was a descendant of Caleb, so there must be family connections still in the area. Evidently the family history, including slave family history, has been preserved even though Princeton was the last Broussard to own the Oaks. So what about the ancestry of Jean Paul Broussard? Did they come to Louisiana with La Salle, or the d'Iberville brothers? Maybe they fought with Lafayette during the Revolution. Surely there's more history than dueling and cheating, Cayce."

"The history says nothing is known about Jean

Paul's family. He never talked about them, but he obviously came from France because he spoke with an accent, although he refused to speak anything but English. Must not have been too proud of his French ancestry. He married Marguerite Galvez, who was from a prominent New Orleans family, related to the governor of Louisiana during the Spanish period. She was quite a beauty. Maybe that's where the dark hair and eyes of Jacob and Princeton Broussard came from."

"But what about the coat of arms on the cookbook? Sophia mentioned she would show the tour the coat of arms and talked of the significance of the fleur-de-lis, the lily. What was all that about if Jean Paul was not proud of his French ancestry?"

"Well, Jacob must have been proud of it even if his father wasn't. I guess it's another mystery, Harri. Anyway, the last chapter is on Spanish Oaks today and talks about ghost incidents. Like I said, I'm saving that one."

"Ghosts, huh? I guess Sophia was right." Harri smiled and propped her chin in her hand.

"Right about what, Harri?"

"When I went down to report the box and your locket missing last night, Sophia told me about things happening in Lily's room but said nothing had happened in a long time. Her exact words were, 'Spanish Oaks is breathing again.'"

"Breathing…breath…I haven't heard that term in a long time, at least not in that context." Cayce smiled, remembering the term.

"I've never heard it. Not a clue what either one of you is talking about. What did she mean by 'Spanish Oaks is breathing again?'" Harri asked.

"Okay. Here goes." Cayce looked around, lowered her voice, and stretched across the table closer to her sister like she was afraid someone might hear what she was about to say.

"It was once believed ghosts were composed of mists or air, like breath, and were possibly a person within a person, a ghost as part of a living human being—that is, until the person died. If the ghost 'within' then manifested itself, the person was considered to be a 'breath' of life again—in the paranormal sense. Supposedly, this is derived from the Latin word '*spiritus*' meaning 'breath.'"

"Well, that's as clear as—a foggy mist." Harri frowned.

"'Spanish Oaks is breathing again.' The spirits are alive and, thus, breathing." Cayce rose from the table and headed for the door. Harri followed, still looking perplexed with her sister's knowledge of the Latin "*spiritus*."

"Well, now that I'm sufficiently stuffed and feeling really icky from all that sweet icing, let's go see what…" Harri paused and looked at Cayce. "What breathing spirit left the prize in my box."

Cayce and Harri were glad to see their door was still locked when they got back to their room. Once inside, they found everything just as they'd left it. Most important, the chair was still propped under the closet doorknob.

"I swear I have goose bumps just thinking about having to get that knife out." Cayce pulled the chair away, retrieved the suitcase from the closet, and placed it on the bed.

"Should we take it in the suitcase or just wrapped

up in the towel?" Cayce hoped her sister would say "take it in the suitcase." She did not want to touch the knife even with the towel as a buffer.

"We could wrap it in another towel, just to make sure we don't cut ourselves." Harri got another towel off the rack in the bathroom and handed it to Cayce, who was taking her time unlocking the suitcase.

"You can do the honors. One bandage is enough for me."

Cayce opened the suitcase and gingerly reached in to take out the wrapped knife, but when she put her fingertips under the towel's corners to lift the knife, the towel fell limp. The knife was gone. The sisters butted heads again as they stared into the suitcase.

Cayce reacted first. "I don't believe it!"

"Obviously, someone has been in here while we were eating breakfast. This is ridiculous! I'm going to give the management what-for, this time!" Harri put her hands on her hips and huffed.

In answer to her sister's anger, Cayce held up the key to the suitcase, dangling it before Harri's eyes.

"Not possible. I had the key with me."

"So now what do we do?" Harri dropped down on the bed.

"Nothing. We just wait to see what happens next. But I do believe someone, or some *thing*, wants us here and is looking to us for help. It's time to get serious, Harri. This is all happening for a reason. Maybe it's time we started seeking real answers for—the breath of Spanish Oaks."

Chapter Five

Harri and Cayce put on their walking shoes and exercise clothes to walk off some of the emotions they were feeling, not to mention the huge cinnamon rolls they'd devoured at breakfast. After finding out from Monica the best place to walk was the gravel road beginning behind the slave quarters, the sisters bought bottles of water from the gift shop and headed in the direction of the slave cabins.

As they rounded the first cabin, they heard the rumble of a giant truck coming up the road. Moving far to the side, the sisters watched as a huge truck pulling a long flatbed trailer rumbled past, carrying a monster bulldozer. The driver waved his thanks to the sisters.

"Looks like the bog is about to be dug up and concreted. I'm not sure how I feel about that. What do you think, Cayce? Can you picture a swimming pool on this old historic site?"

"Depends. If the owner has really put a lot of thought into it, as Sophia says he has, maybe it won't be noticed. It would be nice to be able to cool off after walking, but I guess you'll have to come back in a few weeks to see the results and let me know."

The two started out at a slow pace but quickly sped up until they were power walking, with Cayce huffing as she tried to keep up with her petite sister.

"Either you will have to slow down some or just go

on ahead and let me catch up on your way back. You know I have a set of twenty-pound weights spread over my body that you don't have."

"Okay. I'll slow up. We can just walk a little farther to make up the difference. Besides, I really don't like walking on gravel. It's a good way to turn an ankle."

After ten minutes of walking, Cayce noticed a path heading into the woods. It was well worn and groomed, as if inviting guests to take the path less traveled, and it took very little persuasion for Cayce to get her sister to change routes. The path was fairly wide and clear of debris and was outlined with railroad ties. On the outside of the ties, day lilies bloomed profusely. Cayce thought someone had gone to great effort to make the path inviting.

"I know we're still on the plantation grounds. We couldn't possibly have covered two hundred acres even at the speed you had us going. Do you think this is private property?"

"If it is, there were no signs. But if a Great Dane runs out yapping, remember you're the brave one, Cayce. I'll meet you back at the inn—the old 'I don't have to be fast, just faster than you' philosophy."

"Thanks a lot. I really don't think we need to worry. I doubt we're the first guests to traverse this awe-inspiring path."

After walking for ten minutes, the path opened up to a beautifully manicured yard overflowing with more Spanish moss trees. Under the trees sat a small, weathered, board-and-batten cabin with a high-pitched tin roof hanging over the front of the house to make a deep porch, bayou style. Day lilies and camellias covered the yard and formed deep flowerbeds on either side of a long stone walkway leading to steep front steps. On the porch sat three well-used rockers, their natural patina allowed to age to an ancient golden brown. Flowered cushions filled in the sunken cane-bottom seats, ready for visitors to sit a spell as giant elephant ears planted in antique iron wash pots stood guard at each end of the porch.

The sisters stopped at the end of the walkway and were about to turn and retrace their steps, afraid of intruding on someone's privacy, when the front door opened. Mama Tee stepped out on the porch and yelled, stopping them before they had a chance to leave the yard.

"Welcome, sisters! Please don't leave. I make fresh lemonade and teacakes. Come. Join us on de porch."

Just as the sisters started up the stone walk, the door opened again and a man appeared, carrying a tray with a pitcher of lemonade and four glasses. He was a combination of Harrison Ford and Dwayne "The Rock" Johnson, tall and muscular, with the complexion and build of a golden surfer, although there were tinges of gray shining along the sides of his thick, dark, curly hair. The red knit polo shirt he wore with his tight jeans showed off the muscles in his upper arms as he set the tray on the primitive table at the end of the porch opposite the rockers. He extended a hand to each of the sisters, who could not help but stare at one of the most handsome men they had ever seen. Cayce stared even longer when she realized he had on very expensive western boots.

"I'm Joshua Devaux. Sherone was just telling me about meeting you ladies in the gift shop. What a nice coincidence you showed up just at this time—that is, if you believe in coincidences, and Sherone does not. In fact, for some reason, she just happened to put four glasses on the tray. Sherone has 'insight,' as she calls it, and thinks there is purpose in your being guests at the Oaks. I know better than to argue with her. Anyway, welcome to Spanish Oaks."

"Thank you, Joshua. I'm Harri, and this is my sister Cayce. Sherone, uh…Mama Tee gave us each a wonderful and unique doll in the shop."

"We don't mean to intrude. We asked Monica where would be a good place to walk, and she told us about the gravel road. When we saw the path, we couldn't resist taking it, and I can't say I'm sorry we did. It is so beautiful here. Our curiosity always gets the best of us." Cayce was quick to make the explanation.

"At Sherone's house, visitors are always welcome. As you can see, her porch has three rockers, one for solitude, two for companionship and three for society. And I'll pull over one of the straight chairs from the table, and we'll make it four for a very pleasant crowd."

"Henry David Thoreau. Although I don't think he mentioned the crowd part. *Walden Pond*, right?" Harri and Cayce each took a rocker as Joshua pulled over a very worn straight chair.

"So true, Cayce. Are you a fan of Thoreau? I've read all his works."

"Yes, I am, as a matter of fact, although I haven't read everything he wrote. I was introduced to him when I was in graduate school and did a research paper for an American literature class. I am also a lover of nature like he was. Your place is so beautiful." Cayce directed her comment to Mama Tee, still not sure as to what name she should use.

"Thank you, and call me what name you wish, but my friends call me Sherone. Mama Tee my business name. Joshua, my distant cousin, call me by my Christian name, Sherone. Joshua de owner of dis beautiful estate and rightfully so. He is a direct descendant of one of de first residents."

"Don't mince words, Sherone. My great-great-grandfather Caleb Devaux was a slave. I am proud to be his descendant. He took himself from the bottom and made himself a prosperous man. He was very intelligent, by all accounts known."

"Now I see the resemblance. You are related to the beautiful young tour guide Sophia. Let me guess. Sophia is your daughter. Am I correct?" Harri looked to Joshua for confirmation and guessed by the big smile on his face she was right.

"Soppy is my pride and joy. She's my only child and, thus, heir to Spanish Oaks. She works here in the summer but is working toward a business degree at Mississippi State during the school year. She has one year left and then, hopefully, will go on for a Masters Degree. Her mother died of breast cancer when Soppy was fifteen, and we both promised her mother that education would be top priority."

"Well, I can certainly see why you're proud of her. She is both beautiful and personable and will do well whatever her endeavor. Her love for Spanish Oaks radiates when she talks of the plantation and her ancestors. Harri and I were fortunate enough to check in just as she started her last tour yesterday."

"Then you were there when the little girl Molly saw Milla in the mirror?"

"Yes. The whole encounter was spine-tingling. We had to leave before the tour was completed, but we hope to finish it before we leave at the end of the week, and we will definitely wait for Sophia's tour. Hearing a family member give the history adds a valuable personal touch." Harri matched Joshua's smile of thanks with her own.

Mama Tee left her chair and began pouring glasses of lemonade. Joshua handed each visitor a glass and then passed the plate of teacakes. The teacakes were not round like most but were square, showing they had been intentionally placed on the baking sheet touching each other so the gooey rich batter would run together and form a thin cake layer that had to be cut apart.

"Even though I'm still full from the cinnamon roll Cayce forced me to eat at the Stables, there is no way I can resist a teacake. There is a special place in my heart for the little delicacies, not to mention a big part of my bread and butter. I own a tea shop in Germantown, Tennessee called The Teacake."

"Aha! Now I know who owns the red BMW convertible. So it's you I have to thank for putting the idea of a BMW convertible as a college graduation present in Soppy's head! I just did a walk-around first thing this morning as my daughter oohed and ahhed over your car and assured me hers would have to be red now that she's seen her dream car."

"My apologies, but it is a wonderful car. I'm sure Sophia would be very happy with it, as would you in seeing her enjoy it."

"Just don't you go encouraging her, even though she'll probably get what she wants. She's a wonderful student, even if she is a wee bit spoiled."

"Oh, my gosh! Harri, this teacake melts in your mouth. I hate to say it, but it's even better than our grandmother's recipe, and it's chewy like Mammaw's rather than crunchy like most." Cayce took another bite, savoring it as she moaned in pleasure. Harri followed her sister's lead, copying her enjoyment but with much smaller bites, chewing each one like a bunny, savoring each tiny morsel.

"Okay, Sherone. I taste real butter, more cream than milk, eggs—probably the rich brown kind—but there is something very different going on here, and if you tell me it's a secret, prepare to bury me in one of your day-lily beds."

"It is secret ingredient, but I share it with you some time. You much too young and important to push up lilies yet, I think."

"Well, that's a relief! I was thinking of entering my family teacake recipe in the contest, but after tasting this, there's no way. Is this a family recipe, and if so, is it served in the Stables? I didn't see teacakes anywhere on the menu."

"Indeed, it is a family recipe from Victoria Broussard, but de special ingredient come from my ancestors from de Caribbean. One was Affie, de mother of Caleb, but you won't find it in de Stables."

"Oh, I thought she was from New Orleans, from the family of Jean Paul Broussard." Noticing the surprised look on Joshua's face, Cayce explained where she got her knowledge.

"I read about Affie in the *History of Spanish Oaks Plantation*. I bought it in the gift shop."

"I've read the book. It's actually very accurate, even though the history was originally commissioned by owner number three, who was not related to the family. It doesn't give all the details. I'm writing another history from the perspective of my ancestors, but I'm so busy with my work it will probably take years to complete. Affie's mother was from the Caribbean and was an ancestor to Sherone. Her mother was imported illegally, stolen from her village in Saint-Domingue, present day Haiti, along with her child—or was allowed to be stolen by one of Jean Paul's French counterparts in the black market trade, according to stories passed down through Sherone's family. Affie was a young child when she arrived in New Orleans. I'm sure you read about the unsavory character of Jean Paul Broussard. Sherone can add much to the story if you're interested."

"We would welcome any information you're willing to give us—both of you. Harri and I are blessed, or sometimes cursed, with paranormal senses and feel we were guided here by our 'gift,' as we prefer to think of it. We've had several experiences in the short time we've been here."

"You see, Joshua? Mama Tee is right. With Joshua's permission, I help you all I can. Many mysteries not solved, and maybe de time is now."

"Of course. Just promise me you three won't scare the guests off or endanger yourself or others. I should warn you—not all of our spirits are nice. Also, I would prefer you not share your discoveries with anyone other than Sherone, Sophia, or me. Do we have a deal?"

"Absolutely." The sisters answered as one, as they did on many occasions when tuned in on the same wavelength.

"I have to go now. I've got a lunch meeting with

my pool contractor. It was a pleasure to meet both of you, and I hope to get to know you better while you're here. Oh, and Cayce, if you want to catch up on Thoreau, come by my office and I'll loan you anything you want. My office is upstairs over the Stables."

Harri smiled at her sister, who was blushing from Joshua's seeming interest in her as a fellow Thoreau admirer. When Mama Tee got up to carry the tray inside, Harri gave a thumbs-up to her sister before getting up to help.

"Please come in. I show you my lovely home." Sherone held the door open for the sisters.

The cabin had the quaintness and furnishings of its over-one-hundred-fifty-year history—every piece of furniture a valuable primitive antique, with the exception of the Early American sofa. The cabin's main room—a keeping room—was living room, dining room, and kitchen all in one, with a stone walk-in fireplace as the great room's centerpiece. The master bedroom was off to one side of the great room, and a tall, plain but beautiful antique bed with a feather mattress plumped high could be seen through the doorway. A loft overlooking the main room was accessible by a very narrow, steep set of stairs clinging to the back wall.

Sherone directed Cayce and Harri to sit at the sawbuck table with its natural scrub top. As Cayce headed to the table, she stopped and ran her hand over a large red kitchen press, worn with age and history.

"This press is beautiful. It's even put together with wooden pegs. Is it original to the cabin?"

"Oh, yes. It pre-Civil War. Legend has it Nathan Bedford Forrest took refuge here, waiting for Yankee troops to pass. I can picture him opening one of de doors to remove sugar or honey for his coffee. But den, you probably can, too." Mama Tee smiled, noticing how Cayce was absorbed in the piece.

Realizing she could be standing next to "Get there firstest with the mostest" Forrest if she continued to fondle the cupboard, Cayce jerked her hand away and sat beside Harri at the table.

"Many of de furnishings original in de plantation house, as well, but for dis cabin, every piece original except for de sofa. I add it when I take possession. Since I know you both believers, I will tell you about de mojo attached to dis cabin and to some areas of de plantation home and surroundings."

"Black magic?" The sisters spoke together as each waited for Mama Tee's explanation.

"It is no shock to you dat my family have certain talents. Voodoo, I believe is what you call it de night I met you. I try to be positive, and most of my family members with de gift do likewise, but if pushed, well, it is not always good mojo. De cabin abandoned for fifty years, from 1920 to 1970. No direct female descendant of de original Mama Tee desire dis place or its history and responsibility, but de first Mama Tee plan for dis and use her charm to guard de cabin against outside intruders. But before I get to dat part of Mama Tee story, I should explain about my home."

Harri and Cayce leaned closer to their hostess, propping their elbows on the table and supporting their chins in their hands while Mama Tee took on a serious look as if not sure she should be disclosing this.

"De cabin part of de plantation, yet not part of de plantation. Princeton Broussard know it just a matter of time before it is sold, especially since he produce no living heirs. He slowly sell off acreage as he get old in order to have income, and he live to be old man in his seventies, a very unhappy old man, who depend on Mama Tee and her descendants for spiritual guidance. Before he die, he leave dis house and surrounding twenty acres, mostly swamp, to Mama Tee and her direct female descendants. It can never be sold. Dis is how I come to inherit it. My mother and her mother in denial about de family talents and return to de islands to try to come to terms with de ancestry. But den I come along. It obvious to my mother I inherit de gift and intend to use it. She try to change my mind, but she give up and pass de place to me. When I turn twenty, I come here and never leave."

"So you were here before Joshua bought the place. Were the two of you in contact with each other?" Cayce asked the question, wanting to get everything straight in her mind before Mama Tee explained what Cayce knew was going to be a bombshell. She was sure the information they were getting would not be found in a souvenir history of the plantation.

"I never know Joshua exist 'til he come see me five years ago and tell me he going to buy Spanish Oaks. He know dis piece of property not included and want to size me up before closing de deal. De magic strong between us when we shake hands, and we both know we kin even before we share our ancestral bloodlines wi' each other. I now guide Joshua as past Mama Tees guide owners who sought help."

"So there have been owners who did not seek your advice?" Harri, too, was eager to get as much information as possible.

"Yes, but da would have fared better if da had. No

matter now. For now, I want to answer some of de questions I know you have. Such as, why can de furnishings never be removed from Milla's cabin. Am I right?"

"That and many more questions. Cayce and I feel we were drawn here for a reason. Our gift is similar to yours but without the black magic, and we are willing to use it to help if we can."

"Den I will help you by answering de first of your questions. De first Mama Tee die at close to one hundred, something very rare in 1800s. She outlive two husbands but have only one child, a daughter, Tamara, who receive de gift from her mother. Seeing how her daughter try to deny de gift, Mama Tee become frightened would come a time when de spirits of de ancestors not have protection. Mama Tee protect the spirits wi' black magic. Are you sure you want to know de rest?"

Harri and Cayce both nodded their heads. There was no turning back now. Their curiosity had to be satisfied.

"She concoct magic dat guard any place or item of importance to de spirits of her family members she know remain trapped at Spanish Oaks. De family members were Affie and her descendants. You see, de first Mama Tee and Affie's mother were sisters, stolen from de same village in the Caribbean by Jean Paul Broussard. Jean Paul realize his mistake taking Mama Tee when bad things happen to him. When he give Affie and Caleb to Victoria, Mama Tee insist on going too. At first he refuse, but after some persuasion, in de form of sickness and loss of high stakes in his gambling, he give in."

"So when an object is taken from Milla's or Affie's cabins, they mysteriously reappear because of Mama Tee's magic?" Cayce asked, seeking clarification.

"Like the rope bed Sophia told us about. And even the sag in the floor came back. Remember, Cayce?"

"'Tis true. And you could talk to some locals who try to steal things from de spiritual places or who broke in out of curiosity or mischievousness. One teenage couple decide once to make use of Milla's bed after breaking into her cabin and consuming alcohol when plantation not inhabited. But as soon as da lay on de bed, it levitate and da find demselves inches from de ceiling. When de bed settle down, da see Milla's body hanging from de ceiling with de chair knock over. Of course, people not believe de story, thinking dem in drunken stupor, but it still talk about in River Town."

"What about items stolen? What kinds of things happened to people who took things?" Cayce looked at Harri, who understood too well where this question was coming from.

"Let me think." Sherone put her finger to her lip as if in deep thought.

"Ah, yes. A man wi' questionable background who own a small antique shop try to steal stoneware from Affie's cabin one night. As he ran wi' it, he look back, and run smack into de cistern dat stand near de willow tree. He claim he pulled into cistern by forces not seen. He stay in de black, murky water all night, screaming for help, keepin' a death grip on a brick that stick out, 'til he rescued by de caretaker next morning. As I sure you guess, de stoneware not in de cistern but back in Affie's cabin. De owners not press charge since de stoneware still in de cabin and not support de thief's story, his attempt to come clean. The curse is why Affie and Milla's cabins never rent out. Is just too dangerous."

A short time later, Cayce and Harri thanked Sherone for her hospitality and left, not wanting to wear out their welcome. The information they had gained and the blessing given them by Joshua Devaux to gather more information for the benefit of whoever or whatever had beckoned them here gave a new sense of urgency to their mission.

Before allowing them to leave, Sherone gave the sisters a tour of the yard. At the edge of the backyard by the woods stood a small one-room cabin surrounded by yellow lilies. On the porch walls hung all kinds of dried plants, some looking like weeds and others like onion and garlic bulbs. No rockers lined this porch. It looked like a jungle, completely covered with massive elephant ears. On the door, more of the dried bulb-like plants were crisscrossed, tied together with scarlet and purple rope. The cabin, though quaint, lacked the inviting appeal of Sherone's main cabin and had an aura about it that said "no trespassing" without the aid of written words.

"You guess right. Dis is where I mix potions. Big magic come from here. No one go in but me. When I conduct business wi' clients, I do so in de big cabin, at de table where we sit earlier. But don't be frightened. Good magic, remember? Look instead at de beautiful lilies dat surround de shed. Yellow lilies from France, almost as old as de Oaks and very rare, a treasure dat grows only here, and planted by Princeton Broussard in memory of his Lily. Yellow lilies multiply all through de swamp."

"I thought he did not love Lily. What happened to her after her mother's death?" Harri felt compelled to ask this question even if it meant delaying her and Cayce's leaving.

"You know of de tragic death of Beatrice?"

Cayce and Harri looked at each other, realizing this information came from Cayce's vision and not from information gained on the tour. They had left early and did not know what information was included in the tour. Before either had to answer the question, Sherone continued.

"Of course you do. Princeton love Lily in his own way, but de child did not respond to him. It was a distant love. He try, but no good. Affie care for Lily after her mother's death, but when Lily about nine years old, she take to running away. Many hours spent chasing 'til Princeton have to lock her in her sleeping room at night and in de big attic room every day, wi' every imaginable means of pleasure for a young girl. But Lily only sit and rock and stare."

"That is so sad, but I guess it was all he could do if she was running away. Sending her to a hospital for the insane would have been out of the question. I know how horrid those places were back then." Harri looked to Cayce for confirmation, and she shook her head in agreement.

"No, Harri. He would not think of it. Affie spend much time in de attic wi' Lily, but one day, Lily bolt through de door when Affie try to enter. Princeton away in town, but Zed run after her. Lily run into de woods and disappear. Her daddy and de hands search for two days, only to find her body face down in de swamp water. Lily die at ten years. Her daddy take to drinking again for months, 'til Mama Tee take control here in dis shed. Her magic save him like it did when he lose Milla and Chloe."

"Where is Lily buried?" Cayce knew she had not seen the family cemetery, but like all plantations it was sure to have one.

"De edge of de grounds, past de quarters. Lily beside her mama, Beatrice. Princeton buried on other side of Lily, not by his wife. De child come between her parents even in death. But enough sad stories. Finish your walk, but be careful to stay on de path. Swamp goes for miles past my place."

"Thank you, Sherone. Harri and I hope to visit with you again, if that's okay."

"Yes, and I'm still counting on finding out what that secret recipe is." Harri smiled but did not wait for a reply as she turned to walk with her sister back down the path.

"I hope for many visits, sisters. The breath of Spanish Oaks whispers. You were meant to come here." Sherone waved and reentered her cabin.

****

The woods on either side of the path and to the back of Sherone's house were not inviting and, according to Sherone, were full of bogs, swamps, cypress knees, quicksand, and creepy crawly things including water moccasins and alligators. Cayce's fear of snakes elevated her adrenaline, and she outwalked her sister on the return trip. When they reached the gravel road, neither of them could talk until they stopped to catch their breath.

"Those day lilies are deceiving, aren't they? Can you imagine what a horrible death that must have been for poor Lily? You would think there would be some warning signs up for guests like us who walk the grounds."

"Cayce, look! I don't know how we missed it, but there's the sign right there."

To the left of the path was a sign nailed to a tree warning people to stay on designated paths only. It even mentioned quicksand, snakes, and alligators.

"I bet Mama Tee doesn't get much business because of her location. I hope she has another source of income. Then again, I'm sure there are explicit warnings on staying on the path to her house. Mama Tee and her home both have a mystique about them that would be a drawing card, but let's not linger. You know I still have to register for the cooking contest."

"Yes, and I need to finish reading the history and see if any other information on the family is available. Maybe I'll find Sophia and ask her, or I could go and ask Joshua." Cayce gave an impish grin her sister understood only too well.

"He's definitely your type. Boots, jeans, but no ten-gallon hat to tip and say 'Howdy, ma'am.'"

"Oh, well, this is Mississippi, not Montana. Besides, the muscles make up for the lack of a hat. I'd like to know if there's a way we could get into the attic room. There must be a key somewhere. Do you think I heard the spirit of Lily? If so, she sings in death when she never even spoke during life."

"If I had to bet, I'd bet on Chloe, even though she didn't die at Spanish Oaks, or at least I don't think she did. To be continued."

Chapter Six

When Cayce and Harri entered the lobby, they noticed a man, obviously a well-to-do businessman by the expensive suit he was wearing, registering at the desk. He was short, with jet-black hair all one length and slicked back with mousse. The dark Armani suit gave him a sinister, mobbish look helped by a thick mustache and a goatee, and bushy eyebrows running together like unmowed grass. When he saw Cayce and Harri, he smiled and his whole façade changed like a human chameleon. Beside him sat a leather suitcase, a briefcase, and a large thin box that looked as if it contained a picture or a mirror. The sisters glanced past him and saw Sophia working the desk. Not wanting to interrupt her at work, they smiled and waved before heading up the stairs.

"Oh, Ms. McCallister and Ms. Wellington, wait up! I'll be finished here in just a minute." Cayce led the way back to the desk and assumed maybe they had found her necklace.

"Beatrice's room is ready for you as always, Mr. Fowler. I'll get Albert to take your things up."

"That won't be necessary, Sophia. I can manage, but you should call your dad to send someone for the portrait. It should be locked in a secure place. The museum says it's worth a chunk."

"Of course. I'll call him right now." Sophia picked

up the phone and dialed a three-digit extension. Putting her hand over the mouthpiece, she smiled at Harri and Cayce and said, "I'll be with you in just a second."

"Hi, Dad. Mr. Fowler just arrived. The portrait is here at the desk, and Mr. Fowler says you need to lock it in a secure place. Yes, it's right here in front of the desk. Cayce and Harri? Yes, they're standing right here. You want to tell them yourself, or do you still want me to give them the message? Okay. I'll keep an eye on it until Mack gets here. Bye."

"Dad was on his way out to the pool site with the contractor but wanted me to tell you he'd like to treat you to dinner at the Stables tonight. Seven o'clock, if that's okay with you?"

"That's very nice of him. We'd love to. We'll meet him there." Cayce smiled at Harri as she answered for both of them.

"So you're working days now? I hope that doesn't mean you're not guiding the tour anymore. You know, Cayce and I never got to finish it."

"Just for the next two days. Monica took some time off, but you don't need to pay for the tour. My dad says I'm to show you any part of the house and grounds you want and to give you any information you desire. You two really made an impression on my dad and on Sherone. I had the same feeling when you were on the tour with me. I just knew you were sensing something, especially after I saw you get upset and leave the tour in Milla's cabin, Ms. Wellington."

"Please, Sophia, call us Harri and Cayce. We're very informal people. But now that you mention it, there is one place we'd really like to see. Cayce heard what sounded like a small child rocking and singing in the attic room last night, and we'd like to go there and see if we can make contact with the owner of the sweet little voice."

"Oh, that's great! No one but me has heard our little ghost girl in over a year. We thought she had left for good."

"So others have heard her? Harri seemed to think I was hallucinating. She even accused me of sleepwalking when I went up the stairs to get a closer listen."

"Yes, even I have had encounters with her. In fact, she was with us on the tour the other evening, but I ignored her voice, afraid I'd lose the group before we got started. She sometimes follows me and calls 'Mama' in the sweetest voice I've ever heard. At first I thought it was Molly until I turned around and saw Molly at the back of the group. Anyway, she only called a couple of times and then disappeared again. But that was small stuff compared to Molly seeing Milla in the mirror. I still get goose bumps just thinking about it."

"Is Molly's family still here?" Harri asked. "We haven't seen them all day."

"Oh, yes. They're here for the week. They just went to the coast today to see the devastation from Katrina. Molly's mother loves the Oaks. She came with some of her friends last summer and brought her husband and Molly back this year. Molly's encounter with Milla gave her a little concern, but she and her husband decided to stay. Molly's dad said it made it even more memorable."

"Back to the attic. Is there a time you could show Cayce and me the attic? Do you even have a key to it?

The door seemed pretty rusty, and the knob won't budge."

"No, we have never come across the key, but there is another way to get to the attic room, through Lily's day room. The door you tried has not been opened in the five years we've owned the Oaks. I tell you what. I get off at four o'clock. Meet me here, and I'll show you how to get to it. And by the way, Dad says you have the run of the place. You can explore anywhere that isn't rented, even Milla's and Affie's cabins, but I'll have to give you a key for those. Of course, you'll have to explore when tours aren't going on, which means before nine a.m. and after eight p.m."

A tall, well-built man with a shaved head and a dark Fu Manchu beard appeared, and Sophia came around to the front of the desk. A huge ring of keys hung from one of the man's belt loops.

"This is it, Mack. Be careful with it. Dad said to lock it in the storage room behind his office."

"Will do." Mack turned the bill of his cap around to face backward before picking up the box. The box didn't appear to be heavy, just awkward, but Mack carried it as if it were a box of candy, his muscles protruding beneath his black T-shirt with the sleeves rolled high.

"It's strange you find the attic so interesting. About six months ago, when I was still at school, one of the guests on the second floor said they heard a big thud in the attic and someone running down the stairs. It was after midnight and really scared them. Rodney was working nights and went up to check it out, and he found the door open and evidence that someone had been rummaging around inside. This is an area never open to the public, not even on tours, so whoever was there was up to no good, probably trying to steal antiques. Rodney called Dad on the radio, and he and Tom came running. Some of the beaded ceiling panels and a panel of wallboard had been loosened, and the wallboard had fallen on the floor. Tom took down the wallboard and found a storage area we didn't know existed behind it."

"The thud the guest heard. Lucky for your dad. Was anything stolen?" Harri looked at Cayce and knew what she was thinking. It was probably the same thief who had stolen the cookbook.

"A valuable antique doll was missing, but nothing else they could find, but what was important was not what the thief took but what he left behind. Behind the wall panel, they found a concealed storage area with several wooden trunks full of old clothing, letters, and all kinds of stuff. It was quite a find, but the most valuable thing found was the portrait."

"Would that be the portrait Mack just took to be secured?" Harri asked the question, sensing what the answer would be.

"Yes. It was an oil portrait of Beatrice Broussard, the only portrait painted of her except for the one with Lily, hanging in Beatrice's room. No one knew about this portrait, but we think it was a gift to Princeton on his twenty-sixth birthday, celebrated with a dinner party the night Beatrice died. Dad can tell you more about this. He found reference to a portrait in a family letter, but no such portrait had ever been found until the thief discovered its hiding place."

"Did your dad send it off to be restored? The heat in the attic couldn't be good for oil."

Cayce was an art enthusiast, but her passion was Native American and western art. She had several old paintings in her collection and knew how delicate oil could be.

"The heat had damaged it some, but the worst damage was done about a century and a half ago. It had been slashed. Two gigantic cuts crisscrossed the portrait. Dad didn't know if it could be salvaged, but lucky for him, Mr. Fowler was here at the inn at the time and knew about a museum in New York specializing in art restoration. Once Dad had the painting insured, he contacted the museum. It has taken this long for the restoration to be completed, and right on schedule for our biggest weekend of the year."

Sophia seemed to think the sisters already knew about the weekend so gave no explanation. Cayce prodded Sophia to continue.

"And that weekend would be…?"

"Oh, I'm sorry. I thought that was probably why you were here. May thirtieth is Princeton Broussard's birthday. That's this Friday night. Dad got this idea the first year he owned Spanish Oaks, and it's become a local tradition. You did bring your formal gowns, antebellum attire mandatory? It's the one night we all get to be Scarlett O'Hara, and my dad makes the most amazing Rhett Butler you've ever seen. It all takes place in the ballroom, with the Stables furnishing the food and drinks. It is quite an affair! It's for guests staying here. Anyone else who comes is by invitation only. A few dignitaries usually show up."

"No, we didn't know, but it sounds exciting. However, neither of us has an antebellum gown, I'm afraid. Any idea where we might get one on such short notice? Then there's the problem with shoes, since I mostly wear boots and Harri brought only flats and walking shoes."

Sophia came around the desk and began sizing the two up. She put her back to Harri, surmising they were about the same size.

"I think I just might can fit both of you. I'll have to get back with you later." Sophia had an impish smile on her face.

Cayce decided to finish the history book while awaiting the four o'clock rendezvous with Sophia. Harri brought in her computer to start going through her recipes and trying to figure out what her contest entry would be.

"I can't believe you're not going to use a recipe from the cookbook."

"There's a big part of me that wants to, but I would feel dishonest. It would not be original to my family."

"Monica said any 'old, preferably antebellum family recipe.' She did not say it had to be *your* family recipe. Besides, don't you think it would be appropriate since it's Princeton's birthday? You should go through and see if there's one marked Princeton's favorite. If there is, that's a sign you should use it."

Harri put her finger to her cheek as if in deep thought and then shut her computer down. Donning her white gloves, she pulled the cookbook from the locked suitcase, where it had been kept ever since its disappearance, and began carefully turning pages.

****

"Here! Here it is! Read this, Cayce!" Harri held the book in front of her sister so she could read the entry without touching the book.

Citron Delight. Princeton's Cake
*Created by his adoring nanny for Princeton's sixth
birthday and every birthday after, and on any occasion
deemed worthy of such libation by the overindulged
young master, occasions too numerous to name. The
exception to this being on his fifteenth birthday upon
which he suffered scarlet fever, able only to consume
chicken broth and cold, sweet tea, both of which he
never allowed to touch his lips again. Upon his
recovery, Nanny Affie baked him a monstrous Citron
Delight, a belated celebration of birth and life allowed
to continue through our Lord's infinite grace.*

"And, I might add, it sounds delicious. Finding
citron could be the problem in River Town, Mississippi.
Maybe the head chef in the Stables has some." Harri
returned to her desk with the book.

"What in the heck is citron? I know I've never seen
that ingredient listed on Lean Tasties."

"It's similar to lemon but its peel is very bumpy.
Citron is not used much today because it needs to be
imported if you want the best. It originated in Asia and
the Mediterranean but found its way to the Caribbean
with the French explorers. The strange thing about it is
you don't use the pulp but use the white rind, the
albedo. It's a complicated process that I wouldn't know
how to begin, but it is used in some gourmet desserts
today. It would be a real gamble in a recipe I've never
made, especially to be entering in a contest."

"I bet you could figure it out, Harri. Does the
recipe give you good directions?"

"Good directions for the 1800s, but I'd be guessing
on some of these measurements, and there is no oven
degree. I guess for that period it would have to say 'low

blaze, hot ashes only.'"

"Speaking of the cookbook, I've been thinking as I've been reading. Joshua is being so open with us that I wonder if…" Cayce hesitated.

"Yes, I agree. We should." Harri answered without hearing what her sister was about to say.

"We should what?" Cayce asked wrinkling her brow.

"Show Joshua the cookbook and tell him how it came into our possession."

"Pop would be so proud of you, Harri." Cayce walked over to her sister and gave her a hug.

"For reading your mind or for giving up the cookbook? You know we will have to offer it to him. By rights, it is his. I just hope he offers to reimburse us for it."

"You're right, Harri, but either way I would not feel right if we didn't tell him. Maybe if we share, he'll let me look at some of the family diaries and any primary sources he has that might help us to know what 'the breath,' or maybe 'the breaths' want us to know."

"Well, you have my permission, if that's what you're wanting. Do you want to carry it with you when you go to dinner with Joshua?"

"What do you mean when I go to dinner? You're coming, too."

"I think I'll pass on the invitation. Two's company, three's…"

"Society? Remember it takes four to be a crowd, Harri. You do want to be sociable, don't you? Besides, I think we should both go. We're in this together, Sista."

****

At four o'clock sharp, Cayce and Harri met Sophia at the front desk. Sophia rummaged in the drawer and withdrew two keys, a regular room key and a smaller key. As she closed the drawer, a young man who looked to be a little older than Sophia took Sophia's place behind the desk.

"Rodney, this is Cayce and Harri. I'm going to show them around. I've got my radio, if you need anything." Sophia patted the radio at her side and moved from behind the desk, motioning for Harri and Cayce to follow.

"The entrance to Lily's day room is at the end of the hall on the second floor, the opposite end from the attic room where you heard our little ghost girl. There's no way you would know it was here from the outside, because of the door that looks like all the other room doors."

As the three reached the second floor, the door next to Cayce and Harri's room opened and Mr. Fowler emerged, locking the door behind him. He had changed from his business look to casual khakis and a knit shirt, softening his hard features somewhat.

"Have a pleasant evening, ladies."

"Thank you. You, too," Harri answered for the group.

"Mr. Fowler is a nice man. He and my dad have been friends for a long time. He's the accountant for my dad's construction company, but he also helps Dad find pieces for his art collection. Mr. Fowler has quite a collection of his own, even though his taste and my dad's are total opposites. Mr. Fowler likes modern art with a little Van Gogh thrown in, and my dad is into cowboys and Indians, another of his passions stemming from his childhood fantasies."

"Your dad has a construction company? I thought Spanish Oaks was his main business." Cayce now understood the boots and jeans, having been married to a small rancher turned construction tycoon. But in the end she had gotten the ranch while he got the construction business, and nobody got the shaft with the two parting as friends.

"No, Spanish Oaks is his passion, as he calls it, his dream realized after finding out about his family history as a teenager, but he makes his money in commercial construction. He is away more than I like for him to be, but since he added the office in the Stables, he has been able to conduct much of his business from here. Mr. Fowler and two other associates help keep the business going so Dad can spend more time here. We try to keep Beatrice's room open for Mr. Fowler. It's his favorite."

After unlocking the door to the stairway, the three began the steep climb to Lily's day room. Another door was at the top of the stairs, and Sophia took out a small key that unlocked a padlock added after the burglary.

"I love this room! Some day I hope to have a little girl who will love this room as much as I do. It's hard to believe it started out as attic storage space."

Sophia pushed open the door and stood back to let Cayce and Harri enter first. She intentionally waited until they were inside the dark room to turn on the light, sort of a grand introduction.

The sisters gasped as the room was illuminated. It was full of every type of antique toy imaginable, including an oversized rocking horse, two identical intricately carved rocking chairs, one adult size and one child size, a full doll nursery including a Jenny Lind crib, a wicker bassinet, a high chair, a doll carriage, and a dresser complete with glove boxes and beveled mirror. A line of dolls, mostly china and bisque, sat on a bench next to one wall. A small table with two chairs sat ready for a tea party with an elegant child's china tea service.

On the inside wall a mural was painted, depicting a scene of two children playing by a lake with a forest surrounding it while angels guarded overhead. The little girl most prominent in the mural looked very much like the picture of Lily with her mother in the book Cayce had bought in the gift shop. Another little girl in the mural was African American and guessing was not needed to identify the light-skinned little girl.

On the opposite end of the room was a Jenny Lind rope bed complete with a featherbed fluffed so high it looked as if it could take flight and join its cloud friends floating outside the window. On the bed, a china doll dressed in a white French lace baby gown and cap lay sleeping on its side with its delicate little hands folded under its cheek. It looked as if it were waiting for the return of the little girl who never played with it.

As Harri and Cayce stood staring with their mouths open, Sophia gasped and ran to the bed.

"I don't believe it! This is the doll stolen! How did…"

She was interrupted by a creaking noise coming from a small door on the opposite end of the room.

"Someone is up here…in Chloe's nap room! We should get Dad!"

Realizing Sophia was frightened, Cayce moved to her side, and Harri followed in her sister's footsteps.

"Stay with Sophia, Harri. I'm going to look in the

room."

"No, Cayce! We should wait for Dad. I'll get him on the radio."

Sophia grabbed the radio from her belt and pushed the button. Nothing happened. After shaking the radio, she pushed the button again, but again nothing happened.

"It can't be dead! I just charged it!"

Before they could stop her, Cayce walked to the door and opened it, entering without hesitation. She walked a few feet into the room and stopped.

"We're here, Chloe. What is it you want to tell us?"

Harri followed her sister, knowing she was tuned in to the vibes of the departed, but she stopped just inside the door. Harri had seen this happen many times and put her finger to her lips, warning Sophia to remain quiet. Sophia stood still, watching, clutching Harri's arm in a death grip.

Chloe's room was small, with a slanted ceiling that followed the contour of the roof. The one small window was raised about a foot, and a breeze blew the cotton domestic curtains, making them look like small ghosts floating, keeping watch over whoever was in the room. Cayce pointed, directing the attention of Harri and Sophia to the small, plain rope bed covered in a patchwork quilt similar to the one in Milla's cabin. The featherbed beneath the quilt had the imprint of a small child with her head resting on the soft down pillow. The three stared at the bed as if mesmerized, and no one moved or said a word. Without anyone touching the bed, the feather mattress rose and the pillow fluffed. The quilt was pulled straight from the side as if signifying naptime was over. On the small primitive table beneath the window stood a lamp, and Cayce and Harri recognized it as the one that had been burning from the third-floor window their first night at the Oaks.

Cayce stood transfixed, and Sophia had tears running down her cheeks as she continued to clutch Harri's arm. The primitive child's rocker began to rock, slowly at first, giving the creak, creak, creak Cayce had heard the night before. Then the rocking became faster and faster until the chair toppled forward as if the child were in a rage.

"I know you're upset, Chloe. We are here to help you, but you must let us know what you want us to do. Give us a sign to let us know if you want us to help you."

Cayce's heart was pounding, but she dared not move for fear of stopping the spirit's attempt to communicate.

The breeze through the window became stronger, and the curtains stood almost straight out as if intending to grab Cayce, but she did not flinch. Then, with a giant bang, the window slammed shut. Cayce jumped as the window slammed, but she remained frozen in her spot. Sophia was shaking, and Harri put her arm around her. Then the lamp began emitting a faint light that grew stronger and stronger as if trying to direct Cayce's attention to it. Its light reflected off something on the table. Reaching out, Cayce grasped the object, clutching it to her chest. The light flickered and died.

"I understand. I will help you, Chloe. I'll help you get back to your mama." Turning from the lamp, Cayce walked to the small door and left the room, followed by

Harri and Sophia. The door closed gently behind them although none of them touched it.

Just as they entered Lily's day room, Sophia's radio crackled loudly, and all three jumped. Rodney's voice came on.

"Sophia, your dad said to call him when you get through up there."

The three stared at the radio and then at each other.

Chapter Seven

By the time the three retraced their steps down the stairs, Sophia was shaking out of control. Harri and Cayce held on, consoling her.

"It's okay, Sophia. We were never in any danger. The little spirit is just distraught," Cayce explained.

"It's not that I'm afraid. I've just never had an encounter like this before. It's so sad. How did you know it was Chloe and not Lily?"

"Didn't you say the small attic room was Chloe's nap room?" Sophia shook her head. "Then there you have it. Lily was a poor little lost soul even when she was alive. She did not connect with anyone in life. Chloe, on the other hand, was loved and gave much love in return, especially to her mother. She is lost and we need to find her and get her back to her mother. And here is the sign that she wants our help." Cayce held up her missing locket.

"Inside this locket are pictures of my mother and father. That is the only reason it was important for it to be returned to me. Chloe let me know she needs to be returned to her mama. She's lost between worlds."

"Milla is lost, too, without her baby girl. That's why she stays in the cabin where she died. She's waiting for Chloe." Sophia wiped her eyes one last time and relocked the door to the stairs. "I'm not sorry for this experience, and I know you're right. It's Chloe. I think I've known it since the first time she whispered 'Mama.' I am glad you got your locket back, but what I don't understand is how the doll got back in Lily's day room. Do you think some of our staff stole it and then felt guilty and returned it?"

"It is possible, but Sherone gave Cayce and me another explanation for it the other day that makes sense, but without knowing who the thief is, we'll never know."

"You mean black mojo, the first Mama Tee's spell. Sherone told me about that when I first came, but I didn't really believe it until Tom told me about the oak bed in Milla's cabin. But this was Lily's doll, not Chloe's. The spell guards spiritual places of descendants of Affie."

"Yes, but Affie spent a great deal of time taking care of Lily, so it could be another location where her spirit is trapped. I'm sure Affie loved the child even if Lily could not show her love, and Affie possibly felt guilty for Lily's escape. Also, Lily's day room and Chloe's nap room are attached. Have there been any ghostly encounters with Affie?" Harri figured she knew the answer already.

"Actually, some guests have reported seeing a stocky slave woman walking the grounds at night holding a lamp. We always refer to the apparition as Affie, but there's no way to be sure. I believe it is Affie looking for Lily or Chloe. And there's the drastic lowering of temperature in her cabin, as well as objects moving on their own much like what we witnessed in Chloe's room."

"I think we have not heard the last from Chloe. She is trying to tell us something more than she wants her mama. We just have to let the Way find us. Right, Harri?"

Harri and Cayce returned to their room after leaving Sophia. They needed to record these events, beginning with their trip to Natchez. Cayce got out her computer and clicked away at the keys, with Harri helping to remember everything in proper sequence. When they finished, twelve pages had been recorded, with many more anticipated, considering they were only into their third day of this adventure.

Harri turned from her computer and faced Cayce.

"I wonder how Joshua will take the news of Chloe's channeling you. Do you think he'll still be as hospitable after you nearly scared his daughter to death?"

"Sophia is strong, and she's a believer. If she truly loves the Oaks, and I know she does, she wants the spirits of those in pain to be at rest, and the only way to make that happen is to solve the unknown, whatever that may be."

"Let's think about this, Cayce. What questions do you think need answering in order to let these spirits rest?"

"I'll tell you what mysteries have never been solved, from what I read in the *History of Spanish Oaks*, but if Joshua lets me read some of his family documents, there could be more. First of all, what happened to Chloe when she disappeared in March 1848, and what made Milla give up all hope of finding her and thus take her own life on May 30, 1848?"

"You never told me what the book said about the death of Beatrice Broussard. Did it say she was murdered?"

"Yes, but it gives very few details. Big Zed found Beatrice after midnight on May 30. He supposedly heard a horse and rider leaving at high speed and saw a light in the kitchen. When he entered, he found Beatrice stabbed. They never found out who murdered her but surmised she was killed for a valuable necklace she was wearing at the dinner party celebrating her husband's birthday. What was ironic was Beatrice and Milla died the same night. Shortly after Zed found Beatrice, Caleb found Milla hanging from the rafters in her cabin. Of course, there was speculation Milla had murdered Beatrice and then taken her own life, but Princeton discounted this when he realized his wife's necklace was missing, and he figured Beatrice was murdered by the thief."

"What about guests at the party? Were any of them suspects in Beatrice's death?"

"There was no mention of it in the history. I guess question number three is who killed Beatrice and why?"

"I know you don't want to go there, but you could open yourself up to another visit to the murder scene. Would you be willing, Cayce?"

"I'll have to think about that one. It was one of the most terrifying visions I've ever entered. Speaking of the murder scene, I wonder where the kitchen is where Beatrice died. We can ask Joshua tonight. I'm glad you brought your printer. I'm going to print out our record of happenings and give Joshua a copy. He needs to know what we know, and perhaps Sherone needs to know too."

****

Cayce and Harri dressed for dinner in their usual opposite fashions but were a little dressier than they had been on the trip thus far. Cayce was still the cowgirl from Montana but with fancy red boots, while her sister was the business owner from Tennessee and dressed for the part.

Joshua was waiting for them when they got to the Stables and had a table reserved in a private area in the back. He looked scrumptious, and Cayce was glad to see he still wore his jeans and boots. Dinner was a formal affair always at the Stables, and the table was set to perfection, with a bouquet of fresh flowers in the center of the table. Joshua had taken the liberty of ordering a sampler of appetizers, served as soon they were seated.

"Would either of you care for wine? We have several excellent ones, both white and red."

"Just the wine of the South for me, Joshua—iced tea with two lemons." Harri took control immediately while Cayce glanced at the drink menu.

"I think I'd like some raspberry tea with one lemon. I'm not much of a wine drinker either, but thank you for the offer." Cayce put the drink menu away and smiled at Joshua.

"I sort of favor the wine of the South myself. To tell you the truth, I've steered clear of alcohol for five years now. Went a little overboard when my wife died, until Soppy brought me back to reality."

The conversation continued as healthy small talk through the appetizers and salads, but became serious while waiting for the main courses.

"Soppy told me what happened in the attic today. How do you feel about all of this?" Joshua glanced from sister to sister.

"We should be accustomed to it, given our

experiences with paranormal elements, but it can still be frightening. I feel we are dealing with a positive spirit, but one never knows for sure. I hope Sophia was not too upset. Harri stayed in the background with her when the encounter was taking place, but it seemed to shake Sophia."

"Soppy is a softie where children are concerned. She feels such a bond with the little spirit and has been hearing her almost ever since we took possession of the Oaks. Her calling for her mama brings back memories of Sophia's own mom. This encounter was much more real but in a way was reassuring. Now Sophia knows none of her experiences were the result of an overactive imagination. I started off as a real skeptic but changed my perception fast after a couple of personal experiences of my own. But one of mine was not a positive encounter. Remember, I warned you not all of our spirits are nice."

"Cayce and I would like to hear about it, if you'd like to tell us."

"I don't mind, and I think you need to know what you could be dealing with."

Cayce and Harri gave Joshua their undivided attention as he began telling of his experience.

"When I bought Spanish Oaks, there were no desirable living quarters for Soppy and me, and I didn't want to be in the hubbub of all the guest traffic. Being the outdoors lover I am, I built a comfortable log cabin on the back fifty acres, away from the inn and traffic. It's a good piece behind Sherone's cabin and on the backside of the swamp. I keep horses at the cabin and frequently trail ride along the river.

"On one particular late afternoon, I was riding

along the river when I thought I heard a scream coming from the swamp. I knew a black panther had been sighted in the swamp a couple of times, and they can sound just like a woman screaming, but after I heard it again, I had to check it out. I turned my horse into the swamp along a trail I had ridden on a couple of times until the day I almost got thrown when a water moccasin struck at my horse and spooked it. I didn't go near the swamp after that and didn't think I ever would again."

"Oh, my gosh! I thought black panthers were in the jungle, not Mississippi swamps. It gives me the cold chills to think about riding into the swamp!" Cayce gathered her jacket tighter around her as she shivered.

"My sister is very brave, not afraid of mountain lions, bears, charging moose, or ghosts, but just mention a snake to her, and a yellow streak appears."

"I can relate to that. Nobody knows how the panther got in the swamp, but the old-timers swear there have been panther sightings in that swamp for almost two hundred years. But back to the story. I had to help whoever was in distress and was terrified it might be a wandering guest. Now this will really scare the wits out of you, Cayce. It was getting close to dark, and I don't know my way around that swamp and neither do I care to, but I forced myself to head in. I'd ride a little ways and stop and listen. Thinking I heard a child whimpering, I turned down a path I'd never been on." Joshua paused, glancing at each sister, and noticed the servers bringing their main course and whispered the next line. "That's when I saw it."

Harri and Cayce were no longer anxious to try the delicious meals put in front of them, and Joshua smiled, knowing he had left them with a cliffhanger.

"Lobster casserole with steamed vegetables?" the server announced, and Harri held her hand up.

"And fettuccine Alfredo with grilled shrimp for you, ma'am." When the server placed the wonderful-looking entrée in front of Cayce, her appetite returned in full force.

"And Mr. Devaux, very rare T-bone, as always, with a loaded baked potato."

"Thank you, Carl, and give my compliments to Andre." After Carl left, Joshua continued. "Andre came here from a fancy restaurant in New Orleans less than a year ago. He named a price and I met it, and I've not been disappointed. Speaking of which, how about we eat first so this delicious food won't get cold, and I'll finish the story while we wait on dessert."

"Dessert? I'll gain five pounds by the end of the week if I keep eating like this."

"Oh, right! That should put you up to a whopping hundred and ten, Harri," Cayce remarked with sarcasm as Joshua laughed at the sisterly ribbing.

"You both look great, and five pounds wouldn't hurt either of you. If you want, you can come riding with me tomorrow and work off some of this." Joshua cast an eye at both Harri and Cayce, gauging any interest in his offer.

"You're not talking to me, Joshua, but Cayce is always ready to cowgirl up. My experience on a horse goes back to high school when Pop bought Queen for us. Problem was, I never got to ride in the saddle because my baby sister wouldn't let me. I can only ride cheek to cheek, behind the saddle."

"Well, that was only fair, my dear sister. I was the

one who wanted a horse in the first place. You were lucky I let you tag along."

"But, Harri, I promise you can have your own horse and saddle. How can you pass up a deal like that?" Joshua winked at Cayce, and they both laughed.

"Easy! Besides, unless it has one foot in the grave, I wouldn't go near it. I'm scared to death of horses. I need to go through my recipes anyway and decide what my contest entry will be."

Very little talking took place as the three cleaned their plates. When they finished, Joshua beckoned Carl to the table.

"Carl, I want my friends to try the crème brulee. I know you'll like it, Harri, since you're the gourmet cook. You can have it plain or with your choice of raspberry or muscadine sauce. I prefer the raspberry myself, but the muscadine, being unique to the South, is probably the most popular."

"Crème brulee is my favorite. Regardless of how full I am, there is no way I could pass it up. Plain for me." Harri was quick to respond.

"I'll have muscadine. My sister introduced me to crème brulee when she visited me in Montana one summer. We had crème brulee with huckleberry sauce at Montana Hannah's Trout Hole Restaurant in the Nye Valley, and I swear it was the best dessert I've ever tasted. I'm sure Andre's version will change that idea, though, if it is as good as the rest of the meal."

After Carl took their plates, Joshua propped his elbows on the table and looked seriously at his guests.

"Now for the rest of the story. I followed the crying sound and rode deeper into the swamp, knowing I should have turned around and gone for help, or at least for a light. I had no flashlight and no cell phone. I'm sure you can guess what happened next. I became disoriented, lost as a goose in a whiteout. Realizing what a dangerous place I was in and knowing I would not be able to find my way out in the dark, I found the highest spot I could locate and got off my horse. I gathered up as much dry brush as I could, and lucky for me at the time, I still smoked so had a lighter in my pocket. I started a fire, not because it was cold but to ward off creatures. I tied my horse so he would be in the light of the fire, took the saddle off, and sat on it, knowing I'd be spending the night there. I knew Soppy wouldn't miss me since she was staying at the inn so she could sleep late. She was scheduled to take over the desk early the next morning. As if the swamp itself wasn't enough, a fog drifted in, and I could barely see even though the moon was full. About midnight, it started."

Joshua lowered his voice for dramatic effect and stared across the table directly into his guests' eyes. Cayce and Harri leaned closer, ready for what they knew would be a suspenseful recounting.

"I heard the horse before I saw the apparition. A man wearing a long black coat with the tail flying out in the back, like they wore in the 1800s, galloped past, not fifty feet from me. I stood and yelled out to him, but he never looked toward me or acknowledged he'd heard me."

"Could you tell anything about his features? Did he have a beard?" Cayce asked the question hoping the apparition could be identified if it was a ghost from the past.

"It was like the fog followed him. I couldn't see his

face, but he rode a huge black stallion. I was pretty shaken by it but tried to settle myself down, knowing there were still several hours before first light. Then I heard another horse. This time, it was a man on a big bay with a blaze on its face. He galloped fast, as if chasing the first rider. This rider had on a coat with a tail, too, but it was light gray. I couldn't see his face, but his hair was longer and flopped in back when he was galloping. Once again I stood and called out, but he, too, ignored me. I don't mind telling you it 'bout scared the britches off me."

"I would have had a heart attack!"

"No, you wouldn't, Cayce, because scream or no scream you wouldn't have gone in there with the snakes and 'gators in the first place."

"Well, not unless it was somebody I knew screaming."

"Not even, Sister. Remember the time we were walking with Pop by that old muddy pond? You saw a snake lying beside it and pushed me toward it trying to get away. You and Pop both took off running and left me there. I don't know which one was more afraid, you or Pop."

"Oh, yeah. I did do that, didn't I? Don't mind us, Joshua. Go on with your story, even though I'm shivering so bad I need a goose-down jacket." Joshua stood up, pulled his jacket off, and put it around Cayce's shoulders.

"Thank you. Now…continue."

"I sat back down, trying to settle my nerves, but kept looking around. That was when I saw something black running through the swamp, low like the panther I'd heard about, and this wouldn't be the only time I saw it. I wore myself out looking and listening, and a couple of hours later, believe it or not, I dozed off with my head on the saddle, as close to the fire as I could safely get. I don't know how long I slept, but something woke me up. I sat up and there the guy was, sitting on that black horse, looking down at me. This time I saw his face. He had a thick dark mustache and a long scar that ran the full length of his right cheek. But it wasn't his face that scared me the most. He had a pistol in his hand, one of those old-timey ones you have to put the powder in, and it was aimed at me. He cocked the gun, and I shut my eyes, sure I was going to die in that swamp and never be found. The gun clicked but didn't go off. Then he turned his horse, threw back his head, gave a laugh that would curl an executioner's toes, and galloped off. I could hear him laughing for several seconds, until I couldn't hear his horse anymore. Needless to say, I did not go back to sleep. Between the man and the panther, there was no way I'd shut my eyes. I didn't know which one to fear the most. As soon as it got light enough for me to pick my way out, I left, and I don't plan on going back there. That was a couple of months ago."

"Does Sophia know this story?"

"No, Harri. I haven't told her but have warned her not to go near that swamp. I also had warning signs put up at every possible entrance. Eventually, I'm going to have the whole area fenced off, at least the part on my property. The swamp goes for miles beyond my property lines, but it's state property now, a wildlife reserve. I have it fenced along most of the gravel road, and I have No Trespassing signs all along it. From what I hear, a few people have disappeared in there over the last hundred fifty years, but that would have been on the original Spanish Oaks property, about two thousand acres in the original deed."

"What did Sherone say? She's been living on the edge of that swamp for thirty years, so she must know there are spirits there." Cayce knew she wanted to visit Sherone again to ask her about the swamp but hated the thought of walking down that path.

"She warned me about the bad mojo in the swamp and told me to stay away and never to react to anything I heard coming from it again. Now you know why I warned you not all of the spirits are good. Do you think you two can help? Everyone loves a good ghost story, but I don't want anyone getting hurt."

"There is much paranormal activity going on here, Joshua. Harri and I talked about it this afternoon after the experience in the attic room. I'm not sure we can help with the bad mojo in the swamp. That seems like something Sherone would be better at handling, but I do think Chloe needs our help. We think if we can solve some of the mysteries, the spirits will be at peace. Do you want us to try?"

"Yes, I do. Maybe in the course of helping Chloe the evil spirit will be put to rest, although he might rather stay in the swamp than go where I think he'll be going. Sophia really believes in you two, so what can we do to help?"

Cayce and Harri looked at each other and knew it was time to disclose their buy in Natchez. Cayce gave Harri the nod, and she told Joshua about the cookbook and about her sister's vision. When she finished, Joshua sat back, looking stunned.

"Wow! We have a thief among us, don't we? I

don't know if the cookbook was stolen from here, but there is a way we can find out. When I bought Spanish Oaks, I needed to know how much to insure the furnishings for and hired a very reputable antique dealer in Jackson to come and inventory every antique here and to price each item. Several of his staff spent days and days here and covered every nook and cranny to make sure everything was photographed and listed. Every four years, the inventory is redone and any new pieces bought are added. The fourth-year inventory was finished back in March of last year. I have two volumes of inventory, with pictures, at home in the vault. When I get a chance, I'll see if the cookbook is listed. I'll be happy to reimburse you to have the cookbook back, especially if it's in Affie's handwriting. What a find! When can I see it?"

"I'll bring it to you tomorrow, if that's soon enough. I would like to copy some of the recipes, if you don't mind. There's one in particular I'm thinking about entering in the contest."

"I'll tell you what. Why don't you bring the cookbook up to my office tomorrow morning? I'll take you two to my house and show you where I keep all of my family documents, as well as the Broussard documents, so you can use them for your research. You can have access to the cookbook and all of the documents any time you want. If you come tomorrow, I'll take you for a ride, Cayce. You, too, Harri, if you change your mind."

"Thanks, but I'll pass, although I wouldn't mind looking at your family documents. Maybe I can do that while you and Cayce indulge in your western fantasies."

"Sure. How about you two meet me in my office about nine in the morning. I'd like to show you Beatrice's portrait while you're in the office. It's quite a find."

****

The next morning, the sisters were finishing up coffee and a light breakfast at the Stables, waiting for their meeting with Joshua. Cayce was wearing her boots and jeans, anxious to get back on a horse but also anxious to see the portrait. Harri made sure she wore an outfit not conducive to horseback riding.

"Good morning, ladies. Are you ready to go up to my office?" Joshua led the way through the restaurant and out the back entrance to a steep set of stairs. Once at the top, he unlocked the door, reached inside and turned on the lights, and then stood to the side to allow the sisters to enter.

"Wow! This is amazing!"

Cayce found herself totally immersed in the West even though she was in South Mississippi. And Harri was also impressed with how tastefully the office was decorated, although it was not her style. Most of the furniture was oversized yet elegant in a rustic sort of way. The office was huge, running the full length of the restaurant, but was separated into sections, each section serving a different purpose. One section was a library with bookshelves on both sides filled with books and western art including bronze sculptures, some pieces by Cayce's favorite Montana sculptor, Mary Michael. On the wall directly behind the desk, large pictures of different commercial projects Joshua's company had built dominated, but on all other walls, the theme was the great American West with a huge Kevin RedStar original taking center stage.

On a wall to the right of Joshua's desk was a large oil portrait of Sophia and her mother. Her mother was beautiful, with long dark hair hanging over one shoulder and eyes the same color as Sophia's. The daughter looked like a younger version of her mother and appeared to be about twelve years of age in the picture.

"Your wife was beautiful. Sophia looks just like her."

"Thank you, Harri. Soppy has her mom's personality and sweetness, too. Jeannie was half Choctaw, grew up on the reservation in central Mississippi. Her dad was a principal and her mom a teacher. Jeannie followed in their footsteps and taught school when we first married, until Sophia was born. Fortunately, the company was doing well by that time and she was able to be a full-time mom. What do you think of my collection, Cayce?"

"It's fabulous! My wee collection of western art is no match for this, but we do have common interests in art and sculpture, although yours is far pricier than mine. My buying days are pretty much over."

"Don't let her kid you, Joshua. She's always in the market."

"Speaking of oil paintings, are you ready to see Beatrice?" Joshua took his keychain from his pocket and unlocked a door in the corner behind the office area. The portrait had been removed from the box but was wrapped in heavy material. Joshua brought it out, removed the cover, and turned the portrait toward Cayce and Harri.

The two stood with their mouths open. The woman

in the picture far surpassed Scarlett O'Hara, alias Vivian Leigh. Her thick red hair hung long over one shoulder and her well-endowed chest. Deep cleavage detracted from a waistline so tiny it didn't look real. Cayce stood spellbound, having a staring contest with the emerald green eyes that seemed to cut right through her. The eyes were the same green as the elegant taffeta gown, the narrow sleeves worn off her ghostly pale shoulders.

But it wasn't the eyes attracting the most attention. Around her neck hung the most fabulous piece of jewelry either of them had ever seen, equaled only by the crown jewels of France or England, or perhaps the jewels of the Romanovs.

"I'm not an expert on jewelry, but I know enough to know that necklace is priceless. Harri, on the other hand, knows everything about jewelry. Demonstrate, Harri. Tell us what you see in this portrait hanging around this perfect neck that has never known sunshine or hard times."

Harri took her place at the side of the picture after picking up a ruler off Joshua's desk. Using it as a pointer, she began her description, sounding like a specialist in treasured heirloom jewelry with Sotheby's.

"The necklace is a diamond-and-emerald link chain made up of fifty or more diamonds, at a minimum of two carats each. Four deep green oval cabochon emeralds of fifty to sixty carats, total weight, are evenly dispersed, two on each side of the chain." Harri moved the pointer as she described each section, looking to her audience to make sure she had their full attention. Her voice took on a sophisticated city, almost snobby, tone and was devoid of her usual southern accent.

"Hanging from the center is a remarkable pendant about three inches in diameter, in the shape of a fleur-de-lis, with Pavé-set diamonds, rose cut and flawless, the total of which is…" Harri glanced at the written description. "One hundred carats." She paused, letting the excessive value sink in with her audience of two.

"In the middle of the pendant is a bigger dark green cabochon-cut emerald, enthroned, as three briolette emeralds dangle from three separate points beneath it, total weight about seventy-five carats."

Harri placed the ruler on the desk, bowed curtly to her audience as they applauded, and she smiled and gestured to direct attention to the portrait and signify the real star was the fabulous necklace adorning the beautiful Beatrice.

"This necklace would certainly be a motive for murder. I think the history book was right, Cayce."

"So you know the story of the lost necklace?" Joseph cocked his head to one side and looked from Harri to Cayce.

"Yes. I read it in the history, but it doesn't give any details. Was it a family heirloom of Beatrice's family or of the Broussards?"

"Therein lies yet another mystery. It is thought to be from Princeton's family. He refused to give the sheriff much information about it except to say it was valuable, an understatement, judging by Harri's description. Beatrice's family disclaimed any knowledge of it, so if it had been given to their daughter, they knew nothing of it. I got this information from a letter written by the sheriff who investigated Beatrice's death. No one knew it existed until the portrait was unveiled at Princeton's birthday dinner party on the night Beatrice died. Beatrice was wearing the necklace as she descended the stairs, a grand entrance timed to be in sync with the unveiling of the portrait. The portrait and the necklace disappeared after midnight along with the murderer. Then we found the portrait six months ago behind the wall in a secret compartment in Lily's day room, with two slashes running from corner to corner across Beatrice's amazing bosom." Joshua made a crisscross across the painting without touching it. Cayce and Harri moved closer to get a better look.

"Amazing!" Harri exclaimed and looked at Joshua. "The necklace, that is! Matter of opinion, Joshua."

"So where will you hang the portrait, Joshua?" Harri asked.

"Oh, that's an easy one. It will be hung at the head of the stairs, looking down on the lobby, the same place it was hanging when it was unveiled the night of May 30, 1848. It will be the grand finale this Friday night when we have the annual celebration of Princeton's birthday as the last Broussard to own the Oaks. I just hope it won't make the spirits restless, at least not the ones from the swamp. But here, I want you to see something else about the portrait." Joshua lifted the portrait so that it rested on the edge of his desk.

"Walk to the other side of the room and watch Beatrice as you pass."

"Oh, my gosh! Not only her eyes follow you, her whole body shifts. How in the world did the artist do that?" Harri walked back and forth in front of the painting, even darting quickly at one point as if she thought she could fool Beatrice.

"It's an optical illusion involving the artist's use of

linear perception that focuses on a single point." Cayce had moved in front of the portrait and stared into the eyes of the mysterious Beatrice. When she noticed Joshua watching her with his eyebrows arched in wonder at her knowledge, she explained.

"My daughter Piper is an artist. On one of our many trips to art museums, Piper explained the process of linear perception to me, not that I completely understand it, by any means. I can toss around the terms, but please don't ask me to explain it in depth."

"Speaking of artists, who signed the portrait?" Harri asked.

Cayce leaned down and looked at the bottom corner of the portrait, where a very fancy signature had been written. "R. Fairchild. Have you ever heard of him, Joshua?"

"I don't know anything about him, but he also painted the portrait of Beatrice and Lily hanging in the room where Don Fowler is staying. You'll have to get Don to let you see that one. Beatrice shifts in that portrait as well. Uncanny, isn't it?"

"Gives me the chills." Harri shivered.

Cayce continued to stare at the portrait, absorbing every detail.

"The museum did a wonderful job of restoring it. You can't tell where it was patched."

"You better not be able to tell, after what the restoration cost." Joshua covered the portrait and returned it to the storage room, locking the door before turning back to Cayce and Harri.

"Now then. I believe you have something to show me?" Joshua smiled as he rubbed his hands together in eager anticipation.

Harri was carrying a large cloth bag. Before she took out the cookbook, she removed a pair of white gloves.

"These are way too big for Cayce and me, so maybe they'll fit you. The book is very fragile." Walking to the table in the library area, Harri put on the other pair of gloves and gingerly lifted the wrapped cookbook and placed it on the table.

"Oh, my! Would you look at that! The Broussard coat of arms is hand-painted on the leather cover." The gloves were snug, but Joshua pulled and pushed until he got them on enough to touch the journal. He took his time turning pages and became totally absorbed in it.

"We think the fancy script belonged to Victoria Broussard and the simpler print to Affie." Cayce took a seat in one of the mission chairs, keeping her distance from the table.

"Yes, I recognize Affie's handwriting. I have a Bible where she recorded births, deaths, marriages, and so on."

"Toward the end of the cookbook, there are pages missing, but they most likely were blank. I've gone over the whole cookbook, but the date stops before the fatal night." Harri took over the explanation.

"Do you think the pages that are stuck together would tell us anything?" Joshua asked.

"I think they have already told me more than enough." Cayce thought back to her experience in the antique shop. "And I don't think the dark stain is spaghetti sauce like I tried to convince my sister before I came in direct contact with the book."

Joshua continued to turn the pages with interest, becoming more intense with each page. As he came to the dark stained pages stuck together, he fingered the edges to see if there was any way of getting them apart, but it was useless.

"These pages are thick, like there's something else with them, but there's no way to get them apart without tearing the pages, and I won't do that. I don't guess there's any chance you'd submit yourself to another vision, Cayce?"

"Harri asked me the same thing, and like I told her, I need to think about it. All I know for sure is the body was Beatrice, lying in a pool of blood, murdered by a butcher knife that I think was shown us and then made to disappear. And the necklace was on her at the time she died, the same necklace in the portrait. That means the murderer was still in the kitchen, since he took the necklace before leaving. If I go back, I'll have to confront him, and I don't know what would happen. Give me some time to find answers in other ways, in the present."

"So what do you think it all means? Do you believe you and Harri were led here for a reason?"

"Harri and I have a philosophy we live by, passed down from our father, who had the gift. He always said, 'Keep an open mind and an open path, and the Way will find you.' The night we met Sherone in the gift shop, she said, 'May the Way find you' as she left the shop."

"I think I was led to the cookbook, and it is all a sign: Cayce seeing the knife in the vision and then being introduced to it in person; the knife disappearing as mysteriously as it appeared. Both signs are needed to answer the question of who murdered Beatrice and why."

"We just have to wait and see what is brought to us next. Harri and I are keeping our minds open for all possibilities."

"I believe you." Joshua closed the book, wrapped it back in the bubble wrap and paper, and put it back in Harri's bag along with the gloves. "I'll secure this at my house with the other rare documents. Hopefully, it won't mysteriously disappear like the knife when it was locked in your suitcase. If you're right, I think the journal is meant to stay with us." Holding on to the bag, Joshua locked the storage room door and turned to the sisters.

"Now, let's go to my house. Time for that exercise I promised. Sorry we can't ride out in your Beamer, Harri, but we have to take the Jeep. The cabin is in a pretty isolated spot, and I haven't gotten the road paved all the way yet."

"Oh, I'm used to roughin' it. I grew up with a tomboy sister, remember?" Harri smiled at Cayce.

****

The three headed down the gravel road, passing the path to Sherone's house, following the fence both sisters knew contained the deadly swamp. The top was off the Jeep, and Cayce and Harri enjoyed the scenic ride through a combination of Spanish moss and giant oaks. They had not gone far when the road become rougher, turning sharply to follow the river. A few minutes later, they were going up a long, paved driveway through giant oak and poplar trees.

After climbing a hill, they got their first look at Joshua's log cabin, which was by no means a simple, comfortable cabin. The logs were square and stained gray, not round like most log homes out west, and they had thick white chinking between them. The house was two-story, with a wide porch running the length of the house on the front. The roof looked like the old tin roofs from a hundred years ago. Four doghouses sat on top that must have provided a magnificent view from the upstairs rooms.

"Comfortable, huh? I think that's a bit of an understatement. So where are the stables?" Cayce was anxious to start their ride.

"It is comfortable, a comfortable five-thousand-square-foot home. You'll see the stables soon enough, and I'll take you for that ride. I'll get Harri set up in the study first and show her where the kitchen is. It's well stocked with the most fabulous frozen leftovers you'll ever experience, courtesy of Andre. Just pop them in the microwave and it's like you're sitting in the Stables again. I never cook except for the occasional steak on the grill. After our ride, I'll treat you both to a heavenly lunch, via freezer and microwave."

The great room of the cabin was furnished like Joshua's office but with much more of the Southwestern theme. Wide, pine, plank floors were covered in rugs with Native American motifs in reds, blacks, turquoise, and rich earth tones. A loft under a steeply pitched ceiling looked down on the great room below.

Joshua led his guests through the great room to the study, bigger than the library section of his office but decorated the same with bookshelves filled with books, bronze sculptures, many family pictures, and walls covered in western art.

Joshua went to a door located mid-center of the back wall of shelves and unlocked it. Motioning for his guests to follow, he turned on the light to reveal shelves of very old books.

"These were all removed from the library at Spanish Oaks. Eventually, I'll return them, but I do my research here and needed them secure, especially after the attempted robbery. This room is actually a fireproof vault and serves as a tornado shelter as well. I don't know if it would help if there was another Katrina, but it would stand up against any tornadoes resulting. You are both welcome to spend as much time as you want with these books and documents while you're here, and it's not necessary to wear the gloves unless you want to. I'll even show you where a key is hidden outside so you can come in the house when I'm not here. The Jeep stays parked behind the office, with the key under the floor mat, so just use it any time you want to come out." Joshua walked to the back of the vault and motioned for the two to follow.

"This section contains the really valuable stuff. There are journals from Victoria and Jacob Broussard, a business journal or ledger kept by Princeton, some family letters and other correspondence, and local documents I found by word of mouth after I bought the Oaks. I haven't had time to go through all of it, but I'd be willing to bet a lot of answers can be found in these pages. If I were you, Harri, I'd start with the journals of Victoria and Jacob. In this box on the same shelf there is correspondence between Victoria and her mother-in-law in New Orleans, and also letters Beatrice received from relatives and acquaintances in Louisiana. You'll find plenty of paper and pens in the desk, if you want to make notes. Oh, yes, the door locks automatically when closed, but if you lock yourself in, don't panic. The door will open from the inside."

Leaving the study, Joshua showed Harri the kitchen. When she walked in, she was as speechless as she had been when she got her first look at the Spanish Oaks mansion. It was every cook's dream kitchen, with nothing left to chance.

"I can't believe I'm seeing a kitchen like this in a man's house, a man who cooks with a freezer and a microwave. Did you plan this, Joshua?"

"Actually, my wife designed this years ago. She kept a scrapbook of her dream kitchen. She liked to cook like you do, Harri, but she never got to see her dream reach reality. I would never have put this much into a room I have no intention of using, but Sophia wanted it. Since this will be hers some day, I let her use her mom's ideas, and here it is."

"I've always said the kitchen is the heart of the house. It has to be warm, family friendly, and feel like a gathering place for friends and family every day, not just on festive occasions. This kitchen is perfect. It's therapeutic and tranquil." Harri stood in the middle of the kitchen, turning 360 degrees and staring in awe of the most beautiful kitchen she had ever seen. Cayce joined her sister, stopping in front of a massive fireplace and gazing up at an antique crazy quilt displayed above it.

"This quilt is beautiful. I'd say it dates pre-Civil War. Am I right, Joshua?"

"You are correct, Cayce. You know your antiques. The quilt was one of the few things Caleb took with him when he headed North. I was fortunate to have a long line of ancestors who recognized the value of family pieces for the history they represented."

It was hard to convince Harri to leave the kitchen, but Cayce pulled her away so Joshua could give them a quick tour of the rest of the house. He also showed the sisters the two guest rooms with an adjoining bath and said if they ever wanted to research late, they were welcome to stay.

"Now, Cayce, to the stables!" Joshua rubbed his hands together like an excited little boy as Cayce smiled and followed him.

Harri had her dream kitchen, but Cayce found her dream barn. The barn was huge, with a high pitch like the house, and had a hayloft like barns of the 1800s. It was painted a dark barn red with white trim and was located down the hill behind the house, several hundred feet away. Every stall had a self-waterer and a self-feeder for giving just the right amount of grain and hay. A large tack room took up one whole end of the barn, and Cayce was sure it looked like a western store inside. Mack was working on the plumbing in one of the ten stalls.

"How's it going, Mack? Did you find the problem with the self-waterer?"

"Yep. The drain had a root growing into it, but I'll have it cleared out in no time. I'm replacing the pipe."

Only four horses were in the barn, but it was obvious Joshua planned on having more. Joshua led Cayce to the back and opened the tack room, removing a blanket and saddle he placed on a double sawhorse in the wide hallway. Repeating his actions, he placed another blanket and saddle beside the first.

"Mack must be a jack of all trades." Cayce couldn't help but notice how Mack seemed to be struggling with the wrench.

"Not really, but he's willing. He's learned a lot from Tom, the head maintenance man. Mack's been working here a couple of months. Tom hired him when he was in a bind. It's hard to get help, with all the construction work going on in New Orleans and on the coast. Mack is retired military."

Cayce stopped to rub a buckskin gelding's head as he leaned over the gate of his stall, nickering as if trying to get her attention.

"Hey, boy. Need a good rub?"

"That's Dakota. He's Sophia's horse, but she never has time to ride much anymore. Wanta ride him?"

"Sure. What are you riding?" Joshua went into a stable a brought out a gorgeous palomino stallion.

"That is a fine stallion, but I like the looks of Dakota here."

"Good. The old boy needs the exercise, not to mention a little feminine attention. He's kind of like me in that department, as well as being gentle but spunky." Joshua gave Cayce a playful smile and winked.

Cayce did a double-take, giving her host a questioning frown as Joshua threw back his head and laughed.

"I don't know about Mr. Devaux, but Dakota looks like my kind of horse. Let's get you out and get you ready, boy." Cayce took the halter tied to the outside of the gate and entered the stable. After putting the halter on Dakota, she led him out, tied him to a hitching post, and began brushing him with the brush Joshua handed her.

"Here, I'll throw the saddle on for you." Joshua lifted a blanket and saddle from the sawhorse and headed toward Cayce.

"Thanks, but I can handle it." Cayce took the saddle from Joshua and carried it with little effort. "You saddle yours. I'm long overdue for a ride."

Admiring Cayce's independence, Joshua turned back and picked up his blanket and saddle. He smiled over his horse as he watched Cayce pull the girth tight and then reach for the bridle.

"These stirrups are just right." Cayce had finished and mounted Dakota just as Joshua finished saddling his horse. "Sophia and I must have the same length legs."

"She's long-legged like her mom even though she's shorter. I'd like to make Soppy into a cowgirl, but she told me a long time ago she'd rather shop. She gets that from Jeannie as well."

"Lead on, Massa." Cayce put on a little slave dialect, to Joshua's amusement, as she held back on the reins to allow him to lead the way.

"You better be careful. I might lead you into the swamp."

"I don't think so." Cayce smiled as Joshua looked back at her and motioned her to move up beside him.

The two headed for the river, walking their horses and talking the whole way after Joshua asked Cayce about her ranch in Montana. Cayce was glad to have a reprieve from the paranormal circumstances of her visit and didn't have to be encouraged to tell Joshua all about the ranch, her Beartooth Mountains, and the Nye Valley. She also told him about her daughter Piper and how she was in Europe at the moment, off on an adventure of her own.

"You should come and visit Montana and bring Sophia. I'll take you on a trail ride you'll never forget, into my mountains. Have you ever fly fished?"

"No, but I'd love to try. I go deep-sea fishing on the coast quite a bit and have done a little fishing in the river, spin fishing, that is. At least I'm not the worm-in-a-coffee-can kind of guy, but I'll have to admit I grew up that way."

"Don't apologize. I can still remember worms in a can and minnows and crickets bought from the bait shop. Those were good memories with my dad."

After riding for about twenty minutes, Joshua stopped his horse.

"There's the path that goes through the swamp. I don't guess you want to investigate?"

"Not a chance." Cayce was quick to respond. "I'm watching for snakes even on this scenic river trail."

"There is one spot on the other side of the swamp I would like to show you. It's over behind Sherone's house, not too far in. It's like an oasis in the midst of hell, quite spectacular, but I guess you aren't game."

"You'd have to tell me more and assure me there is no chance of getting lost."

"Did you see the yellow lilies behind Sherone's house?"

"Yes, I did. They're beautiful. She said the bulbs were imported from France by Jacob Broussard."

"That's right. Well, imagine a whole field of those surrounding a clear pool of water where you could see goldfish and turtles swimming around lily pads."

"And snakes and alligators?" Cayce added.

"You know, I've been there a couple of times with Sherone, and I've never seen anything creepy. Are you game?"

"I'll have to take a peek at the trail before I give

you an answer."

After a few more minutes of riding, Joshua turned down a side trail leading to Sherone's yard.

"We'd say hello to Sherone, but I know she's not here. She told me she was going to New Orleans today to visit a cousin—more like a partner in crime. Her cousin Jaleel is a fortuneteller, too. Sherone told me she needed more lizard tails and possum hearts." Seeing the shock on Cayce's face, he added, "She likes to joke around. At least I think she was joking." Joshua laughed as he led the way to the entrance to the swamp.

"We have to ride about five minutes through the swamp, and then the path clears out, leading to the lily patch. What do you think? Can you handle it?"

Cayce rubbed her thighs nervously and raised up in the saddle to look beyond Joshua, trying to make up her mind.

"You guarantee Dakota won't be spooked by a moccasin?"

"I promise to go first and clear the way. You can't get lost. There's only one way in and one way out, and no side trails. Both of these horses have been in here before. I've even taken Sophia in here. If you feel uneasy at any time, we'll turn around and leave. I promise."

Getting an approving nod from Cayce, Joshua reined his horse into the swamp with Cayce reluctantly following. The trail was narrow, and she took shallow breaths, often holding her them and looking at her watch to see when five minutes was up. On either side, cypress trees grew out of slick black water, intermixed with willows that seemed to weep more than normal.

"How much farther? Five minutes is up." Cayce

was losing her trust in Joshua as she kept her focus on his back, not looking to either side, and she was wishing she had not given in.

"We're here. Ride up beside me. The path is wide here."

As she peeked around Joshua, Cayce caught a glimpse of yellow and knew he was telling the truth. The sight in front of her took her breath. As far as she could see, there was a jungle of yellow lilies.

"You're right! An oasis in the middle of hell. How can this be?" She stood in her stirrups and leaned up on the saddle horn to get a better view. "The lilies go for yards and yards. Why are there so many?"

"I guess they multiplied over the century and a half since they were planted."

"I wonder why Princeton planted the lilies here."

"Another mystery, my dear. Follow me. This path leads through the lily field to the clear pool I was telling you about."

A path opened up in the middle of the lilies, reminding Cayce of the story of the parting of the Red Sea from the Bible, except this sea was yellow. When the path stopped, the pool Joshua had told her about appeared and was several yards across, surrounded on all sides by yellow.

"It's safe to get off here if you want. You will be amazed when you look into the pool. You can put your reins on the ground. The horses will stay put."

Joshua and Cayce walked to the edge of the pool with Cayce just a little leery of snakes even in the midst of the yellow heaven.

"There! See that huge goldfish?"

As Cayce looked in the direction Joshua pointed,

the fish disappeared into a thin mist that drifted in over the water, swirling around in the hot, muggy air like a phantom being. The pool turned slimy and black, the lilies changed to gnarled trees, and ghostly cypress knees and tangles of weeds and vines blew in the stifling breeze, giving off a pungent smell that choked her. The sun no longer ricocheted off the yellow as the swamp transformed into a darkening hell. She heard steps like a small deer, and before she could yell a warning, the little girl in her muddy once-white dress stumbled in, beating the water with her hands but not trying to hold her head above the water. Cayce tried to get to her, but something was holding on to her, something weighting her arms, holding them to her sides. All she could do was scream before the blackness overtook her.

"Cayce! Cayce! Are you all right, sweetheart?"

She awoke as Joshua shook her back into reality. Joshua had lowered her to the ground and was holding her head in his arms, dabbing her forehead with his handkerchief he had wet in the pond.

"My god, you scared me to death! What happened, Cayce? You kept trying to jump into the pool. I had to hold you."

"This is where Lily died. Right over there." Sitting up, she pointed to the opposite side of the pool as Joshua helped her to her feet, holding her around the waist.

"You had a vision?" Joshua looked stunned.

"Yes. But this was a terrifying dark swamp then. No lilies. No clear pond."

"I am so sorry I made you come in here. I had no idea. I knew Lily drowned in the swamp, but no one has known where until now. Are you okay? Maybe you need to sit down for a while." Joshua held tight to Cayce's waist to make sure she was steady.

"No. I'm fine. Just let me sit here for a while and enjoy the beauty and try to get over what it looked like when poor little Lily was lost."

After several minutes of sitting still, Joshua helped Cayce onto her horse, and they rode out of the swamp with Joshua constantly looking back to see if she was all right. When they reached Sherone's yard, Joshua got off his horse and helped Cayce down.

"Sherone never locks her house. Let's get you something to drink before we ride home."

Cayce did not argue. She led her horse past the yellow lilies of the shed and ground-tied him in the front yard. Joshua went inside, leaving her sitting in one of the rockers. Cayce put her head back and closed her eyes. She did not want to forget what Lily looked like. It would be the last time the little girl was seen alive. Joshua handed Cayce a glass of cold lemonade and pulled one of the straight chairs over close to her.

"This is good—just what I needed." Noticing the worried look on his face, Cayce smiled and rubbed his cheek with her fingers. "I'm okay, Joshua. And I'm glad I went to see the lilies, especially the Lily I had no idea I would see. You needed to know where she died. And I'll bet that's the reason the lilies grow there. Her daddy probably planted them to memorialize the spot where Lily died."

"You're probably right, but I feel guilty I made you go in."

"Joshua, no one makes Cayce McCallister do anything she doesn't want to do. Understand?"

Joshua smiled as he picked up Cayce's hand. He surprised her more when he leaned over and lightly kissed her on the lips.

"How about we get back to the back fifty and see if your sister found anything. She won't believe what we found, will she?" Still holding to Cayce's hand, Joshua stood and helped Cayce up, only then letting go of her hand.

"She won't be surprised, I can assure you."

After Joshua and Cayce put the horses away, they headed inside to see what Harri had found. She was sitting at the kitchen table, drinking an iced coffee, totally engulfed in Victoria Broussard's journal as the Food Network blasted from the big screen TV mounted on the wall on the opposite side from where she was sitting.

"You won't believe what I've found." Harri barely looked up as Cayce and Joshua entered but moved the journal over so they could see the page she was reading.

Joshua looked at Cayce, waiting for her to respond with what they had learned, but she only looked at him and smiled.

"Let's have it, Harri. No, wait a minute. I want one of those iced coffees. As you can see, we always make ourselves right at home, Joshua."

Harri left the table, retrieved two more small bottles from the refrigerator, and proceeded to fill two glasses with crushed ice and the coffee drink. Handing each of the new arrivals a glass and a napkin, she led them back to the table, talking the whole time about looking through each journal before deciding to start with Victoria's. Cayce picked up the remote and muted the on-screen cook, leaving her to make banana pudding in silence with her two handsome sons beside her.

"Now, are you ready?" Harri looked from Cayce to Joshua.

Joshua and Cayce took a seat at the table opposite Harri, who was glancing over her notes, trying to find what she had written. "Here it is. On June 1, 1822, Victoria wrote:

Jacob held Princeton for the first time today. His eyes filled as he looked into his firstborn's face, so proud our Heavenly Father has bequeathed to him an heir to the Broussard name and estate. When Nanny Affie took the baby to the nursery, Jacob left the room only to return a few moments later, smiling and hiding something behind his back. To my astonishment and overwhelming disbelief, Jacob entrusted to me The Flower. And even though I knew I could never disclose this to anyone other than my son, my heart was full.

Joshua looked from Harri to Cayce with question marks hovering on his brow.

"And giving his wife a flower at the birth of his son is unique and important because…?"

"*The* Flower. *La Fleur.*" The sisters spoke simultaneously.

"*La Fleur?*" Joshua repeated what he heard, still not understanding.

"The Flower. The fleur-de-lis necklace Beatrice was wearing the night she was murdered." Harri was ecstatic over her find. "Now we know it belonged to the Broussard family, a family secret. Something tells me Beatrice did not have her husband's permission to pose with his mother's pendant adorning her fabulous bosom."

"And you know where else we heard *La Fleur*?" Cayce looked at Joshua, who still seemed to be in the dark.

"You two have lost me completely. But I trust you are onto something, after what I witnessed today."

"Witnessed today?" Harri looked at Cayce.

"In a minute, but first I need to explain about *La Fleur* to Joshua. In the history book, it told about Jean Paul Broussard having many duels, but it only gave details of two, the one with the original owner of the land where Spanish Oaks sits and the other with a P. Bruser who spoke with an accent—a French accent, I'm sure. He was challenged to a duel he lost, right after accusing Jean Paul of being a thief, of stealing '*La Fleur*,' a good reason for Jean Paul to keep it a secret and a reason not to talk about his French connections."

"Yes, now I remember. I just never made any connection since no one knew what Princeton was talking about when he said the murderer stole an expensive necklace from his wife's body. If we hadn't found the portrait of Beatrice, we still wouldn't know. I've read Victoria's journal and remember the passage, but as far as I was concerned, it was a rose from the garden. Jacob and Princeton were interested in horticulture. I remember thinking at the time Jacob must have grafted a new type of rose and named it after Victoria, but then I'm just a construction hand, not a horticulturist."

"Anything else of interest from Victoria?" Cayce asked, glancing at her sister.

"I'm only a quarter of the way through it, but I'd be willing to bet we'll learn more."

"Take all the time you need. Remember, you can

come here any time you want," Joshua offered.

"That reminds me. Joshua, I have another favor to ask of you."

"Anything, Harri. I'm at your service."

"It's about the contest. Do you think I could borrow your kitchen? I need a place to try out the recipe in the cookbook."

"On one condition. I get to be the taste tester."

"Deal. How about tomorrow? I'll get all the ingredients today."

"Check out the cupboards here first. It's pretty well stocked, even though I don't cook. And the cookbook is right here, unless it disappears like the knife. I just hope the book doesn't magically return to wherever it was hiding."

****

It was almost two o'clock in the afternoon when Joshua pulled out frozen leftovers that would taste nothing like leftovers. Cayce performed the microwaving, licking her fingers as some of the finished entrée spilled, and she announced she thought Andre should work for Lean Tasties. Lunch consisted of chicken tetrazzini, Italian spinach, potato rolls, and peach sorbet for dessert. Cayce told Harri about her experience in the swamp over dessert.

"That's what you get for doing what you said you wouldn't. Will you ever learn?" Harri was playing big sister.

"I'm glad Joshua talked me into it. We know more after this one visit than we would have gained in hours of reading through documents, and there is no guarantee this information could be found there."

"If you say it's worth it, then it is, but you scared

the ba-jiggers out of me." Joshua reached and picked up Cayce's hand, something Cayce found very enjoyable.

Harri laughed at Joshua's choice of words. "I haven't heard that expression in so long, but I bet it fits. What are ba-jiggers anyway?"

"Not a clue. You'll have to look that one up. When you find out, let me know." Joshua chuckled as he answered.

****

When Cayce and Harri returned to the inn, they noticed Molly sitting on the side porch, rocking her doll.

"Hi, Molly. Is your baby asleep?" Harri stopped and looked down at the precious little girl. She was holding an African-American rag doll like those sold in the gift shop, but this one looked old and worn.

"Shh…!" Molly put her fingers to her lips. Then she whispered, "She's almost asleep."

"I'll be very quiet." Harri whispered her reply as she tiptoed on by. She and Cayce met Molly's mother coming out.

Cayce smiled and warned the mother not to wake her daughter's baby.

"Baby?" The mother looked surprised as she approached Molly. "Molly, where did you get that baby doll?"

Hearing the mother's question, the sisters stopped at the door.

"The little girl gave it to me. She said I could play with it if I took very good care of it."

"What little girl, Molly?" The mother looked anxious.

"The one by the willow tree." Molly pointed to the

lone willow beside where the new swimming pool would be set.

"Well, you need to find her and give it back. Daddy said he'd buy you one from the gift shop, remember?"

"Okay, Mama. I'll give it back to her when I see her again."

"What's your friend's name?" the little girl's mother asked.

"I don't know, but she dresses kinda funny," Molly replied.

"That's not a nice thing to say, Molly. She must have been nice, to let you play with her baby doll."

Cayce and Harri looked at each other and then walked back to Molly and her mother.

"I'm sorry. We couldn't help but overhear what Molly told you. Is it okay if we ask Molly a question?" Harri waited until Molly's mother nodded in agreement and then asked, "What did the little girl look like, Molly?"

Harri and Cayce both knelt to be closer to Molly.

"She had two long pigtails like mine and wore a long dress. It was all dirty, but she was really nice. Can I stay here a little while, Mama? My baby is almost asleep. I just need to sing to her a little bit." Molly's mother hugged her little girl while giving Harri and Cayce a questioning look.

"Sure, sweetie. I'll just sit here in the rocker by you and wait, but you need to find the little girl and return her baby."

Harri and Cayce sat in rockers on the other side of Molly and her mother and listened as Molly resumed rocking her baby and began singing in her sweet little girl voice.

"Hush-a-bye, don't you cry,
Go to sleepy little baby.
When we wake, you'll have cake,
And all the pretty little horses.
Way down yonder, down in the meadow,
There's a poor wee little lamby.
The bees and the butterflies pickin' at its eyes,
The poor wee thing cried for her mammy."

"Molly, where did you learn that verse? I've never heard it before." Molly's mother put her hand on her daughter's, waiting for her answer.

"She taught it to me. My friend, the little girl who had the baby doll. She said her mama used to sing it to her and tell her to stay in the yard or something bad could happen to her."

"I don't like it, Molly. Please don't sing that verse anymore. It's a beautiful lullaby, but that part is too frightening." Again, Molly's mother looked to Cayce and Harri as if hoping they could help explain this.

"It's all right, Mama. I'm not scared, but I won't sing it anymore." Molly then sang the verse her mother had taught her.

"Black and bay, dapple and gray,
Coach and six little horses,
Hush-a-bye, don't you cry,
Go to sleepy little baby."

Cayce had cold chills, remembering the first time she had heard the lullaby at Spanish Oaks. Harri and Cayce knew who Molly's friend was but did not disclose the information to Molly's mother just yet.

"We need to visit the slave quarters, Harri, and go back to Lily's day room and Chloe's nap room. We have to make a mental inventory of everything in those places, everything 'spiritual,' as Sherone called it."

"Yes, and we forgot to ask Joshua about the kitchen where Beatrice died, not that I think you're ready to go in it."

Cayce nodded her head in agreement. The experience that afternoon with Lily had been quite enough for one day.

Chapter Eight

The next morning found them well rested, with no experiences from the night. When Cayce and Harri came downstairs, they were surprised to see Monica at the front desk.

"Good morning, Monica. Sophia said you would be gone a couple of days."

"Good morning, Harri, Cayce. I thought I would, but I started feeling better last night and decided to come back to work. It must have been food poisoning. I heard you two had some excitement while I was out. I'm glad it didn't scare you away."

"Interesting, but nothing could scare us away at this point. Besides, I've got a contest to win."

"Well, two more days and you'll get your chance. Have you decided what you're making?"

"Oh, yes. The problem is finding all of the ingredients. It's from a really old cookbook."

"Really! Is it from your family?" Monica seemed genuinely interested in Harri's entry.

"No. It's from a cookbook I found in an antique shop in Natchez. I hope it doesn't have to be from my family."

"Oh, no. It just has to be from an old recipe, preferably the nineteenth century. Is it that old?"

"Early nineteenth century," Harri answered.

"Cookbooks that old are rare. I bet it cost a pretty

penny, especially being in Natchez. I hear those antique shops are expensive." Monica seemed very interested in where they had bought the cookbook.

"We found it in a shop on Franklin Street. Have you ever been to Natchez?" Cayce asked the question, wondering why Monica was so interested.

"No, I keep meaning to get up there but just never have made it. When I get a day off here, I just seem to have too many other things to do." Monica looked past Harri as the front door opened.

"Mr. and Mrs. Grantham? What a pleasant surprise! So you recuperated from your injuries?" The couple looked to be in their late sixties or early seventies. Both had scratches on their faces, and Mrs. Grantham limped and held on to her husband for support as they walked to the desk. Cayce thought Mr. Grantham looked familiar but could not recall where she had seen him. He wasted no time telling why they were at the Oaks.

"We recuperated faster than we thought and considered going back home to New Orleans, since we were so close, but decided to come on after renting a car. We didn't want to miss Princeton's birthday celebration. I hate we gave up our room, but we didn't think Mary would be released from the hospital so soon. We got hit on her side, so her injuries were a little more serious than mine. I don't guess there's any chance you still have our room?"

"No, Mr. Grantham, I'm sorry. In fact, these two ladies here rented it the same day you cancelled. But I'm sure Mr. Devaux would be happy for you to come to the ball Friday night. If you'd like, I can check with him. Do you have reservations elsewhere?"

"Yes, we do. John made them just in case our room was gone. I'm not sure I could make it up two flights of stairs anyway, but we do love Lily's room, and John said he'd help me. I hope the cancellation won't hurt our standing reservations."

"Of course not. I've kept you booked for the last week of every month through August, just like you requested." Monica excused herself as she picked up her radio and headed into the office behind the desk. Cayce and Harri had stopped, pretending to look at the reading material guests could check out. Both were curious to see the couple that had been jinxed by the paranormal forces needing the sisters to occupy Lily's room.

"I'm sorry to hear about your accident. I'm Cayce McCallister, and this is my sister, Harri Wellington. We can see why you like Lily's room. We are enjoying staying in it very much. I hope you're not too disappointed by having to go to a hotel."

"Well, we are disappointed. We feel like Lily's room is ours, since we're here so much. In fact, before I leave, I'm going to book through December. I don't suppose you'd like to trade with us. I'd make it worth your time." Mr. Grantham looked at his wife with hope written all over his face. "I'd gladly pay for your room. We booked at a new hotel in town. It overlooks the Mississippi River. I'd be willing to pay for your meals and everything if you'd let us have Lily's room back."

Harri looked at Cayce to see what she thought. Cayce shook her head, indicating she was not interested.

"No. It's a generous offer, Mr. Grantham, but we'd really like to stay at the Oaks. We've gotten attached in the three days we've been here and won't be able to come back for a long time. We really like old historical inns. Sorry." Harri answered without a hint of guilt.

Cayce and Harri headed for the door, wanting to avoid any additional efforts the Granthams might make to try to convince them. Mr. Grantham did not appear too happy with their decision to stay, but Cayce and Harri had too much invested in the form of emotional attachment to bow out now. As they entered the Stables, Joshua motioned for them to join him at his table.

"How're my two favorite ghost hunters this morning?"

"Rested. The ghosts slept, too, thank goodness. I died when I went to bed, and so did Harri. However, died is probably not a good term to use, all things considered."

"We just saw the Granthams, the couple who cancelled just in time for Cayce and me to get their room. Mr. Grantham tried hard to persuade us to give them back their room, but we resisted."

"Yes, Monica called me. But don't worry about it. I told them they are welcome to attend Princeton's ball Friday night and invited them to brunch on Saturday. That should appease them. Besides, they come at least once a month."

"I guess New Orleans is not that far, but I can't believe they came on, seeing Mrs. Grantham's condition. Cayce and I hurt just looking at her."

"John Grantham must have a lot of money but not a demanding job, since they're here from three to five days every time they come. But who am I to complain. It's that much more in funds to put back into Spanish

Oaks. So what's on your agenda today? I'd offer to take you to the swamp, but I've got to go to Jackson and check on a project." Joshua smiled at Cayce.

"Not funny!" Cayce tried to look serious but returned Joshua's smile after Harri poked her under the table to let her know it was obvious Joshua was flirting with her.

"If you're sure you don't mind, Joshua, I'd like to use your kitchen today. But first we have to go into town to a specialty shop we found listed in the directory, in hopes it has citron, the one ingredient I'm missing for the cake I'm thinking about entering."

"Citron! Is that what you're worried about? Why didn't you say so? You don't have to go into town. You just have to visit Sherone. Here. I'll call her for you." After a quick exchange with Sherone on the phone, Joshua put his cell phone back in the holder on his belt. "You're all set. Mama Tee will be home all day and is looking forward to your visit."

"What in the world is she doing with citron? Never mind, I'm sure there's a story there, so we might as well wait for her to tell it." Harri changed the subject as she looked at Joshua's plate. "That omelet looks divine. That's what I'm having."

Before Cayce and Harri finished their breakfast, Joshua excused himself but reminded the two to help themselves to his freezer full of entrees. Harri assured him they would be happy to oblige and promised to leave something for taste testing when he returned from Jackson.

Cayce drove the Jeep out the gravel road, enjoying the feel of the rough 4x4 that reminded her of the old Army Jeep she often drove on the ranch. She was not as happy when they reached the path, knowing they would have to walk the rest of the way to Sherone's house. As they walked down the path, a soft breeze started, welcome in the day that had begun hot and humid. The day lilies waved, encouraging the sisters to continue. Only a fluorescent lizard scampered across the railroad ties and into their path, giving Cayce a good scare, much to her sister's delight. When they reached Sherone's house, she was waiting for them on the porch.

"Welcome, again, sisters. Ice tea waits for you, with muffins hot from de oven."

Even though they were full from breakfast, Cayce and Harri forced themselves to indulge in poppy seed muffins with chunks of candied fruit adding a light and very different taste.

"These muffins are delicious, Sherone. Let me guess. There's citron in them, and citron is the secret ingredient in your teacakes, right?" Harri took pride in her ability to identify ingredients and was pleased she had figured out the special ingredient.

"You are correct. Now, if you will follow me to de back yard, I will show you where it come from." At the side of the shed not visible from the yard stood several tall shrub-like trees containing green fruit similar to lemons. Sherone picked two and gave one to each of her guests.

"Dis is de beginning of a long process. De citron plants brought by first Mama Tee from de islands, but de process was much longer den, wi' salt water boiling, fermentation in barrels for days, and den sugar bath and candying. I give you some citron for your cake. I have both candied and a special citron flavoring I use in teacakes. What cake you bake for de contest, if I may ask?"

Harri looked at Cayce, not knowing whether to tell the truth or not, but then decided Sherone needed to know about the cookbook and everything.

"Citron Delight. Princeton's Cake." Sherone looked startled and leaned against the shed as if fearful of fainting.

"Is something wrong, Sherone?" Harri moved to her side, prepared to help her if she started to fall.

"Tell me how you know dis cake. No, wait. We go inside." Sherone hurried into the cabin.

Sitting at the table as if they were clients, Harri and Cayce told Sherone about buying the cooking journal. Cayce also told about the vision in the shop and about all that they had experienced since arriving at Spanish Oaks. Mama Tee sat quiet, not interrupting to ask questions or to make comments until the whole story, even Cayce's experience in the swamp, had been disclosed.

Mama Tee sat without saying anything for several seconds. When she did speak, she leaned across the table and put a hand on each of the sisters' hands folded on the table.

"De Way has found you, but I not think you understand fully what dis mean. Neither do Joshua understand. He should not have taken you to de lily patch. As you now see, bad mojo can hide in beauty."

"We want to understand, Sherone, and we are willing to help ease the pain of those who have called us, if we can. What do we need to understand?" Cayce looked into the dark eyes that stared into hers from across the table.

"Citron is powerful in hands dat can feel it. Princeton's cake not made since de night Beatrice die in 1848. You not find de recipe. De recipe find you. If you make dis cake on May 30, it will open many portals, some you may not want open. You must think dis through, no quick decision. I think de time has come, but you decide. Dat all I can tell you now."

Cayce and Harri finished their refreshments and said goodbye to Sherone. Once she had warned them, the conversation had become light, like on their first visit, with no more mention of the Way or mojo.

"You are going to make the cake, aren't you?" Cayce asked the question as she drove.

"I am today, but I don't know about on Friday. Maybe I should just do my take on the red earth cake you like so well. It's one of our old family recipes, you know."

"Harri, we've come this far, so let's not turn back now. I think it was an important part of the plan from the start. Let it continue unabated, and see what happens."

While Harri was in the kitchen baking, Cayce decided to dive into the documents. Leaving Victoria's journal for Harri to finish, she took out the box of correspondence but with the use of the white gloves Harri had left for Joshua. Cayce was not going to risk entrance into another vision at this time.

The first letter she took out was from Victoria's mother-in-law, Marguerite Galvez Broussard, dated February 3, 1832. In it, Mrs. Broussard thanked Victoria for the lovely handkerchiefs she had sent and told her she was not feeling any better. She told her daughter-in-law she was unable to leave her bed and felt her end was near. Her life had been "full and happy" with her only regret not being able to watch her grandchild grow to adulthood. There were no more letters from the first Mrs. Broussard.

Cayce dug deeper in the stack and pulled out a form letter, an invitation, not in an envelope. It was not Victoria's handwriting but was elegant in the fashion of the time.

May 1, 1848
You are cordially invited to attend a dinner party
honoring the birthday of Princeton Broussard
on May 30, 1848.
The festivities will begin at 6:00 p.m.
at Spanish Oaks,
the plantation home of
Mr. and Mrs. Princeton Broussard.
Please RSVP by May 18 to
Mrs. Beatrice Broussard
Spanish Oaks Plantation
River Town, Mississippi

"Harri. I think I've found a way to know who all attended Princeton's dinner party. Look at this." Harri left the kitchen and came to the study with a batter-smeared spatula still in her hand. Cayce handed her the blank invitation.

"All I have to do is look through these letters and find the replies for Princeton's birthday dinner party. As formal as plantation owners were in the 1800s, I'm sure they all replied."

Cayce began going through the letters, separating replies from other correspondence. When she finished, she had a stack of twelve letters. Of the twelve, only one was a regret, and that was from a Captain and Mrs.

Charles Langford of River Town. Taking out a legal pad, she began listing names of guests, most of whom were couples.

One name and address caught Cayce's attention, and she called Harri to come as she read the name and address aloud: "Mr. Rathbone Fairchild, Fairchild Plantation, Bayou Meade, Louisiana."

"R. Fairchild, the artist who painted the portraits. Now we have a name and address. He's the only one invited who did not bring a wife, Harri!"

"That is an amazing discovery, Cayce, but I need to get back to the kitchen. I've got something cooking." Harri hurried out, spatula in hand.

"That smells so good. How much longer until it's done?" Cayce raised her voice so Harri could hear her from the kitchen.

"Thirty minutes," Harri called back. "Maybe Joshua will get here in time for the taste test. I'm putting a boiled icing on it just like Affie did. It's really more or less an old-fashioned pound cake, but with citron and icing. It's awfully plain for a contest entry, but with all that real butter and eggs, it has to be good."

"Just remember there might be more at stake here than a contest. But it's your entry, and I won't try to influence you. After all, you are the cook."

"So true, but don't worry. All will be considered." Harri tried to reassure her sister.

After another hour of reading letters, Cayce decided to put away the box. She was just about to take out Milla's journal when she heard a loud pickup truck pull up out front. Before she could get the gloves off, Joshua bounded in, cowboy hat and all.

"Something sure does smell good!" As he laid his

hat on the sofa, he saw Cayce standing in the study with her gloves still on and couldn't resist.

"Is this a black tie affair? I see you've got your gloves on." Joshua put his hand on Cayce's shoulder giving her his most serious look.

"Your boots and hat will do just fine. We'll do a taste test if that sister of mine ever gets finished. She's killing me." Cayce yelled so Harri could hear her in the kitchen.

"Almost ready. Just need to drizzle a little more icing."

Harri had found fresh strawberries in the fridge and decided they would be the perfect complement to Citron Delight. After putting a big serving of each on china dessert plates she found in the dining room, she called Cayce and Joshua in. Coffee made from freshly ground beans accompanied the cake, and they all took their first bite together. The cake was perfect, and the citron gave it the difference in flavoring to make it a potential winner.

"You've got my vote, but only if there are seconds."

"I can't believe you could actually eat another piece, Joshua. I'm stuffed, but it was delicious, Harri."

Joshua made it through half of his second piece before pushing back from the table.

"Well, that was dinner, except for maybe a bedtime snack. So what did you do, Cayce, while your sister slaved in the kitchen?"

Cayce showed Joshua the list of guests for the dinner party. Joshua had the idea Fairchild was invited as the delivery person for the portrait, but there was no way to prove or disprove his theory.

"What I wonder is when did Beatrice pose for the portrait. Those eyes had to be looked into for a long time for them to be that realistic and spooky."

"I think you're right, Cayce. I wonder if there was any hanky-panky going on between artist and subject." Joshua rubbed his chin as if in deep contemplation.

"Spoken like a true man, Joshua. No offense meant."

"None taken, Harri. But you have to admit it's a possibility. After all, Princeton didn't show his wife much attention, according to the information we have. She was a beautiful woman. Maybe she looked elsewhere for attention."

"I wonder if Fairchild Plantation still exists."

Joshua's answer to Harri's question was immediate. "There's one way to find out."

After turning on his computer, Joshua did a search for the plantation. A website was found on Louisiana historic plantations, and Joshua scrolled down until he found Fairchild Plantation. All that was left were two cabins from the slave quarters and the burned-out ruins of the once-large home. Two stubs of chimneys stood at either end of the house remains. From the short narrative, they learned the large plantation home was left abandoned for over one hundred fifty years and burned in 1998. The original owner, Rathbone Fairchild, had been a well-known artist who painted portraits for several prominent people in Louisiana in the early 1800s, one of whom was the governor of Louisiana. The portrait was bought by a museum in Baton Rouge in 1900.

"Listen to this." Joshua read aloud: "'R. Fairchild disappeared when he was forty-five without a trace and left no heirs to the plantation. Speculation at the time was he owed many people money and had none to repay his debtors. Another theory was he had made many enemies in his lifetime as a 'shrewd businessman.'" That usually means cheater. 'He was possibly murdered by one of these enemies and his body buried or disposed of in a place where it was never uncovered.' It seems our Mr. Fairchild was not a popular man except for his artistic abilities. I wish there was a picture of him. Too bad he never painted a self portrait."

Joshua looked at other websites of Louisiana plantations but found even less about the Fairchild Plantation. Seeing he'd hit a dead end, he closed the computer and turned to Harri.

"So, Harri, is Princeton's Citron Delight a go for the contest? It sure tastes like a winner. I assume you got the citron from Mama Tee?"

"Yes, and a lot more." Harri told Joshua about Sherone's reaction and about the warning.

"I think she's not telling us everything. Maybe she's afraid of scaring us off. She truly thinks we're meant to be here but warned Harri that baking Princeton's cake on his birthday could trigger something—'open portals,' as she called it. She wouldn't explain what portals."

"I love my distant cousin dearly, but she is a strange one. Are you really reconsidering your entry, Harri?"

"Not yet. I guess it depends on how many ghost stories I get stuck in the middle of between now and Friday."

"Speaking of ghost stories, Joshua. I want to go

back into Lily's day room and Chloe's nap room. Chloe interrupted us and we didn't get to look deep for clues. Don't worry. We'll leave Sophia out of it, in case we have any surprises we don't want."

"Of course you can, but don't think you scared Soppy off. You just made her hungry for more. Just ask Monica for the key, but promise you'll be careful. I really worry about you, Cayce, after the episode in the swamp, and I wish you would wait until I can go with you, but I guess there's no chance of that."

Cayce liked Joshua taking such an interest in her well-being but knew she would not listen to his warning.

"I appreciate your concern, Joshua, but I need to be searching for clues. Speaking of which, did you look in the loft for any other paintings or artifacts?" Cayce asked the question but was sure Joshua had made a thorough search.

"Yes, but we only found the one portrait. At some point, I need to take down the other walls and see if I can find what the burglar was seeking. I just can't imagine why someone started stealing from the Oaks. To my knowledge, this didn't happen with the other owners, but then, they may not have known what was there, like I didn't know about the cookbook. Tom might actually know if anything has ever been stolen from the Oaks. He's worked here longer than anyone. Have you two met Tom yet?"

"No, we haven't," Harri answered.

"Tell Sophia to call him on the radio. She's working for Monica today. Tom is quite a character and knows everything about Spanish Oaks. He'll talk your ear off."

"Oh, Monica is back. She told Harri and me she had food poisoning. I hope she didn't get it in the Stables. That would be hard to believe, with Andre being the perfectionist chef he is."

"Is that right? I didn't know why she was out. Monica is always dieting, so I doubt it was the Stables. She thinks the food there is too rich to be healthy. She's so thin, it's hard to believe she got food poisoning, but I have no reason to question her absence. She rarely takes a day off. So what are you two doing this evening? More research?"

"Speaking of research, where is the kitchen where Beatrice was murdered? Harri and I have not been all over the grounds yet, but we'd like to see it."

"It's out back of the present kitchen. It partially burned in 1897, shortly after Princeton died, and is used now for storage. Like all the old plantation homes, it was not attached to the house, thank goodness. When the new kitchen was built, it was attached. The new kitchen is only used for morning coffee and the occasional bedtime cookie treat. All of the main meals are prepared in the Stables. Check it out along with the rest of the house, but be careful. I haven't been in there in several months, so I don't know what kind of shape it's in. If you need a guide, get Tom to show you."

"Maybe we'll do that tomorrow. For right now, I think I'd just like to go back and relax on the porch. We'll park the Jeep back behind the Stables." Cayce gave Joshua's arm a squeeze. "Thanks for the use of your house and the Jeep. Ready to go, Harri?"

"I'm leaving the cake for you, Joshua, just in case you get hungry later."

"Thanks, Harri. I doubt there will be much left

after tonight. My pool contractor, J.T. Lewis, and Don Fowler are coming over later. I want to go over the drawings again before the digging starts on Saturday. I'll offer them a piece, but knowing Don, he won't stop with just one, and from the look of J.T.'s gut, he'll follow Don's lead."

"So you're starting the digging on Saturday?" Cayce asked. "That's unusual."

"J.T. wants to start tomorrow, but I don't want a mess with the big evening coming up. He will start at two p.m. on Saturday, after the morning brunch is over. Speaking of which, just wait until you see the spread Andre puts out. It's the only meal we serve after Princeton's Night. Andre serves the brunch from nine a.m. until noon, and there will be a line, so you better get there early. It's served buffet style, and guests are invited to take their plates and eat on the porches or anywhere on the grounds they choose. We use it and Princeton's party to kind of kick off the tourist season. Andre cooks all night the night of the party, so we shut down after the brunch is over to give the staff a little rest before the vacation rush hits."

"Don't worry. We'll be first in line. So when is the contest winner announced?" Harri was anxious to hear Joshua's answer.

"That will be on the night of Princeton's ball. Speaking of which, I believe my daughter has gathered up some gowns for you to try on, some very special gowns. You'll both be gorgeous, but you probably need to find Sophia and try them on in case some alterations need to be made. And Don and I have discussed this already and would love to escort the two of you to the ball, unless you already have escorts."

"No, we don't. Speaking for myself, I'd love to have an escort. How about you, Harri?"

"Of course I don't mind. I assume you two cowpokes will be a couple. Do you think Don would mind being my escort?"

"I know for a fact he would love that. He thinks you look like a petite glamour doll. And don't worry. Don has been divorced for years and has no current attachments. I'm not sure he can dance the waltz, but usually, at some point, the band moves a hundred years or so ahead to at least the seventies and eighties."

"Glamour doll, huh? Well, I guess it's better than 'perty as a speckled pup.'" Harri put on a cowboy drawl and made Cayce and Joshua laugh.

"The waltz, huh? Are you sure they can't throw in a little 'Cotton-Eyed Joe'?" Cayce tried to look serious as she asked the question.

"I just bet they can, Cayce, for the right tip. Are you planning on wearing your boots under that fancy gown and hoop? I wouldn't want you hanging a dogging heel. Oh, that's right. You wear Fatbabies. All I know is the Rhett Butlers sure had the more comfortable attire back then, not to mention a whole lot of fun." Joshua winked at Cayce.

"I'm sure I can figure out my footwear. You just concentrate on looking debonair, Mr. Butler, and as for my attire, I'll worry about it tomorrow." Cayce did a Scarlett turn, holding a limp wrist as she prissed out of the room.

Chapter Nine

Sophia was sitting outside the Stables when Cayce and Harri pulled up in the Jeep. With her was a lady who appeared to be in her forties.

"I've been waiting for you. Dad called and told me you were on your way. I took the liberty of hanging some gowns in your room for you to try on. Oh, this is Janine Nabors. Janine, this is Cayce and Harri. Janine works in the Stables during the daytime but has an alteration service on the side."

"Pleased to meet you both. Maybe you'll luck out and find a gown that fits perfectly."

"That would be lucky for you, too, since we need them Friday night. Can you get them altered that quickly, Janine?" Harri was thinking about where she lived and how long it took just to get something hemmed.

"Oh, yes. I'm used to getting things done in a hurry. It actually helps my business, and I need all the business I can get. Actually, my friend Monica works the front desk, and she helps me, too. I don't know what I would do without her."

"Well, Harri and I appreciate your willingness to help us, Janine."

"Are you ready to check out the gowns? I even have shoes for you to try, if you're game." Sophia led the troop up stairs, talking the whole way about how

166

much fun the ball was going to be. Cayce unlocked the door and let the others enter first.

The closet door was open, exposing yards of elegant red, white, and even yellow taffeta. Two hoop underskirts lay on one bed, overhanging by a good foot.

"Oh, my goodness! These are wonderful, Sophia. Where on earth did you come up with them?" Harri immediately took out the red gown and held it up to herself.

"I just knew you'd like the red one, Harri, the color of your BMW. Try it on, and let's see how close it is to fitting. Janine is ready with pins, if it needs anything."

Harri took the gown off the hanger and went into the bathroom to change.

"These are really old, Sophia." Cayce took out the yellow gown that looked like it might be okay in length, once stretched over the hoop. "Where did they come from?"

"I didn't have to look far. They were hidden in the storage room we discovered six months ago behind Lily's day room, in massive wooden trunks looking way too much like caskets. I couldn't believe they were never sold, but I guess the other owners didn't know they were there. But then, the place is full of original furnishings and personal effects from the Broussard family, including the family documents and books Dad keeps under lock and key now."

Harri came out of the bathroom humming *Tara's Theme* as she danced around the group as if practicing for the ball. She stopped and turned her back to Sophia for her to button the long row of buttons.

"Would you do me the honors, please?" She made the request in the worst Scarlett accent ever heard.

"Suck in, Harri. It's a little snug at the waist." Sophia tugged on the dress and then motioned for Janine to take control.

"We can let these darts out here, and that should give you plenty of room, or at least it won't cut your breath off." Janine spoke through lips holding at least a dozen pins.

"But not the least bit snug in the boob section. Whose dress was this, Beatrice's?" Harri held on to the top as it ballooned away from her. "To think they had no cosmetic surgery back then. Those suckers were real!"

"You are so right. Well, it needs to be let out a little in the waist and taken up a whole lot in the bust. Slip a hoop under it and let's check the length." Janine handed Harri the hoop skirt.

The length proved perfect, and Janine added one more pin to the top as Cayce waltzed out of the bathroom in the yellow taffeta. The dress fit perfectly, like it was made for her.

"And whose was this? Any idea, Sophia?" Cayce asked.

"Not for sure, but I think it might have belonged to Victoria Broussard. I remember reading in her journal her husband's favorite color was yellow, and I know she was not as petite as Beatrice," Sophia motioned for Cayce to turn. "Gosh, could it be a more perfect fit?"

Even the length was right after Cayce added the hoop under it.

"So do I wear my cowboy boots as your father suggested, or borrow a pair of Harri's flats?"

"Depends." Sophia opened a box sitting on the floor of the closet. "Check these out."

Sophia pulled out two pairs of women's antique lace-up shoes. Cayce took one pair from her, held them up, and laughed.

"I didn't know southern women ever practiced binding their children's feet from birth in order to prevent the growth of clod-hoppers. These couldn't be more than a size four, if that. Got a six and a half in there or maybe even a seven? I suppose that might be a man's size, looking at these."

Sophia dug through the box again and pulled out a bigger black pair.

"Try these. How about you, Harri? What size do you need?"

"A six, if you have it. But then, I'm sure sizes were different back then. Let me look through and see if anything looks like it might fit."

"These are okay, but I'm not so sure about dancing in them. Maybe I'll just wear my walking shoes and make sure the hoop doesn't fly up when I sit." Cayce held up her hoop to peek under it at the odd-looking shoes.

Harri decided on a pair of black shiny lace-ups with a little bit of a heel to them. Cayce kept the pair that felt snug, with the idea that if they became too uncomfortable she'd have an excuse to come back to the room and change.

"I'd better take your gown and get started altering it, Harri. I'll actually take both of them, if you want me to, and drop them off at the cleaners on my way to work in the morning."

"Yes, I'm afraid they're a bit musty from being in the trunk for a century and a half. Janine's cousin owns the cleaners we use for guests here. We can get one-day service, and he'll have them back here about mid-afternoon tomorrow, plenty of time to get ready for the ball on Friday. Oh, wait a minute." Sophia reached back into the box. "Take these two pairs of long gloves, too, Janine."

"Actually, the gowns don't smell that bad, considering how long they've been in those trunks, but there is a really pungent smell to Victoria's, like old lavender mixed with lemon juice, or maybe it's citron." Cayce smelled the gown again and then held it out to Harri. "What do you think, Harri? You're the citron expert."

"Could be either. I'm not an expert yet, but I will be by the time I get through baking for the contest."

As Sophia was unbuttoning Harri's gown, Harri ran her hand down the side and discovered a small pocket concealed in the seam. Putting her hand in, she felt a piece of paper and retrieved it. It was yellow with age and folded several times until it fit snugly in the point of the shallow pocket. Carefully, she unfolded each section, afraid of tearing the aged paper.

"Would you look at this?"

Sophia and Cayce leaned over Harri's shoulder to get a closer look. The note was written in old ink that looked as if it had been written with a quill. The note was short, but the writing had elegant strokes. Cayce put her hands behind her, afraid she might be tempted to touch it. Sophia began to read its message aloud:

I long to hold you in my arms again. Meet me in the stables at midnight.

R

"I think I recognize that handwriting. Very artistic, don't you agree?"

"I think you're right, Cayce. 'R' for Rathbone. Joshua was right. There was definitely some hanky-panky going on between the two even though he was almost twice Beatrice's age. I wish we could date this, but unless there's some mention of an occasion when Beatrice wore this gown in some of Joshua's documents, we won't know. I'll add this to your father's collection, Sophia. Better check and see if there are pockets in the other gowns."

The yellow gown also had a pocket, but it concealed nothing other than a fancy lace handkerchief with the initial "V" on it. At least they knew for sure now that this gown had belonged to Victoria.

After Janine left with the gowns, Sophia sat down on one of the beds.

"I hate to have to push Janine to alter Harri's gown. I know she must be tired after working at the Stables all day." Cayce pulled on her boots as she talked.

"Janine is a workaholic, but not because she loves work. She has a hard time sleeping at night and likes to keep busy. Back in March, she lost her only child in a terrible car wreck. His name was Buddy, and he was her life, even though he never made it easy on her."

"That is so sad. How old was he?" Harri sat down beside Sophia, and Cayce took a seat on the other bed.

"He had just turned twenty-one, finally legal. Janine gave her old car to Buddy and put it in his name, always afraid he'd be involved in a vehicular homicide and she'd lose her home, pretty much all she had. Buddy's dad left them when her son was just a baby. Buddy stayed in trouble, drank a lot, and word in town was he was dealing drugs. His mother was frightened he would end up in jail. Right before his wreck, he had opened up a bank account and had several thousand dollars in it. After his death, Janine was given the money by the bank, a total surprise to her, but one that caused her even more grief not knowing where he got it."

"Didn't he work? I always said my children would be required to work just like Harri and I did when we were still at home. My daughter Piper was no exception."

"Actually, he worked here. He helped Tom in maintenance. Tom said Buddy was a quick study. Tom encouraged him and was always teaching him new skills. Tom was really upset when Buddy died and had no idea where Buddy got the money."

"What about his friends?" Harri asked. "Were they questioned about the money?"

"Buddy's two best friends were in Afghanistan. Buddy had wanted to enlist with them, but Janine pitched a fit. After the wreck, she said he would have been safer in the military. Buddy had a girlfriend, Shelly Winthrop. She worked here, too, at the desk. Monica took her job after she left. Shelly told me she and Buddy were going to get married as soon as they could save enough money."

"I guess she was heartbroken. Is that why she left?" Cayce asked.

"I'm sure she was, but we really don't know. Shelly never came back to work after Buddy's death. In fact, she didn't even show up for his funeral. She just disappeared. Dad sent her last paycheck to the permanent address she had put on her application, an Alabama address. He never heard from Shelly or her sister, but his letter wasn't returned."

Sophia got up to leave.

"I better go. There's still a lot to be done to get ready for the big night. Is there anything else I can help you with before I get busy?"

"Oh, yes. Your dad said Harri and I could go back to the attic rooms. We really didn't get to look around much the other day. Could we get the key?"

"And when we finish there, if you could call Tom on your radio, we'd like him to show us the original kitchen."

"Sure. Come on down, and I'll get the key and call Tom."

Tom agreed to meet the sisters at the old kitchen in an hour, so Cayce and Harri had time to go to the attic rooms while they were waiting. Before Sophia let them leave with the key, she handed them a radio and showed them how to use it.

"Hopefully, it will work this time if you need it."

Harri clipped the radio onto her waistband, although neither of the sisters really wanted to deal with it. Sophia was so insistent they gave in and took it just to appease her.

After unlocking both doors, Cayce and Harri flipped on the light. The room appeared just as it had the day before.

"Okay, Harri. Where do you want to start? We need to look at every piece in here, inside and out, and make sure there are no hiding places. Do you want to take Chloe's room, or should we do that together?"

Harri surveyed the room before answering.

"This room is so big, we better both search it. If it gets close to time to meet Tom, we can wait until later to search Chloe's room."

Harri began checking out the rocking horse for secret compartments, then stopped and looked at her sister.

"Uh, Cayce, what exactly are we searching for anyway?"

"Not a clue, but we'll know it when we see it. Also, we're making a mental inventory of what's here, just in case the burglar comes back."

They continued turning over every toy, feeling under and around the mattress on the Jenny Lind bed and along the walls in case there was a way to get into any secret nooks. When they felt they had thoroughly searched the room, the sisters stopped and took another last look around to see if they had missed anything. The mural caught Harri's eye.

"Look at the mural, Cayce. Do you see anything strange in it?"

Cayce stood back to get the full effect of the large mural. It was a pleasant scene, with two little girls playing but not together. The Lily look-alike had a jump rope, something highly unlikely considering Lily's state of mind, and the Chloe look-alike was sitting under a willow tree playing with a homemade doll.

Cayce walked closer to the mural. "Does this doll look to you like the old doll Molly was playing with?"

"Yep. It sure does. Interesting, huh?"

"Yes, but not surprising." Cayce looked at her watch. "We've got time to do a quick look-around in Chloe's nap room. Are you game?"

The sisters had to duck to enter through the small door. Both stopped at the door to survey the scene, which appeared nothing like their first time there. The window was closed tight, the lamp was not burning, and the bed had no imprint of a child napping.

Harri walked to the window, intending to raise it and give a little ventilation in the stuffy room, but she couldn't budge it.

"See if it's locked," Cayce suggested.

Harri checked, but there was no lock on the window. Holding back the curtains, she felt along each side of the window and above it.

"As if the mystery could get any spookier, one of the old ropes that guides the window up and down is broken. See, it's hanging from the top. Which means there's no way this window could open—but it did." Harri held up the dangling cord and turned to look over the small room. Cayce read her mind.

"Pretty sparse, huh, especially compared to the other room? Do you think Princeton felt a little guilty where Lily was concerned? Anyway, this shouldn't take long. I'll check the bed, Harri, and you check the wardrobe."

Cayce felt all over the featherbed, under the quilt, and looked under it, but found nothing of interest. She even checked the bedposts to see if they might screw off to disclose a hiding place beneath, but they were all one piece. She also checked the door leading to the narrow steps, but it was still locked tight, the doorknob rusted like the stair side.

"Check this out, Cayce."

Harri was going through the drawer in the bottom of the small wardrobe. She held up cotton pantaloons and a cotton gown with a nightcap to match. Then she found two bonnets with big bills that would have protected Chloe from the hot sun. One was made from a plaid woolen fabric, homespun, and the other was a light domestic cotton yellowed with age. Both had wide ribbon ties that must have once been bright colors but were now faded. Digging deeper, Harri held up a book, a copy of a *McGuffy Reader* like the one in Milla's cabin. Under it was a slate tablet, with pieces of chalk wrapped in a handkerchief and tied with a ribbon. Beside this was an old-fashioned homemade abacus, the beads cut to precision and dyed different colors before being threaded onto a thin leather cord. As she started to put the slate back into the drawer, Harri noticed some letters written on the slate that had not been completely erased.

"M-O-L— Oh, my gosh! Do you think Molly has been in here?" Harri held up the slate for Cayce to see.

"Surely not. The doors are all locked. But stranger things have happened."

"I wonder if the *McGuffy Reader* is the one in Milla's cabin. We should check it out, Cayce."

"She could have had one in each place. Milla seemed to be determined for her child to be educated, slave or not. Kids today have it so easy." Cayce smoothed the bed where she had mussed it.

Harri replaced the clothing and the other objects and closed the drawer, turning her attention to the top of the wardrobe. She pulled on the homemade knobs, but the wardrobe doors were stuck.

"Help me with this, Cayce."

Together they tugged, even propping a foot against the drawer for leverage. Finally, both doors opened at the same time, causing the two to fall backward on the bed. Laughing, the sisters helped each other up and stared into the child-size primitive piece.

Two dresses hung in the wardrobe. They were plain cotton, one brown and the other gray, with simple off-white domestic pinafores to wear over them. Folded and lying on the bottom were pantaloons from the same domestic fabric, with a single ruffle stitched around the hem to show under the dress that hung to probably six inches or more from the top of her shoes. Beside the pantaloons, a tiny pair of brown worn lace-up shoes stood ready for the little girl to wear as she skipped under the magnolias, rocked her homemade baby to sleep, or pulled the expressionless little Lily up and down the stairs pretending she was a real playmate, or sister.

Cayce looked at her watch as Harri closed the wardrobe doors.

"We need to head down. Tom should be waiting for us."

"Cayce, are you sure you want to do this? What if you have another vision while you're in the kitchen?"

"It's a chance I'll have to take. Don't expect me to actually touch anything, though. I just want to get a feel for it and see if I recognize it from the time I was there in the antique shop."

Tom was a tall thin man with gray hair and beard. He smiled as the sisters approached, and held out his hand to each of them.

"You must be Cayce and Harri. Joshua has told me a lot about you and gave me strict orders to show you whatever you want. It's good to meet you both." Tom had a pleasant smile and friendly demeanor, and the sisters liked him immediately. His firm handshake proved an added bonus to his positive introduction. The sisters' father had always told them to show strength of character as well as body when shaking hands. "No wimpy girls in my bloodlines," he always chided and made them practice giving the correct amount of firmness. Thanks to him, they could also recognize a firm handshake in return.

Tom led them to the back of the inn, to a small building constructed of old brick probably made on the plantation. The outside had been kept up, but after entering the large room, Cayce and Harri realized it was outward cosmetics only. Cayce stood just inside the room to get a feel for it before exposing herself to its full force. Harri marched right in, with Tom behind her.

The brick walls inside looked as they must have in the late 1800s, with a large fireplace in the center of one wall. Any primitive pieces left in the kitchen had been replaced with stacks of boxes, wooden crates, and barrels. The wall and ceiling surrounding the fireplace were coated in black soot, evidence of the fire of 1897.

"Owners number two and three both had the idea to restore the kitchen, but their plans never really got off the ground. Joshua's goal is to restore it eventually, but that project got replaced on the to-do list by the swimming pool. I guess you know the story about what happened here?" Tom asked.

Harri looked at Cayce, waiting for her to respond.

"I've read the account of Beatrice's murder in the *History of Spanish Oaks,* but I bet you can add some additional tidbits not in the book."

"The only tidbits I have are what I've been told by the owners of the place during the time I've been here, and a few unexplainable occurrences I've been privy to, most when I was caretaker in between owners. There have been a lot of sightings—I believe that's what ghost hunters call them—if you believe in such, and I'll tell you right off I do after working here for twenty years. Anyway, when there is something needed from here or if something has to be stored, I'm the only one who'll come near the place. You're the first guests that have asked to see the original kitchen."

"Really? I would think with the murder being such a popular part of the whole Broussard story it might even be included in the tour. Has it ever been?" Cayce asked.

"Oh, no, at least not since I've been here. There is a story of a son of one of the owners coming in here one night, bringing some of his friends and trying to scare them, but they evidently had such a fright a huge lock was placed on the door and the windows were boarded up. Owners who followed left it that way until Joshua bought it."

"What did the boys see?" Cayce figured she knew firsthand but wanted verification.

"Story goes they saw Beatrice lying on the floor with a trail of blood leading to the door. Supposedly, the owner's son actually had blood on his shoes when he ran into the big house screaming for help. The two friends with him said somebody ran out the back door, but they didn't see him, and then they heard a horse galloping away like a ha'nt was chasing him. And that's just one story."

"So do you know where exactly Beatrice was lying?" Harri kept watching her sister to make sure she was still with them.

"Oh, that's an easy one. Come over here in the center of the room in front of the fireplace." The sisters followed Tom to a spot on the old stone floor. "If you look right here, you'll see a big dark splotch with a long dark stain leading from it to the door where we came in. According to the legend, no matter how many times the stain has been removed, it keeps coming back. One owner had the idea to restore the kitchen and use it, but after the stain kept coming back and then his son's experience, he gave it up."

"What happened to the old scrub-top table that was here originally?" As soon as Cayce asked the question, she realized what she had done. Tom looked confused by the question.

"How do you know about the table? It's been gone from here a long time. In fact, I'm the one who moved it to Affie's cabin right after I started working here."

"If you'd been to as many old antebellum homes as we have, you'd know every kitchen has a primitive scrub-top table. So it's in Affie's cabin?" Harri tried to steer Tom away from his question. Cayce smiled a thank-you to her quick-witted sister.

"Something I know was in here but don't know where it went was a long butcher knife, but then I was never sure if I really saw that or not."

"Butcher knife? Was that the weapon used to stab Beatrice?" Cayce looked at Harri in eager anticipation of the disclosure Tom was about to make.

"Possibly. All I know is I saw the knife, or thought I did, covered in blood and lying on that table the day before I moved it to the quarters. I brought the owner out here to show him, and it was gone. Of course he didn't believe me." Tom looked at his watch as if there was someplace he was supposed to be.

"You ladies seen enough yet?"

Tom opened the door and stood back for the sisters

to pass. Cayce stopped and took a quick glance back at the room, surprised she had not experienced anything different from what Harri and Tom had seen.

A few minutes later, when Cayce and Harri started in the front door, they noticed Molly sitting under the willow tree. She was holding a new doll like the ones from the gift shop and was talking away to her. The sisters changed directions to talk to Molly.

"Well, I see you have a new baby. She is very pretty. Do you mind if I hold her?"

Molly handed the doll to Harri, smiling like a proud new mother.

"Daddy bought her for me. I had to give the other baby back to the little girl."

"Oh, you saw the little girl again? Where did you see her, Molly?"

Molly looked at Cayce but only shrugged her shoulders.

"Was she here at the willow tree?"

"No, but I can't tell you where she was. It's a secret." Molly whispered the last part of the answer.

"Do you see her much?" Harri handed the doll back to Molly.

Molly shrugged her shoulders again as she cradled her baby in her arms.

"Molly! Come in, sweetie. You need to get ready for dinner," Molly's mom called from the side porch where she had been sitting. As Molly trotted toward the porch, her mother waved at Cayce and Harri.

"Do you have your gowns for the ball?"

"Yes. We got them today. How about you?" Harri and Cayce walked toward the porch.

"Oh, yes. We came prepared, and you should see

what Miss Molly is going to wear. Molly, tell Miss Cayce and Miss Harri about your beautiful dress your grandmother made for you to wear to Princeton's ball."

"It's Cinderella blue, with big fat sleeves and a skirt I can twirl in, like this." Molly twirled to show her admirers.

"You will be the belle of the ball, Miss Molly. And does your dress have pantaloons to go under it?" Harri asked.

"Does it, Mommy?" It was obvious Molly was not sure what pantaloons were and so couldn't answer Harri's question.

"Yes, indeed, it does, and they have rows of ruffles at the bottom. Tell the ladies goodbye, baby. We need to get ready. Daddy says we're going into town to eat tonight."

"Oh, goody! Hamburgers!"

"Oh, no, little one. Not hamburgers." Molly and her mother headed inside with Molly protesting because they were not going to have her favorite meal.

When the sisters got inside, they saw Sophia with two women carrying briefcases.

"Harri, Cayce. Come over here. I want to introduce you to someone." The sisters smiled at the strangers.

"This is Nicole and Stephanie. They're from Jackson. Dad said he told you about the inventory their firm did for him. This is Harri and Cayce, the ones with the cookbook."

"Yes, he did. Are you going to check and see if anything is missing?" Cayce asked the question, hopeful of the answer.

"Yes. Actually, we've already started. We got here early after Joshua called and told us about the cooking journal you bought in Natchez." Stephanie seemed to be the one in charge and did all the talking.

"And did you find it listed on the inventory?" Harri asked, anxious to hear the reply.

"No, we didn't. That is so strange, considering what you paid for it. It should be in the rare books section, but it was not here when we did the inventory," Stephanie answered.

"Maybe Joshua was right. Another owner could have sold it, and it has made the rounds."

"I don't know about that, Cayce, but I do know we've already found some very valuable pieces missing from the dining room and the women's parlor. I guess it's okay if I share this information with them, isn't it, Sophia?"

"Oh, yes, Stephanie. Dad would tell them anyway. Cayce and Harri are doing a little investigating on their own."

"So what kinds of things are missing, if you don't mind telling Harri and me? Perhaps the missing pieces were also sold in Natchez."

"We know two valuable pieces of eighteenth-century Paris Porcelain are missing. These pieces are very rare, museum quality, and are among the earliest of Paris Porcelain pieces found in the United States. The French royalty kept a tight rein on this particular porcelain, and it should not have been accessible in the late 1700s when Jean Paul Broussard obtained it. We're just getting started, but Stephanie and I feel there is definitely a thief in the house, or there has been. We know there were two other pieces here that are not as old as these but are even more valuable because of their rarity. The four pieces we know are missing so far would be worth a minimum of fifty thousand dollars and could go higher in the hands of the right collectors."

"We did see some Old Paris pieces in Natchez, but I don't know if it's like what is missing here. Do you have pictures of it?" Harri got an answer immediately as Stephanie pulled out two sheets of paper and showed them.

"I'm not really into china and porcelain, so I don't know for sure, but it certainly could be what I saw while my sister was stalled in the rare books section. Is Joshua planning to send someone to investigate?"

"I can answer that. Yes, I am. How about playing detective with me tomorrow, Cayce? Mind if I cart your sister off for a day, Harri?" Joshua had entered behind the group and stood beside Cayce, putting his hand on her shoulder.

"Joshua, I didn't see you come in." Cayce smiled, pleased to see him.

"Well, what's your answer? Are you ready to do a little more antiquing in Natchez?"

Cayce looked at Harri.

"Please take her. I need to borrow your kitchen again, and she'll just be in my way. I've got to turn my entry in by Friday at five p.m., and I want to bake it one more time to perfect the icing."

"Good. We'll leave about seven in the morning, if that's not too early." Joshua looked to Cayce for an answer.

"I'm a rancher, remember? I'm used to getting up early." Cayce couldn't think of a better way to spend the day than with the good-looking Joshua Devaux.

"I'll see you then." Joshua gave Cayce's shoulder a

little squeeze before turning to Stephanie and Nicole. "Now, let's see what you've found so far."

As Cayce and Harri headed for the stairs to their room, Cayce was called back to the desk.

"Cayce, I couldn't help but overhear what was being said. So things have been stolen from the Oaks?" Monica seemed concerned.

"It appears so. Have you noticed anyone acting strange, any of the guests?" Cayce asked.

"No, not really. It's a little disconcerting to know there's stealing of that magnitude going on here. People have killed for less than the amount of money they were talking about. Do you think we could be in danger? I mean, it could be professionals."

"I have no idea, Monica, but it would pay to be on guard for anyone who acts suspicious, guests or staff," Cayce added.

"Do you have any idea how long this stealing has been going on?"

Monica's question seemed peculiar to Cayce.

"No, I don't. I don't think anyone knows at this point."

"And the cookbook where your sister got her contest entry. You think that was stolen from Spanish Oaks?"

"We know it came from Spanish Oaks, and we also know it ended up in an antique shop in Natchez. That is all we know right now."

Cayce thought about her conversation with Monica all the way up the stairs. It was a strange line of questioning, and she seemed almost too interested in the whole situation. But maybe Monica was right. It could be a dangerous place to work with the amount of money that could be made in a major heist like this. This was grand theft, not petty, and it could involve professionals, and they could be armed and dangerous. As she entered their room, she told Harri about the conversation.

"I just had the strangest conversation with Monica. She asked me several questions about the burglary or burglaries, and one question in particular really didn't make sense."

"What was that?" Harri stopped looking at her recipes and gave Cayce her full attention.

"She wanted to know when the burglaries started. I wonder why that is so important. She did make a good point, though. She said people have been killed for less, and we don't even know what all is missing at the moment."

"You're suggesting this could be a big-time operation with people who play rough?"

"I hope not, but anything is possible." Cayce looked worried.

Chapter Ten

The next day Cayce found herself sitting across the console from the best-looking man she'd ever known. And not only was he good-looking but he had much in common with her. Joshua got her to talking about Montana again and began making plans to visit.

"I really want you to come, Joshua. I'd like nothing better than showing off the state I love to people I care about. But don't forget, Sophia is invited, too."

"I'm not so sure I want my daughter to come with me. Do you think we need a twenty-year-old chaperone?" Joshua moved his arm that had been resting on the console and reached over and picked up Cayce's hand, locking his fingers in hers. Cayce smiled and did not withdraw her hand.

"I hope I didn't offend Harri by not asking her to come along, but I really wanted some time with just you. You're the most interesting woman I've met in a while. It's hard to find a good-looking cowgirl in my age range in South Mississippi."

"I'm sure you have plenty of interesting women in your life, Joshua, and I bet none of them come with the baggage I have."

"By 'baggage' you mean your psychic powers?"

"Yes. It's not something I can always control. I would prefer not to have Pop's gift most of the time and would like just to be normal, but I do have it, so I have to make the best of it. My husband, ex-husband that is, could never accept it. We're still good friends, but to put it bluntly, I scared the hell out of him."

"Oh, I think that's part of the reason I find you so intriguing. Anyway, I wish you were staying longer. You're leaving Sunday, right?"

"Yes. I really didn't plan to be away any longer than that. Harri and I do a trip every summer. Usually it's for two weeks, but she has her business to run, and I have my horses to tend to, so we're only doing a week this summer, with another week later on in the fall."

"I don't guess I could convince you to stay an extra week."

"Joshua, you know as well as I that the inn is booked for the summer."

"Yeah, but my place is not." He raised his eyebrows as he looked at Cayce to see what her reaction would be.

"I don't think we're to that point just yet, cowboy. Maybe I'll take a rain check. We'll see how things pan out. In the meantime, keep the thought alive." Cayce smiled and gave Joshua's hand a squeeze.

"Oh, it's alive. Don't you worry." Joshua gave her a playful grin.

As they reached the outskirts of Natchez, Cayce became entranced again at the historic river town and looked forward to returning to Franklin Street, even though the reason for coming was not for total enjoyment. But any trip with Joshua was enjoyable, and Cayce hoped this would be the beginning of a close relationship, something more than friendship. As they made the big curve going into Natchez, Cayce looked over at the spot where she and Harri had witnessed a wreck less than a week earlier.

"There was a pretty bad wreck right there when Harri and I were leaving the other day. I hope the people were okay." Just as she said it, she had a flashback, one of her "cheap shots," as she called them. She let go of Joshua's hand and rubbed her temple.

"Got a headache?"

"No, just some of that intrigue I have."

"Another vision?"

"More like a recurrence." Cayce put her head back and closed her eyes.

"Is there anything I can do?" Joshua looked worried.

"No, I'm fine. Just trying to get it to play back. I think it was important."

Joshua fell silent, but Cayce was aware he was watching her and the road simultaneously. Concentrating, she blanked out everything around her, willing the scene to replay. In a matter of seconds, she saw him, the man with the bloody face and shirt who made eye contact with her just before climbing into the ambulance. Then the scene left her again, but not before his face was engrained in her mind.

She jerked her head away from the seat back, opened her eyes, and almost yelled, "John Grantham!"

"What?"

"John Grantham! The guest who cancelled in Lily's room! He was in the wreck in Natchez, not New Orleans like he said."

"Are you sure, Cayce?"

"I'm positive. I saw him getting into the ambulance. His face and shirt were bloody. I even made eye contact with him."

"Was this in a vision maybe, like foreseeing something happening somewhere else?"

"No, Joshua, this was reality. Harri and I had to slow to a stop because of a wreck, and when we got beside it, I saw John Grantham. I knew he looked familiar that day he and his wife tried to convince us to give up our room, but I couldn't remember where I'd seen him. I had a cheap shot just now when we passed the wreck site."

Joshua looked at Cayce with a giant question mark on his face.

"A cheap shot is what I call a really quick scene change. It happens in a flash and leaves just as quickly."

"Okay, and this means what? You've lost me."

"It means he lied about where he and his wife were when they had the wreck. Why would he do that?"

"I don't know. You tell me." Joshua was confused but felt Cayce had an explanation in mind.

"Damn! I wish I had remembered before we came here. I would have sneaked his picture and brought it with us. Maybe he's involved in the thefts."

"Whoa, Sherlock! Not so fast! The Granthams are my best customers. They've been coming for several months and staying days at a time."

"I rest my case, Watson." Cayce held her hands up to indicate it was an obvious conclusion.

"Uh, huh! And how would we go about proving the very nice paying couple are cat burglars, my dear?"

"I'll have to figure that out, but where there's a will, the Way will find you." Cayce emphasized the word "Way."

"Nice play on words there, Sherlock. Let me guess.

Pop's philosophy."

"Yep! And it usually proves true." Cayce looked past Joshua and saw the police station and yelled, "Stop, Joshua! Pull in here!"

Joshua jumped but turned in at the police station without slowing down.

"Damn, Cayce! You're gonna kill us both before we get to the first antique shop!"

"I'm sorry, but maybe I can get some information from the police about the wreck." As Cayce opened the truck door, she looked back at Joshua. "Well, aren't you coming?"

Joshua opened his door and followed Cayce into the police station. A round-faced, balding dispatcher sat at the desk. He put aside his foot-long submarine sandwich, began to chew the bite in his mouth fast, and with a dribble of mayo on his lip asked if he could help them.

"Earlier in the week, there was a wreck on the big curve by the river. My sister and I came by right after it happened and saw the driver of the SUV getting into the ambulance. We have since found out it could have been a friend of ours. We wondered if he and his wife were all right. Can you give me any information about them?"

"Oh, yeah. I remember that wreck. I'm not supposed to give out information, but it was in the newspaper the next day." He turned to a stack of newspapers and started digging through the pile. "Here it is. Made the front page. Tells you there's not a whole lot going on in our little town."

"Yep, there's his SUV." Cayce showed Joshua the picture. "May I take this with me?" She directed her question to the police officer.

"Sure. I don't have a puppy or a gerbil."

Joshua thanked the man as he opened the door for Cayce, who was engrossed in the paper already.

"Says here the couple's names were Janet and David Rigby and they were from Baton Rouge. I could have sworn it was Grantham."

"Have you ever had a cheap shot steer you wrong before?"

"No. Not that I know about anyway. Says they were hospitalized with minor injuries. Continued on page eight." Cayce flipped through the newspaper. "Ah, hah!"

"Ah, hah? Must mean you hit pay dirt."

"Pull over, Joshua. You need to look at this snapshot some passerby took."

Joshua pulled into a quick stop parking lot and took the folded back paper from Cayce. The picture was a side shot of the man watching as his wife was pulled from the SUV.

"Well, I'll be damned! It's Grantham, all right. You're good, Sherlock."

"Thank you, Watson. All in a split second's work."

"Your Way is talking to you, my dear. Here. Let me take a picture with my phone and enlarge it. We can show it in some of the antique shops and see if he's a dealer."

"Make that a dealer who buys from estate sales. We better make up some story of why we're asking questions. If we find any of your stuff, they might not want to answer questions for fear of being charged with selling stolen goods. I'm sure no one would know Grantham was dishonest. You didn't."

"True. So what should we say, or do I just act like I did in the police station, the sidekick with no balls and even less brains in this daring duo?"

"No. You need to take the lead this time, Joshua. Everyone I saw working in those antique shops was female. You just pour on your handsome cowboy charm and they'll tell you anything you want, including their personal address and phone number."

"Well, thank you, ma'am. I think." Joshua pretended to tip the cowboy hat he was not wearing.

As they drove down Franklin Street, Cayce looked for the antique shop where they had bought the cooking journal.

"There it is! On the corner." Cayce pointed to the shop.

Joshua parked the big truck, taking up more than one space, and looked at his partner.

"You really think this will work, Cayce?" Joshua reached across and took Cayce's hand again.

"I'd bet my greatest gift on it." She reached into the back seat and got Joshua's cowboy hat and handed it to him. "Here you go. No woman in her right mind could deny a handsome cowboy anything he wanted— not even information."

"Does that include you?" Joshua raised his eyebrows.

"That includes me, cowboy." Cayce squeezed Joshua's hand again. "Now, back to business. You got the story straight?"

"Yep. Let's do it." Joshua got out of the truck and walked around to escort Cayce into the shop and held the shop door open for her. Cayce recognized the woman as the one who had waited on her and Harri.

"Hello. I was in here a few days ago and…"

"I remember you very well. I hope the cookbook was everything your sister thought it would be."

"My sister is very excited about it. This is my friend, Joshua." Joshua tipped his hat and gave his most charming smile. "He is a collector and has some particular pieces he's looking for. Harri and I were so impressed with your shop I just had to bring him here."

"Well, thank you. My name is Linda Johnson." She held out her hand and gave Joshua a huge smile as she shook his hand. "My husband and I own this shop. I'm glad you came, Joshua. What kind of pieces are you looking for?"

"Old Paris Porcelain, preferably eighteenth century, if you have any. Actually, I recently bought an old plantation home in River Town, and I'm trying to refurbish it in period pieces from the late 1700s and early 1800s."

"Oh, I see. You have excellent taste, Mister…"

"Just call me Joshua. You will probably be seeing a lot of me, from what I'm seeing so far." Joshua winked at Cayce as the woman directed them to follow her. She stopped at her desk and got a ring of keys from the drawer.

"You know, there was a lady from River Town who came in the shop just two days ago. She had a picture of a pretty young lady she showed me to see if I might have bought any antique pieces from her back in February or March. I didn't remember ever seeing her. She seemed pretty disappointed. From what some of the other dealers told me, she went in every antique shop on the street and asked the same question. I believe she said the girl was her sister."

"Did she give her name?" Cayce asked the question, interested in the reason for another sleuth from the small town.

"No, she didn't." The owner continued walking to the back of the shop, taking Cayce and Joshua past the rare books counter where Cayce had entered another century and past the Civil War memorabilia that had distracted a daddy from his overactive son, who had started this whole saga.

"The kinds of pieces you're talking about are very valuable and extremely fragile. We don't display them out in the open. The most valuable pieces are secured in a fireproof vault in the back of the store. There is one estate dealer in particular that we buy many of our best pieces from. Actually, he's the one who sold us the cooking journal. I believe the last estate he bought from was an antebellum plantation home in South Louisiana." She stopped in front of a back room with a heavy lock on the door.

"I guess you can't give us the dealer's name?" Joshua knew it was a shot in the dark and Linda would think he was trying to eliminate the middleman or woman in order to buy at a better price.

"No, I'm sorry, Joshua. It's a policy my husband and I have. I'm sure you understand."

"Of course. I was just wondering if it was a dealer I've bought some pieces from before." Joshua tried to clarify his reason for asking.

"Come in, but, if you don't mind, you'll have to wait at the door. The vault has a combination lock." The woman made sure she kept her back between her customers and the door, as if afraid they might try to memorize the combination.

"Step inside and I'll show you our pieces of Old Paris from the eighteenth century." She stood back and allowed her customers to enter.

Joshua and Cayce found several shelves of porcelain on display, as well as boxes and cases they could not see inside, some probably containing jewelry. Joshua looked at Cayce when the saleslady was not looking and knew she had read his mind.

"Would there possibly be heirloom jewelry in those cases? I am looking for something special for Cayce. She's a little more than a friend, as you've probably surmised." Putting his arm around Cayce, he drew her to him, giving her a kiss on the cheek. Cayce smiled up at Joshua and gave him the evil eye. This was not part of the script they had practiced in the truck, but Joshua's action did give Cayce a little jolt, the struck-by-lightning variety.

"Oh, yes, indeed. We have several pieces. Any stones in particular you like?" She directed her question to Cayce.

"I absolutely love emeralds and diamonds set together, the bigger the better. Do you have anything like that?"

"Let's see. There is this one really magnificent necklace. I'll warn you, though. It is very pricey, museum quality." Cayce looked at Joshua and saw the anticipation on his face.

Their hope faded when she opened the case to display a small necklace with one very large emerald in the center and probably a dozen large diamonds on either side. Leading up to the centerpiece was a strand of smaller diamonds and emeralds.

"This is beautiful, but I've got something a bit

more extravagant in mind for my girl. Anything else?" Joshua took Cayce's hand.

"Extravagant. Let me think. I'm afraid everything we have right now is smaller than this one."

"I'll give you my card before we leave. If you come across anything like we've described, would you call me?" Joshua was thinking ahead, and Cayce was impressed.

"Of course. I was promised a piece a few months ago from the same estate dealer who sells me most of my valuable pieces, but it never transpired. It was almost priceless, from the way he described it. In fact, I had already contacted a friend of ours who is a museum curator in Philadelphia, Pennsylvania about it. He wanted me to call him the minute I got it and not to show it. But it might have been out of your price range. Are you ready to look at the Old Paris Porcelain?" Joshua looked at Cayce and frowned, showing he was insulted by the woman's remark about his price range.

"Oh, yes. I have quite a collection already, so it will be interesting to see if you have any rare pieces I don't have." Joshua turned to bragging to make the woman eat her words.

"Rare." Linda looked as if she was thinking out loud. "We do have two pieces from the 1800s that are quite rare. They are portrait pieces, but unfortunately, the dealer was not able to identify the portraits. I can show you these, but my Philadelphia museum curator friend is coming next week to look at them, so even if you wanted them, I couldn't sell them to you. To be honest, I don't know how to price them. If they are what he thinks they are, my husband and I will be a lot nearer to closing down the shop and retiring to the

Caymans. Would you like to see them?"

Joshua and Cayce followed her to the back of the vault, where she carefully took down a box from a middle shelf and brought it to the table in the middle. After unwrapping several layers of bubble wrap, she held up a porcelain plaque edged in gold. In the center was a portrait of a beautiful dark-haired woman who looked to be Spanish, dressed in an elegant red gown. She was sitting in the center of a Classical Federal sofa of mahogany with black horsehair upholstery, her hands clasped on her lap.

Being careful, the shop owner placed the plaque on the table and began unwrapping the other plaque. It too was edged in gold but had a picture of a very distinguished-looking man on it dressed in a fine black suit, probably silk and satin. He was posed on the same sofa with his arm resting on the arm of the sofa.

"Are these not magnificent? My husband would be angry with me for showing them, but I know you two know value when you see it."

"So you can't give me a price? I am really interested in these two pieces." Joshua rubbed his finger along the gold edges, admiring the plaques.

"I'll have to talk to my husband, but I know what he'll say. We have to wait for Michael, the friend from Philadelphia. If he does not buy them for the museum, I will certainly be glad to price them to you, but that will be the end of next week."

"What about the other Paris Porcelain pieces? Could I see those?"

"Most of what I have is from 1820 to 1850. They are nice pieces but fairly common to South Mississippi and Louisiana, not rare like this other piece I am going to show you. When we leave the vault, I'll show you those pieces. We keep them in a locked glass case."

The lady pulled out several pieces Joshua did not find interesting and then pulled out a bedside tea warmer, called a *veilleuse*, with "J.P." marked on the bottom.

"Ah, hah! Now this interests me. Jacob Petit, one of the few pieces of Paris Porcelain with markings. I need one of these for my collection. What do you think, darling? Wouldn't this be perfect beside our bed? What is the price on this?"

"You do know your Old Paris. Let's see. This is three thousand dollars."

When the woman turned to put two of the less expensive pieces back on the shelf, Cayce gave Joshua a good boot kick in the shin.

"Ouch!" Joshua stopped rubbing his leg when the lady turned back around and pretended his outburst was a reaction to the price. "That is steep, but I have been wanting a piece of Petit. I'll give you twenty-five hundred for it."

While the owner was wrapping up the porcelain, Cayce wandered over to the rare books case and motioned for Joshua to follow.

"You're not gonna kick me again, are you?" He had pulled her to him and whispered this into her ear as if he were whispering sweet nothings. He kept his hand on her neck, massaging it.

"If you keep on, I'm going to do more than kick you."

"Is that a promise?" Joshua smiled at Cayce with the impish grin he'd been giving her all day. She realized she was just beginning to see the true Joshua

Devaux and found him entertaining, in a rude sort of way, as well as handsome.

"Would you stop playing around and show her the picture like we planned before you started your comedy act?"

"Oh, yeah, but for all you know, it might not be an act." Joshua headed back to the cash register to sign his credit card receipt, leaving Cayce shaking her head.

"I have this picture and wonder if you'd mind taking a look at it. He's an estate dealer, and I'm hoping you might know him. He might even be the one you bought the cookbook and some of the other pieces from." As Joshua unfolded the paper and handed it to the lady, he added to his explanation. "I was supposed to contact him about some duplicate pieces I want to sell, but I've lost his card and forgotten his name. Someone gave me this photograph. I really need to contact him."

"He looks familiar, may have been a customer in the shop at some point, but he's no dealer that I know. Sorry." She handed the picture back to Joshua along with the box containing the Paris Porcelain. "But if you can't get in touch with him, bring your pieces by. We might buy them or negotiate a trade, now that I know what your interests are."

"Thank you. I'll consider it if I can't locate him. Oh, by the way, do any of the other shops have pieces of the quality you have? I don't want to waste my time if they don't."

"I feel bad about answering you this way, but no, none of them deal in pieces of the quality I showed you. Most of their Old Paris pieces are from the Common Era, early 1800s, but it might pay you to look. The other dealers are my friends, and I don't want to steer business away from them."

****

"You are such a snob!" Cayce gave Joshua a push with her shoulder when they got outside the door.

"Am not. I'm just a good actor." Joshua opened the truck door for Cayce and helped her in before jogging to his side, grinning at Cayce's reaction all the while.

"Oh, no. You're a snob, Mr. Jacob Petit expert. Are you sure you're a descendant of Affie and not Jean Paul?" Cayce continued the conversation when Joshua got in the truck.

"I'm sure. Speaking of Jean Paul, did you recognize him from the portrait piece?"

"Oh, yes. After recognizing the beautiful Mrs. Jean Paul Broussard's face displayed on the other plaque, there was no need to guess who the stately gentleman was—or should I say sharkster? I assume they belong to Spanish Oaks?"

"Indeed they do. They're two of the missing pieces from the inventory. I'm glad to know the museum isn't coming until next week. That gives me time to get the law involved. I will be getting those pieces back, but it's more important I find out first who stole them. I guess the Granthams are a dead end after all."

"Yes. That was a disappointment. But we're not giving up yet. The clues are waiting for us, Joshua."

****

As they headed out of Natchez, Joshua decided it would be a good time to introduce Harri to Don.

"How about we cook some steaks tonight at my place. Do you think Harri might like to get to know Don before the big bash on Friday night?"

"I'll call her and see. She's probably cooking away at your house." Cayce pulled out her cell phone and dialed her sister. After a very brief conversation due to the entry cake being frosted, Harri agreed to Joshua's suggestion.

"Harri says don't plan on dessert. She's got a reject waiting for us."

"Something other than Princeton's favorite, I hope? It should not be a reject. I think she's got a good chance at winning with that one."

"I'm pretty sure it's her chocolate cake filled with whipped cream and strawberries. I forget the name of it, but it is so good it's almost immoral."

"That ought to get Don's attention. Not that Harri needs any help in that department. I believe he is quite smitten with our miniature glamour doll."

"Well, he better not fall in love, because my sister likes her single life. She was married to a sweet guy, Stan, and it didn't hurt he was a well-to-do doctor and spoiled her rotten. Stan died a couple of years ago and would be a hard act to follow. She keeps telling me she's not looking, but she still likes to have fun."

"What about her sister? Is she looking for a follow-up to…?"

"Cody. His name was Cody, and believe it or not, he owns a construction company—builds oil refineries, chemical plants, and other stinky but lucrative endeavors. I bet you didn't know you had so much in common with my ex."

"I know one thing I'd like to have in common with him, if she'd give me half a chance." Joshua took her hand again.

"Remember, I scared Cody away, but we are still

friends."

"And therein lies the difference. You don't scare me, Cayce. You fascinate the hell out of me. Will you give me a chance? I promise not to make any other crude remarks, at least not for the rest of the day."

"How could I resist a deal like that? Let's shake on it." Cayce held out her hand.

"I've got a better idea." Pulling to the side of the road, Joshua pulled Cayce across the console and kissed her, a long passionate kiss.

"Now that's out of the way! Let's go cook those steaks." Joshua pulled back onto the highway while Cayce tried to catch her breath.

Chapter Eleven

Cayce and Harri got back to their room close to midnight. Joshua had stuffed his guests with T-bones, T standing for tyrannosaurus, and Harri had made potato salad and baked beans to go with them.

"So you seemed to hit it off okay with Don?" Cayce couldn't wait to hear Harri's response as they drove back to Spanish Oaks in Joshua's Jeep.

"Not as much as you seem to be hitting it off with Joshua. It's really not fair. My escort to the ball looks like a pirate, or an actor playing one, and not the handsome version of the red carpet but in full gosh-awful makeup, gold teeth, and costume for his ugly roles. Those black eyes of Don's peeking out from under those bushy eyebrows are more than a little scary, even though his personality somewhat makes up for his looks."

"Oh, Don doesn't look that bad, but he's definitely not the looker my escort is." Cayce smiled just thinking of the handsome Joshua Devaux.

"Do I detect a little romance in the air?" Harri grinned as she asked the question.

"Possibly. He is quite a hunk. But the best part is Joshua is not terrified of me."

"Give him some time. He hasn't seen you in the midst of one of your bloodcurdling visions yet. If he gets to experience you in another butcher knife nightmare and still doesn't find you terrifying, marry him. It might be your last chance."

"Let's not jump the gun here, Harri. I'll take it slow and easy. But Rhett Butler is going to be mighty tempting. I just hope I can pull off Scarlett."

"Changing the subject, tell me all about what you and Joshua found out in Natchez. Joshua didn't seem to want to talk about it. Does he not trust me, or Don? You'd think he just went there on a shopping spree or a date with my sister, to hear him tell it."

"I think he's just being cautious. I'm sure he'll tell Don eventually, but he told me not to tell anyone but you about seeing the Old Paris portrait plaques. It's probably a good idea, since it could be someone who works for him that's heading the ring of thieves. I still can't believe the Granthams are not involved."

"Speaking of the Granthams, Monica said he called again and wanted us to contact him. He is still trying to persuade us to give up our room. What's the deal with that?" Harri asked.

"Maybe he's planning on boozing it up at the ball and doesn't want to have to drive to the hotel."

"The only way I'd move from here is if Victoria and Jacob's suite comes open. I hear it is the most elegant two rooms in the whole place." Harri loved elegance as much as her sister loved rustic.

"I keep hoping they'll leave the door open so we can take a peek, since it's just down the hall, but I guess we won't get to see it. Maybe we can reserve it for next summer." Cayce looked at her sister to see if she would react to her suggestion. She knew Harri knew the real reason she wanted to return.

"Or maybe you can get your man to let you stay in

it sometime. He'd probably want to play Jacob, though."

"Nah. He's already tried to convince me to stay an extra week…at his place."

"You're kidding! He moves fast, doesn't he?"

"Well, at our age, it doesn't pay to wait too long or arthritis, or something more debilitating in the romance department, might set in." Cayce laughed when she saw the look of disbelief on her sister's face. "I'm not staying, Harri. Not that I might not come back at some point, but he needs to come to Montana first. It's the ethical way to be immoral."

Neither of them could ward off the high-calorie-induced sleep coming within minutes of heads touching pillows, but before they were ready for it, sunlight was poking at their eyelids, trying to pry them open.

"You can have the bathroom first. I'm dead." Cayce spoke through grogginess without opening her eyes.

"No, you can." Harri's mumbling was barely interpretable, so Cayce knew she would be the one to go first, as it had been since birth.

When they finally made it downstairs on their way to the Stables for coffee and only coffee, Monica stopped them at the desk.

"I've got a proposition for you, one I think you will jump at."

"A proposition?" Harri's interest was piqued.

"Yes. Mr. Grantham is driving me crazy trying to get me to talk to Joshua and get him to make you give them back their room. Of course Joshua won't hear of it, but he told me if anybody leaves for any reason to offer you that room at no charge. He said he'll even refund any guest who leaves early, something strictly against his usual policy, as you know."

"Okay. So you're about to tell us that a room has come open?" Cayce looked at Harri and knew she was thinking about their conversation from the night before.

"Not a room. A suite of two rooms." Monica smiled as she said it.

"Jacob and Victoria's suite!" The sisters spoke at the same time and high-fived with both hands.

"How did you guess? Anyway, the Denmans left at about seven this morning, and the staff is already cleaning the suites. So what do you think?"

"Do we look like we're crazy, Monica? Of course Harri and I will take the suite, and the Granthams are welcome to Lily's quaint little room."

"When do we need to get our things out of the room? Cayce and I can pack before we go for coffee, if we need to." Harri wanted to hurry before the Granthams got wind of it and asked for the suite instead of Lily's room.

"Go on and have your breakfast. With your permission, we'll relocate all of your belongings and have you set up in your new room by the time you get back."

The sisters were giddy over coffee, thinking about getting to stay in the elegant suite.

"Oh, my gosh, Cayce! We'll get to dress for the ball in Victoria's room. Oh, god! I just thought about something. What if her ghost is still in there, and she doesn't like you wearing her yellow gown, Jacob's favorite color?"

"Don't worry. The worst that could happen is I'll die in my sleep in a magnificent four-poster bed with a canopy looking like it belongs to an Arab sultan's favorite wife."

"Wait a minute! I'm wearing Beatrice's gown. You don't think…"

"Oh, don't be such a worry wart, Harri. At least it's red. It won't show stain as bad as the green." Cayce took a drink of coffee, eyeing her sister over the rim of the cup and laughing through the sip, almost choking.

"That is not funny, Cayce! Think about everything that's going to happen this year. Beatrice's portrait will be unveiled again on Princeton's birthday, the same night she pissed somebody off enough to make them take a butcher knife to the portrait and her. I'm baking Princeton's cake, the first time since the fatal night, against a warning by the family voodoo princess, and we're wearing gowns previously owned by the living dead. Damn! How much more fun can two middle-aged sisters have?"

"A lot more, and that's just what we're going to do. At six o'clock Friday evening, I'll turn into Scarlett awaiting the handsome and debonair Rhett Butler Devaux, and…"

"I'll turn into Beatrice the Bitch waiting on my pirate and death by taffeta."

After the sisters finished their coffee, they stopped by the desk to pick up the keys to their new suite. Monica was turned facing the wall behind the desk and was rubbing her finger over one of the photographs in a group she had just finished hanging, the hammer still in her left hand. She was so engrossed in the photo she didn't hear Harri and Cayce approach the desk.

"Monica?" Harri whispered her name, fearful of startling her.

Monica jumped, dropping the hammer. "Oh, I am so sorry. I didn't hear you come in the front door. I guess you want the keys to your suite. Tom and Mack helped move your things while you were having breakfast." Monica picked up the hammer and laid it on the desk.

"Those pictures are new, aren't they? Do you mind if we look at them?" Cayce especially wanted to see one photograph that looked like the entire staff dressed in antebellum costume, probably from Princeton's birthday celebration the year before.

"Of course not. Here." Monica opened the desk gate. "Come on around so you can get a closer look."

"Is this the whole staff?" Harri got closer, as did Cayce.

"Yes. Well, the staff from a year ago."

"Oh? Are they all working here now? Some don't look familiar." Cayce picked out a nice-looking young couple in the front, figuring she knew who they were. "I don't think I've seen these two."

She pointed at the two young people. The boy was dressed in a gray coat with a long tail and top hat to match. The girl wore a long flowing white gown, her long blonde curls hanging over each shoulder. Her gloved right hand was holding on to the boy's left arm as if he were her escort. They both wore big smiles, showing they were having a good time.

"The boy is Janine's son, Buddy Nabors. He was killed in an automobile accident in March."

"What a terrible thing to happen, especially to one with so much life ahead of him. I think Sophia told me he worked with Tom. Is that right?" Harri looked at her sister, not knowing where her questioning was going.

"Yes, he did. I just started working here at the end of March so didn't know Buddy, but Janine has become my dearest friend. She is still distressed by the loss of her son. Any parent would be."

"And the girl by him? My goodness, she is beautiful. They look like they might have been a couple." Cayce continued to pick Monica for information.

"Yes, she was beautiful."

"Was?" Harri looked at Monica as she asked the question, catching on to the reason for her sister's questioning. "Was she killed in the same accident?"

"No!" Monica answered abruptly. Seeing that her reaction made no sense, she lowered her voice. "The girl is Shelly Winthrop. She worked the front desk but quit right after Buddy's accident. Janine thinks Shelly just couldn't stay here after Buddy died. Buddy and Shelly were planning to get married when they'd saved enough money."

"I'm sure Shelly will be all right. Young people are resilient, even after the worst tragedies. As beautiful as she is, I'm sure she will find love again." Harri was sincere in her statement. "Well, if Cayce and I can have those keys, we'll go visit Victoria and Jacob."

"You think Monica has a special interest in Shelly, don't you?" The sisters were at the top of the stairs out of earshot when Harri asked the question.

"Yes, I do. The way Sophia told us, Shelly more or less disappeared, didn't even pick up her last paycheck. When Joshua and I were in Natchez, Linda, the owner of the antique shop where we bought the cookbook, said another woman from River Town was there earlier in the week showing a picture of her sister and asking if she'd sold any antiques to her back in March."

"And you think the girl in the picture was Shelly. Do you think Monica is Shelly's sister? Monica's last name on her ID is Pearson, but that doesn't disprove it."

"She could be her sister, and we have a way of proving it. I just need to get their pictures from the personnel files, the ones they used for their Spanish Oaks ID badges, and get copies of them to Linda for confirmation. I'll call the antique shop and get her email address and tell her what I'm sending. That will be the fastest way to find out."

Sophia let Cayce and Harri into Joshua's office after lunch and showed them where the files were kept. Joshua had ridden to River Town with Don but told Sophia to give the sisters access.

"Just lock the door when you finish. I've got a tour to conduct." Sophia started to leave, then turned back. "Oh, yeah, Cayce. Dad said to tell you that Watson will expect a full report over dinner tonight, the Stables at seven. He said to call him on his cell if that's not okay." Sophia gave an approving smile as she closed the door.

After calling Linda, Cayce scanned the photographs of Monica and Shelly and emailed them to Linda, using one of the computers in Joshua's office. It only took ten minutes to get a reply from Linda confirming Monica was the lady showing the photograph of her sister earlier in the week, and that the other picture looked like the girl in the picture the woman was showing. Linda also took the opportunity to thank Cayce and Joshua for making their purchase and invited them to come back soon.

"Now what, Cayce? Do we confront Monica?"

"I want to talk to Joshua first and see what he

thinks. He might want to be with us if we talk to her, since she's his employee."

As they approached the door to their suite, the Granthams came out of Lily's room. John Grantham was all smiles as he met them in the hall.

"Thank you so much for moving. I can't tell you how pleased we are to be back here at the inn."

"You're more than welcome. We're thrilled to get to stay in Jacob and Victoria's suite." Harri looked past John Grantham and smiled at his wife, who returned her smile. She was much more pleasant than her husband and seemed to almost cower behind him. "You look so much better, Mrs. Grantham. How are you feeling?"

"Actually, I'm feeling better and walking better every day. The stairs are not bothering me nearly as much as I thought they would."

"My wife is more concerned about not being able to dance at the ball tomorrow night than she is about walking up the stairs, but we are limiting that as much as possible."

Mrs. Grantham followed her husband to the top of the stairs but did not go down.

"Just bring me back whatever you get for dinner, dear. I'll just lie up here and read until you get back." After her husband got down the stairs, Mrs. Grantham turned to go to Lily's room. Cayce called to her as she and Harri approached.

"Mrs. Grantham, I heard you and your husband have been coming here for quite a while. You must really love it here." Cayce began the conversation while Harri stood silent, not knowing where her sister was heading.

"Yes, we do. We come as often as we can. New

Orleans is not that far away, really."

"And you always stay in Lily's room? It is a lovely room, but there are so many more rooms more luxurious. I just wondered what the appeal is."

"We like the simplicity of Lily's room. We also like having separate beds. I have restless leg syndrome, and it drives John crazy."

"My sister and I were wondering if, during your visits here, you ever saw anyone who looked or acted strange." Cayce had decided to plunge ahead and see how Mrs. Grantham reacted. Harri did not know how big a plunge her sister intended, so provided support and no information.

"Strange? In what way?" Mrs. Grantham propped on her cane, waiting for Cayce to continue.

"Well, I don't know if you've heard or not, but there have been some thefts at Spanish Oaks. Quite by accident, Harri and I found some pieces in Natchez in an antique shop that had been stolen from here. Since you are here so much, I just thought you might have seen someone who gave you reason for concern."

"No, I haven't." Mrs. Grantham seemed anxious to end the conversation and turned to go into her room. Harri and Cayce started to walk away when the woman began to speak again. "Please don't let my husband know about the thefts. I'm afraid he would never want to come here again, and I truly love coming."

"Of course we won't, Mrs. Grantham, but Mr. Devaux may ask him." Harri turned away and then decided to add to her sister's questioning. "Speaking of Natchez, have you ever been there, Mrs. Grantham? It has some lovely bed and breakfast inns that I bet you would find just as intriguing as Spanish Oaks." Mrs.

Grantham remained turned facing the door to Lily's room.

"No, we haven't been to Natchez, but maybe we will some day. I really need to rest now. Have a nice afternoon and evening." The woman entered the room and closed the door. Cayce and Harri heard her turn the deadbolt.

The information they had gathered took backstage as the two stepped into Jacob and Victoria's enormous suite. Standing in the middle of Victoria's room, they took tiny steps as they turned on the massive Oriental rug, absorbing every fine detail of the most magnificent bedroom either could ever imagine.

"Would you look at this white marble mantel, Cayce? This family was obsessed with fleur-de-lis. I think it's a calla lily design like one Stan's mother had in her house." Harri ran her hand along the exquisite mantel. "And, oh my, take a gander at this mirror; the gold edging matches the chandelier." Harri looked up. "What do you think? Sixteen-foot ceilings, or more?"

"At least. I know more about primitives, but I'd bet that chandelier is a Louis XV, and I know those sofas in front of the fireplace are Empire." Cayce moved to sit on one of the sofas. "I can imagine Victoria sitting on one of those in her formal ball gown, maybe the one I'm going to wear. Or I can also see her in a white lacy nightgown, holding her young son and reading him bedtime stories."

"Considering the Broussards were French, you're probably right. I bet it was a wedding present for the couple from rich Daddy."

Harri turned her attention to the huge ornate rosewood bed.

"Oh, my gosh! I wonder how much white taffeta it took to make that canopy. It is beautiful." Harri walked to the bed and ran her fingers along the headboard. "Look, Cayce! The lilies on the headboard match the ones on the mantel. Everything matches to perfection."

Cayce and Harri moved to the side of the bed and felt the white silk duvet that covered a fluffy down comforter, piled even higher with down pillows.

"It looks like…like a combination of super-soft marshmallows and billowy clouds. It makes me want to…to…"

The sisters looked at each other and, at the same time, dived into the middle of the bed, sinking into the clouds of fortune-filled days gone by.

"This is my room, remember, Harri. You need to go look at your room while I lie here and pretend I never have to leave."

"You'd leave your Beartooth Mountains for this? You've got to be kidding."

"Well, maybe for a little while." After closing her eyes for only a minute, Cayce jumped up and pulled her sister to her feet. "Let's check out Jacob's pad."

Jacob's room was as elegant as Victoria's but more in line with king than queen. His furniture, too, was hand-carved rosewood but was much more ornate than his wife's. His bed was king-sized, half-canopied, with two posts at the foot to hold a mosquito bar. Harri stared at the bed with her mouth open, surprised by the size.

"Do you reckon this is a California king?" Harri felt the bed to make sure it was as soft as Victoria's, and was not disappointed.

"I think it's probably a New Orleans king, a gift

from Daddy, probably won in another high stakes poker game." Cayce made the statement while looking around the room.

"Check out the sitting area." Harri directed Cayce's attention to another part of the room as she rubbed her hand across the black marble mantelpiece. It, too, was carved, but the design was the fleur-de-lis of the family crest. A huge armoire almost covered one wall, and opposite it was an oversized, ornately carved desk.

"I wonder what Jacob used the desk for? There's a huge office downstairs."

"It was probably just for looks, to show how rich they were." Cayce turned around just in time to see Harri jump to try to get on her bed. On the third try she made it and lay across it, her hands behind her head, testing it for comfort.

"I wonder how they decided whose bed they were going to share on those special nights." Cayce asked the question as she sat in one of the chairs surveying the room.

"Maybe they took turns, or did an eeny-meeny-miny-mo." Harri slid down from the bed and joined her sister in the chairs in the sitting area. "So back to reality. What did you think of Mary Grantham's reaction to your questions?"

"She's lying. They're up to something, but what I don't know. Time to pull a Nancy Drew."

"I thought you were Sherlock, judging by Watson's request for your company. Which reminds me. Don asked me to eat dinner at the Stables tonight too, but I know I'm too busy. Help me with this, Cayce. What am I too busy doing?"

"Nothing. You should go, Harri. It's not a date, just

dinner. You don't have anything else to do."

"I could remove the polish from my toenails, or Ped Egg my heels, not to mention shave my legs."

"Harri, don't be such a hard ass. He's a nice guy. I'll call Joshua, and we can all eat together. Besides, I don't want to be too late finishing dinner. I've got something else in mind for us to do." Cayce gave Harri the look her sister knew only too well.

"Do I have to hear this? Something tells me I'm not going to like it."

"There are two places we have not searched. Think about it."

Harri thought for a minute and then looked at her sister.

"Milla's and Affie's cabins. Right?" Harri knew she was right even before Cayce answered.

"Right. But we can't get in them until after nine o'clock tonight. That means we'll be way after dark, and there is no electricity in those two cabins. We'll have to use flashlights or light the lamps in them. It could be spooky." Cayce watched for her sister's response.

"Could be? Forget the gloves, Cayce. We might need full body armor for this. You know I've already had an experience in Milla's cabin, and I didn't have to touch anything. It was more like she touched me, in a spiritual sense."

"It's a chance we'll have to take. I am not afraid, for some reason. It's like this is what we are here for and everything is going to be all right. The Way has found us, Harri, and we've got to use our gifts to help. It's what we do."

Joshua met Cayce and Harri at the entrance to the

Stables and led them back to their usual table. He explained Don would be a little late and had asked that they not wait on him. "He said he'd be here by the time we got our entrees and told me what to order for him. He's meeting some old friend in town but said it wouldn't take long. So what sounds good to you two ladies tonight?"

Just as the three were finishing up their salads and waiting on their entrees, Joshua looked up and saw Sherone entering with a very attractive woman who looked to be in her late forties. Sherone was dressed in her usual colorful fashion with a long, bright, red-and-black tunic over black pants that bagged in the legs and tapered to a tight fit at the ankles. A lightweight black shawl lay loosely over her shoulders. She wore gold-strapped sandals and her usual oversized jewelry but did not have a scarf wrapped around her head. Instead, her long, dark, wavy hair was contained in a ponytail adorned with an inch-wide gold band secured around the base. Her friend was tall and thin and dressed in a sophisticated American style, not Caribbean. Her outfit was pale yellow, with simple black strap sandals completing her outfit.

Joshua motioned for Sherone to come over.

"What a surprise to see you in the Stables, Sherone. I thought you didn't want to have anything to do with Andre or his food."

"And I don't, but my cousin Jaleel, here, is visiting and had heard about de establishment. Only for her would I enter dis place." Jaleel smiled at Harri and Cayce and turned to her cousin for introductions.

"Please meet my cousin Jaleel from New Orleans. Dis is Harri and Cayce and my cousin Joshua, all dose I have told you about." Harri and Cayce each shook Jaleel's hand across the table.

"Sherone has told me about you, Jaleel, but you don't look anything like what I imagined. You are a pleasant surprise, and I'm pleased to finally meet you." Joshua held out his hand to Jaleel and seemed to be staring at her, causing Cayce to feel a tinge of jealousy.

"I bet you thought I was a fortuneteller like Sherone. Am I correct?" Jaleel smiled at Joshua and put her hand on his arm.

"Yes. That would be the case, but I take it this is not exactly true?" Joshua seemed to be groveling, afraid he had insulted Jaleel with his shocked look and fumbled words.

"Jaleel is Dr. Jaleel Crawley, a professor of psychology at de university, but she does often see de past and de future, just in an educated, more socially acceptable fashion." Sherone showed great pride in her cousin's accomplishments and was also enjoying the shock on Joshua's face.

"My passion is extra sensory perception and paranormal occurrences. I'm presently doing some research with the University of Louisiana, as well as teaching a couple of graduate classes, but I am a practicing psychologist in New Orleans."

"That is a very interesting field. I'd love to hear about your research some time." Cayce broke the tension. "Would you like to join us? We're waiting on Joshua's friend, Don, but we can always move to a larger table. Isn't that right, Joshua?" Joshua stood up to call the server over, but Sherone stopped him.

"Oh, no. We have a table reserved already and have much to talk about. Besides, Joshua knows I don't take to Don any more dan I take to Andre. But I do like you two sisters and would like you to get to know Jaleel. I have told her of your gift."

"Yes. I'd really like to interview both of you at some point, for my research, if you don't mind. Maybe I'll see you before I leave. I'll be at Sherone's for the whole weekend."

"Cayce and I would love to talk to you, Jaleel. Yours is a field of great interest to us. I'm glad we got to meet you."

"Oh, please be sure and come to the ball tomorrow night. I'm sure Sherone can help you with a suitable costume. If not, my daughter Sophia can help you as she did Cayce and Harri." Joshua was still trying to make amends to the attractive woman.

"I would love to attend. Thank you, Joshua. It was nice meeting all of you."

Sherone saw Don at the front of the restaurant and began to move away from the table, hurrying Jaleel to leave.

"Yes, the same here." Joshua stood as the ladies walked away. He waved to Don to let him see where they were sitting.

"Well, Jaleel certainly doesn't look like a lizard-and-possum-guts kind of woman, does she?" He glanced at Cayce, who was propped on the table giving him one of her "I can't believe you" looks.

"What?" Joshua stared at Cayce as if not understanding the expression she was giving him.

"Nothing." Cayce moved her salad dish away from her and looked across the table at Harri, knowing her sister was reading her mind.

Just as Don sat down, Andre, complete with chef's

hat, arrived at their table.

"And are these the two lovely ladies I've heard so much about, Joshua?" His voice gave away his lifestyle, and Cayce wondered if he ever tried to share fashion secrets with Joshua. She was sure Andre did not approve of cowboy boots unless they were knee high, brightly colored, and were used to accessorize just the right outfit.

"Yes, Andre. This is Cayce McCallister and her sister Harri Wellington. Ladies, may I present Chef Andre Genet."

"Oh, Andre, your culinary talents are so very impressive. Your name is French and your crème brulee is to die for, but you don't sound French."

Cayce couldn't have agreed more with her sister. Andre didn't sound French. He sounded gay. But Harri was ecstatic to get to meet Andre and wished he would just pull up a chair and talk culinary secrets for the rest of the night.

"I hear Joshua stole you from a famous restaurant in New Orleans."

"Actually, I found Joshua, but it did not take much persuasion once I fed him a few meals on the house." He patted Joshua on the arm, and Joshua winked at Cayce. "As for the lack of a French accent, I can put on an authentic one when needed, but I'm actually second-generation American. My family all speak French when we have our gatherings."

"Harri had her own restaurant at one time and studied at a culinary institute in New York." Cayce bragged on her sister every chance she got.

"Yes, so I heard from Joshua. I also hear you have an entry in the contest. I'm not one of the judges, but I wish you luck. If you win, you'll have to share all your secrets with me so I can perfect it for our menu. Maybe we can rendezvous in the kitchen before you leave."

"I'd like that. Thank you, Andre. It was a pleasure to meet you."

Andre took Harri's hand and kissed it.

"Zee pleasure is all mine, mam'selle." Using his best authentic accent with a twist, Andre bowed and bid his adieus before returning to the kitchen.

After he left, Cayce stared at Joshua. Joshua gave his wholesome laugh that echoed through the room.

"I never said he was a stud. I just said he was an amazing chef. Okay, so he has a flair for the dramatic. It doesn't take macho to stir up a good pot of vittles, does it, Cayce?" Joshua's cattle trail lingo made the group laugh.

The foursome ate a leisurely dinner, and even Harri seemed to enjoy the evening. When they finished, Don announced he was going over to one of the casinos on the river and asked Harri if she would like to go with him. Harri thanked him but said she was tired and thought she'd curl up in Jacob's big comfy bed and read herself to sleep. It wasn't a total lie. She had every intention of doing just that as soon as she and Cayce had finished their little escapade in the slave quarters.

After Don left, Joshua turned to Cayce.

"Sophia told me you want to go to Milla's and Affie's cabins. Do you mind if I tag along? I'd like to see how two sibling ghost hunters work. That is, if it's okay with you, Harri."

Joshua acted as if he thought Cayce liked having him around. She knew she had been a little cool during dinner, but she wanted Joshua to come with them. She could tell he didn't want to intrude on the sister act unless his presence was okay with both of them.

"I would welcome your presence, Joshua. If Cayce continues to have visions like she's had this week, I might need a strong arm to hold her."

"Harri, I told you I feel very positive about tonight's venture. I'm not saying I won't get in tune with Milla or Affie, or both, but it won't be dangerous. Speaking of which, I'm ready to head to the quarters. Do you have a flashlight, Joshua?"

"I do, but we can also burn the oil lamps. That'll make the cabins the way Milla and Affie experienced them when the dark fell, but I'll get a flashlight out of the Jeep in case you need extra light. Who knows? The flashlight might even work even if the electricity never has."

"Harri, you pick. Milla's or Affie's cabin first? You were the one Milla communicated with on the tour that day," Cayce remarked.

"Let's go to Milla's first."

After stopping at the front desk and picking up the keys from Sophia, Joshua joined Cayce and Harri on the stone walkway to the slave quarters.

"It's nine-thirty, in case you two want to make any mental notes. I'll have to admit this is a first for me. I've been in both cabins plenty of times in daylight but never after dark. Hold my hand, Cayce, so I won't get scared." Cayce was pleased to detect a little interest in her after the way Joshua had stared at Jaleel.

"So much for the 'strong arm' theory, Harri." Cayce took Joshua's hand without hesitation.

After unlocking the door, Joshua unfastened the rope that kept tour groups away from the furnishings and led the sisters to the table he could see by the moonlight coming through the wavy-glassed windows.

"Thank goodness for a full moon...I think." After finding the box of matches, Joshua lit the lamps.

"Sophia was right. The coal oil flame gives an aura of suspense—almost foreboding, and makes me feel as if I've stepped back in time to 1848." Cayce almost wished she could sense what Milla was feeling that night so she could understand the desperation it took for her to take her own life.

"So what do we do now? I'm the ghost-hunting rookie. Teach me." Joshua said it lightheartedly, but Cayce and Harri knew he was serious about wanting to help.

"We have to search every piece of furniture and every inch of this cabin. That includes feeling for loose stones in the fireplace and loose boards on the floor and walls. Harri, do you want to start with the bed?"

"Sure. The furniture won't take long. Milla was given only the bare necessities. You know that really doesn't make sense, does it? If Princeton loved her, why didn't he make sure she was comfortable? Beatrice, the wife he abhorred, lived in luxury. But then, everything about this chapter of Princeton's family history seems unfair." As if someone was trying to react to Harri's statement, the lamp on the table began to flicker as if it was going out.

"Whoa! Did you feel that? It was like a breeze blew through the cabin, and the door and windows are all shut. It must have dropped several degrees in here." Joshua looked more than a little apprehensive. Cayce moved to the table, where she took Joshua's hand and gave it a squeeze, warning him that she was about to do something. Joshua looked at Harri and took her lead in standing still and quiet.

"Milla! We're here to help you. If you're with us, give us a sign."

As soon as Cayce got the last word out of her mouth, the candle on the mantel flickered wildly. Joshua clutched Cayce's hand and reached for Harri's, not wanting her to feel he wasn't there for both of them if they needed him. Harri gave him a reassuring smile to let him know she was fine and moved to the bed, where she began to feel under and all over it. Feeling a lump under the quilt, she turned it back.

"Recognize this, Cayce?" Harri held up a rag doll. "It's the one Molly was playing with the other day. Do you think Molly has been in here?"

"Not unless she came with the tour again. This cabin is locked at all times. The tour guides have to unlock the door before bringing a group in." Joshua answered Harri's question, but they all knew locked doors meant nothing to desperate spirits.

"What about the *McGuffy Reader* we saw in here when we took the tour? Do you see it anywhere, Harri?" Harri looked around and under the bed.

"Nope. I don't see it. It seems to have moved to Chloe's nap room."

"You mean the little room in the attic off Lily's day room?"

"Yes, Joshua. Harri and I saw it in there yesterday. And no, we don't have any idea how it got there. I think it's another sign we are on the right track. I want to try to reach Milla again. Are you two okay with it?" Joshua and Harri both nodded their heads and stood still, waiting to see what she had in mind. Still holding

Joshua's hand, Cayce began.

"Milla, tomorrow is Princeton's birthday, and there will be a big celebration. I know that was a terrible night for you, but there is something we need to know. Did you kill Beatrice that night so long ago? Is that the reason you took your own life? If you did kill her, give us a sign." The three stood very quiet, waiting to see if the lamp would flicker again. Nothing happened. Cayce looked at Harri and nodded to let her know she needed to ask a question.

"Milla, you showed me the last time I was in here how sad you were that night. You looked out the window at the stars and asked God to let you be with your baby girl. Did you take your life because you missed Chloe and you thought you could be with her in death? If this is true, give us a sign." The light on the mantel flickered and went out, leaving them with only the light from the lamp on the table. Harri continued her questions.

"Is there anything you want to tell us about that night, Milla? If you have something to tell us, leave the lamp burning, but if you cannot tell us who killed Beatrice, then make the lamp go out like you did the other one." Harri looked at Cayce and Joshua in eager anticipation. All three of them were hoping Milla wanted to tell them something, but in a matter of seconds, the lamp went out. Joshua took the small flashlight from his pocket and turned it on, lighting their path to the door.

Once they were outside, Joshua took a deep breath. "I've never experienced anything like that before, with the exception of being harassed by a dude on a black horse in the swamp. But this was not terrifying. Milla really communicated with you two. That was amazing!"

"Yes, and in her own way, she told us a lot. Milla did not kill Beatrice."

"That's right, Harri, but we didn't find out if she knows who did. She only answered there is nothing she wishes to tell us about that night. Either she doesn't know or she doesn't want to tell." Cayce felt they had learned much in the visit, but there was much more to be learned, possibly in Affie's cabin. "Shall we carry on to Affie's cabin?"

Joshua held up the key ring in the moonlight and singled out a very old key like the one to Milla's cabin. But after inserting the key and turning it, the door did not open.

"What the hell is wrong with this key? It worked not an hour ago, because Affie's cabin was part of the last tour. Sophia would have told me if there was a problem with it." Joshua tried turning the key again, but the door would not budge. "Here, Cayce, you try."

Cayce tried turning the key, but the door would not open. Then Harri took a turn, but it was futile.

"Do you think Affie doesn't want us in there tonight?" Harri looked at Cayce, who only shrugged her shoulders.

"Give me your flashlight, Joshua. I'm going to peek in the window." Cayce held the flashlight up and peered through the window but could see nothing. As she turned to go back to Joshua and Harri, she saw a shadow approaching on the stone path.

"You are just in time, and I don't think it's a coincidence. Am I right?" Joshua and Harri turned to see the person Cayce was greeting. Sherone was almost to the end of the path.

"What are you doing here, Sherone?" Joshua looked past Sherone. "Where is your cousin?" Joshua took the flashlight from Cayce and shined it toward Sherone.

"Jaleel is waiting for me in de inn. I was summoned here."

"Summoned? By whom? Did Sophia tell you we were here?" Harri asked.

"I was summoned by de one you seek. But she will only speak through one who knows."

"Knows what? Sherone, you're about to piss me off. Get to the point and stop speaking in mumbo jumbo." Joshua's irritation surprised Cayce and Harri.

"Dis is not you speaking, Joshua. You are affected by bad mojo dat guards dis place—t'ings you do not understand." Sherone held out her hand to Joshua, but he backed up, bumping into Cayce, who did not move from her spot behind him. She ran her hand down Joshua's arm and took his hand, finding it tight with tension. Sherone moved closer and put her hand on Joshua's shoulder. Cayce felt Joshua relax.

"I'm sorry, Sherone. I don't know what made me speak to you like that."

"It's okay, Joshua. Not your fault." Sherone passed by Joshua and climbed the steps to the cabin porch.

"We can't get the key to work in the door, Sherone. Would you like to try?" Harri held the key out to Sherone, but she did not take it. She walked to the door and stopped, turning back to the others, who followed her.

"When we get inside, you mus' all stay quiet and calm. I know what you want to know and will communicate wi' Affie's spirit if she will allow.

Regardless of what you see or feel, remain calm. And you mus' wait at de door 'til I have permission for you to enter."

Sherone put her hand on the doorknob and turned it. It opened without a key. The foursome entered the darkness, but only Mama Tee walked into the room, no one making a move to light the lamp sitting in the middle of the table. Sherone pulled out a leather pouch from under her tunic and began to sprinkle something around the room. Her mouth was moving, but none of the three who waited at the door could understand what she was saying. She took a seat at the primitive table, the one Tom had moved from the old kitchen, and motioned for Cayce and Harri to sit on either side of her. Joshua moved behind Cayce and rested his hands on her shoulders, maybe for her security, or maybe for his own.

"Mama Tee is here, Auntie. Let your presence be known." Without anyone touching it, the lamp began to cast a faint glow. Joshua squeezed Cayce's shoulder.

"De people wi' me are here to help you and yours, but da mus' know what you wish of dem." The lamp's flame grew brighter and then lowered to the faint glow again. Joshua squeezed harder. Cayce put her hand on top of one of Joshua's, locking her fingers in his, and he released his grip.

"De cookbook find de sisters. Is dis your will?" Once again the lamp glowed brighter for a few seconds. As soon as it died down, Mama Tee continued.

"Tomorrow is Princeton's birthday, and his cake will be baked again from your recipe. De portrait of Beatrice will be hung again at de head of de stairs tomorrow night." This time the lamp's flame leaped from its globe, sending off a hissing sound that surrounded the whole cabin like a monster snake. Cayce and Harri recoiled, leaning back as far as possible without moving from their chairs. Joshua held tight to Cayce, but he wanted to grab her and Harri and rush from the cabin his fear was so great. Mama Tee remained calm, and as quickly as it started, the lamp settled again to a low blaze.

Mama Tee was quiet for a few minutes as she pulled something from beneath her tunic and placed it on the table. The bloom of a yellow lily rested in the light of the lamp. The flame swayed, dying slowly as if weeping, and then extinguished itself, leaving them in darkness again with only the moonlight as a nightlight.

Everyone looked to the spiritualist for direction, wondering if it was over. But the woman stayed focused, staring at the lamp. Mama Tee tilted her head back and lifted her hands as if beckoning, but without saying anything. As she channeled Affie, the floor began to sway as if the cabin were sitting on top of the San Andreas Fault, the table tilting first one direction and then the opposite. The lamp slid from side to side on the tabletop. The stones in the fireplace cracked, several of them falling from just under the roughhewn log mantel. As abruptly as it began, the movement and the sound ceased, the silence and stillness deafening.

Mama Tee rose from the table and motioned for the others to stand.

"She is showing us something, and we must be quick to find it. Joshua, take your flashlight and go to de fireplace. She wants us to look where de stones have fallen."

Joshua turned on the flashlight and headed for the

fireplace with Cayce and Harri at his side and Sherone watching from her post at the table. He directed the light to where the stones had broken loose.

"There's an opening under the mantel, and look at these stones. They are flat on the backside, chipped away to allow space behind them." Joshua reached his hand into the opening and could feel something but could not pull it out. Cayce and Harri began pulling the rocks away. Something in the stones reflected in the moonlight.

"Be careful, Joshua. Shine your light in there before you put your hand in." Harri knew only too well what could happen if you stuck your hand in something without looking first. Taking great care, Joshua stuck his hand in part way.

"I've got it!" Joshua pulled the object clear of the broken stones, took it to the table, and laid it gingerly in the middle beside the lamp. The long butcher knife had brass brads on the rosewood handle and a razor-thin blade that looked as if it had been hard at use for decades before being retired after its last deadly project.

"Is this what I think it is?" Joshua stared down at the brutal-looking weapon.

"It's the butcher knife that was in the box with the cookbook. It makes my finger throb just looking at it." Harri shivered at the thought of how it must have felt as it was plunged into Beatrice's petite body. She shivered again as the lamp relit. Mama Tee began talking to Affie again.

"We are here, Auntie. What more do you have for us?"

Once again the room began to shake and again more stones fell from the fireplace.

"There is more, Joshua." Sherone motioned to the spot where Joshua had found the knife. Joshua held the flashlight down inside the space left deeper by the falling stones.

"There is something else in here, caught on a ledge at the bottom of the opening. Stand back. I'm going to pull more stones off." Joshua used all his strength to remove the stones and reached into the space left open. He held his hand out and directed the light to it so they could see the item in his hand. Harri shrieked, and Cayce moved closer to get a better look at the most beautiful and largest emerald stone she had ever seen. It was a deep green, and oval in shape.

"I think we all know where this came from." Joshua turned the jewel over in his hand so all sides of the huge stone could be seen.

"La Fleur!" Harri and Cayce spoke in unison.

"Yes. I believe it is a stone from the necklace, but the rest of it is still missing."

Sherone took her shawl off and placed the butcher knife in it, careful to roll it up in such a way that the sharp blade would neither be exposed or able to cut through the scarf's thickness. Joshua took out his handkerchief and wrapped the emerald in it before putting it deep in his pocket.

The group did not have to wait long to know what was to happen next. The front door flew open, banging against the wall inside as a strong breeze blew through the cabin. The door continued to tap against the wall like the foot of an impatient woman waiting on her children. Mama Tee handed the shawl to Joshua, who seemed reluctant to take it. Cayce took the shawl, and they all walked toward the door. Mama Tee walked through first, followed by Harri, Cayce, and Joshua as protector bringing up the rear. As Joshua cleared the door, it slammed behind him, and he leaped forward, almost knocking Cayce off the porch. He heard the heavy door lock behind him.

Once clear of the quarters, the group stopped. Everyone was shaken, with the exception of Sherone.

"I'm not so sure I'm as into this ghost hunting as I thought I would be. That was almost as bad as being in the swamp with the count." Joshua was breathless, his heart racing like a new jogger.

"It was even a little unnerving for me, Joshua, so don't worry. Now you know why Cody was scared of me."

"De portals are opening. You must be ready. Will you make de cake, Harri, on Princeton's birthday?" Harri looked from Cayce and Joshua to Sherone.

"Yes, I will. It is time to find out what happened here. I think Affie, Milla, and Chloe are ready, too."

Chapter Eleven

The thief's tiptoeing was soundless; not even a board creaked, the intruder proceeding like a stealthy lion stalking its prey. First stop, the attic room...again. This time the professional would work alone, not with a careless amateur, and the job would be completed. Enough time had passed, and no one watched any longer for the return of the doll burglar, the nickname for the one who left with only an antique doll worth pennies compared to the real target. The blueprints from 1815 were specific in showing the hidden spot for the small safe. The letter found by the thief, addressed to Princeton but never opened, indicated Jacob Broussard had told no one, not even his wife, about his hiding place. He had meant to share the information with his son when he felt he was mature enough to handle the valuables, but Jacob had waited too long, due to his son's careless nature. Jacob Broussard carried the secret to his grave. It took a master thief to know where to look, and the blueprints would lead to the safe.

The first door was opened easily, as it was that night six months ago, even though the lock had been changed, a small obstacle for a master. The second door lock, a padlock, was also no obstacle. Anyone with a hairpin could have done the same with only minutes of training. Once inside, the thief stepped to the loose wall panel barely reattached once the hidden storage area had been emptied of its hidden treasures, or so they thought.

The old trunks full of gowns and letters were of no interest in this venture, although the portrait had been, not for the beautiful woman depicted, and not even for the value of the portrait itself, but for what she wore around her neck. But that treasure was lost again, thanks to the same foolish efforts of the amateur turned greedy, unless the girl could be found. But all efforts to find her had failed. How the amateur had found it in the first place was a mystery. He had not been able to get back in the attic, so he did not find it there, but he would not disclose where it had been hidden, only saying he had found it by accident.

But there was no need to think about it anymore. The amateur had paid a price for his greed, and so would the girl, whether she had it or not. The girl knew too much and had to be silenced.

Feeling along the back wall, the thief felt the trigger and pulled it. A floor panel, camouflaged with oak matching the rest of the floor, opened with a low squeak that caused a moment of panic. Hurrying now, the robber dropped the penlight into the hole, where its light disclosed a wooden box. The thief retrieved the box but did not take time to open it here, not wanting to risk the two nosy women hearing what was going on above them. The floorboard was pressed down gently to keep it from squeaking as the trigger reset itself. The wall panel was replaced, and the two doors were relocked as the genius backtracked, leaving no evidence of ever being there.

In the shadows of Lily's day room, she stood, no

longer invisible as she had been while the intruder completed the devil's handiwork. The phantom woman showed no emotion as she shuffled over to the rocker and sat as one who was tired and needed a long rest, eternal rest. Slowly she rocked, unconcerned with the squeak of the chair, and hummed softly, her voice barely above a whisper.

Way down yonder, down in the meadow,
There's a poor wee little lamby.
The bees and the butterflies pickin' at its eyes,
The poor wee thing cried for her mammy.

****

In the room below, Harri and Cayce awoke at the same time, each sitting up in their beds in separate rooms, neither knowing the other had been awakened. Each one listened, turning her head in all directions to figure out what had awakened her, but hearing nothing, they lay back on their fluffy pillows, each falling asleep to the rhythmic creaking of a desperate old lady's rocking and grieving.

Chapter Twelve

Cayce yawned big, stretching her arms out from under the plump down comforter. She gazed up into the heavenly silk folds above her and smiled, knowing she was lying in luxury, Victoria Broussard's luxury. In the adjacent room, her sister was still sleeping, but soon the big day would begin. What the day would bring, she did not know, but she and Harri felt ready for it. The gift had never exposed them to more than they could handle, and there was no reason to think this time would be different.

After showering in the modern bath that had been added in one corner of the massive room, Cayce woke her sister. There was much to be done before getting dressed for Princeton's birthday ball later in the day. Joshua would be picking them up in an hour.

As the sisters were leaving their room, they met Don on his way to the Stables.

"Good morning. Care to join me for breakfast?" He directed his invitation to Harri.

"Oh, thank you, Don, but we're meeting Joshua. Today is the big day for me, you know. I've got a cake to bake." Harri opened the door and walked back into her room, pretending she had forgotten something. She rejoined her sister after Don had plenty of time to get down the stairs and out the door.

"You are so rude, Harri."

Harri just shrugged her shoulders as she led the way to the stairs, but before they reached the first step, they heard a door open and looked back expecting to see the Granthams. It was the door to Beatrice's room.

"Uh, oh! Looks like Don didn't close his door all the way. We should go back and close it for him."

Harri headed for the door, but as she reached it, she walked in rather than closing the door. Cayce stared, waiting for Harri to come out, but she just popped her head out and motioned for Cayce to come.

"What are you doing, Harri? This is trespassing." Cayce stopped by her sister, who was gazing up at Beatrice and Lily's picture. It was hanging crooked over the bed.

"Look. Beatrice does that same weird following thing she did in the other portrait, but Lily only stares in one spot and doesn't shift. How weird is that? Rathbone might have been a womanizer, but he was also a damn good artist." Glancing from the picture to the bed, Harri did a double take. "Oh, gosh, would you look at that?" A pair of silk boxers, black with huge red polka dots, lay casually over one of the pillows.

"See? I told you. Disney character." Harri pointed to the boxers, and she and Cayce started laughing. They stopped when the closet door opened without either of them touching it. Cayce hurried to the room door and checked down the hall. Seeing it was clear, she closed the door and turned the deadbolt. Harri stood at the closet looking in and motioned for Cayce to join her.

"Look! Up there! It's some kind of opening that has not been closed all the way. Give me a boost, Cayce, like you did when I wanted to climb that pecan tree you were always hiding in when we were kids."

Cayce locked her hands and held them down for Harri to step in. As she lifted her up, Harri steadied herself by holding to the shelf in the closet as she lifted the loose ceiling board. She felt around and grabbed hold of something that felt like paper. Once she had retrieved the object, she moved the board back to conceal the hiding place again.

"Get me down!" She whispered as if afraid someone would hear her.

Cayce lowered her sister and stared at what was in her hand.

Harri held a stack of thousand-dollar bills held together with a wide rubber band.

"Well, now, there's something you don't find in just anybody's closet." Harri stared at the money. Hearing a bumping noise coming from the top of the closet, she motioned for Cayce to be quiet. It sounded like the Granthams were climbing the wall Lily's room shared with Beatrice's. Harri gingerly closed the closet door, half expecting John Grantham's head to appear in the ceiling hole.

"We better get out of here, Cayce. They might have heard me." Harri whispered to Cayce while stuffing the roll of money in the waistband of her pants and wishing for a brief moment they were old-lady elastic. She tiptoed behind Cayce to the door. Cayce cracked the door enough to see and hear if anyone was in the hall, and then the two left the room, pulling the door closed behind them. They hurried down to their end of the hall and then slowed to a leisurely walk, talking small talk as if they had not just found a stash of money in a secret compartment in a room that had once belonged to a murder victim.

The two sat in rockers on the side porch, waiting for Joshua to pick them up. Harri felt bloated and took a cushion from behind her and covered her stomach with it. When Joshua pulled up in the Jeep, both of them practically ran to get in.

"Now that's what I like to see. Two beautiful women eager to be with me."

"Hit it, Joshua! We have to talk."

Joshua looked at Cayce's expression and juiced it, spinning his tires like a teenager. Cayce and Harri were talking at the same time and both so fast Joshua couldn't understand either of them. When they got down the gravel road out of sight of Spanish Oaks, he pulled over and held up his hands to silence them.

"Now, one at a time," he admonished.

Cayce motioned to Harri, who leaned over the console from the back seat and showed Joshua the stack of money while explaining what she was doing with it. Joshua rubbed his hand through his hair in disbelief.

"Holy shit! What the hell is Don up to?"

"I don't know, but with all that's been going on here, you might need to find out. Maybe you should call the sheriff?" Harri looked at Joshua, waiting for an answer.

"I already did, but only to tell him about the thefts and that I needed him to go to Natchez and retrieve my valuable pieces of Old Paris. He said he'd get the sheriff there to go with him to visit Linda, but he's waiting for some information Sophia is gathering for him. It's really gonna piss me off if Don is the estate dealer trying to make a fast buck off me, like he doesn't already get a chunk for his services." Joshua leaned back in his seat. "I need to stop and think about this.

Don't want to jump the gun until I know more, but this stack of money sure puts him in the prime suspect category."

Joshua drove the rest of the way in silence, obviously upset by evidence that pointed to the person he trusted most in the world.

When they got to his house, he led the sisters into the library and opened the vault.

"Let's put the money in here for right now. I just don't know what to do other than wait for the sheriff to report back. I don't want Don to know we have the money until the time is right. Damn! I trusted him completely! And I've got him escorting you tonight, Harri."

"Well, there's nothing we can do until we find out what his game is. I think you need to play it cool, but don't you two get out of my sight tonight. What is it they say? Never trust a pirate?"

Joshua looked at Harri, puzzled by her remark.

"It's a private joke, Joshua. You wouldn't understand." Harri offered no further explanation.

"I've got fresh coffee made, and I nuked some muffins, if you want one." Harri and Cayce poured themselves big mugs of coffee but decided to pass on the muffins. They drank the coffee in a rush, anxious to get to the mission at hand, both research and cooking.

"Okay, girls, let's have a good look at what Affie gave us last night." Joshua directed them to a section of shelves that was mostly empty. He had wanted to keep the knife and the emerald separate from the other documents and items, but the knife and the emerald were no longer alone on the shelf.

"What the hell is going on?" Joshua sounded

angry, and Harri and Cayce moved closer, afraid the items had disappeared.

"I know they were on this shelf all by themselves, but there's some other stuff with them now." Joshua picked up the additional documents. "Here's the Plantation Ledger. It's where Princeton kept up with purchases and supplies he either bought or needed and listed jobs that had been finished or jobs he wanted done on certain days. I've never even read through this completely." Joshua handed the ledger to Cayce. "And what's with this? Looks like some of the old letters that were in the box of family correspondence. I don't know who's been in here; nor do I know *how* they got in here. The key was with me. With all that's been happening, I was afraid to leave it in the desk."

"Joshua, I think these were put here for a reason, but I don't think it was anyone that a locked vault door could stop." Cayce looked at Joshua and nodded toward the knife.

"Affie. You think she's trying to tell us something."

"Yep, and I think the sooner we get started, the more we're going to find out what it is she's trying to tell us. I also know I'm not touching anything without gloves on."

Joshua handed Cayce the white gloves.

"Harri, do you need a pair, too?"

"No. As much as I want to know what's in those documents, I have to get going on Princeton's birthday cake. I just hope Affie will direct me with the boiled icing. I had to cook it three times the other day before I got it right." Harri turned and headed out of the vault, then stopped.

"Just let me know when you get to the good stuff."

Joshua put on the other set of gloves, stretched to fit his large hands, and handed the ledger and letters to Cayce. While she headed to the table in the library, he removed the cookbook from the other shelf and brought it out.

Joshua opened the book and it fell open to the bloody splotch that had acted like glue, binding several pages together. But this time, the pages fell open. Cayce and Joshua stared at what was between the blood-soaked pages. A folded piece of stationery was wedged between two pages, and on it the immaculate handwriting of Beatrice Broussard was easily identified. It looked as if it had been sprinkled with blood, but the droplets did not prevent it from being read. Cayce picked up the piece of paper and read aloud:

May 30, 1848

My dear Princeton,

It is with my deepest regret I write this. I can go on no longer. Your actions tonight were despicable, to ruin my portrait merely because I wore the jewel you thought you had hidden from me, an heirloom that rightfully should be mine as your dutiful wife.

I am leaving you, Princeton. Rathbone has asked me to go with him and I have conceded. He is twice the man you could ever hope to be.

I will send for Lily as soon as I am settled. Live your life as you want with your slave whore in your bed, but you will never shame me again by ignoring Lily or me. Your bastard child is de—

"Is what? Don't stop now!" Joshua looked over Cayce's shoulder, anxious to hear what came next.

"That's it. She stopped before finishing. Maybe someone came in and prevented her from completing it." Cayce sounded frustrated.

"Yeah, like the husband, the half a man. Princeton must have been one angry man, and probably drunk to boot, and if he caught her writing this, probably mad enough to shove that butcher knife into her," Joshua concluded.

Cayce leafed through the cookbook to see if anything was written on the other pages that had been sealed shut with Beatrice's blood, but all she found was more recipes.

"Recipes! Nothing but recipes!" Cayce closed the cookbook and laid it on the table, folding her arms across her chest.

"Okay. I know it's frustrating, Cayce, but let's not give up. Affie is giving us pieces of the puzzle, but she wants us to put it together. I'll start with the plantation ledger, and you go through the letters." Joshua handed Cayce the small stack of letters and opened the ledger.

"I'm starting with March 1, 1848. If I don't find anything from there, then I'll backtrack."

Cayce took out the first letter, dated March 10, 1848. It was written to Beatrice from a cousin in Louisiana and was mostly family gossip until the last page. One part caught Cayce's attention, and she began reading aloud:

It is unfortunate you had to resort to such drastic measures as to separate the child from her mother, but you must remember your husband drove you to it. You must think no more of it. The slave woman got what she deserved, and you will get a wonderful likeness of yourself from a master artist in return.

"Joshua! She gave Chloe to Fairchild! What a cruel, cruel woman!" Cayce showed Joshua the passage.

"Sounds like she bartered the little girl for Fairchild painting her portrait. I bet that's not all she gave him as payment."

Joshua went back to the ledger, and Cayce opened the next letter, dated April 1, 1848. This one was from the same cousin in Louisiana and was telling Beatrice she was looking forward to her and Lily's visit. In it she said, "I have arranged for a nanny for poor little Lily, as I am sure you will be spending many days with Rathbone as you sit for your portrait. I envy you having the handsome devil stare at you for hours on end and know I would not be able to retain my feminine virtues under such circumstances. Hopefully, you, my dear cousin, are stronger than I."

When Cayce read this passage to Joshua, he laughed.

"Feminine virtues, my ass! I'm afraid our delicate Bea had none."

Before reaching for the third letter, Cayce asked Joshua if he was finding anything.

"I'm just getting to the part where Chloe has gone missing. Princeton was pretty frantic. He hired every man in the county, practically, and offered a sizeable reward for whoever found the little girl. It also has where he paid the newspaper in town to print up posters. He paid for six dozen posters and then paid several men to put them up in South Mississippi, Louisiana, and Alabama. Princeton forked out some money looking for his little girl."

"Sounds like he was pretty upset, and to think his

own wife had given his and Milla's child to Rathbone Fairchild, a man who was close enough to the couple to get an invitation to Princeton's birthday dinner party—or maybe that was Beatrice's idea and not her husband's." Cayce put her finger to her lips as if she were thinking. "You know, I bet Princeton found out that night about her giving Chloe to Fairchild. Now, there's another motive for murder. I'd say love of a child would surpass the monetary value of an heirloom necklace, wouldn't you?"

"You bet. I know I'd kill for Sophia, and I'm sure you would for Piper. Any good parent would do anything to protect their child, and to revenge their child, as well."

The last letter was written by Victoria in December 1848 and seemed to be almost a last will and testament but without the legal ramifications. She gave details for her burial and expressed wanting to be placed on the right side of Jacob in the family cemetery, nearest to an ancient cedar tree she loved. She told Princeton to do as he wished with her personal effects, with the exception of La Fleur. When Cayce got to this part, she called Joshua over and read the statement aloud to him:

Upon my death, which I fear is close, I do not want Beatrice to have The Flower. I am sorry I encouraged you to marry her, but I had no idea what a selfish and deceitful creature she is, spoiled by her own parents. Beatrice openly covets everything of value from my personal estate as I lie dying. Just this week Affie caught her going through my secret drawer and was sure she saw her holding the precious gift your father gave me upon your birth. But when I confronted her about it, she denied it vehemently.

"Ah, hah! Now we know Beatrice was not wearing her own necklace the night she died, unless Princeton had gone against his mother's last request. Highly unlikely, don't you think?" Cayce asked.

"Definitely. Is that the last of the letters, Cayce?"

"Yep. What's next?"

Joshua walked to the soft leather sofa and patted the seat beside him.

"Come over here and read through this part with me. I'm up to April. Maybe your sharp eyes will see something I missed. Besides, I want you close to me." Cayce smiled and took her seat by Joshua.

"And you think I'll be able to concentrate, sitting this close to you?"

"Here, this will help." He put his arm around her and pulled her closer, nuzzling her ear.

"Oh, yeah, that's a lot better." Together they devoured each page, not turning a page until both had finished reading it.

Joshua started to turn one page when Cayce stopped him.

"Look down here at the bottom." Cayce pointed to a section that mentioned material for a new well at the slave quarters. "Didn't we just read where he bought materials for a new well at the quarters about two pages back?"

"Yes, we did." Joshua turned back and found it on the page dated May 4. "It's continued on the next page, so let's see. Maybe he dug two wells, which is strange."

"Aha! Here we go." Joshua followed the words with his finger as he read and then summarized. "It says there were heavy spring rains, and the other well caved in before they got the brick cistern completed. It also says Beatrice insisted the well was too far away from the quarters, like she gave a damn how far the slaves had to carry water, and the first well could be seen from the main house. She wanted it moved so it was 'less obtrusive,' so Princeton, giving in as I'm sure he always did when tired of her bitching, had the new one built several yards from the first."

Joshua and Cayce continued to read until the ledger stopped on May 29, 1848.

"Looks like the old boy didn't give a damn about business after his big night. Go figure." Joshua laid the ledger down and was in the process of kissing Cayce when Harri walked in with a spoon loaded with something that smelled heavenly.

"Pardon me, but I need a taste tester, if I could redirect your lips for a minute. Which reminds me, aren't you two supposed to be researching?"

"We just finished. Give us that spoon and sit down, and we'll fill you in." Joshua grabbed the spoon before Cayce had a chance and took a huge bite out of its contents.

"Oh, my goodness, Harri! That is the best praline I've ever tasted. What'd you do—change your mind about Princeton's cake? You know you might slam the portals shut if you do that." After taking one more bite, he handed the spoon to Cayce with orders for her not to eat it all.

"Nope. Just made a mistake that could be my ticket. It's Affie's boiled icing recipe, but I cooked it a little too long because I was engrossed in the pumpkin pie recipe they were making on the television and forgot to look at the clock. Anyway, it tasted like the richest praline ever, so I threw in some of those pecan halves I found in your freezer, stirred it up, and dropped it by spoonfuls on waxed paper, and—*voila*! Harri's Pralines by Accidenta."

Joshua immediately jumped from the sofa and headed to the kitchen, with Cayce on his heels.

"You bring us a spoonful to fight over when the counter is covered in them?" Joshua looked the counter over for the biggest praline and took it, handing Cayce a little one. She hit his arm but took the praline anyway. Before she got the second bite, Joshua was reaching for a second one.

"I don't care if your cake wins or not, I want these for Spanish Oaks. Let's make a deal, Harri." Joshua spoke with his mouth full.

"Cayce, do you remember what I said the first night at the Oaks when Chloe turned our room upside down?"

"Oh, I do indeed. You said something to the effect of 'a chocolate mint on the pillow would be nice but a pecan praline would be better.'"

"That's right, and Affie has provided the solution. I'll make these in the Teacake and package them and sell them to you, Joshua, and you can put them on your guests' pillows when you turn their beds down at night and have them for sale in the gift shop, too. I have a friend whose daughter is a graphic designer. Sarah will design the package for the pralines using a logo that represents Spanish Oaks, like maybe a fleur-de-lis. You can help make that decision. I promise they won't be too exorbitant in price."

"It's a deal. I'd shake your hand, but I need another praline first." Just as Joshua was reaching for another one, Sophia walked in.

"Do I smell pralines?" Sophia joined the group at the counter, and by the time they were finished, half the pralines had disappeared. While everyone was on praline overload and before Harri began trying again with the boiled icing, the group went into the library so Joshua and Cayce could fill them in on what they had learned. The three also had to tell Sophia about their experiences at Milla's and Affie's cabins the night before.

"I hate I missed that. That's even better than Chloe in the attic. Hey, that sounds like the name of a ghost story. Maybe I'll write it and sell it in the gift shop." Sophia looked at her dad for his nod of approval.

"You write it and I'll sell it, sweetheart. Now, Sophia, did you get your homework done?" Sophia retrieved her backpack and began unloading.

"I'll say I did, and you owe me a lot of overtime. I was up until two a.m. getting all this together. All of the staff photos from the past year have gone with the sheriff to Natchez. He says he'll try to get you a report later today, if he can finish making the rounds. Here's the list of missing items from the inventory and the estimated value, and remember, Dad, there are three ladies present, so don't blow a gasket." Joshua took the pages, looked through them hastily, and immediately jumped up from the sofa.

"Damn! One hundred sixty thousand dollars, and that's just an estimate? There are eight, nine, there's nearly a dozen items missing! How the hell?"

"Dad? Don't get your boxers in a wad. We know where two of the most expensive pieces are, remember?"

Cayce had a vision of Don's bed and hoped

Joshua's boxers weren't polka dot. She looked at Harri, and she was laughing so hard she snorted. Joshua and Sophia stared at her.

"I'm sorry. I was just thinking of something that happened earlier." Harri excused herself to the dream kitchen where she had been held a happy prisoner all day. Cayce could hear Harri still laughing in the kitchen.

"And here is a list of every guest who came several times and stayed for any length of time over the last year." Sophia took out some papers and started going over what she had found.

"The Granthams you already know about. I have their address as New Orleans, and when I called information, I did get confirmation on the phone number but can't verify the address as yet. They are by far the best customers we have, 'best' meaning they come the most and have a standing reservation once a month, always toward the end of the month, and they always stay in Lily's room, a definite pattern there.

"The second best customer is Louise Habersham, a librarian from New Orleans who has been coming regularly for about eight months. You know, Dad, she's tall and skinny, real dark hair. She always wears her hair up in a bun and wears big old-fashioned glasses. She's a nice lady but kind of frumpy-looking, like she knows what the television stereotype of a librarian is and tries to make herself fit it. Her phone and address info check out."

"Does she have a favorite room?" Cayce asked the question, finding this guest particularly interesting.

"Yep. Beatrice's room, but she has stayed in Jacob and Victoria's Suite when nothing else was available.

She was booked for three more times in April and May, but she cancelled at the first of March. She never called back to rebook, so we can probably take her off the list of suspects. She didn't really have a pattern to her staying anyway, but she couldn't with Mr. Fowler taking Beatrice's room the last of every month."

Cayce looked at Joshua and knew he was reading her thoughts.

"That's right. Don comes at the end of the month every month, and we go over all the accounts, including the Spanish Oaks books. He has to come sometimes in between, but if the inn is booked, he gets a room in town or just comes for the day."

"That's pretty much it for the best customer scenario. Most of our regulars come during Pilgrimage every year, or for Princeton's Birthday. Is any of that information helpful?" Sophia always wanted her dad's approval.

"Yes. You did good, sweetheart. Now let's spend the rest of our time going through documents. Each one of us can take one and skim through. That's all we have time for today. Maybe Affie will throw something at us again like she did the ledger and the letters."

The three headed back into the vault, each one taking a different set of documents. Cayce was exploring a set of old books that came from the mansion's library when she saw a clear plastic bag full of what looked like dried mud, sitting on the floor under the shelf.

"What is this, Joshua?" She held up the bag.

"Oh, you know my story about the swamp? Well, when I was on that little knoll that night, I found this sweatshirt. It's covered in mud. We can unwrap it if you want to see it, but we better do it out back on the deck. I don't know why I kept it, but something made me."

"What night in the swamp, Dad?" Sophia looked at her dad with a puzzled expression.

"Oh, damn! I'm sorry, Soppy. I never told you because I knew you'd be frightened. I'll tell you about it on the deck." Joshua took the bag and grabbed a pair of scissors out of a drawer as he went through the kitchen. As he cut the tape that sealed the plastic bag, he gave Sophia a quick synopsis of the night back in March but left out some of the scarier details.

"I can't believe you did that, Dad. You know Sherone told us never to go in that swamp unless she was with us. She even got mad when you took me to see the lily patch, remember?"

"Yes, and she was right, Soppy. I'll never go in that swamp again, and I want you to promise me you won't either." Joshua took the sweatshirt out and stretched it on the deck table. The hooded shirt was maroon, with "Mississippi State Bulldogs" in white letters on the front. Cayce looked closer and picked up one sleeve with her fingertips.

"What's this on the sleeve? It looks like dried blood."

"It does look like blood." Joshua picked it up to look at it closer. "I never noticed that with all the mud on the bottom half, but I didn't really look at it that closely."

Cayce looked inside at the label on the back of the neck. "It's a size large but that doesn't mean anything. I even wear a large in a sweatshirt, just because I like them big."

Sophia began looking more closely at the sweatshirt and turned it partly wrong side out.

"Here, on the underside of the waistband—a laundry tag like they use at Mississippi State. Some students put their initials or name on them so the university laundry won't get their laundry mixed up with other peoples'. I put my initials on mine. This tag is so muddy I can't even make out the number."

Joshua went inside and came out with a glass of hot water. He picked up the sweatshirt and dunked the tag in the water, rubbing it between his fingers. The water looked like skim chocolate milk.

"Now let's see what we have." Joshua held it in the sunlight. "It looks like SW."

"Oh, my god!" Sophia had to sit down in one of the chairs at the table. "Shelly Winthrop! It's Shelly's sweatshirt! I remember her wearing this all the time. She went to State one year but then quit when she started working at the Oaks. You don't think…"

"I don't think anything, Soppy. Maybe she went in there at some time, but she must be all right, since no one ever contacted me after I sent her last paycheck."

"I'm glad you didn't wash this, Joshua, or dispose of it. If this is blood, it could be important. Let's wrap this up and put it back in the vault for now." Cayce opened up the plastic wrap so Joshua could put the sweatshirt back in.

"There's another reason to keep it." Joshua began to reason. "If Monica is Shelly's sister, like we think, then maybe Shelly's whereabouts are not known and that's the reason Monica is asking about the girl instead of being afraid Shelly stole from the Oaks. That's a terrifying thought, considering where I found this."

"Monica? You think she's Shelly's sister?" Sophia looked at Cayce, and Cayce told her what she had found out in Natchez.

"We don't know for sure, Sophia, but it is a definite possibility."

"I hope Shelly didn't disappear in the swamp. That would mean she's…" Sophia stopped in dismay.

Joshua put his arm around his daughter and hugged her.

"We don't know that, Soppy. Just think good thoughts. I know you two had become pretty close before she left."

After they put the sweatshirt back in the vault, Sophia told them she had to go. She had promised to let Rodney off for a couple of hours to get ready for the night. Monica was off today, and Rodney would have to work the whole day until the ball was over.

****

When Cayce went in the vault to put the box of correspondence back, she noticed some long, rolled-up papers that looked like the Declaration of Independence they were so discolored. Pulling these out, she realized they were blueprints.

"Are these the original blueprints to Spanish Oaks, Joshua?" Joshua looked up from his computer.

"Yes. Tom found those in a barrel in the old kitchen. Most of that stuff in there was moved from the Stables when it truly was the stables. I had him go through and throw some of the junk away when I thought I was going to renovate there, back in December. Buddy brought them to me when Tom found them, but so far I haven't even had a chance to look at them."

Cayce unrolled the prints and laid them out on the table, using a book to hold each corner down. They were out of order, so she began putting the pages in order from one to twelve. "Did you know you're missing two pages?"

Joshua left his computer and came to the table. He checked through the stack, making sure Cayce hadn't overlooked any. "Well, I'll be damned. There's no page five, or page seven. Let's look through these. I should be able to tell what parts of the house are missing." Joshua scanned the pages. "Huh! The attic floor is missing, and there is nothing here for the old kitchen."

"How about the second floor? Would there be a close-up to show a hidden compartment if there was one, like the hidden storage room in the attic?"

"You mean like the one in Beatrice's closet?" Joshua asked the question, and Cayce nodded her head. "That compartment wouldn't be on these blueprints. Remember, old houses didn't have closets back then. Closets are pretty much a phenomenon of the twentieth-century, as are bathrooms."

Joshua looked at each page closely until he found the one Cayce was talking about, Beatrice's room.

"See, there's nothing on the blueprint but wall." As he began to really pore over the blueprint, he pointed to something in Jacob and Victoria's Suite. "Now, this is interesting. This shows an under-floor safe in Jacob's room, under where his bed is. How about I come check that out, say around midnight?" Joshua smiled at Cayce as if he were joking, but she suspected he was not.

"Of course you can. I'll tell Harri to expect you. She's in Jacob's room. I'm in Victoria's."

"It's okay. I already knew about the safe, and I

know it's empty. But there might be one under Victoria's bed that I haven't checked." He reached for Cayce, pulling her to him and giving her a big kiss.

"Later, Watson. Much later." Cayce's answer was ignored as Joshua kissed her again but this time more passionately.

"Why is it I always walk in at just the wrong time? Maybe it's a big-sister thing, looking out for my innocent little sister. Anyway, Joshua, I would like to borrow a beautiful crystal cake stand I found in your china cabinet, and two of the dessert plates for the judges' pieces, the cream-colored ones covered in gold fleur-de-lis motif, if you don't mind?"

"Of course you can. The fleur-de-lis is pure magic around here, you know. Maybe it will bring you luck, not that I think you need it. Besides, you're already a winner with the pralines, and you didn't even have to compete."

"Thank you, kind sir." Harri curtsied to the gentleman. "Now continue with whatever it was you were doing. I need to finish up and get this baby to the Stables. Will you two be unlocked in about thirty minutes?"

Harri brought her entry into the library a few minutes later and set it on the table for Joshua and Cayce to admire. The cake looked perfect as it sat royally on the crystal stand. The hollow center of the cake was filled with a combination of sliced strawberries and fresh whipped cream. Around the cake lay clusters of three strawberries, each cluster topped with a sprig of fresh mint. Harri used her best TV dramatization style to describe how she would display the pieces for the judges.

"A big slice of moist, citron-enriched cake is positioned in the middle of the fleur-de-lis-emblazoned dessert plate. Fresh sliced, succulent strawberries caress the crown, lathered with rich, heavenly, boiled icing with just a hint of citron. A dollop of whipped cream completes the serving, with a touch of mint on top to enhance its appeal. The sweetness of the boiled icing and the slight tartness of the strawberries eject a burst of flavors that together create sheer unadulterated harmony and ecstasy."

Joshua sat with his mouth open, watching and listening to Harri give the most seductive description of cake he had ever heard.

Cayce saw Joshua's amazement and knew what he was thinking. Leaning close to him, she whispered, "Cooking does that to her. She practically has an orgasm basting a turkey, but only if it's a Tom."

Joshua gave one of his giant, hearty laughs as he jumped to his feet and herded the women out the door and into the Jeep, Cayce in the front and Harri in the back trying to balance her prize-winning entry as they bounced along the gravel road.

Chapter Thirteen

*The thief gazed at the velvet bag filled with jewels.
It had been a lucrative night, no amateurs bumbling the
endeavor. It was not the mother lode, but it was worthy.
The bag held sixteen flawless diamonds, none smaller
than two carats, but it was the emeralds that took the
breath, two brilliant emeralds with a total weight of
maybe thirty carats. It was a good job, one worthy of
genius.*

*There was nothing else of value in the wooden box,
only a yellowed envelope sealed with the Broussard
wax seal. "To be given to Caleb upon obtaining his
freedom at twenty-five years of age" was written on the
outside, but this was worthless and thus put back in the
box to be destroyed later. If only The Flower had been
in the box, the genius could shake the dust off and leave
Spanish Oaks forever, leaving no trace of ever having
been there.*

*But until the girl was found, no chances could be
taken. How was it possible for her to hide for so long
and so well? How long must the genius endure this
charade? If The Flower ever surfaced again, it would
not be shared with the dealer. The genius alone would
be rewarded for effort spent, reward for the toil of the
master and for no little insignificant people. Until then,
the archaic birthday celebration would ensue, and the
commoner part would be played to the fullest,*

259

continuing the next day and the next until the girl was terminated and The Flower possessed by the only one who deserved it.

****

Cayce sat on the sofa, wondering how on God's green earth women had endured the tight, lace-up shoes and the hoops that practically hit the ceiling to expose everything but ladylikeness when a lady sat wrong—and Cayce was sure to sit wrong. It took only minutes for her to shower and pile her hair on top of her head, held loosely with antique-looking combs she had found in the gift shop. Applying her makeup took even less time, since she wore very little of the stuff. She put off donning the gown until the last minute and sat in her camisole, hoop slip, and pantaloons, looking down at the ugly shoes killing her feet already. She kept looking at her watch. Harri had started getting ready at four o'clock and still wasn't ready. It was five thirty, the hour of transformation when Annie Oakley had to bite the bullet and get ready to play Scarlett.

After pulling the yellow taffeta over her head, she began trying to place it over the hoop, but she could not reach that far. Reaching under the dress, she pulled the hoop up and lowered the dress over it one small section at a time until she had completed the circle. Holding the hoop and the dress up on each side, she made long strides to Jacob's bedroom to get Harri to fasten the back. When Cayce saw her sister, she had to stop and stare.

Harri stood in front of the long mirror, her blonde hair perfection—up in the back, with long ringlets hanging down each side. Her makeup looked like a professional had done it, and her elegant red dress clung to her body like it was made for her. All she needed on her pretty smooth neck were the pearls Stan had given her. Cayce went to her sister and began zipping the back of her dress, glad the rows of tiny buttons had been replaced with a modern-day zipper.

"Thank goodness Janine had the forethought to replace all those buttons. I'd die of claustrophobia if I thought I couldn't get out of this dress in a hurry. You look elegant, Harri. I wish Stan could see you."

"Maybe he can. Anyway, if he can, he certainly won't be jealous when he sees me holding on to my pirate's arm. Let me zip yours, Cayce." Harri zipped the yellow gown and then turned her sister around. "What is it cowboys say? 'Ya clean up good,' or is that somebody else?"

Cayce curtsied to her sister to acknowledge she took the remark as a compliment.

"Really, Cayce, you look beautiful. Joshua will want to stay lip-locked all night."

"I doubt that. He'll be too busy looking at his staff and guests, trying to figure out which one is robbing him, unless Sherone's cousin Jaleel is there." The two sisters stood looking in the mirror at their image.

"You know, Harri, I think this is the best twin trip ever."

"You say that every year, Cayce. You better wait until tonight is over before you make that decision. The portals may open and we might all drown."

"Are you ready to go meet our escorts?" Cayce asked, knowing Harri's answer already.

"When you put it like that, no, I'm not, but since I don't have a choice…" They each grabbed up their long white gloves and started to the door when they heard a ruckus in the lobby. Harri opened the door, and they both stepped out and looked down at the lobby, where a group of staff and guests had formed.

"She was in the room thirty minutes ago, and now she's gone. I thought my husband had taken her out on the porch. She complained of being hot in her dress, but he said he thought she was with me. He's looking down by the lake. Oh, God, please don't let anything happen to my baby!"

"Is Molly missing?" Cayce called over the railings.

"Yes, we've been searching for about twenty minutes, but no one can find her. My husband has several of the other guests searching the grounds."

"We'll check all the rooms up here. Don't worry, I'm sure she'll be found." Harri was trying to reassure the panic-stricken mother.

"Let's check the attic doors, Cayce." Cayce and Harri tried to walk side by side, but the hall wasn't wide enough for them and their hoops, so Harri stopped and turned to Cayce.

"You take the little stairway, and I'll check the door to Lily's day room."

Cayce knew the door was locked but felt she had to check it, knowing Molly had possibly been in Chloe's nap room before. With Harri's fast steps, she made it back to the stairs before Cayce got past the third step, her hoop not cooperating.

"That door is locked. This one should be, too, but we need to check it out, just the same." Cayce kept trying to go up the stairs but couldn't make the turn with the hoop on. Harri was behind her but couldn't see where she was going since Cayce's hoop kept popping up and hitting her in the face. Tired of seeing her sister's pantalooned backside, Harri backed down the stairs.

"You go. I've almost been knocked unconscious twice by that hoop of yours. I'll wait at the bottom."

Cayce heard a noise coming from up the stairs. It sounded like a little girl's voice.

"Tell her mom I think she's up here. I'm going up." Realizing there was no way the wide hoop was going to make it, Cayce pulled her dress up and pulled the hoop slip down, stepped out of it, and then half rolled and half threw it down the stairs. Then she reached through her legs and grabbed the back of her dress and pulled it to the front. Holding the yards of fabric gathered in a wad in the front, she started up the stairs.

The door was open, and Molly was sitting in the little rocker holding both dolls, the old one and the new one; the *McGuffy Reader* was in her lap. In no time Molly's mother was standing at the door, squeezed in beside Cayce and shocked by the sight of her daughter. Cayce put her fingers to her lips to tell her mother to wait before confronting Molly.

"Now, pay attention, babies, and I'll read you a story." Molly used her best motherly voice to her babies.

Molly's Cinderella-blue dress lay in a pile on the floor at the foot of the rope bed, her ruffled pantaloons and shiny patent leather shoes lying on top of the pile. Molly was dressed in one of Chloe's cotton dresses, the off-white pinafore over it and the simple pantaloons showing above the worn lace-up shoes. As they watched, Molly opened the book and began to read.

"Lesson One. Here is John. There are Ann and

Jane. Ann has a new book. It is the first book. Ann must keep it nice and clean. John must not tear the book. He may see how fast he can learn." Molly's mother tiptoed to the rocker and knelt beside her little girl. Molly turned and smiled at her mother.

"Molly, you scared me. I didn't know where you were."

"I'm sorry, Mommy. I thought you saw the little girl when she came in our room to get me."

"What little girl, Molly?"

"The one who gave me this dress to wear to Massey's birthday party. She said only Lily is allowed to wear pretty dresses, and I should wear this one or Lily's mama will get mad."

"Let me see your book, Molly." The mother looked at the pages. "Molly, you can't read yet. How do you know these words?"

"The little girl taught me. She can read the whole book. We read together sometimes." Molly's mother looked at Cayce. A lone teardrop slid down the mother's face. After wiping her cheek, she took Molly's hand.

"Let's go find Daddy. We need to put your pretty dress on for the party now. We can leave the little girl's dress here for her."

"But we shouldn't dress like that, Mommy. We have to serve at the party. I want to wear this one."

"We'll talk to Daddy about it, Molly. Let's go now. Leave the book and the doll here." The mother picked up Molly's party outfit and led her daughter to the door. Cayce followed as they all squeezed through the narrow stairway. When they were almost to the curve in the stairs, the attic door closed behind them and locked.

Harri met Cayce at the bottom of the attic stairs, holding her sister's cast-aside hoop slip. Harri smiled at Molly and her mother as they walked past, and the little girl reciprocated with her own angelic smile.

"Lose something, Cayce?" Harri held the hoop with one arm through it and the rest slung over her shoulder.

Cayce was still holding her dress in a wad in the front when she looked down and saw Joshua looking up from the lobby. He took off his shorter version of the top hat and bowed to her, barely able to contain his laughter at the comical sight she posed. She curtsied back, still holding her dress in front as Harri shook her head in disbelief. At just the same time, Don came out of his room wearing a top hat perfectly matching his scarlet long-tailed suit coat. He looked at Harri, who smiled politely.

"I'll be down in just a few minutes, Don. I have to redress my little sister." Still fake smiling, she whispered through clenched teeth, "Move over, pirate. The dude has arrived."

****

Stepping into the ballroom was like stepping into Victoria's journal. The only difference was that many of the glamorous women were suffering from the discomfort of unaccustomed wearing apparel, and Cayce was leading that pack. Harri, on the other hand, was in her element. It was like she belonged in the Old South with all its pomp and glory, but Cayce knew her sister also fit well in the twenty-first century. In fact, Harri fit into any period of time or any scenario requiring a flair for fashion. Harri was talking to everyone and had danced with Don only once. He seemed to be playing host as well, but his days of importance at Spanish Oaks could be numbered.

Cayce had always felt she was a reincarnation from the 1800s, but not the southern plantation mansion scene; she was from the 'creaking wagon over muddy mountain passes' scene of the western pioneer movement. Those women were the real heroes, and yes, they wore long hot dresses and inhibiting sunbonnets, but they were not above hiking those dresses up to lead the horses over a stream, or helping their men as they fixed broken axles while standing knee deep in mud.

Cayce stood to one side, watching her escort mingle as if he were Princeton Broussard reincarnated. She was brooding and felt out of place, and as she looked up, she saw more reason to brood. Jaleel walked in looking like the real sister to Harri Wellington, at least from a fashion standpoint. Her dress was elegant, a pale peach color, with ruffles to spare. All she needed was a parasol to twirl as she walked under the Spanish Oaks—Joshua's Spanish Oaks. She carried herself with the grace of a southern belle. Joshua met her at the door, bowing low and taking her hand as if the two had rehearsed their parts. He ushered her over to where Cayce stood, sure the two had so much in common they could entertain each other for hours while he played host. Cayce returned Joshua's smile as he drifted back into the crowd.

"You look lovely, Cayce."

"Thank you, Jaleel. You do, too. Your dress is beautiful. Did you have any trouble finding it?"

"No. I had to go back to New Orleans this morning, so I picked it up in a costume shop downtown." Jaleel's eyes seemed to be watching

Joshua's every move.

"Is Sherone coming?" Cayce had been watching the door when she wasn't watching where Jaleel was watching, but she had not seen Mama Tee.

"She's coming later, closer to eleven, she said. I think that's the bewitching hour. I plan to leave about ten. It's been a long day. Sherone said she'd come to the ball after I got back to her house."

"Is there another way to her cabin? Surely you don't have to walk that long path at night, especially in that gown."

"Actually, there is. A road comes fairly close to the back of her shed, so it's only about a two-minute walk to it, thank goodness. I don't like snakes, and that swamp is way too close for me."

Cayce had run out of things to say, so she continued to watch Jaleel through her peripheral vision.

"You don't need to worry, Cayce."

"Worry? About what?" Cayce looked at Jaleel, who did not return the look.

"Remember, I'm a psychologist. I promised Sherone I would keep my eye on Joshua while I'm here. She is quite fond of him and is scared something major might happen to him or Sophia tonight. Besides, just between you and me, I'm taken." Jaleel never took her eyes off Joshua, even though she knew Cayce was watching her.

"She really thinks the portals are opening, huh?" Cayce chose to ignore the other part of Jaleel's remark.

"That's what Sherone says. Anyway, she thinks it will be later tonight, probably when Beatrice's portrait is unveiled and hung, or should I say re-hung?"

"I can hardly wait." Cayce was being sarcastic,

uneasy about what the event might trigger. "I hope Sherone brings that pouch she had the other night. Did she tell you about our visit to Affie's cabin?"

"Yes. You and your sister definitely have a gift. I hope Harri was serious when she said you would let me interview you for my research."

"We both are. Maybe you can answer some of our questions, too. Our dad was the one with the psychic powers, but he shared very little with us. His talents supposedly came from a shaman ancestor."

"Inheriting psychic powers can be a problem. Sherone tells me you have a daughter. Does she have the powers?"

"If she does, she hasn't admitted it to me yet. We are continents apart, literally, but we always seem to know what is going on in each other's lives. I call her when she's sick, and she calls me when I'm sick or down for any reason. My dad and I had the same relationship, and so do Harri and I." Cayce stopped as she saw Joshua approaching, but she wondered which one of them he wanted to be near.

"Do you mind if I take my beautiful lady away for a few minutes, Jaleel? I'd like to dance with her."

Joshua took Cayce's hand and led her to the ballroom floor, erasing all her jealous thoughts. Cayce was hoping she would not have to waltz. It had been a long time since she took ballroom dancing as the only P.E. class she could get into during her freshman year of college. To her good fortune, it was only a slow dance. Joshua held her tight and nuzzled her ear until she began to tell him some of what Jaleel had told her.

"Sherone evidently thinks there is danger for you and Sophia tonight. She will be here later for the 'bewitching hour,' as Jaleel put it. Where is Sophia anyway?" Cayce looked around the ballroom.

"She should be here shortly. She was going to pick up some shrimp for Andre in town. It seems my head chef ran short for some appetizer he was making. She was ready except for putting her gown on. She wants to be fashionably late. Oh, yes, she asked me if she could dress in your room. She wants to make an entry down the staircase."

"Of course she can. Did you bring your cell phone? Call her and tell her."

"It's okay. I told her you wouldn't mind." Joshua pulled her close again. When the dance ended, he kept Cayce's hand and led her to a different part of the room, away from Harri and Don but where they could still see them. Joshua warned Cayce he was having a hard time making conversation with Don and felt it might be better to keep his distance until he knew what his accountant was up to. Joshua took Cayce to a small sofa in the back corner.

"Aren't you supposed to be playing host?" Cayce didn't want to take Joshua away from his responsibilities.

"I did that already. Even welcomed the Granthams. Did you notice Mrs. Grantham is not using her cane tonight? Reckon that was a cover-up for some big heist they have planned for later?"

"Joshua, don't feel you have to babysit me. I know you have plenty you should be doing."

"Cayce, will you please stop. I am where I want to be." He hugged her, pulling her closer and leaving his arm around her shoulder. "But there is something I want you to promise me."

"What's that?" Cayce looked into Joshua's eyes and saw his seriousness.

"If there is trouble tonight of the paranormal variety, please take care. Don't try to be a hero—or is that heroine? I don't mean to show gender bias, but I get the politically correct terminology confused." Joshua took Cayce's hand and held it to his lips, kissing it as he stared into her eyes. "You mean a lot to me, Cayce. I don't want anything to happen to you."

"Joshua, you know I'll do what I am led to do. I'll make no promises, because I don't know what or if anything is in store, but I will be careful."

Just at that moment, the crowd became quiet, with everyone looking to the entry to the ballroom. Molly and her parents walked in, and not only was Molly wearing Chloe's dress, but her mother and father were dressed like a slave family on their way to church. Cayce and Joshua stood staring at the brave family and began clapping. The other guests followed suit. The applause was deafening, and Joshua continued clapping as he went to welcome them.

"You don't know how many times I've almost done what you did tonight. Thank you for having the courage to show our ancestors' place in history. I try never to forget about them—Affie and Big Zed, Milla and Caleb—and their importance in making Spanish Oaks what it is today, but I've never had the courage to do what you are doing. You make me ashamed of the pretense I'm showing."

"Oh, don't be ashamed. Our closet upstairs holds costumes just like what we're seeing here. Our daughter showed us the error of our ways. Isn't that right, Molly?" Her daddy picked her up and hugged her.

"It was Chloe's idea." Molly hugged her baby doll.

Molly's mother looked concerned. "Is that what she told you her name is, Molly?"

Molly nodded her head.

"That's the first time she's called her by name. If I never believed in ghosts before, and I didn't, I certainly do now."

Joshua's cell phone rang, and he excused himself from the family. After putting it away, he led Cayce aside.

"That was Sophia. It seems she had to go to another town to find shrimp. I am so pissed off at Andre. I told Sophia to forget the damn shrimp and come back here. She's missing the ball. She said she'd try one more place and that would be it."

****

Sophia was driving way too fast trying to get back to Spanish Oaks. She decided to take the shortcut road that went by the back of Sherone's house. As she passed the turnout where Sherone always parked, she saw Sherone getting out of her old minivan. Stepping out on the passenger side was a young girl with long blonde hair. As Sophia passed, she started to honk her horn but stopped when the girl turned to look toward the road.

Sophia almost fainted. It looked like Shelly Winthrop. Sophia almost wrecked trying to get another glimpse of the girl, just to make sure it was Shelly. She wanted to go back and talk to her, but she didn't have time. It was already 9:15, and she wanted to be back by ten o'clock, in time for the unveiling of the portrait. She had a special reason for wanting to make a late entrance, but she hadn't meant for it to be this late.

"I wonder why Shelly is with Sherone." Sophia was thinking out loud as she sped toward Spanish Oaks. The parking lot and the road were jammed on both sides with cars, and she had to park at the end, down the gravel road. She was glad she had left her costume with Monica and told her to put it in Harri and Cayce's suite. She just hoped she didn't smell like shrimp when she made her entry.

After dropping the heavy bag of shrimp off at the Stables, Sophia ran to the mansion. Not wanting anyone to see her, she ran past the ballroom and took the stairs two at a time. It was 9:30. She had to hurry. As she headed up, she saw Monica coming down the stairs. She was dressed in a white taffeta gown that looked like the one Shelly had worn in the staff picture from last year.

"Monica, if you aren't busy, I could sure use some help. I'm running late, and I have to get my gown on before the portrait is unveiled."

"I'm not busy at all, Sophia. In fact, I feel a little out of place, still the new girl, you know." Monica followed Sophia up the stairs.

Sophia scrubbed her hands with soap until she finally got the shrimp smell off. Seeing Harri's perfume, she grabbed it and squirted a generous amount on, just to make sure the shrimp was covered up. Monica was taking the gown off the hanger as Sophia put on her camisole, pantaloons, and hoop slip.

Monica put the gown over Sophia's head and helped her straighten the full skirt over the hoop. The row of buttons on the back of her gown had not been replaced with a zipper, and it took a while for Monica to button all of them. When she finished, Sophia gazed at herself in the mirror.

"Well, too bad I don't have an emerald necklace to go with this beautiful gown like Beatrice did, but I guess my mom's simple gold locket will do." She lifted her hair while Monica fastened the clasp.

"That is a stunning gown, Sophia. Wherever did you get it?"

"It was in a wooden trunk in the attic, in an area we didn't even know existed until six months ago. Janine had to take the top up quite a bit. Beatrice was well endowed, if you know what I mean. And Janine repaired a patched piece that was in the bodice, a little bit disconcerting. It's the gown Beatrice wore in the portrait and most likely is the one she was wearing the night she was murdered. Monica said the patch looked as if it had been sewn hurriedly, probably not something a person wanted to spend much time on, considering. Fortunately, there were no bloodstains left on it." Sophia slid her hands over the well-hidden patch, then turned her attention to Monica.

"I love your gown, Monica. It looks just like one a girl who once worked here wore to Princeton's ball last year. I don't guess it's the same one, is it?"

Monica buried her face in her hands and began to cry. Sophia handed her a tissue from the dressing table.

"I'm sorry, Monica. Did I say something wrong?" Sophia thought she knew why the woman was crying.

"I just can't hide it any longer, Sophia. Shelly is my little sister. She's been missing since March. I don't know if she's alive or dead."

"I'm so sorry, Monica. We thought she was just upset over Buddy's death and couldn't stand to come back to work here. Dad sent her last paycheck to the address she had in her personnel file. We just assumed she got it, since we never heard anything more from there."

"I came here and took this job to find out what happened to her. I was afraid if I told who I was, I wouldn't get as much information. I miss her so much. I raised her after our parents died when she was just twelve. She's my life, but I'm beginning to think she's dead. Janine doesn't know Shelly is my sister, so please don't tell her. She told me Shelly's purse was in Buddy's car the night he died, but I don't know if that means anything. I just want to find my sister and bring her home, even if it's just to bury her by our parents."

Sophia didn't know what to do. She felt she needed to talk to her dad about seeing Shelly, but she also wanted Monica to know her sister was alive. She had started to tell her when Monica began talking again.

"When I was putting on this gown this evening, Janine was there, and she told me you and Shelly had started doing some things together right before she left. Do you have any idea where my sister might have gone?"

Sophia opened her mouth again to tell Monica, but there was a knock on the door. When she opened it, Cayce rushed in and plopped on the sofa.

"I thought I saw you come up the stairs, Sophia." Cayce started unlacing the tight shoes and noticed Monica standing by the dresser. "Hello, Monica. Your dress is beautiful." Cayce noticed the woman looked as if she had been crying. "Are you all right?"

"Yes, I'm fine. I'll just use the rest room while I'm here, if you don't mind, and then I'll go on down. I just helped Sophia get her gown on. Isn't she lovely?"

Cayce threw the shoes away from her and held her feet up, wiggling her toes as she gave out a big sigh.

"That's better. If I'm going to be able to keep up with your dad on the dance floor, I've got to change shoes." Cayce finally got a good look at Sophia.

"Oh, my gosh! It's the green taffeta gown from the portrait! All you need is La Fleur, but I'm glad you're not wearing it. You look fabulous, Sophia, but I can't help but be just a little alarmed at your wearing that dress tonight."

"Don't be superstitious, Cayce. I'll be fine. Is Dad ready to hang the portrait?"

"He's moving it from his office now. Are you ready to make your entrance? Your dad says he wants to escort you down the stairs. He's got a photographer waiting."

"My dad is way too cool! Yep. I'm ready." Monica came out of the bathroom and said she'd see them downstairs.

"Thanks, Monica, for helping me."

Cayce went to the closet to get something else to put on her feet, and Sophia headed to the door.

"Wait, Sophia. I want to be down the stairs when you come down. It's going to be quite a production." As Cayce was about to open the door, there was a knock.

"Are the two most gorgeous ladies at the ball ready to come down?" Joshua entered with a black velvet box in his hand. Cayce smiled, knowing what was in the box.

"This is for you, Soppy, from your mom and me." Cayce felt out of place and thought this should be a father-daughter moment, so she told them she'd wait downstairs.

"No, wait, Cayce. I need a mom here even if she's not mine." Sophia opened the box and gasped. Inside was a gold chain set with many diamonds and holding a big emerald drop in the center.

"Daddy, it's beautiful! Is this Mom's drop that was on the necklace you bought for her when she turned forty?"

"Yes. I had the stones from it and two others of her necklaces made into this for you. It was something your mom wanted me to do for your twenty-first birthday, but I just felt you needed it tonight."

"Cayce, will you help me get it on?"

Cayce replaced Sophia's other necklace with the new one and gave the girl a hug. "It's perfect, Sophia."

Sophia turned to her dad and ran to him, giving him a big hug and kiss. "Thank you, Daddy. I'll wear it every year on Princeton's birthday."

"Okay. I'm going downstairs to wait for you two to make your entrance. Sophia, my dear, you put Beatrice to shame in beauty and integrity. Good job, Joshua." Cayce gave them a thumbs-up as she left the room.

Chapter Fourteen

It was an inspiring moment when Sophia came down the stairs on her dad's arm. The photographer hired by Joshua snapped pictures one after another. Most of the guests left the ballroom to be part of the historical moment and clapped with approval as the beautiful young lady descended the stairs. She stopped on the third step from the bottom, as was planned, and Rodney handed her a cordless microphone. Joshua darted into the office behind the desk and brought out the portrait draped with a black velvet cloth. After placing the covered portrait on an easel at the right of the stairs, he gave his daughter the nod.

"On behalf of Spanish Oaks Plantation, I would like to thank all of you for coming. This is our fifth year to celebrate Princeton's birthday, but this year is very special. Six months ago, quite by accident, a famous portrait was found in the attic, but it had to be restored, a process that was painstaking, long, and yes, Dad, costly." The guests laughed and looked at Joshua, who smiled and nodded in agreement.

"You all know the story of the tragedies that occurred on that night in 1848. Two people died— Princeton's wife, Beatrice, and the one he loved even more than his wife, Milla, the mother of the little lost girl, Chloe. Even though Beatrice's character proved flawed, my dad felt it only proper to return her portrait to the spot where it hung for only that one night. We hope the spirits agree, but we won't know for sure until we hang the portrait. Dad, would you unveil Beatrice?"

Joshua removed the drapery and stepped to the side so everyone could see. The guests were awed by the portrait. Beatrice, the beautiful young woman with flaming red hair to match her fiery spirit, had the guests each straining for a better look, some drawn to her beauty, others drawn to the magnificent La Fleur, but all curious to see the treasure hidden for over a century and a half.

"As you see, the gown I am wearing is Beatrice's gown, the one she wore when she sat for the portrait. It is not, however, the one she died in, nor is it a perfect fit, as you can see." The audience laughed, looking from the heavy-bosomed Beatrice to the petite, athletic Sophia. "The portrait will be hung at the head of the stairs, where it was placed originally on that night, but we will wait until exactly eleven o'clock, which is the time this event ended in 1848. And, no, we won't be running you off at that time. You are free to dance until midnight. In the meantime, hors d'oeuvres will be served in the dining room." The guests started toward the refreshments, but Sophia stopped them. "Oh, and don't forget. In just thirty minutes, we will announce the winner of the annual Stables cooking contest. Now, please enjoy yourselves."

The guests clapped, and Joshua beamed as he took his daughter's hand and led her the rest of the way down the stairs. Many guests stopped to get a closer look at the portrait.

"Nice job, sweetheart." Joshua kissed his daughter's cheek.

Harri and Cayce hugged Sophia and congratulated her on a job well done.

"Thirty more minutes. Why am I so nervous? You'd think I was on one of those reality cooking contests." Harri wrung her hands.

"If I were a betting man…"

Joshua didn't finish his statement. The band had started playing music from the sixties, and he grabbed Cayce, rushing her to the dance floor. Don followed suit, and Harri was surprised to see the man could actually bop. Molly's parents were bopping even though they weren't old enough to remember it. They were definitely the most comfortably dressed for sixties dancing. Cayce was wishing she had dressed as an 1848 pioneer woman. She would have been more comfortable and certainly closer to her real character.

Joshua stopped the band at 10:30, after it finished playing "Rock Around the Clock." Getting everyone's attention, he introduced Andre, who would announce the winner of the contest. On the table in front of them was the winning dessert, covered by a white cloth.

Andre began, "It is my pleasure to announce the winner of the fifth annual Stables cooking contest. We had twenty amazing entries this year, and the judges had a difficult time choosing a winner, and remember, we have no first and second place. Only one person has the honor of having their winning entry placed on our menu for the next year. So without further adieu, I'd like to present to you this year's winner."

He took the cover off the dessert as Harri and Cayce strained to see over the crowd. Cayce held Harri's hand in a death grip, with fingers crossed on both sets of hands.

"Citron Delight, made by Harriet Wellington."

Cayce screamed, and she and Harri hugged and tried to jump up and down without getting all tangled in their hoops. Joshua took Harri's hand and led her through the crowd to the front of the room. From the back of the room, Don yelled, "Speech," and Joshua handed the microphone to Harri. Before she began speaking, Joshua whispered something in Harri's ear.

"This is such an honor for me and is totally unexpected. Joshua asked me to tell you how I came upon this recipe. Believe it or not, it is Affie's cake recipe she baked every year for Princeton's birthday. Citron Delight was always his favorite. The last time it was baked was on May 30, 1848. I came across her cooking journal in an antique shop and it, literally, would not let my sister and me leave the shop without it. Our interest in the cookbook is what brought Cayce and me to Spanish Oaks. I knew nothing about the contest until we registered as guests. Anyway, Citron Delight is Princeton's Cake. Happy Birthday, Princeton, wherever you are, and thank you, judges, for choosing Affie's cake."

The guests applauded as Harri made her way back to her sister. Andre took the winning entry and placed it in the center of the refreshment table in the dining room.

A few minutes before eleven, Sherone came in, dressed in full Caribbean regalia, the original Mama Tee attire. The only thing unusual was that she came to the celebration at all. This was not something she had attended in the past.

Harri and Cayce met her as she entered the ballroom.

"I hope you brought a pouchful of magic like you had in Affie's cabin. It won't be long until the portrait is hung. Do you feel uneasy, Sherone? Jaleel said you had some concern." Cayce asked the question but knew the answer already.

"It is de only reason I come here. And I know already de portals are opening. I feel it. You must be very careful, Sisters. Much will be expected of you, but if you trust your instincts and do not t'ink too much before you act, de end will be good."

Joshua directed everyone back to the lobby to witness the fixing of the portrait in its place of honor. Tom and Mack were at the top of the stairs, ready to hang it on the waiting hook.

Cayce looked for Sophia but did not see her anywhere. This was unsettling. She wanted to keep her eye on her in case there were any paranormal occurrences. Harri was by her sister's side.

"Harri, do you know where Sophia is?"

"I saw her going out the front door with Monica a few minutes ago. Why?"

"I am just a little uneasy and wanted her where her dad and I could see her, especially with the portrait about to be unveiled. I can't believe she's not in here for it."

Cayce walked to the front door to see if she could see her anywhere. No one was on the porch with the exception of Molly and her dad.

"Did you see Sophia come out?"

"Yes, she went down that way with the lady who works the front desk…uh…what's her name?"

"Monica?"

"Yeah, that's her."

Cayce walked to the edge of the stone sidewalk and looked toward the parking lot. Down toward the end, where the last cars had parked, she saw a car pulling away. Joshua stepped out on the porch.

"Cayce, have you seen Sophia? It's almost eleven."

"I've been looking for her. She came out this way with Monica. I hope that wasn't her I saw leaving. A car just pulled out down the road."

"That's strange. I know she wanted to be here when we hang the portrait. Oh, well, she'll just have to miss it. We need to get this over with. Come on inside." Joshua held the door open for Cayce.

The guests were all congregated at the bottom of the stairs. Mack was up on a short ladder ready to do the honors, while Tom held the portrait.

"Go ahead, Mack. Hang her up." Joshua yelled up the stairs.

Harri moved beside Cayce, and they both noticed Sherone with her pouch open. She was sprinkling something in the room, probably the same potion she had used in Affie's cabin. Harri was rubbing her arms like she had a chill, and Cayce was watching the door, hoping Sophia would walk through it.

Tom handed the portrait to Mack, who leaned to put it on the wall but was having trouble reaching the hook. He climbed up one more rung on the ladder and reached again, stretching his arms while balancing precariously. Tom locked his feet and legs against the ladder as Mack went higher. Just as he almost had it hooked, special effects began.

The lights flickered, reminding Cayce and Harri of the lamp in Affie's cabin. Joshua moved over and put his arm around Cayce's waist. The lights flickered several more times, fast like they were angry, and then they went out.

Guests screamed, afraid to move in the dark. Even the dim hall lights on the second floor went out, and they had backup batteries. Joshua heard a thud on the stairs, and when he heard a man moan, he ran up blindly. He caught Mack on the landing between the sets of stairs.

"Somebody get a flashlight! Tom, are you up there?" There was only silence and darkness above.

The lights flickered again and came on. Mack's head was bleeding, but he was conscious. Tom was trying to get up from the floor at the top of the stairs. Cayce ran up to take care of Mack so Joshua could see to Tom.

"What happened?" Mack asked as he sat up, groggy from his fall. Cayce yelled for Harri to bring her a wet cloth.

Upstairs, Tom stood but held on to Joshua.

"I don't know what happened, Joshua. One second I was holding the ladder and the next I was on the floor like somebody had knocked me down." Tom searched the area and then looked down the stairs. "Is Mack all right?"

"He's got a bump and a cut on his head, but he's conscious." Joshua had Tom sit on the top step and turned to see if he could figure out what happened. The ladder had fallen over and the portrait lay face down on the floor. Joshua picked the portrait up and leaned it against the wall.

"Well, would you look at that! Damn!" The portrait had been slashed diagonally from the two upper corners, crisscrossing Beatrice's bosoms—exactly as it had been when they found it six months earlier.

Rodney called 911, and within minutes the paramedics arrived. Mack went in the ambulance to get checked out but assured Joshua he would be back in a few minutes. Tom said he was okay and refused to go. Mack told them he'd almost had the portrait hung when the lights started flickering. When they went out, something like a big wind knocked him off the ladder, and he and Tom both went down. Mack fell, dropping the portrait in the process, and rolled down the first part of the stairs, stopped by Joshua on the landing. He apologized to Joshua, thinking he had somehow cut the portrait when he dropped it, but Joshua assured him it was not his fault.

The guests were visibly shaken, and a few decided to leave early, going to their rooms or back to their homes or other hotels. Andre was furious because he now had to do something with a ton of leftover food. One thing he did not have to put away was the Citron Delight Cake. The cake had disappeared from the table.

Cayce and Harri walked out on the side porch to get some air and found Sherone sitting in a rocker, staring toward the quarters.

"It has started. The portals are open." She pointed to Milla's cabin. Through the window, Harri saw a lamp burning low, and hanging from the rafter was the silhouette of Milla's limp body.

Harri reached for Cayce, but she was walking toward the old kitchen. Harri knew her sister was going back in time and called to her. Sherone told Harri to let her sister go.

As Cayce continued her path to the kitchen, Sherone trailed behind her with her arms outstretched, chanting something Harri could not understand. Cayce took off the long gloves and dropped them on the ground as she walked trance-like to the murder scene. Harri was frantic and ran back into the mansion to get Joshua.

Before she reached him, the whole plantation was shrouded in dark fog as the lights once again went out.

Chapter Fifteen

Sophia hated to leave the ball, but Monica didn't know where Sherone's cabin was and begged her to take her to it. Sophia had watched Monica all night and couldn't stand seeing her sad expression any longer. When she told Monica she thought she had seen Shelly with Sherone earlier that night, Monica was overwhelmed. She said it was like someone you love rising from the grave. Sophia decided the reunion of the sisters was more important than Beatrice's portrait and left the ball to take Monica to her sister. Before leaving, Sophia told Rodney to tell her dad she was going to Sherone's. She hoped Rodney would remember.

Sophia went the back way to Sherone's cabin, so they would not have so far to walk in their long, awkward gowns.

"It's just a few minutes' walk from here, but the path is narrow. You might want to leave your purse in the car, since you're going to need both hands to hold your gown up."

"I'll just put the strap around my neck. A few minutes of walking is a small price to pay to know your sister is alive."

"I just hope you're not disappointed. It certainly looked like Shelly, but I did go by pretty fast. I don't know why she would be with Sherone. Shelly hardly knew Sherone."

As they reached the shed in Sherone's backyard, Sophia heard a terrible sound coming from the swamp. Monica moved beside Sophia and looked into the woods.

"What was that? It sounded like a woman screaming."

"Dad says there's a panther in the swamp, and they're known to sound like a woman screaming. I know I'm not going in there to find out."

A light was burning in Sherone's cabin, and Sophia could see Jaleel sitting on the sofa reading. Sophia knocked on the door, and Jaleel answered, looking surprised to see anyone visiting so late.

"You're Sophia, Joshua's daughter, right?" Jaleel smiled but looked uneasy.

"Yes, I know it's late, but could we come in? It's really important." Jaleel hesitated, glancing back into the cabin. Sophia noticed the light in the loft go off and was sure Monica had seen it, too.

"Of course, come in. Is the ball over already? Sherone hasn't made it home yet." Jaleel directed them to sit at the table on the opposite side from the sofa and the loft.

"Jaleel, this is Monica Pearson, Shelly Winthrop's sister. She's been working here ever since Shelly disappeared and has been trying to find out what happened to her."

"I'm afraid I don't know Shelly Winthrop. Could I offer you some iced tea or lemonade?" Jaleel got up and headed to the kitchen but was stopped by the sound of Monica's voice.

"You can stop the charade. I know she's here."

Sophia got out of her seat and moved to Jaleel

when she saw Monica pointing a revolver at them. "Monica, what are you doing? Don't you want Jaleel to help you find your sister?"

Jaleel took Sophia by the arm and pulled her behind her. "What do you want? I told you I don't know Shelly Winthrop."

Monica walked to the stairs leading to the loft, never taking her eyes off Sophia and Jaleel.

"Unless you want your friends to meet the same fate as your boyfriend, you better come down. Now!" Monica yelled up to the loft.

Shelly descended the stairs, holding to the wall and looking terrified.

"That's better. Now join your friends, where I can keep my eye on all of you at once."

"I don't understand what's happening. Why are you doing this?" Sophia looked at Shelly and Jaleel for answers.

Shelly spoke up. "She's not my sister, Sophia. I don't know who she is. Buddy wouldn't tell me who hired him to find the necklace and steal all those pieces, but I suspect she's a thief and a murderer."

"Shelly's sister just got back from a missionary trip to Honduras." Jaleel took over the true explanation. "She's coming for her sister tomorrow. Shelly has been with me in New Orleans, hiding from whoever caused Buddy's death."

"Why did you kill Buddy, Monica?" Sophia looked deep into Monica's eyes. "He was just a young guy trying to make enough money so he and Shelly could get married."

"You are so naïve, Sophia. Buddy was an amateur, a wannabe, who turned greedy and took something that is mine. I told him I'd give him twenty thousand dollars if he could find the necklace, but after he found it, he turned greedy and demanded a hundred thousand. Then he decided he'd keep it for himself, a stupid move. I'm the treasure hunter who found out about the missing La Fleur from the Bruser family who lived in France in the 1700s. I'm the one who researched and dug until I discovered Jean Paul Broussard, Broussard being a derivation of the name Bruser, and followed the history of La Fleur to the last place it was hidden, Spanish Oaks Plantation, and the last person who knew where it was, Princeton Broussard. And I'm the one who will have it in the end. I know Buddy didn't have it when he died. The men I hired to convince him to turn it over to me searched the car before they left him, the night he wrecked trying to outrun them. But your purse was in the car, Shelly, and that means you have it. And you are going to get it for me if you want to live."

"I don't have the necklace. If I did, you'd kill me anyway, so what good would it do to give it to you?"

"Shelly is telling the truth, Monica. She's been with me for almost three months. I'd know if she had the necklace." Jaleel moved between the two young women, trying to protect Shelly and Sophia.

"The necklace—you mean The Flower, the necklace Beatrice wore in the portrait? Is that what this is about? You killed Buddy for just a piece of jewelry?" Sophia was frightened but was also angry at the magnitude of Monica's greed.

"Are the Crown Jewels just jewelry? I think not. Sophia, come over here. Perhaps you can help me persuade your friend." Sophia's eyes filled with terror as she looked at Shelly for help. As she began walking toward Monica, Shelly reached out and pulled her back.

"Wait! I don't have the necklace, but I know where it is."

"Go on." Monica moved closer and sat in a chair, totally at ease and in control.

"The night we were being chased, Buddy made me get out and take the necklace. I was to hide in the woods until he came back for me, but he never made it back, thanks to you. I ran into the woods, but it turned into swamp, and I got lost. I was terrified and thought I saw a man, but he wouldn't help me. He just laughed and rode away on his horse. I tried to catch up with him, and I got stuck in quicksand. I threw the strap of the bag containing the necklace over a cypress knee that stood in the middle of the quicksand and tried to pull myself out. I started to panic and fought it, and kept sinking and sinking until I had to let go. The more I fought, the faster I sank until I was all the way under. I thought I would suffocate, but a hand reached in and pulled me out. I don't know who he was or how he reached me, but he was a big African-American man. He pointed, and I dragged myself out of the swamp in the direction he showed me and ended up in Mama Tee's yard. Mama Tee and Jaleel saved me. The necklace is still in the middle of the quicksand, hanging on that cypress knee, unless someone found it, and I doubt anyone has been in there."

"You expect me to believe that fairy tale?" Monica raised her voice in anger.

"My dad found Shelly's sweatshirt in the swamp, but he didn't know it was hers until I told him, and I know Dad doesn't have the necklace." Sophia emphasized the word "know."

Monica sat silent for a few minutes and then gave them a sadistic smile.

"Then you two will find it. You!" Monica stood and motioned to Jaleel with her gun. "Get clothes for Sophia and me, something a little more suitable for exploring in a swamp at night. You two come over here by me. If you try anything funny, Jaleel, I'll shoot these two, starting with Sophia." She cocked the revolver and pointed the gun at Sophia.

****

Cayce heard a scream and heard Affie crying, "My baby, my baby! Get de Massa! Quick!" In her subconscious, she knew Caleb had taken the news of Milla's suicide to his mother. Without looking back to the slave quarters, Cayce continued to walk, letting the Way lead her through the fog. Soon, she saw Caleb run past her without seeing her. Caleb stopped at the door to the kitchen, where loud voices could be heard coming from inside—voices of a man and a woman. Cayce watched as Caleb stopped, concealing himself under the window to listen.

Cayce reached the kitchen door next but did not stop. The door opened on its own, not giving her subconscious a chance to reconsider. Stopping in the doorway, Cayce found herself enveloped by fog as loud voices echoed off the brick walls.

****

"So you're leaving me, going with that bastard Fairchild? You were just going to leave word in a note, like the cowardess you are?" Princeton threw the note onto the table, on top of the cookbook Affie had used to prepare his birthday feast.

"Yes! Don't act as if you care, Princeton. You

proved how much you hate me when you destroyed my portrait because of a necklace that rightfully should be mine, a necklace not even your friends knew you possessed. You only care for your whore Milla. Well, now you can have her, and I'll have a real man, a man who will love me and take me to bed and treat me like a wife! I loathe you!" Beatrice stepped toward Princeton and raised her hand to slap him, but he grabbed her hand and pushed her against the table.

"You'll not go with Fairchild! You'll stay here and care for the pitiful child you bore."

"Pitiful child? Is that what you think of Lily? I suppose you would rather it were Lily stolen, and your bastard Chloe still be here to harbor all your attention. Well, you won't have Lily, and you will never have Chloe. She is dead! Do you hear me? Dead!"

"What do you mean? You're hysterical and playing the part of the cunning witch you play so well. You don't know what happened to Chloe any more than I do." Princeton propped on the table, distraught at the thought of losing Chloe forever.

"I gave her to Rathbone, and she is dead. You'll never see her again. Your bastard child is dead. I saw her die, and I am glad!"

Princeton started toward Beatrice with hatred and anger in his eyes, but the sound of a horse galloping away broke his spell.

"Fairchild! I'll see him in hell before this night is over."

Princeton took his pistol from the mantel and stormed out the back door. Seconds later, his horse was heard galloping after Fairchild's. Beatrice walked to the fireplace and put one hand on the mantel and the other to her heart, leaning as if she would faint.

Cayce watched as Caleb stole in through the door, stopping by the table. His face was distorted. Hot tears of rage boiled in his eyes, staring straight and hard at his master's wife. He looked to the table at his left and saw the butcher knife. Picking it up, he moved toward the woman who was responsible for the deaths of his niece and now his sister. As she turned and saw Caleb with the knife in his hand, her eyes glazed over in terror and she began backing away.

She stood with her back to the fireplace and opened her mouth to scream, but the strong young man was too quick as he plunged the knife deep into the belly of the woman he despised. Beatrice staggered toward the door and fell onto the table, holding her wound as if trying to stop the flow of blood. But it was useless, as the deep wound gushed blood, drowning her in death. She lay on the floor, her hair tumbled over her face and her other hand held to the necklace she would never enjoy.

Caleb backed away, staring at the horror he had created. Realizing he had killed another human being, the usually gentle young man began sobbing. Seeing the bloody knife in his hand, he threw it on the table, knocking over a pitcher of milk. He stood frozen in his steps, wanting to run but unable.

Cayce wanted to comfort Caleb. He had killed out of desperation and revenge for an even greater crime, the murder of a helpless, sweet child, but she knew it was not her place in time. She could only watch and remember. The door opened behind her, and a big black man entered. He looked at Beatrice lying in her own blood and then looked at his son. Caleb, sobbing, told his father what he'd heard and confessed to the crime he had just committed. Big Zed held his son in his arms, consoling him and trying to think of what to do. He released Caleb but held on to his shoulders, making him look him in the eyes.

"You must never tell yo mama. You hear me, Caleb? It would kill her to see you hang for dis. Dat a bad woman. She kill Chloe and she cause yo sista to kill herself, but de white man court won't see yo side. Dis devil woman get what good nuff for her. Wash yo'self and go take care of yo mama. I take care of dis."

Caleb did as his father told him and left the kitchen. His mother would never know the depth of her son's grieving because he would not tell her Chloe was dead. Nor would she ever know of the guilt he would carry for taking a life, even the life of one who deserved to die.

After Caleb left, Big Zed took the necklace from Beatrice's neck and put it in his shirt. He would hide it where no one would ever find it. Massa Princeton would find his wife lying dead and think someone killed her for the necklace. Big Zed left the kitchen, closing the door behind him, and disappeared into the fog.

****

The kitchen dissolved into the mist as it had done the first time Cayce was there. She could feel herself falling into the thick mass as the darkness swallowed her.

"Cayce! Cayce!" Joshua called, frantic to make sure she was all right. "Get me some water, Harri!"

Cayce opened her eyes and saw Joshua staring down into her face. He was sitting on the stone floor of the old kitchen with his back propped against one of the wooden barrels and was holding her head in his arms like he had done that day at the lily pond. She smiled at him, and he returned her smile, pulling her to him as he hugged her tight.

"Are you okay?" He helped her to sit up.

"Yes, I'm fine. Help me up." Joshua held on to her as she stood, while Harri came running up with a glass of water and handed it to her sister.

"Let me stop shaking, Cayce, before you tell me what happened. And for gosh sakes, let's get out of this spooky old kitchen."

When they got outside, the lights were back on and guests were strolling the grounds or sitting on the porch drinking wine and mint julep while the band continued to play in the ballroom.

And the world of Spanish Oaks was about to know who killed Beatrice.

****

Joshua sent Harri upstairs to pack bags for the night for herself and Cayce. He was not about to leave them at the inn. Cayce had given him a real fright, but even after the vision, she did not scare the hell out of him. In fact, she intrigued him more than ever. She had become important to him in a short period of time, and he wanted to protect her.

Joshua left Rodney and Andre in charge of shutting down for the night and piled Cayce and Harri and their yards of taffeta and hoops into the Jeep to take them to his cabin. Sherone disappeared as soon as she knew the portals had closed again, and Sophia had still not returned.

Before leaving, Joshua left his daughter a message with Rodney, telling her to come to the cabin. It was then Rodney remembered the message Sophia had left for her dad. Joshua drove the Jeep too fast, angry and concerned his daughter had left the grounds without telling him.

"Sophia went to Sherone's house for some strange reason. I'm going to call her on her cell phone and give her what-for for leaving the ball early. It's just not like her to act so irresponsibly." Joshua had a hard time shifting gears with an ocean of taffeta and hoops smothering his gearshift, but he managed to get them on the road and dial Sophia at the same time. He let it ring several times before hanging up. He decided to try again when they got to the cabin. Right now he had to fight a hoop skirt for control of the steering wheel.

****

Jaleel heard the cell phone ringing but couldn't get to it. Monica had bound Jaleel's hands and feet with duct tape and put tape over her mouth before dragging her into a closet and leaving her there, with a chair propped under the doorknob of the closed door. Jaleel felt so useless and could only imagine the ordeal the two young women were going through in the swamp. As she twisted her hands trying to get free, she smelled it—Gas fumes were coming under the closet door, and she knew Monica had turned the burners on the heater and the kitchen stove wide open before leaving. Her only hope was that Sherone would show up soon.

Sherone drove her usual fifteen miles per hour as she headed down the gravel road, but when she rounded the big curve, she saw him and knew something was wrong.

The panther stood on a pile of brush at the edge of the swamp as if waiting for her. She stopped beside the animal and rolled down her window. The panther's red eyes met hers, and they talked their talk, the talk of mojo and secret pacts, curses, and transformations. He raised his head and screamed, and she knew she had to hurry.

Sherone stomped the accelerator like a NASCAR driver and turned into her parking spot, slamming on the brakes without first slowing down. Leaping out of the van, she ran to the cabin. The lights were off, but she sensed all was not well inside. As she opened the door, she smelled the gas fumes. Covering her mouth with the tail of her dress, she rushed into the cabin, turned off the gas, and threw open windows and the back door. It was then she heard the banging on the closet door.

****

Harri sat on the porch, waiting for Joshua and Cayce to come back from the barn. Joshua had said they needed to check on the horses, but Harri had a sneaky suspicion he just wanted to be alone with her sister. He'd left his cell phone with Harri just in case Sophia called, and Harri had orders to tell Sophia to get to the cabin tonight.

Harri could hear Cayce laughing and was proud her sister had met Joshua. He was a good, decent man who was not frightened by Cayce's psychic gift. Harri wasn't in the market at the moment but wondered if she'd ever find anyone as good as Stan. Surprisingly, her night with Don had not been that bad, but she'd kept her distance, thinking about the money and wondering if Don was playing a part in the robberies.

Harri was just about to go in and get the gown and lace-up shoes off when Joshua's cell phone rang. It was

Sherone, and she was hysterical.

"They're in the swamp...with Monica?" Harri repeated everything Sherone said to make sure she was understanding Sherone's thick Caribbean accent. "Oh, my god! I'll get Joshua! I'll tell him right now and call you back!"

Harri pulled the hoopskirt up as high as she could get it and started running to the barn, screaming for Joshua. Joshua and Cayce heard her scream and ran to meet her. Harri was panting by the time she got to them but was able to relay Sherone's message.

"It's Monica! She's the thief! Shelly's alive, and Monica has taken Sophia and Shelly into the swamp! She said something about quicksand!"

"Slow down, Harri! Tell me exactly what Sherone said." Joshua held to Harri, helping her to catch her breath.

"Okay! I remember now! Shelly left the necklace in the swamp the night Buddy died. She was caught in quicksand and left the necklace there! You've got to get them, Joshua! Hurry! Monica has a gun!"

Joshua took off running back to the barn with his long-tailed coat flapping behind him. Cayce was right behind him. As she ran, she began ripping off her taffeta gown and hoopskirt, so that by the time Joshua had the horses out and bridled, she was down to pantaloons, camisole, and red boots.

"No time for saddles. Can you ride bareback?" Joshua was too anxious to even notice Cayce's attire.

Cayce answered Joshua's question by grabbing Dakota's mane and doing a pony express, leaping onto the horse's back as it began to move. Together they galloped toward the swamp.

****

Sophia and Shelly trudged through the black water with Monica prodding them on with the butt of her gun. When one of them fell, she made the other one help her up. Monica held the gun in one hand and a flashlight in the other and kept a stream of light ahead of Shelly, who led the way.

Sophia couldn't help but think about the alligators and snakes all around them just waiting for the opportunity to strike. She hoped the creatures would get Monica first. *One good 'gator bite for the thief and I'm an animal activist for life!*

****

Shelly could only think about the quicksand and would take her chances with the creatures any day over that. She remembered her last gasp of breath and how she knew her lungs were going to explode as she sank into the petrifying darkness. Then the big hand reached through the mire and grabbed her by the hair. She had managed to get her hand up, and he grabbed it, pulling her to safety. She could still see him smiling at her but not saying a word. He was a giant of a man, dressed in old worn clothes, but he looked like a guardian angel. She'd used swamp water to wash enough of the grime off her face so she could see the path he was showing her. Half walking, half dragging her exhausted body, she followed her instincts and remembered how to pray.

She remembered passing a pond surrounded by yellow lilies and stopping to wash more of the quicksand off her face and hands. A few minutes later she was in Mama Tee's yard. She didn't remember calling for help, but Mama Tee was there in seconds. The next thing she remembered was waking up in

Mama Tee's bed, washed clean of the swamp gore and dressed in Mama Tee's flannel gown.

****

"How much farther? You better not be taking us on a wild goose chase." Monica nudged Sophia hard, pushing her into Shelly and making them both fall into the murky water.

"I don't know." Shelly got to her feet and helped Sophia up. "We have to see the lilies before we get to the quicksand."

"Lilies? Are you crazy? This is a swamp, not Botanical Gardens!" Monica screamed at Shelly.

"She's telling the truth, Monica. I've only been in here once, but my dad showed me a large patch of yellow daylilies. It's not far in. We should be getting close."

Monica shined the flashlight up ahead and saw a reflection of yellow. "Well, I'll be damned! Maybe you'll get to live after all."

Shelly led the group around the lily patch and stepped into deeper stagnant water, cringing with every difficult step. The flashlight was not reassuring, considering it was in the hands of a murderer. Shelly knew the quicksand was not too much farther and only wished she and Sophia could talk so they could come up with a plan of escape.

****

Joshua rode like a madman until Cayce made him slow down.

"You won't do her any good if you kill yourself before you get to her. Pick your trail. Think, Joshua. They're coming from Sherone's house, so what is the route you think they'll follow?"

Joshua slowed down and looked at Cayce. The moonlight was bright at the moment, and he could see the tension on her face.

"You're right. I've got to think how we would get to the lily patch from here. I've seen a forestry map of this area. I just need to get it in my mind."

Joshua's thinking was interrupted by the scream of the panther off to the left. In the moonlight, Cayce saw the animal leap from a tree and head off into the woods, but as its feet hit the ground, it changed into a large black man. She knew Zed was visible only to her and did not tell Joshua.

"This way, Joshua. Follow the panther."

Joshua knew better than to second-guess Cayce. Her instincts had proven true so far. Besides, he knew no alternate routes.

****

The three stood looking at the large area of quicksand. Monica shined the flashlight around in it and saw the cypress knee in the middle. A leather strap could be seen around the knee, but the pouch was hidden in the quicksand, concealed by fallen branches.

"Is there another way to get to that cypress knee, maybe a path that doesn't go through the quicksand?" Monica directed the question to Shelly.

"I don't know. I only know I was in it right there, a few feet from the cypress knee."

"Well, then, Shelly. You put it there, and you will get it out." Shelly shook her head as Monica nudged the girl toward the quicksand.

"No! I won't go back in there! I won't! You can just go ahead and shoot me!"

"Oh, you won't? Then I'll just shoot your friend

first." Monica put the gun to Sophia's head, and Sophia closed her eyes tight.

"No, don't! Please!"

Monica moved the gun. "Sophia, grab that log over there and drag it over." Monica yelled her order, and Shelly helped Sophia drag the log.

"Now lay it across the quicksand and see if it will reach to the cypress knee." The girls did as they were told, and the log reached.

"Okay, Shelly. Hold on to the log and start across. Take slow steps and don't panic and you won't sink. Drowning in quicksand is a myth, for movies and stupid girls who kick their feet and flail their arms."

"Don't let me go under, Sophia! Please!" Shelly's face tightened with fear.

"I won't, Shelly. I promise. Just keep your left hand on the log and don't panic."

Shelly stepped into the sand and water that would change to quicksand with the weight of the intruder. She was crying as she moved farther away from solid ground and could feel herself sinking with each step.

"Just a little farther, Shelly. You're doing fine." Sophia spoke softly and tried to calm Shelly but knew if she were the one out there she'd be terrified.

When Shelly got within a few inches of the cypress knee, she sank to her waist and began to panic.

"Stop, Shelly! Stop moving now!" Sophia yelled to get Shelly's attention.

Shelly froze as Sophia yelled at her and willed herself to look up at the stars and the moon. In her mind she was praying. Slowly, she began to move toward the knee again, moving forward an inch or two at a time.

"Get the bag, Shelly, and quit your whimpering.

The sooner you get it, the sooner you can get out," Monica screamed at the girl, and Shelly continued praying and proceeding forward one inch at a time.

"Keep holding to the log, Shelly. You're almost there." Sophia spoke in a low tone, trying to keep Shelly calm.

"You won't let go of the log, will you, Sophia?"

"No, Shelly. I won't let go. I promise you."

Shelly moved another tiny distance and sank to her chest, but she managed to grab the bag. Holding on to the log with her left arm and pulling with the strap, she pulled herself out of the quicksand enough to reach the cypress knee. She kept a death grip on it as she worked the strap of the bag over and off. After securing the bag by hanging it around her neck, she started back across the swamp. The distance seemed twice as far as it had been on the way to the cypress. She glanced toward the bank and saw Monica pacing, with her gun pointed at Sophia. The thief was frantic to get her hands on the bag.

"Hold on to the damn log with both hands, Shelly. Sophia is going to pull you to the bank." Shelly held tight, and Sophia pulled hard, inching her over until she could reach her by stretching out her hand.

"Give Sophia the bag." Monica pointed the gun at Shelly.

"No. Get me to the bank first." Shelly shook her head in refusal.

"Hand Sophia the bag or I'll shoot her right now." Again Monica cocked the revolver and pointed it at Sophia. Shelly pulled the strap over her head and stretched her arm out to Sophia. Sophia had to lie on her stomach and reach far out to get it. Once she had it in her hands, she stood up.

"Now, open the bag and show me the necklace." Monica was anxious to get her hands on the prize she'd sought.

Sophia opened the bag and brought out the heavy emerald-and-diamond heirloom. Just holding it in her hands made her feel sick. Two people had died because of it, or because of coveting it.

"Now throw the bag to me." Monica was smiling an evil smile, and Sophia knew she had no choice but to do as she was told, but she also knew she and Shelly were not going to leave the swamp alive. Sophia made a quick decision. When Monica put the bag over her head, Sophia would rush her and try to get the gun away from her. She took a quick glance at Shelly and saw she was being still and holding on to the log, and then she threw the bag to Monica, making it fall short so she would have to move closer.

Monica walked toward the bag, and Sophia could feel her adrenaline rising. As Monica put the strap over her head, Sophia charged, throwing herself into the woman, knocking her down, and causing the gun to go off, but Sophia was unable to take it away from her. Sophia was strong, but Monica was stronger, and she rolled the girl over, pinning her to the ground. Sophia reached beside her and found a rock and wrapped her fingers around it. Using all the strength she could muster, Sophia brought her right arm up and hit Monica across the face. Monica rolled to the side and Sophia got to her feet, but it was all for nothing. Monica sat on the ground, holding the gun pointed at Sophia.

"That was a stupid thing to do. Not that I would let you live anyway, but I'll feel not even the least bit of guilt now." Monica cocked the revolver.

"You don't have a conscience, Monica, or you couldn't have killed Buddy." Sophia saw movement behind Monica. Something that looked like the creature from the muddy lagoon was crawling from the quicksand onto the bank. Sophia knew she had to keep Monica talking to distract her.

"How did you know about the jewel? You said you came to Spanish Oaks looking for it."

"I'm a librarian, Sophia. I have the world at the tip of my fingers and a genius for finding lost treasures. La Fleur is not the first priceless jewel I've taken. Don't you remember me? Dark hair and ugly black-rimmed glasses? Who would think such a frump could be such a master at, shall we say, *borrowing* valuables from the wealthy? I saw you look down your nose at me when I first came to Spanish Oaks eight months ago, but now you're looking down the barrel of my gun, a gun that is going to end your spoiled young life."

"You'll be caught, Monica. I'm sure my dad is looking for me as we speak. You'll never get away with this."

"Oh, I'll get away. My private plane is waiting for me in New Orleans. By tomorrow I'll be at my little island paradise, taking bids on this new treasure. I am beyond the law, Sophia, the master of the game. And there will be no one to tell where I've gone. But enough talk. It's time for me to get out of this hell hole and leave you two for a 'gator feast."

Monica stretched her arm out and aimed the gun at Sophia, but before she got a chance to pull the trigger, the mud monster waylaid the criminal with a short piece of log, knocking her into the quicksand, her gun flying out of her hand. Monica did a belly flop, landing face down, and forgot her own instructions, flailing her arms and legs, causing her to sink rapidly into the quicksand. Sophia hugged Shelly, mud and all, as they stood on solid ground watching and listening as Monica tried to hold her face out of the quicksand while begging for help.

Shelly and Sophia heard the sound of horses, and Shelly was terrified, thinking it was the man on the black horse, with the long-tailed coat and the laugh of the devil. Instead, she laughed as she saw a man with a long-tailed coat riding bareback on a palomino. With him was a buckskin horse carrying a woman dressed in a camisole, pantaloons, and red cowboy boots. As they reached the girls, Joshua jumped from his horse and ran to his daughter to grab her in a bear hug.

"Sophia, are you all right? We heard a gunshot!"

"I'm fine, Dad, but the next time Shelly asks me to come out and play, I'm saying no."

Sophia pointed to the quicksand just as Monica's head went under. Her arms and feet were barely visible above the quicksand. Sophia walked to the edge and yelled to Monica, "Monica, stop fighting and flip over."

Monica did as she was told and gasped for a breath of air as her mud-caked face resurfaced.

"Now lay your head back, stretch out your legs, and relax. You'll float. Quicksand is just like water but thicker. You'd think a genius would know that. When you have some free time in the prison library, Google quicksand. It's amazing what you can learn with the world at the tip of your fingers. Of course, in prison that's the only way you'll have access to the world."

Chapter Sixteen

The next morning, Joshua drove Sophia, Cayce, and Harri back to Spanish Oaks for brunch. Joshua looked across the gearshift of the Jeep at Cayce and began to chuckle.

"You look good this morning, Cayce, in those tight jeans, but I liked that outfit you put together last night even better." Cayce gave Joshua her aggravated look but changed to a smile when he put his hand on her knee and squeezed it, leaving it there for the remainder of the trip. From the back seat, Sophia hooted, and Harri snorted out of control.

As they drove up, a large group had already formed. Joshua saw a tense Andre issuing orders to his staff as customers chose from five different buffet lines. Sophia immediately went behind the serving line and got herself a white jacket to act as hostess and give out the special menus for the brunch spread on long tables.

"We're not fighting the lines." Joshua took control. "I'll get you each a menu and you can mark what you want. I'll get one of the staff to fix our plates and bring it to us. Find us a spot to eat."

Tables with white cloths were set up on the porches and grounds, and people were free to eat their meals wherever they wanted. Cayce and Harri took a table under one of the magnolias in the yard so they could soak in the view. To the side of the quarters, a bulldozer waited to be able to make its grand entry later that afternoon. Parked in front of the mansion were two sheriff's patrol cars with deputies leaning against them.

When Joshua returned with the menus, Cayce pointed at the deputies.

"Are you expecting more trouble, Joshua?"

"We still don't know who the dealer is, although I think we got the more dangerous element of the duo. I asked the sheriff to send the deputies in case there's trouble. I'll be surprised if my good friend Don is not the next one to ride in a sheriff's vehicle." Joshua handed Cayce and Harri each a menu.

"Maybe he's not. He certainly didn't act like a criminal last night. I was never uneasy with him, except when he got a little carried away doing the dirty dog." Harri turned her attention to her menu.

"Good lord! This is not a brunch. It's a feast! Take a look at this, Cayce!"

"And you'll find every item on it is delicious. I'm lucky Andre hasn't been snapped up by some fancy restaurant that can pay a lot more than Spanish Oaks can, but he seems content." The three continued to look at the menu, trying to make up their minds:

Spanish Oaks Plantation
Brunch Menu
BREAKFAST TABLE
HEAVENLY OMELETTES with bacon, green onions,
mushrooms, peppers, and cheese
INDIVIDUAL ROUNDS OF HASHBROWNS topped
with thin sliced smoked ham, and a poached egg,
smothered in cheese sauce
BELGIAN WAFFLES served with whipped butter and
warm Vermont maple syrup

CHEESE GRITS
AMBROSIA, layers of fresh fruits, coconut and pecans
~
SOUTHERN COMFORT TABLE
MUSTARD GREENS with ham hocks
BLACKEYED PEAS with diced onion
FRIED GREEN TOMATOES
SUGARY CANDIED SWEET POTATOES
MACARONI AND CHEESE made with four cheeses
SOUTHERN FRIED CHICKEN
fried crispy and golden brown
SPIRAL-CUT HAM
with a brown-sugar-and-bourbon glaze
~
BREAD TABLE
FLAKY BUTTERMILK BISCUITS
YEAST ROLLS
VARIETY OF HOMEMADE MUFFINS
SOUTHERN STYLE CORNBREAD, no sugar added
~
DESSERT TABLE
BREAD PUDDING WITH JACK DANIELS SAUCE
FRESH SIX-LAYER COCONUT CAKE
with lemon curd filling
CHOCOLATE PECAN PIE
SWEET POTATO PIE
~
BEVERAGE BAR
COFFEE
TEA, hot or iced
MILK
BLOODY MARY
MIMOSA

In minutes, the three were munching away on some of the best food they had ever eaten. Joshua was so busy eating he didn't notice Don approaching the table. After the ordeal of the night before, Joshua had hoped not to have to confront him first thing on Saturday morning.

Harri was first to see him. "Uh, oh! Are you ready for a repeat of last night? Don is heading this way."

Joshua turned and saw him coming to their table, plate in hand.

"Do you mind if I join ya'll?" Don asked in his charming southern accent that was not so charming this morning.

Joshua motioned to the empty chair at the table. He took his time trying to figure out what he was going to say. After Don exchanged greetings with Cayce and Harri, Joshua dove right in, figuring there was no reason to delay.

"We caught the thief last night. Or do you already know about it?"

Don looked up from his plate with surprise.

"Really? How did you do that? I didn't hear any sirens or commotion—that is, after the commotion with the portrait."

"You want to know *how* I found out rather than *who* it was? That's a little strange." Joshua raised his voice, staring at Don, thinking his one-time friend and confidante already knew who it was so there was no reason to ask. Don put his fork down and stared at Joshua.

"Of course I want to know who the thief is, but I figured in telling how you found out, you'd identify him. Is something wrong, Joshua? You seem a little annoyed this morning."

"Him? Identify *him*? You know damn well the thief is not a him but a her!"

"A woman? How on God's green earth would I know the thief is a woman? What the hell is wrong with you, Joshua? Did I miss something here?" Don looked at Harri and Cayce as if they might explain Joshua's actions.

Joshua looked at Harri and nodded his head. She opened her purse and handed him something under the table.

"I think you know a lot about the burglaries, Don. Why else would you hide a stack of money like this in the ceiling of your closet? Can you explain this? And don't try to say you didn't know it was there." Joshua held up the stack of bills and shuffled through them almost in Don's face. Don scooted his chair back.

"You think I had something to do with the robberies? You know me better than that, Joshua, or I thought you did."

"I would like nothing better than to believe that, but this money says otherwise. How do you explain it, Don?" Joshua looked furious. Don sat with his head in his hands as if trying to think what to say.

"Joshua, I wish I could explain that to you, but I can't right now. You need to trust me for a little while longer. Can you do that?"

"What? And give you time to take your stash and leave? I don't think so." Joshua laughed sarcastically.

"I'm not going anywhere, Joshua. We have your account to go over this afternoon, remember?"

"You won't be going over any of my business ever again, Don. As of this moment, your services are no longer needed. And don't think you can run away and hide. When I get proof from the sheriff, I'll see your ass in jail." Joshua stood like he was going to punch Don, but Cayce took hold of his arm and stopped him. Don stood, pushing his chair under the table.

"Joshua, I promise this will all make sense later. Give me another hour or two, and you'll see. Excuse me, ladies, but I believe I've lost my appetite." Don left the table and headed toward the mansion.

"I'm sorry, Harri, Cayce. I shouldn't have confronted him, but I couldn't help myself. The sheriff should be here any minute with a report for me. Hopefully, Linda identified the dealer. If it's Don, his ass will be the next one to ride in one of those cars sitting out front."

Joshua couldn't eat anything more after his confrontation with Don and excused himself, taking his coffee to his office.

"Cayce, do you have a feeling about Don, one way or another?" Harri put her fork down and looked at her sister.

"Not really. But I don't feel animosity, and that should be a natural emotion if I sensed he was involved, especially with a cruel person like Monica."

"I feel the same way. I just don't think my instincts would let me actually begin to like Don, in a friendly way that is, if he was a partner with someone who had caused a young man's death. I think there's more here than meets the senses."

"Oh, my gosh, Harri! Not changing the subject, but this bread pudding is to die for!"

"No, Citron Delight is to die for, if your name is Beatrice and you have a fondness for the color green and for older men. Speaking of the cake, I wonder how it disappeared? Did you happen to see it in the old kitchen last night, Cayce?"

"No, but I was a little distracted. Do you plan to make the cake again, Harri?"

"Of course. In fact, I'm meeting Andre later today to give him the recipe and explain to him the problem I had with the boiled icing. But I'm not telling him it makes wonderful pralines. I'm claiming that recipe and selling those babies to your man."

As Cayce and Harri finished up their dessert, they saw the Granthams sitting at a table nearby. Mrs. Grantham no longer needed her cane to walk, and the bruises on her face had turned a much lighter purple. Her husband had his plate piled so high it needed three-inch side-planks. When they finished, John Grantham helped his wife out of her chair. As they passed the sisters' table, Mrs. Grantham smiled and stopped. Her husband continued toward the mansion, not realizing his wife was not behind him.

"Congratulations on your winning entry, Mrs. Wellington. Have you enjoyed the Jacob and Victoria Suite?"

"Thank you, and yes, Mrs. Grantham, we have enjoyed it very much. You and your husband should stay in it sometimes. You would each have your own bed, but they would be big and oh, so soft." Harri smiled at Mrs. Grantham. Cayce was thinking it was time to confront the Granthams about seeing the wreck in Natchez.

"I'm glad to see you are recovering from your car accident. Were the hospital facilities in Natchez adequate? My sister and I really liked the little town and might even think in terms of buying there some day."

"Yes, the doctors and nurses were wonderful." John Grantham had retraced his steps and heard the tail end of the conversation.

"She said Natchez, dear, not New Orleans. Our accident was in New Orleans." Mrs. Grantham looked anxious as her husband took her arm and ushered her away. The sisters could tell he was angry with his wife.

"Well, now we know. Poor thing. I bet she gets a chewing out when he gets her inside. Quick thinking, Cayce."

When Cayce and Harri got inside, they saw Rodney at the desk.

"Congratulations, Ms. Wellington. Do you know yet when you would like to reserve the Jacob and Victoria Suite?"

"Thank you, Rodney, but I don't know yet. I'll have to call back."

Cayce and Harri ran into Mack at the top of the stairs, taking down the hook from the night before. Beatrice's portrait was being sent back to the museum to be restored again. Mack had a bandage on his forehead.

"How's the head, Mack?"

"I'm fine, Ms. McCallister. I was back here an hour after the ambulance took me to the emergency room. Tom's back at work, too. That was one scary night, huh?"

Cayce had started to answer when Mr. Grantham came out of his room. He had his car keys in his hand. Mack watched John Grantham descend the stairs and excused himself with Cayce in the middle of answering his question.

"Well, that was rude. He acted like he didn't give a rip about hearing your reply after he asked the question. Did he sound like a Yankee to you?"

"I think you've overdosed on Scarlett, Harri. Let's freshen up and head back down. I have a feeling something is about to break loose."

"You, too, Cayce? I've felt it ever since we drove up and got out of the Jeep."

A few minutes later, Cayce and Harri descended the stairs again to take a seat on the side porch, where they watched the deputies' cars and the grounds. When they were almost to the bottom step, Mack rushed past them, a tool kit in his hands. He looked intense and did not speak to Cayce or Harri.

"Let's go back inside. Something tells me…"

Cayce did not get to finish her sentence. John Grantham entered, carrying a large briefcase. He headed up the stairs without so much as a nod to Mack, who was filling in the hole left by the hook. After Grantham closed the door to his room, Don came out of Beatrice's room and stood at the door, looking down the hall at Mack. Mack took his radio off his belt and called someone, Don re-entered his room, and Mack headed to the door of Lily's room, where he stood with his ear to the door. What came next startled Cayce and Harri, who sat in the entry watching.

Two deputies burst through the front door, drew their revolvers, and headed up the stairs. When Mack saw them, he took out a revolver that had been concealed in his tool belt, and as soon as the deputies reached the top of the stairs, Mack kicked the door in and entered, with the deputies close behind.

"Freeze!"

The voice they heard was Mack's. They could hear John Grantham swearing but could only make out the profanity. Don came out of his room and stood in the hall. In a minute, one of the deputies entered his room also but without his gun drawn.

The front door opened, and this time Joshua burst through.

"What's going on, Rodney? You said on the radio two deputies headed upstairs?" Cayce and Harri walked over to Joshua and filled him in on what they had witnessed. In just a few minutes, one of the deputies escorted John Grantham down the stairs, handcuffed. Mrs. Grantham was not handcuffed but was being escorted by the other deputy. Don followed, last in line, with no handcuffs. He smiled when he saw Joshua, Cayce, and Harri at the bottom of the stairs.

"Look, Joshua. No handcuffs." Don held up his hands.

"Are you ready to tell me what the devil is going on, Don?"

"Come out on the porch, and I'll fill you in."

They sat on the porch away from curious ears, and Don explained what had just happened.

"John Grantham approached me at the end of February and said he had a large amount of cash he needed to be invested or diverted to overseas accounts. He offered to pay big for my services. Grantham also told me he would have additional funds that would be coming in once a month for the next few months. I suspected it was money obtained illegally and that Grantham was looking for an accountant to launder the money for him, so I went to the FBI. The FBI was very interested and had been watching the Granthams for some time. I agreed to help the FBI catch the Granthams and collected the money each month, taking it to the FBI, who set up false accounts and investments."

"And Mack is in on it too?" Joshua asked.

"Mack is an undercover FBI agent. He meant to keep the whole set-up going for a while longer, but I told him I couldn't keep it up, not after finding out about the burglaries. I was afraid the whole thing would come down around me, and I wanted this over. Mack contacted his supervisor, and today was pinpointed for the last transaction."

"I am so sorry, Don. I should have known you weren't a thief, but everything was happening so fast. Please accept my apology." Joshua held out his hand, and Don smiled and shook it. Then Don turned to Harri.

"If you looked up in that closet right now, Harri, you'd really find a stack of money; in fact, several stacks of thousand-dollar bills. I knew Grantham was bringing up another load and contacted Mack. And I believe you witnessed the rest."

"Did we ever! I thought for a minute those deputies were coming for you. I'm really glad it was the Granthams instead." Harri smiled at Don, and he returned the smile. Even his uni-brow seemed to separate, making him look less like a pirate and more like a hero.

"I hate Mrs. Grantham was part of this. She actually seemed like a sweet lady. I believe Mrs. Grantham was under the thumb of her husband and had no control over what he did."

"I think you're right, Cayce. Hopefully, the courts

will take that into consideration. But she did know what was going on. In fact, she often went to Natchez with her husband to pick up money to be laundered." Don looked at Cayce and Harri and shook his head. "It's a shame she's involved, though." Don turned his focus back to Joshua.

"Mack has a lot of questions, Joshua. The FBI needs to identify who was laundering his money before I got involved. They've been coming here for six months, so Mack will probably ask to see your guest records." Don excused himself, saying he would be expected to give a full report to Mack and his supervisor.

"So the Granthams were crooks, but John Grantham is not the dealer, and neither is Don. I wish the sheriff would hurry up and bring me that report." Joshua pondered the mystery aloud to Cayce and Harri.

"So what will you do with La Fleur now that you have it, Joshua?"

"Good question, Harri. For right now, it's in my safe in the office. I'm tempted to leave an armed guard with it. There is still so much we don't know. Like where did Buddy find it? We know Big Zed hid it, but Buddy wasn't the brightest coin in the fountain and had to have found it by accident. I've got Tom going back in his maintenance log to see what jobs Buddy was working on in the days before his death."

"Shelly didn't know where he found it?" Harri figured the boy would have told his girlfriend, since she knew he had it.

"All he told her was that he found it while he was doing a job." Joshua was ready to put this all behind him. He had a construction company to run and a plantation inn to get back on track, with a few more renovation projects in mind after the swimming pool was completed.

Joshua looked across the grounds as Tom came walking fast toward them, his logbook under his arm.

"I know what Buddy was doing, Joshua. He didn't work the day he died. I figure after he found the necklace he didn't think he needed to work for wages anymore, so he must have found it his last day at work. Look here in the log." Joshua looked at the page where Tom was pointing.

"Of course. That makes sense."

"Are you going to keep us in suspense all day?" Cayce was sitting on the edge of her chair, waiting to hear what Tom had found.

"Better than that. I'm going to show you, darling." Cayce didn't know if she should take the "darling" seriously or not, but she liked the sound of it.

Joshua stood and took Cayce by the hand. He started walking toward the quarters but went past them and began climbing the hill toward the family cemetery. He stopped in front of Princeton's grave. The tombstones had all been cleaned and the letters re-blacked so they could be read. Joshua squatted down to look at Princeton's headstone and began his disclosure.

"Back in March, two days before Buddy died, I had the graves of Princeton and Lily dug up and moved. It looked like there was a sinkhole or something, and the graves kept receding. The hill was eroding on that side, too. I was away at the time, so Tom was in charge. The only directions I gave him were to move the two graves to the flat spot on top of the hill and to make sure he put Lily between Princeton and Beatrice. Sherone was adamant this had to be done."

"So Sherone was okay with the move?" It was hard for Harri to believe Sherone approved of disturbing the dead.

"Yes. Surprising, isn't it? Then again, maybe she knew this was supposed to happen. She did her mumbo-jumbo thing and spread something on the graves before they were dug up."

"So you think Buddy found the necklace in one of the graves?" Cayce asked.

Tom spoke up.

"He found it in Lily's grave. I'm sure of it. I remember how antsy he seemed that day when I walked over to see if he needed any help with the digging. He told me he'd finish digging up Lily's grave and would call me when it was time to move Lily's casket to her new gravesite. This was totally out of character. Buddy had a lazy streak when it came to manual labor. I had to help him fill up Princeton's old grave the day before, because he complained so much. Besides, if he had found it in Princeton's, he would never have worked the next day. Buddy must have thought there might be other treasure buried and didn't want to share."

"But Lily died years after the necklace disappeared. So did Big Zed move the necklace from where it was originally?"

"I don't know, Harri, but it would seem so. Maybe Zed was afraid it would be found in the first hiding place. Burying it in a grave would assure it would not be found. Besides, it was kind of fitting for La Fleur to be buried in Lily's grave."

Cayce added her theory on the moving of the graves to the conversation. "Then again, the forces that be, and I can attest to there being many, are probably the reason the graves sank in the first place. Someone or something wanted the necklace found. It's like putting an end to all the unknowns and ending a curse that's lasted for over a century and a half. That's why Harri and I were led to the cooking journal."

After they left the cemetery, Joshua asked Cayce to spend the afternoon with him. Harri had plans to meet with Andre to go over the cake recipe, so she certainly didn't mind. She had told Andre they needed to work on the boiled icing, and he had agreed they would give it a trial run as soon as the brunch was cleared out around two o'clock.

As Cayce and Joshua were heading to the office, a deputy stopped them.

"I've got some things for you, Joshua, but you'll need to get them from the sheriff's office. We searched the house Monica was renting and found a lot of evidence we'll need to save for trial, but there's this one thing the sheriff says you need to take. We've already cataloged it, but the sheriff doesn't want the responsibility of having it at the office."

Joshua and Cayce walked into the sheriff's office a few minutes later.

"Is the sheriff on his way back from Natchez yet?" Joshua couldn't believe it was taking him so long to conduct the investigation.

"Yep. He should be here in a couple of hours, and he said he's got news for you. He's coming to the Oaks as soon as he gets back in town." The deputy opened a safe and took out a wooden box.

"It had a lock on it at one time, but I guess Monica broke it off."

"Any idea where she found it?" Joshua asked the question but was sure the deputy didn't know.

"That woman is being very tight-lipped. She's got an attorney coming up from New Orleans. She's talked to him about five times today already."

The deputy put the box on the table where Joshua and Cayce were sitting. It was a rosewood box with a fleur-de-lis carved in the top.

"I think you're gonna like what's inside." The deputy smiled as he pushed the box to Joshua.

Joshua opened the lid and saw a velvet drawstring bag. He opened the bag and poured the contents into his hand.

"Oh, my gosh! Would you look at these, Cayce?" Joshua put his hand in front of Cayce, and she began to count the stones.

"May I?" Cayce looked at Joshua, who gave his nod of approval. Cayce picked up one of the emeralds and held it where the sunlight could shine through it.

"It is magnificent! Looks like Sophia is going to have plenty of emeralds to go with that green gown next year." She handed the stone back to Joshua, who put them back in the bag.

As he put the bag back into the box, he noticed the yellowed envelope in the bottom. He read the words written on the outside of it aloud:

"To be given to Caleb upon obtaining his freedom at twenty-five years of age."

"And was Caleb given his freedom at age twenty-five?" Cayce looked over Joshua's arm at the elegant handwriting.

"Yes, he was. Princeton gave him his freedom and sent him north with the financial means to start his own business. It was something his father had promised Affie not long before he died." Joshua turned the envelope over and saw a gold wax seal that remained unbroken, but he made no attempt to see what was inside.

"Aren't you going to open it? You are a descendant of Caleb, and it was found at Spanish Oaks, your property."

"I'll wait until I get home. I want Sophia with me, since she's a descendant of Caleb as well. You and Harri should be with me, too. You are part of Spanish Oaks now, with all you've done to help solve the mysteries."

Joshua and Cayce took the box and headed back to Spanish Oaks. It was two p.m., and the contractor was waiting for Joshua to give him the okay to start digging for the new pool. The yellow tape had been removed, and the ground was marked for the excavation to begin. Joshua locked the box in his office safe and headed toward the door with Cayce beside him. He put his hand on the door but stopped, turning to face Cayce.

"Cayce, you mean a lot to me. I hope you can sense that."

"My senses are quite remarkable, remember?" Cayce put a hand on either side of Joshua's face and drew him to her, giving him a serious kiss.

He put his arms around her and held her to him, holding the kiss for a long time. "Are you sure you have to leave tomorrow? I know we haven't known each other very long, but I can't stand the thought of you leaving me."

"Then let's make the time we have left count."

They kissed again, stopping when Joshua heard the

bulldozer start up.

"Damn 'dozer! We'd better go."

When they got outside, Joshua took Cayce's hand and looked at her. "Don't leave my side today, Cayce. Okay?"

"I won't. But don't walk so fast." She had to practically run to keep up with him as he headed across the yard.

****

In the Stables, Harri had just gone over the old recipe with Andre, and they were gathering ingredients for a trial run. Andre insisted they drink champagne to celebrate her winning entry. Harri agreed but had no idea Andre would be such a guzzler.

"Cooking this is the problem, Andre. It's such a simple recipe, but you have to time it, and you have to make sure your heat is the same at each stage, every time you cook it. This can be a problem unless you're using the same stove each time. I had to cook it three times before I got it right."

"I am going to watch, and I'll know when it's ready because I'm using this new invention called a candy thermometer to see the exact temperature, girlfriend. It's the only way to be sure. I can't be making it three times per cake, not with as many cakes as will be needed in the Stables."

Andre pulled out the thermometer and laid it on the counter. Harri was totally pissed off at Andre's sarcasm and couldn't believe she had thought she would like him the night she'd met him in the Stables. The more he drank, the giddier he got, and he was really grating on her nerves. She had many gay friends and a couple of them were chefs, but the chefs were professionals, none of them silly or demeaning like Andre.

Harri combined the egg and sugar, using a wire whisk to blend them well. She added the milk and mixed it in thoroughly, then transferred the mixture to a heavy pot. Harri never stopped stirring the mixture, keeping it on medium heat until it began to boil. Turning the heat down just a little, she continued to stir, refusing Andre's offer to take over if her arm got tired. As she stirred, Andre talked about nothing and about everything, mostly bragging of what "no chef can make it like I do" dishes he had served to what bigwig. Later, Harri would describe the conversation as the "f" word multiplied by five—"famous food for famous folks"— and only Andre could make the dishes.

Andre constantly criticized her technique, telling her to "stir in the same direction, making teeny circles." Harri figured Andre put the "candy" in "candy thermometer" and decided if he mentioned the "no-fail thermometer" to her one more time, she was going to tell the chef to stick his thermometer up his candy ass and see if it could measure rudeness.

****

The bulldozer bit into the hard ground, the first bite of many, as the swimming pool project was begun. Joshua watched in eager anticipation of seeing the large rectangular hole grow. The deep end of the pool would be the first part dug, and the contrary willow tree would be gone forever.

While Joshua stood hypnotized by the large piece of machinery, Cayce looked around to see if any of the guests were out. Molly sat in a rocking chair, her baby doll held tight. She stared at the 'dozer but with a look of panic, not the look of excitement Joshua had. Her

325

daddy came out and tried to get her to go inside, but she wouldn't leave the rocking chair. Finally, he pulled a rocker up beside her and watched the bulldozer at work.

Cayce glanced over the grounds and saw a sheriff's car pull up in front of the mansion. Sheriff Brody got out of the car, holding what looked like a notebook. Cayce took Joshua's arm and pulled him around so he would see the sheriff. Joshua and the sheriff met halfway.

'Let's go into your office, Joshua." The sheriff sounded as if his business was urgent.

Joshua motioned for Cayce to come with them.

Sheriff Brody opened the notebook and took out the staff pictures Sophia had prepared for him and put them on the table.

"I'm sorry I took so long, Joshua, but I wanted to try to find another person who could identify the estate dealer. Linda was the only one who could ID the person in Natchez but said the dealer once mentioned an antique shop in south Louisiana, so I went there. The owner not only identified him but showed me pieces he had bought, more pieces from the missing inventory you gave me. We confiscated all the pieces there, but we didn't find all of them."

"I don't care about the missing pieces. Who is the bastard who's been selling what Monica stole?"

The sheriff pulled one picture from the stack and handed it to Joshua.

"There's your man. Lead me to him, and I'll arrest him."

****

Harri was still stirring the icing when Joshua and Cayce came into the kitchen in the Stables. Andre was standing behind her, checking over her shoulders. Harri gave her sister a look that said she was ready to kill, and there was no need to guess who had brought her to her boiling point.

"Andre, you thieving son of a bitch!" Joshua was furious and started toward the chef, but Cayce held him back.

"What are you talking about, Joshua? And don't you talk to me that way!" Andre raised his voice to Joshua and moved behind the island, putting it between Joshua and himself.

Joshua continued his tirade.

"*You* have been the dealer selling what Monica stole. Did you know she's responsible for the death of Buddy Nabors? That makes you an accessory to murder."

Andre's gasp indicated he did not know, but he reached under the counter, pulled out a revolver, and pointed it at Joshua.

The sheriff began to try to talk him down. "You can't get away, Andre. I have deputies en route. Give yourself up before you get in deeper."

Harri was to the side of Andre, and he was paying her no attention. She took the bottle of champagne and poured some in the boiled icing mixture. Grabbing the hot pad lying on the counter, she put the end of it into the flame under the pot. Once it ignited, she dropped it into the alcoholic mixture. It immediately burst into flames. Holding the pot by its handle, she flung it at Andre.

Andre screamed as his apron caught on fire. The flames consumed the apron in seconds as Andre danced and screamed, dropping the gun and running toward the door. Harri headed him off with a fire extinguisher. With one push of the thumb, Andre was covered in fire retardant and the flames were snuffed out.

As the sheriff's deputy led Andre out of the Stables in handcuffs, Harri began to laugh.

"What are you laughing at, Harri?" Cayce stared at her sister.

"I was just thinking. That's the best praline I've made yet. Overcooked boiled icing covering one giant nut!"

Cayce and Joshua laughed as they led Harri out the door, her snorts louder than their laughter.

****

The 'dozer dug deep, lifting bucketloads of dirt out of the soon-to-be swimming pool. The last bite pulled up the willow tree, and the 'dozer scooped it up to remove it once and for all. But before it could take the next huge bite, Molly screamed from the porch, dropped her doll, and ran toward the bulldozer. Her father took off after her, terrified she would be run over by the 'dozer, since it was so loud the operator could hear nothing.

Joshua saw the little girl running and bolted for her, catching her at the edge of the hole.

"Stop! Stop!" Molly screamed and kicked, trying to get out of Joshua's arms. Cayce ran to the bulldozer and motioned for the operator to stop.

Molly's daddy took his little girl from Joshua. She was hysterical and kept begging Joshua to make it stop.

"Molly, the big machine has stopped. Tell us what's wrong, sweetie." Cayce caressed Molly's hair in an attempt to calm the little girl.

"Chloe is in there. By the tree." Molly pointed to

where the bulldozer had just picked up the tree, leaving a gaping hole.

At the same time, Cayce, Harri, and Joshua ran toward the hole. Joshua motioned for the bulldozer operator to back up. Once it was far enough back, Joshua jumped into the hole and began knocking aside clods of dirt and tree roots. Then he saw it. A black leather satchel sat half buried in the dirt. Joshua pulled the satchel out, and under it he found human bones.

"Oh, my god! Cayce, get Tom and tell him to bring shovels and a tarpaulin. We have human remains down here."

Molly's father took his daughter inside, not wanting her to see the little girl's skeletal remains when they were brought to the surface. An adult skeleton was found with the child's, covering the small skeleton as if still trying to protect the little girl.

Cayce and Harri opened the worn leather satchel and found a piece of oilcloth tightly wrapped around something and tied with a leather strap. When they untied the strap, a rolled-up, thick piece of aged paper was uncovered. After pressing it out, the sisters realized it was one of the posters Princeton had ordered printed in an effort to recover Chloe. On the back of the poster was a crudely drawn map showing a trail that followed rivers and bypassed roads and swamps filled with quicksand, a trail from Fairchild Plantation to Spanish Oaks.

Harri gasped as she felt the adrenaline rush of the slave woman as she got nearer the house and felt the fear and anguish as she disappeared into the ground.

Cayce, in her mind, saw the slave woman with Chloe on her back, running through the downpour toward the mansion, and she heard the abrupt silence as the two were swallowed by the newly dug well as it collapsed around them, suffocating them with mud several feet deep. Cayce could not stop the tears, and Joshua pulled her to him to console her.

"You see it all, don't you, baby?"

"Yes. Beatrice saw them fall into the hole where the first well was dug. She knew the well collapsed on them and did nothing to save them. That's why she had the second well dug in a different spot. Beatrice got better than she deserved."

****

On Sunday morning, a graveside service was held for Chloe and Eliza. Eliza was buried beside the little girl she had promised to protect. Chloe was buried in the grave with her mother. Chloe and Milla were reunited at last. Molly dropped the old rag doll in with Chloe before they began putting the dirt back in. At the end of the service, Molly's mother sang Chloe's lullaby.

Hush-a-bye, don't you cry,
Go to sleepy little baby.
When you wake, you'll have cake,
And all the pretty little horses.

Chapter Seventeen

Joshua and Sophia, Cayce and Harri, and Don sat at the table in the study at Joshua's cabin. With the finding of Chloe and the slave lady who had tried to rescue her, and the identification and arrest of Andre as the dealer in stolen antiques, time had gotten away from Joshua, and he had forgotten about Caleb's letter. Now all of his favorite people surrounded him as he broke the seal to read the letter of his ancestor.

The handwriting was elegant, like those in the documents they had read and reread, yet it was different from the others. Long, bold strokes indicated great strength, someone who was not afraid; someone who was in control. Joshua read the letter aloud:

June 6, 1835

As I grow old and weak and approach the time when I must stand before God and account for the errors of my life, I desire to right the one wrong that has torn at my conscience all these years.

In my older years, at a time when I should have known better, I fathered a son for whom I could not take credit, the son of the young slave woman Affie. My wife, knowing of my transgression, requested I send Affie and the baby boy to serve our son, Jacob, a gentle and caring master who would see to the boy's needs and would find a suitable husband for Affie, a man who would teach the boy strength of character.

Having taken Jacob into my confidence and admitted my sins in my old age, I am leaving this letter in his care to let Caleb know his bloodline. The Broussard blood is strong, and I trust mixing with colored will weaken it little.

I wish Caleb well and have instructed Jacob to make sure the boy is given his freedom when he is twenty-five years of age, along with funds gained from the sale of these precious stones, enough to start a new life in the North. At that time, I wish for this confession to be given to him so he will know his ancestry and his offspring and theirs for generations to come will know of the power of their bloodline. Blood is important. I know that now and regret having distanced myself from my own family in France at a young, irresponsible age.

Jean Paul Broussard

Joshua folded the letter and put it back in the envelope.

"Jacob died before he was able to give Caleb the letter, so Caleb never knew he was a Broussard and neither did Princeton." Joshua became quiet, as if in deep thought.

Sophia left her chair and put her arm around her father's shoulder. "So I guess I have to change what I say on the tour, the part about Princeton being the last Broussard to own Spanish Oaks."

"No, Soppy, you don't. Blood is important, but it is not what makes a father. Caleb's father was Big Zed, a man who held on to his son during a terrible tragedy and risked his own safety to save his son from the gallows. Caleb had the surname his father was given, Devaux, and you and I will carry on that name. Actions and love make a father, not a bloodline."

Sophia kissed her dad's cheek and hugged him again.

"Now. There's one more thing I need to do." Joshua took the cooking journal out of the vault and brought it to the table.

"Harri, I want you to have this. You never got to look at all of the recipes, and there's no telling what you might find you could use in the Teacake. Besides, I don't plan on cooking, and I'll bet Cayce doesn't either." Cayce smiled and nodded her agreement with Joshua's gift.

"But Joshua, it's part of the history of Spanish Oaks. Besides, I don't know if I want Beatrice's blood to remind me of the scary events of the week." Harri rubbed her fingers over the leather cover.

"And I wouldn't give it to you if it had Beatrice's blood in it. You need to look at it. I noticed it this morning when I was returning documents to the vault." Joshua pushed the book closer to Harri.

Harri opened the book. The bloodstains were gone, disappeared as if the night in 1848 had never happened.

"Oh, my goodness! Well, maybe Affie does want me to have it. I bet she's the reason my Citron Delight disappeared. She needed to do a taste test to see if she approved of my take on her recipe. Who knows? Maybe Princeton tasted it, too." Harri hugged Joshua. "Thank you, Joshua. I'll cherish it always." Harri hesitated before continuing. "But does this mean you're not going to reimburse me?"

The group all laughed except for Harri, who was waiting for an answer she would not get just then, as Joshua continued, "There is something else I found in the vault this morning. There was a letter rolled up, tied with a string, and concealed in the bottom of the leather bag that held the necklace." Joshua looked his audience in the eyes and could see they were all anxious to hear what he had learned.

"Affie buried The Flower in Lily's grave." He paused to enjoy the puzzled looks on their faces. "Affie saw Zed hide the necklace under the mantel, the same place we found the butcher knife that night in Affie's cabin, but Zed didn't know Affie had seen him. Affie knew how much Zed hated Beatrice. He always felt the vile woman had something to do with Chloe's disappearance, so when Affie saw Zed hiding the necklace, she thought Zed had killed Beatrice. Affie tried to cover his crime by taking it. She kept the secret but was always afraid someone would find the necklace and Zed would be hanged."

"So Affie confessed her suspicions in the letter?" Harri asked the question but had a puzzled look on her face. "But if Buddy found the necklace in the leather bag in Lily's grave, that would mean Affie wrote the letter years after Beatrice's death."

"Yes. That appears to be the case. Buddy's finding of the necklace and our discovery of it in the swamp months later would be more of Affie's way of putting the evidence in the proper sequence for us to find."

"Affie always felt the necklace had to be moved to a more secure place. Unfortunately, Lily provided her with the perfect hiding place. By the time Lily died, Zed was all Affie had left of her family. Princeton had given Caleb his freedom, and Caleb had moved to the North. Milla was dead, and Affie believed Chloe would never be returned. Affie sneaked out to the cemetery the night after Lily's burial and buried the necklace in the one place she felt Zed's secret could remain hidden."

"Affie's spirit and perhaps the spirits of the others, restless with the pain of that tragic night, and perhaps seeking forgiveness through open confession for the secret she kept all those years, put the chain of events in order, beginning with allowing the cookbook to be found and sold. Affie needed to expose all secrets and thus gain eternal rest. And that, my friends and family, is the rest of the story."

****

It was her last night in Mississippi, and Cayce couldn't sleep. But it was more than reliving the events of the last two days. It was the thought of leaving the next day and not knowing if she would ever see Joshua again. Thinking everyone was asleep in the cabin, she tiptoed barefooted down the hall, stopping at the kitchen to grab a bottle of water as she made her way to the porch, her path lit only by the moonlight coming through the windows. She eased open the heavy front door and tiptoed onto the porch.

The moon was full, highlighting the silhouettes of giant oak trees surrounding Joshua's little piece of heaven. Cayce knew the mighty river was not far away, but she couldn't hear it like she could the Stillwater back home, its water cold and clear, issuing from snowy peaks high in the Beartooths. This time of the year the Stillwater would be loud and raging like the passion she felt for Joshua, passion unfulfilled, but in another month or two, her river would transform into a rippling creek, tranquil and perfect, like the life she coveted on the downward slope of life.

It was now June first, and the Mississippi air hung heavy with the sweet smells of magnolia blossoms and wild honeysuckle, the smells of her childhood. But Cayce missed the refreshing, antiseptic smell of her mountain flora: blue spruce and aspen, sagebrush and wildflowers. Her Way was clear and it led to her home, Montana. Still, thoughts of life without Joshua nagged at her heart. Cayce leaned against the cypress log post, sipping her water and staring into the moonlight, and melancholy overcame her.

****

Joshua had tossed and turned for hours until he gave up, grabbed his sweatpants, and took refuge on the porch. The cool breeze felt good on his bare chest as he reclined on the cushioned pine chaise lounge. He wanted a cigarette and a cold beer, but his daughter had convinced him to give both up, the beer five years ago and the cigarettes just six months ago. So Joshua sat, soaking in the scene of what had been his utopia, his perfect spot on earth. Cayce had come along and ruined it, turning his world topsy-turvy. He couldn't sleep knowing she was down the hall and knowing she'd be leaving in a few hours. Then he heard her as she tiptoed out onto the porch, thinking the moonlight was hers alone.

He stared at her from the shadows, unsure whether to let her know he was there or to just sit and enjoy the sight of her, her long brown hair reflecting the moonlight as it blew wispy in the breeze. She was silhouetted as she leaned against the post, the moonlight complementing her curves, perfect for her age, covered only by pajama pants that bagged below her waist beneath a white tank top. As he drank in the sight of her, he knew he wanted to be nearer. He whispered her name, trying not to frighten her. "Cayce!"

She turned in the direction of the sound but didn't see him, so he whispered again, a little louder.

"Cayce, I'm here." Joshua rose from the chair and walked toward her.

"You couldn't sleep either?" Her heart raced as she saw him, barefoot and shirtless, approaching from the dark. She sensed the ultimate test was about to be thrown at her.

"No." Joshua spoke only the one word as he passed her.

He sat on the top step and patted the floor beside him. Cayce sat, her arm touching his. He put his arm around her and pulled her to him. She laid her head on his shoulder, and they sat silent, looking at the moon.

"Penny for your thoughts?" Cayce spoke first, almost afraid of breaking the spell.

"You know what I'm thinking," was all he said, and silence took over again until Joshua broke it. "Stay, Cayce, at least for a few days. I'm not ready for you to leave me."

"You know I have to go, Joshua. If I stayed a week or two weeks, it would still be the same. Eventually, the mountains would call me home."

Joshua leaned against the post, stretching one leg behind her, and pulled her back against his chest, wrapping his arms around her. She stretched her legs out as she leaned into him, feeling his muscular chest and wanting him. He kissed her head, working his lips through her hair until she turned her face to his. They kissed with passion, their tongues playing like trout fingerlings in a mountain stream. When their lips parted, he held her even tighter and whispered in her ear.

"Come to bed with me, baby."

"You know I can't, Joshua. I want to, but I can't."

"Why not? You're here and I'm here and the moment is now." He kissed her ear, and she felt his body responding to his desires and hers.

"I don't live for the moment, Joshua. If there is a future for you and me, the first time has to be in my bed."

"But your sister is in the adjoining room. My bed is away from everyone."

"No, I mean *my* bed." She meant her bed in Montana. "That way, I'll know I wasn't just a cheap shot."

"You could never be a cheap shot, Cayce."

Cayce sat up and looked into his eyes.

"Then you'll have to prove it, Joshua Devaux. The Way is clear."

She took his face in her hands and kissed him long and hard. Then she stood, caressing his cheek with her hand as he looked up at her. She let her fingers linger on his mouth, and he took her hand and held it to his lips. She began to move away, but he held on to her hand, hoping she would change her mind. She stopped and looked deep into his eyes and he thought she had reconsidered, but then she turned and walked back inside the cabin. The moon disappeared behind a cloud, and he was alone.

****

TEACAKE headed down the long paved road shaded by ancient Spanish oaks whose limbs overlapped, their fingers dripping Spanish moss that danced in the warm breeze, beckoning "stay." The sisters had fallen in love with the old plantation and its rich family history, and they had fallen in love with the family who would most likely be its last caretakers.

Harri knew she would be back to claim her prize and was close enough to come more often if she wanted. Besides, she had praline business to conduct with Joshua.

Cayce sat silent, riding shotgun again, and stared up into the moss with rays of sunlight bursting through in short spasms, reminding her of promised silver linings. Would she ever see Joshua again? Was the relationship they had just a fling, spurred on by the emotional highs of vision quests, hidden secrets, and treasures revealed? She could only hope it was real. He promised he would see her in Montana as soon as he could get away. But time can heal or time can kill. She knew once she saw the Beartooths again, she'd feel revitalized, but there would be a weak spot in her heart for some time.

As the red convertible approached the end of the row of Spanish oaks, the sisters recognized an aged minivan sitting on the side of the road. Mama Tee, in full regalia, stood beside the car, a plastic bag in one hand and a bouquet of yellow lilies in the other.

Harri pulled the car over, and the sisters got out, smiling at Sherone, definitely the most colorful part of their visit. They each hugged their friend, wishing they could have spent more time with her, more time to learn from one who knew so much about them even before they met.

Sherone handed the bag to Harri. It was filled with candied citron.

"For Affie's pralines. Da won't be de same wi'out Mama Tee's citron."

"Thank you, Sherone. I'm sending the first batch to you so you can tell me if I got them right. And yes, I do believe Affie showed me the way to make them. There are no coincidences, Sherone." Sherone smiled and patted Harri's hand.

"And for you, Cayce." Sherone handed Cayce the yellow lilies. "Da are flowers of love. You should have come for your fortune to be told and you would know de answer to your worries."

"No, Sherone. That is one part of my future I don't want to know in advance. Love should be spontaneous. If Joshua and I are meant to be, it will happen. If not, I'm still glad I met him. He's a wonderful man, and my life has been enriched knowing him for even this short time."

"You don't forget de love dolls I give you, did you?"

"No way. I'm depending on mine, but I'm not bringing her out 'til I'm good and ready, and it isn't right now." Harri laughed, and Cayce knew she was thinking about Don.

"I have mine. It's in my backpack I'm taking on the plane, not in checked baggage. It brought me luck already, Sherone. I'm counting on it to keep working." Cayce squeezed Sherone's hand and turned to get in the car, then turned back to say, "The lilies are beautiful. Thank you. At least one of these will be pressed in the book I'm reading on the plane." As Cayce got in the car, she added, "Tell Big Zed goodbye for me, and tell him thank you." Sherone nodded and smiled.

As they pulled away, Sherone yelled out to them. "Keep de Way clear and de heart will follow." Harri and Cayce each threw up a hand, signaling goodbye, while Mama Tee followed them with her eyes until they were out of sight.

****

Harri and Cayce hugged one last time before Cayce headed through security. Just before she was out of her sister's sight, she turned and yelled, "I still say it was the best twin trip ever." Harri nodded and waved before turning to leave.

Cayce put her book away and took out the love doll, looking at it one more time. It was time to board. She was glad she had upgraded to first class. It was a long trip back to Montana, and she hoped she could sleep. How she missed Joshua already. Cayce felt like a foolish teenager instead of a fifty-year-old woman.

She sat in a window seat and was already getting cozy with a blanket draped over her, waiting for takeoff. With her eyes closed, she found her way back to her snowcapped Beartooths. She was riding her horse through a meadow, with Joshua riding beside her, and in her hair she had wildflowers he had picked for her.

"Is this seat taken?"

Cayce started not to open her eyes, wondering why anyone would ask such a foolish question when all seats were assigned. Besides, she wanted to continue her daydream. But there was something about the man's voice… She peeked through one eye and smiled. Joshua stood in the aisle looking down at her, cowboy hat, jeans, boots, and all. He put his hat in the overhead compartment, took the aisle seat beside her, and fastened his seatbelt.

"So I'm heading to Montana to spend some time with my girl. Have you ever been there?"

"I have. It's breathtaking. You're a lucky man to

have someone in Montana. Are you planning to stay long?"

"As long as she'll let me." He put his arms around her and kissed her.

The heart had followed.

VINTAGE RECIPES USED

Citron Cake (Princeton's Favorite)

Six Eggs. Two and a half cups sugar. Four cups flour. Two cups citron. One cup butter. One cup sweet milk.

Cut citron in small bits and mix with all ingredients in a batter as for a pound cake.

Boiled Icing

Three cups sugar. One-half pint sweet milk. One egg.

Boil the whole until quite stiff and flavor with vanilla. When cool, put this preparation between layers of the cake and on top.

*For Pralines, cool a little longer and add chopped pecans. Drop by spoonfuls, pressing each praline flat to desired thickness. Cool on wax paper.

*Footnote: These directions may seem incomplete but are written just as they were written in the late eighteen-hundreds cookbook used.

Tea Cakes

Cream together the following ingredients: Two whole eggs. One cup sugar. One-half cup vegetable shortening. One teaspoon vanilla.

Sift together the following ingredients:

Two cups all-purpose flour. One and one-half teaspoons baking powder. One-half teaspoon salt.

Add to creamed mixture along with two teaspoons milk. Form into a ball and refrigerate for at least an hour.

Remove from refrigerator and knead a couple of times. Roll out to desired thickness. Use cookie cutter for preferred shape.

Bake at 375 degrees. Do not brown on top. Edges should be slightly brown. Check cookies after ten minutes. Do not overcook.

In addition to being a published author, Dr. Sue Clifton is a retired teacher and principal, a fly fisher, and a ghost hunter. After putting her writing career on hold, Dr. Sue followed husband Woody in his career and also in her own career as an educator in Mississippi, Alabama, Montana, Alaska, Canada, New Zealand, and on the Northern Cheyenne Reservation.

Dr. Sue is not new to paranormal investigations and travels all over the U.S. ghost hunting as well as in search of places and material for her new series "Daughters of the Way" with The Wild Rose Press, Inc. *The Breath of Spanish Oaks* is the first book in the series, to be followed by *Keeper of the Lambs*, set in a ghost town in Idaho.

Nyoka Beer enjoys traveling and searching for antique cookbooks to add a big "taste" of intrigue to the Way novels. She is already plotting book number three in the series. Nyoka travels all over the U.S. with her sister, researching and helping write plots with many twists, turns, and surprises for the books.

When not traveling or researching, Nyoka spends time with husband Ben at their home in Tennessee. Nyoka also travels with friends, is an avid reader, enjoys her two grandsons, cantors for her church, and is writing her own cookbook.

Dr. Sue now divides her time between Montana and Mississippi and loves all things vintage. With her vintage camper "Delta Blue," Dr. Sue attends events with the national outdoor women's group Sisters on the Fly. Dr. Sue supports Casting for Recovery (CFR), a national organization providing fly fishing retreats for women with breast cancer. A portion of the profits from all her book sales goes to CFR.

Dr. Sue is the author of six novels in a series with The Wild Rose Press, Inc.; and two nonfiction books and two paranormal mysteries published elsewhere. Dr. Sue appeared in October 2015 in A&E's five-part series for television *Cursed: The Bell Witch* and was also featured in *USA Today* in articles about her nonfiction book which included the truth about the Bell Witch Legend as told through a young clairvoyant, Angel Leigh.

Visit Dr. Sue at:

www.drsueclifton.com

and at Novels by Dr. Sue Clifton on Facebook.

Thank you for purchasing
this publication of The Wild Rose Press, Inc.

For questions or more information
contact us at
info@thewildrosepress.com.

The Wild Rose Press, Inc.
www.thewildrosepress.com

To visit with authors of
The Wild Rose Press, Inc.
join our yahoo loop at
http://groups.yahoo.com/group/thewildrosepress/